Lemur nodded. "I am well aware."

"If this was a definite plan to sneak in, snatch Doc and Krysty and take them back to Atlantis," Ryan stated, "then he knew they were here, he knew what made them of interest and he knew how to get past your sec patrol and into the ville. He knew exactly where we were. There's only one way he could have known all that."

"Spies," Mark said. "Wretches who claim to want freedom but are nothing more than dogs."

"Who are they?" Ryan asked. "Mark, you trained as a Crawler and you knew nothing of spies?"

Mark returned Ryan's stare, unblinking. Finally Ryan nodded. "I believe you. You've put too much in here to be a traitor. But someone is, and if they know about us, then they know about everything you do. If we're gonna get my people back, and get rid of Odyssey, then we're gonna have to move fast—before the information has a chance to find its way back to Atlantis."

He pulled himself to his feet. "Are you ready?"

Lemur shook his head. "No...but we have no choice."

Other titles in the Deathlands saga:

JAMES AXLER

DEATH LANDS®

Atlantis Reprise

ALTERED STATES
BOOK TWO

A GOLD EAGLE BOOK FROM
WORLDWIDE®

TORONTO • NEW YORK • LONDON
AMSTERDAM • PARIS • SYDNEY • HAMBURG
STOCKHOLM • ATHENS • TOKYO • MILAN
MADRID • WARSAW • BUDAPEST • AUCKLAND

First edition December 2005

ISBN 0-373-62582-0

ATLANTIS REPRISE

Of all the causes which conspire to blind
Man's erring judgment and misguide the mind,
What the weak head with strongest bias rules,
Is pride, the never-failing vice of fools.
                              —Alexander Pope,
                                  An Essay on Criticism

THE DEATHLANDS SAGA

This world is their legacy, a world born in the violent nuclear spasm of 2001 that was the bitter outcome of a struggle for global dominance.

There is no real escape from this shockscape where life always hangs in the balance, vulnerable to newly demonic nature, barbarism, lawlessness.

But they are the warrior survivalists, and they endure—in the way of the lion, the hawk and the tiger, true to nature's heart despite its ruination.

Ryan Cawdor: The privileged son of an East Coast baron. Acquainted with betrayal from a tender age, he is a master of the hard realities.

Krysty Wroth: Harmony ville's own Titian-haired beauty, a woman with the strength of tempered steel. Her premonitions and Gaia powers have been fostered by her Mother Sonja.

J. B. Dix, the Armorer: Weapons master and Ryan's close ally, he, too, honed his skills traversing the Deathlands with the legendary Trader.

Doctor Theophilus Tanner: Torn from his family and a gentler life in 1896, Doc has been thrown into a future he couldn't have imagined.

Dr. Mildred Wyeth: Her father was killed by the Ku Klux Klan, but her fate is not much lighter. Restored from predark cryogenic suspension, she brings twentieth-century healing skills to a nightmare.

Jak Lauren: A true child of the wastelands, reared on adversity, loss and danger, the albino teenager is a fierce fighter and loyal friend.

Dean Cawdor: Ryan's young son by Sharona accepts the only world he knows, and yet he is the seedling bearing the promise of tomorrow.

In a world where all was lost, they are humanity's last hope....

Chapter One

The ruins lay smoldering in the valley below them. Worn down by the fight, caught by the searing heat of the fires that had spread through the ville on the wings of the swirling zephyrs, there were few survivors. Not many that were people. A few mules and horses, some dogs—those that had managed to slip their bonds and scrabble their way up the steep slopes, their fear powering their limbs as they attempted to outrun the devastation.

Ryan Cawdor, Jak Lauren, J. B. Dix, Mildred Wyeth and Krysty Wroth had prevailed, with them, Doc Tanner—or possibly not Doc Tanner. Who could tell, in his currently unconscious state, whether he would wake to once more be Dr. Theophilus Tanner, or if he would be Joseph Jordan, the reincarnated or transferred soul of a Scottish trapper from the centuries before the nuke-caust?

For now, it didn't matter. Like all of them, Doc was beyond caring about such matters. While he was still wrapped in the velvet oblivion of unconsciousness, the others began to stir. They had managed to escape from the holocaust that raged beneath them, but the effort had rendered all of them too exhausted to take another step, all sinking into their own sleep of exhaustion.

Yet this wasn't the place to succumb to such measures. The heat rising on spiraling air from the inferno beneath was enough to warm the air around and the earth beneath them, to take the edge from the ever present howling gales that swept unfettered across the barren plains of rock and ice that surrounded them. It was enough to keep them from freezing to an early chill. But it wouldn't sustain them for long: the cold would bite, the fires below subside. When that happened, then the sudden drop in temperature would take a swift and exacting toll.

Should they even survive this, then there was the greater problem: where did they go from here?

First things first. The most important thing was to survive as long as possible, from one moment to the next, until these moments ran together to make a long stretch of time. And to survive, they had to be on their feet and moving.

Ryan was the first to surface from the blackness. Something deep inside him nagged and impelled him to come around from the comfort of oblivion. He was tired, aching, and felt as though he could settle into the arms of Morpheus forever, never to be bothered again by the rigors of having to survive. And yet still there nagged a voice that told him to face the pain and the cold. It wasn't just about him. When he became the leader of his small group, then he undertook the duty to try to guide them through adversity to whatever it was that they had spent so long searching for. That obligation wouldn't allow him to take the easy way out.

Ryan dragged his aching limbs, his legs still suffused with lactic acid burn from their flight, and used his less battered and more responsive arms to propel himself upward, into a kneeling position. It took a moment for him to gain his bearings. He looked out over the empty plain, the daylight already beginning to fade, then back toward the valley, the air around the rim glowing as though casting a benign radiation into the darkening skies.

But there was no mistaking the odor that drifted across the short distance. Cutting through the ever present sulfur burn that always made the air taste sour, there was the smell of roasted flesh, sickly sweet and mixed with the ashes of the woods and brick that had once constituted the ville of Fairbanks.

A glorious folly. Doc had used those words once, when he was Doc. He had been quoting some kind of old song or poem at them, something to do with six hundred men riding into a valley. Mebbe that was why he could think of it now, why it cut through the fog that still partially clouded his mind.

Not knowing what else to do, Ryan hauled himself to his feet and half walked, half stumbled across the short distance to the rim of the valley, so that he could see what was happening below.

Nothing.

Not, at least, in terms of action or life. There were still tongues of fire that whipped across the remains of the ville, crisscrossing over the rubble that was all that remained of the streets and buildings. If anything had managed to stay alive in there, it was trapped and buying the farm in a long, slow, agonizing way.

Not that Ryan cared. Those mad Inuit bastards would only have chilled them after they'd burned the inhabitants of the ville. With only a very few left back at the settlement, he guessed that this meant the end of the Inuit tribe.

Fuck them, they would have taken out his people.

His only concern about who lived was based on the assumption that any still down there may come after them. And if his friends felt anything like he did right now, then they were in no fit condition to take on anyone.

He turned his back on the mayhem below and trudged wearily to where the rest of the companions lay on the ground, some now beginning to show signs of life.

Mildred and Jak had managed to reenter the real world and were no longer blearily staring around them, struggling to make their aching limbs respond to the messages their befuddled brains were sending. By the time that they were able to lift themselves to their feet, J.B. and Krysty were also beginning to respond to their surroundings.

It left only Doc, blissfully unaware of the perils from which he had been rescued, and the perils in which he now reposed, oblivious on the cold, hard ground.

The shock of the cold beginning to hit them as the night crept on and the fires in the valley subsided rapidly, casting up less heat, was enough to focus their minds.

Mildred checked Doc. He was unconscious, but seemingly unharmed apart from a few contusions and cuts, which was no more than the rest of them had suffered during the brief and brutal battle. There was no reason that she could define to explain why he was still unconscious while the others had all managed to recover sufficiently to function.

'What the hell do we do now?' J.B. asked Ryan as the two men stood surveying the wasteland around

them. 'Can't go on to Ank Ridge. We don't know where
it is, don't know how far and mebbe couldn't even pick
up the trail.'

'Even if we could, they'd have some idea of what's
been going on, and how the hell could we explain away
the trail of devastation the Inuit left behind them? We're
all that's left. We'd have to shoulder all the blame and
the shit that would come with it,' Ryan added grimly.
'I don't know about you, but I'm sure as shit not up to
another firefight right now.'

J.B. cast a glance back over his shoulder to where
Mildred was still tending to Doc. 'Not if we've got a
passenger, as well. Whoever the hell he's going to be
next,' he said simply.

'So, a rock and a hard place. Fireblast, whoever
thought that one up must have been thinking of a place
like this,' Ryan murmured. 'J.B., we don't know what
lies off the trails, and we don't know how far anything
is in any direction except one. We've only got the two
choices.'

'Go back past the slopes, all the way back to the redoubt, and then jump.' It was a statement rather than a
question.

'That's only one choice. What's the second?'

Ryan shrugged. 'Lie down, go back to sleep and buy
the farm.'

FACED WITH A CHOICE that stark, even the most tired of
limbs, the slowest of dulled reactions, couldn't fail to
click into gear. Mildred made Doc as warm and comfortable as was possible and then joined the others in
their mission under the fading light.

There were animals roaming, lost around the rim of

the valley. Some of the dogs still had sleds or partial sleds attached to them. The companions' task was to round up as many of the animals as they could, taking care not to spook them. Easier said than done, as the events in the valley had set a wave of fear trembling through those creatures that survived. But they, too were exhausted, and so, with a little patience, the companions were able to round up the surviving livestock and tether it as best as possible.

The plan was simple: from the partial and whole sleds that survived, they would attempt to cobble together enough transport to hook up to the beasts. That would enable them to tackle the distance between their position and the redoubt perhaps faster than they would on foot, and certainly enable them to preserve their energies. The remainder of any salvaged wood they could use for fires along the journey, to warm them and their pack beasts in the darkest, coldest watches of the night.

The beasts could be used to pull the transport. They could also be slaughtered along the way to provide food for both the companions and for those beasts that survived. The slaughter would perhaps put fear into the beasts, but that would be countered by their intense cold and hunger, which would make them perhaps more malleable than usual.

By the time that they had collected the livestock, made a fire for the now imminent night, and begun to hammer together enough sleds to carry them and any animal carcasses they would slaughter for food back to the redoubt, they were exhausted. Unwilling to begin the slaughter so soon and to face a sleepless night with the unsettled livestock, the companions resorted to the remaining self-heats. Whatever else occurred, J.B. and

Mildred always insured that they could keep their essential stocks close to hand. It wasn't even something they thought about: it was a second nature.

The food was foul, but it was nutritious enough to justify forcing it down rather than throwing it to one side in disgust. Their stomachs full, they settled to rest, Ryan opting to force himself awake to keep first watch.

As his companions and the beasts slept soundly into the night, Ryan cast his eye around him. The valley was now a distant glow, the fires finally burning themselves out. Nothing more had emerged from the ruins, and nothing was likely to have survived. Just the six of them and a smattering of livestock.

The one-eyed man wondered at how his friends were able to drag themselves from precipitous situations, coming back time and again from the brink of being chilled. One day their luck would run out, but until then there was little they could do except to keep moving.

But to keep moving across this plain that they already knew to be so hostile? With the sleds and the livestock, they had increased their chances of survival. Nonetheless, it was going to be a hard ride.

THE JOURNEY WAS LONG and hard. Started the next morning, it took two days and well into a third before the area of the redoubt hove into view. They stuck to the trail proscribed by the traffic between villes, now reinforced in view by the detritus left a few days before by the Inuit as they had passed. The pace they set was steady. To go too fast and risk burning out the strength left in the livestock would have been ultimately self-defeating. Nonetheless, it was important that they cover the ground quickly. The wood for fires, the livestock for food—neither would last for very long. Moreover, it was vital for their state of mind that they traverse the trail with speed and get out of that godforsaken territory.

It was almost a pleasure for them to be able to relax and to rest weary and torn muscles as the beasts pulling the sleds took most of the strain. They still had to be steered, which sometimes took its toll on wounded biceps and shoulders. A small price to pay for such a rapid and relatively easy progress.

Along the trail, the few landmarks that existed seemed to come upon them so much faster than before—inevitably, given their mode of transport, but vaguely disorienting after the rigors of the outward-bound march.

The deserted settlements, ripped apart by the plas-ex detonations of their previous visit, stood alone and desolate, their keening loneliness speaking more of the isolation and vast tracts of empty space than the companions could have cared to be reminded of, reliant as they were on exhausted beasts on a trail to nowhere. They were a stark reminder of how close the companions had come to being chilled themselves in such a manner—not once, but several times during the expedition. Even now, they weren't out of danger. The weather had been holding for more than forty-eight hours, the heavy yellow-tinged chem clouds pregnant with rains and snows that could engulf them, lose them in the roaring blizzard, and soak and chill them to the bone, with no shelter within view where respite could be sought.

There were, in the distance, the occasional glimpses of deer or bear as the packs and herds went about the business of trying to survive. They could be a danger if they approached, but hopefully held too much fear of the sleds and those pulling them, based on past experience, to come too near.

The ice and snow plucked from the rock and swirled in the never-ending flurry of winds still numbed and chilled when coming into contact with exposed skin. Despite the layers of skins and furs that still swathed them, the companions were chilled to the bone by the constant crosswinds, this time without the exercise of marching to warm them in any way. It was all they could do not to succumb to the ravages of hypothermia. How ironic if their attempt to increase their speed was to cause their demise. However they chose to make their flight, it seemed as though they faced nothing but life-threatening obstacles.

Two nights huddled by fires built—on the second night—from some of their sleds caused them to double up for the last day, and to put more strain on the livestock—livestock that was becoming more and more unsettled as Jak slaughtered some to feed the others and to feed the companions. Ryan had been correct in his assumption that the creatures would be too hungry and cold to be that distressed by the slaughter, intent as they were on eating their chilled companions to appease the hunger gnawing at their guts; however they were still unsettled enough for their pace to be upset on the following day's trek.

The trail took them along the base of the volcanic slopes that housed the Inuit village. They skirted the rock-enclosed passage and didn't take the trail as it wound up into the wooded slopes, choosing to avoid a possible firefight by keeping to the base of the slope. Ryan hoped that the few remaining Inuit wouldn't be hunting at that point in the day. The way he had it figured, they'd have enough trouble keeping the settlement going, and it was too early for them to be sniffing around for any sign of their warriors returning.

After passing the volcanic region, and watching it recede peacefully into the distance, it was only a matter of a few hours by sled before they reached the area where the redoubt was hidden.

All the while, Doc hovered between conscious and unconscious. Mildred tended to him, but could still find no reason why he shouldn't be fully aware of what was occurring around him. It seemed to her almost as if he were surfacing, taking note of his surroundings, then retreating into his own mind after deciding that he didn't like what he saw.

J.B. took what sightings he could in the appalling conditions, trusting the accuracy of the minisextant and his own skill to attain an accurate reading. Ryan hoped that the Armorer's sense of direction under these conditions was accurate. They couldn't last for much longer without some respite from the weather.

He didn't care where they might end up when they made the mat-trans jump. Anywhere had to be better than this…although, he realized with bitterness it was probably how he'd felt before they ended up in these icy wastes.

J.B. motioned them to change direction and a familiar outcropping came into view. The end of their quest was in sight.

It was almost as if Doc knew. He surprised Mildred by raising himself up on one elbow and looking at her with a quizzical air that was at once all too familiar to her.

A suspicion confirmed when he opened his mouth and said, in a voice that was distinctly his own, 'My dear Doctor, what on earth are we doing out here in these appalling conditions? And why, pray tell, do you look as though you've been on the losing side of a fight?'

Chapter Two

Although nothing had changed within the confines of the redoubt since they had last set foot there a few days before, the atmosphere that greeted them was totally different. Where there had previously been an air of gloom and foreboding, now there was nothing but a sense of relief. Despite the memories that had been stirred by their last incursion, there was no trace of remorse or remembrance. The strange atmosphere that had seemed to drape itself over them, penetrating to their very souls and painting their emotional world a darker shade of black, had now lifted.

Perhaps those ghosts that had been stirred had now dissipated, blown away by the experiences of the past few days. Perhaps those ghosts had never really existed and were just random memories that had fed a deeper malaise triggered by the act of a mat-trans jump. Or perhaps they were still here, but were now kept at bay by the fatigue that ate into their very bones, deadening all thought and all feeling in the effort just to keep moving until they were in a position to fall unconscious with exhaustion.

Ryan punched in the sec code once they were on the inside of the heavy entry doors. The remaining beasts had been freed from the sleds and driven away from the entrance. They lurked at a distance, unsure of what to do and where to go. Born into service, they were wild but with muted survival instincts, wanting to stick close to humans they saw as a source of food. There was only a slim chance that they would survive in the harsh environment, finding their way back to the remaining Inuit if they were lucky. It might have been kinder to have chilled them all, putting them out of their misery quickly and efficiently, yet it would have required an effort that none would have felt they had the energy to discharge.

As the door closed on the lurking beasts, on the snow and ice carried on chill winds and on the barren rock landscape, they felt a collective relief. The slightly musty recycled air, heated to a bearable temperature, kicked in, driving the cold from their bones. It was all they could do to keep from collapsing in the tunnel.

Except, perhaps, for Doc, who seemed filled with a new vitality.

'By the Three Kennedys, I don't know what's been going on—nor, come to that, why I am still with you when I appear to have been in some sort of coma all this time—but I do know that whatever it is, it appears to have taken a hefty toll upon you all.'

'Hefty toll,' Mildred repeated with a short, barking laugh. 'Doc, you mad old freak of nature, I don't think you even know how funny that is.'

'Funny would appear to be a strange word for it, given the condition in which you find yourselves,' Doc replied, a little perplexed.

'You know, it kind of depends on what you mean by funny, I guess,' Mildred answered him. 'I mean, do you see me laughing?'

'That would seem to be the last thing that you are capable of doing right now,' Doc threw back at her with all seriousness.

Mildred fixed him with a shrewd look. 'I don't think you've got the slightest idea what's been going on, have you?'

Doc opened his mouth, but no words came forth. Only Mildred now stood at the end of the corridor with him. The others had wordlessly made their way down the corridor, headed for the showers and the dorms. They moved slowly and with the grim determination of those only kept awake by sheer willpower, a dogged one-foot-in-front-of-the-other approach all that kept them going. Mildred followed the direction of his gaze, read the complete confusion in his eyes.

'No, I don't suppose you have,' she murmured more to herself than to the bewildered old man. Then, in a louder voice, she added, 'Doc, I can't tell you everything now. I'm just too damn tired and aching. Another few hours aren't going to hurt. We just need to rest and clean up before we jump.'

'We're using the mat-trans again, so soon? But surely we should be looking for—'

'Doc, just don't,' she interrupted, holding up a hand to silence him, then turning away to follow the others. She threw a parting shot over her shoulder. 'Just wait, keep it all in until tomorrow, then you'll understand.'

Doc stood watching her, a frown furrowing his brow. Whatever had happened out there—whatever it was that he couldn't remember—it had some kind of effect on those people he called his friends. The only friends he had in this godforsaken land in which he had been forced to strive for survival. Even in the few short minutes that he had been conscious he had noticed that there was some kind of distance that had arisen between them.

Why? He could recall being here and leaving to strike out toward Ank Ridge. But then? He could recall depression, and he could recall a storm that mirrored his mood, a blizzard that obscured the landscape in the same way that his feelings had obscured his ability to observe and function what was happening around him…and after that? A blur of ideas, images and emotions that he couldn't grasp.

The distance he felt was mirrored by the way in which they had left him at the head of the tunnel. As Mildred disappeared around a dog-leg bend, leaving him isolated by the entrance, he felt that the physical distance was nothing more than a mirror.

Reluctantly—for he had no idea what he would face when the others had rested—he followed on from them. By the time that he had reached the showers, they were stripped and washing the filth, ice and blood from their battered bodies.

Doc sat quietly as they finished and dried themselves. Only the barest necessity of communication took place, no more than a few words in each exchange. It was almost as though they were too tired to even acknowledge one another's existence. Certainly, none seemed to acknowledge Doc's presence.

Before too long he was left alone in the shower room, the others having gone in search of washing machines. Automatically, he stripped and washed himself, noting with an almost detached bemusement the signs of combat, the scars of recent wounds and the discoloration of contusion on his body. How he came to have these, he had no idea.

Frankly, he didn't care. It was with no little sense of foreboding that he eventually joined the others in the dorms, where he tried to settle to sleep.

The redoubt was silent and still. Doc tried to will himself to sleep, but his mind was racing. Fragments of what might have occurred, and of the thoughts that had plagued what, to him, seemed like a distant dream, ran through his mind, tripping over each other in the race to assume order and to make some kind of sense.

Eventually the effort of trying to make sense from chaos was enough to tire him and he fell into a fitful, uneasy sleep.

DOC AWOKE the next morning to find that the others had risen before him. Despite the unease with which he had first fallen into sleep, it had proved to move from fitful to deep and dreamless, and he now felt refreshed and less apprehensive. He rose and dressed, going in search of the others. In the quiet of the redoubt, the hum of un-maintenanced machinery the only breaks in the silence, it wasn't difficult to determine where they were.

Doc's sense took him to the kitchens, where the others were attempting to construct some kind of appetizing and nutritious meal from what they had left in the stores before leaving the last time. Which was very little. But they were in no condition to be fussy about what they would eat. Even the remains of the stores beat charred and burned mule or dog meat when it came to a contest.

'Doc, I didn't want to wake you, so I left you,' Krysty said on catching sight of him. 'Hope that was okay. How are you feeling?'

'Do you mean generally? Or are you being more

specific—as in, do I feel quite insane today?' Doc queried with as much of a grin as he could muster.

'It wasn't what I meant, but I guess it's a fair question,' Krysty mused. 'I don't know what you remember, but you kind of lost it for a while there.'

'I'll have to take your word for that,' the old man answered, settling himself among them. 'I have no recollection of any events after first leaving here and being caught in a blizzard.'

Ryan had been watching Doc carefully and had no doubts that the old man was telling the truth. There was something disingenuous about the old man. It was always easy to see when Doc was entering one of his mentally fragile phases, and equally it was easy to see when he had clarity of thought. Now was one of the latter times and Doc seemed genuinely confused about events. If nothing else, Ryan was glad to see the back of Joseph Jordan, whoever or whatever he may have been.

'Dark night, there's a lot that happened since then,' J.B. said with a degree of wry understatement. 'Where do we begin?'

Doc sat entranced while the events of the past few days were relayed to him. The trek across the wastelands, followed by their discovery by the Inuit hunting party when Doc tried to escape them. Their captivity in the Inuit settlement and near sacrifice in pagan- and Christian-inspired ritual to insure the fertility of the waning tribe. From this, the sudden emergence from fever of a new personality within Doc—that of the reincarnated Joseph Jordan. When the story reached this point, all watched Doc closely for some flicker of recognition, yet there was none. The only emotion to register on his face was that of astonishment.

From here, the old man's astonishment mounted as they unfurled his plans to take on the ville of Fairbanks as a large-scale sacrifice to their Lord, and of the war party he had helped to prepare.

By the time that Mildred and Jak were relaying to him the doomed attack on the ville, and the manner in which they had almost been trapped within the burning streets, Doc's face was ashen. Racing through his mind were thoughts of how his own insanity had nearly doomed his companions. Thoughts that jostled for space within his mind with others, that were darker and more introverted: how fragile was his mind, his personality, that it was able to be submerged so easily into some kind of disguise? How easy was it for him to sink into a kind of oblivion where he was able to threaten the very existence of those he valued most with no impunity?

'Doc, Doc, are you okay?'

'Eh?' The old man shook himself from his reverie to see that the others were studying him closely. He realized that their story had ended and he had seemed not to acknowledge this.

'I'm sorry,' he began haltingly. 'I just find it hard to comprehend. That I could have seemed to have functioned so clearly and yet to be advocating such madness. In fact, actively pursuing it.' He shook his head slowly. 'I have no recall of any of the events you have outlined, not even in the sense of a dream from which I was detached, merely the observer. What I recall is so much…less…' He petered off, not quite sure where to begin.

In the ensuing silence Ryan scanned the companions as they sat around the kitchen of the redoubt. Mildred and Krysty, who seemed to have a better grasp of the complexities of Doc's psyche than anyone else, were on edge, waiting for the old man to try to explain what had happened to him in his own mind. It was vital information for them, as they would be able to try to assess just where he was coming from…and perhaps where he was going to.

Jak was impassive. His scarred albino features were as grim and unreadable as they always were. Very rarely did any emotion escape the mask that he used to shield himself from the outside world. But he would be taking it in and making his own assessment.

J.B. looked like Ryan felt—as though he wanted to know what was happening with Doc but doubted that he could assimilate it. The two men had been friends for so long that Ryan was sure that J.B. felt the same way as he did. They were men of action and only used their sharp minds when action was called for. This was something beyond that range of experience.

Doc began again. 'In my mind, I felt as though I were not here. Everything that I experienced on our journey to the Inuit ville was part of some test. I was back in the time from which I originally came. I was insane, locked in a padded room and going through these experiences as a kind of mental exercise. It was as though I were a rat in a maze, running blindly at the behest of some celestial scientist who had a purpose in mind for me, and if I reached the end of the maze I would be rewarded. Not with candy or cheese, but with the truth. A revelation that would explain why I was going through this whole experience…not just since landing here, but in the entire time since you, my dear friends, first saved me from the hands of Cort Strasser.

'It seemed to me that in order to do this, I had to go through some kind of change, some kind of rebirth. I had to be like the butterfly that emerges from the chrysalis…even if that change meant that I had little or no knowledge of the life that I had experienced before that moment.

'I suspect that that was the moment at which this man Jordan first made an appearance. I could not tell you who or what he was, only that once he appeared, I receded not just in your eyes, but in my own mind, as well. I have no recall of anything that happened after that, and only one fleeting memory from then until I awoke on the sled as we approached this place once more.

'If I think about it, I can remember, just for a moment, standing in a log cabin staring at you all, wrapped in furs and skins. I tried to speak, but somehow the words would not come out. It was as though I were watching you through a gauze, as though I could hear you through a fog of white noise. My chest was constrained, making every breath something for which I had to fight, every syllable something that had to be forced from my lips. The words were there, but they would not come out.'

'But it is fleeting, momentary, and after that there is nothing. Nothing until last evening, when I awoke to find myself on a sled, aware that something had happened, but not what that may be.'

Doc stuttered to a halt and shrugged, not knowing where to go.

'I think that being here triggered things you didn't want to remember and made you withdraw into yourself,' Mildred said slowly. 'Strange thing is, although it may sound like madness, it's more a way of clinging on to your sanity.'

'But at what cost?' Doc spit bitterly. 'What does it benefit me if I save sanity at the expense of losing identity? What use is it if I close down whenever things get too much? How does this settle with the notion that I am in some way a useful member of this group. Good heavens, Doctor, if I am to retreat into my own head at the drop of a hat, what possible use could I be to you? In fact, I could be nothing except a complete liability. And this is not a world in which to carry passengers.'

'That's for us to decide,' Ryan cut in.

Doc shook his head firmly. 'I cannot be responsible for such an eventuality.'

'Then what do you propose to do about it?' Krysty asked in a reasonable tone. 'You want to stay here, alone? How long will you cling to your sanity then? You had a set of circumstances that are unlikely to occur again. I can't see why you—'

'But that is not the point,' Doc shouted over her. 'It may have been a one-off occurrence, but I cannot know that for sure, any more than you can. I cannot risk it happening again.'

'Doc, the only way any of us can avoid a risk like that is by buying the farm right here and now, and that's just stupe,' J.B. said. 'It's this fucking place—it messes with our heads. Let's just get the hell out and see what we feel like when we land somewhere else.'

It was a view with which all could agree, even Doc, who approached the idea with some trepidation, yet could see through his own fears how the redoubt may be, once more, exerting its pernicious influence.

They effected the quickest evacuation of all their redoubt experiences. In next to no time, they had collected what little they had to take with them, replenished from

the few supplies left in the stores and were in the mat-
trans chamber.

Ryan stood by the door while the others filed into the
chamber. As he entered and closed the door, Krysty
settled on the disk-inset floor next to an apprehensive-
looking Doc. She could feel the oppressive atmosphere
that had once again been creeping upon them begin to
lift, as if carried on the trails of white mist that began
to spiral around them.

Chapter Three

Jak wretched and sent a thin stream of bile across the floor, where it settled at Ryan Cawdor's feet.

'Jak's coming around,' the one-eyed man muttered, watching the stream of liquid congeal at the toe of his heavy combat boot. He couldn't think much beyond that, having only just managed to clamber to his feet. His head still spun wildly and it was at times like this that he was almost thankful for monocular vision, as it spared him the worst excesses of vomit-inducing blurred and double vision after a jump.

'It's not him I'm worried about,' Krysty slurred, shaking her head as she tried to clear it. The movement only made things worse and she slumped forward from her kneeling position. She felt terrible. Like the others, she had been concerned that with little opportunity to recuperate after a traumatic firefight and flight, the jump would be too much of a strain. Jak always suffered after a jump, but it was the ever-fragile Doc who was the cause of most concern.

She'd worry about him later, though. Right now, her primary objective was to make sure that she was functioning.

J.B. and Mildred had stirred, and while Ryan tried to make out shapes through the opaque armaglass walls of the chamber, Krysty helped the pair of them to their

feet. Jak, as ever, eschewed all help, waving away
Krysty's proffered hand to drag himself upright. He
spit out a sour ball of bile and looked over at Doc.

'He okay?'

Doc lay motionless, on his back.

'I don't know,' Mildred muttered unnecessarily as
she made her way over to him. The reflex reply had been
necessary to cover her own concern. To all intents and
purposes, Doc looked as though the trip might have
been one trauma too much. He was so still, looked so
peaceful, that at first she suspected that he had bought
the farm while being reconstituted. It was only when she
was kneeling over him that she could see he was breathing shallowly. There was still some life in the old bastard.

Something he confirmed by suddenly opening his
eyes. They were wide, staring and alert, with none of
the muzziness that he—or, indeed, any of the others—
usually experienced after a jump.

'Why, hello, my dear Doctor. How pleasant to see
you. I must say, you don't seem to be at all well. I, on
the other hand, feel as though I have had a most refresh-
ing rest.' He propped himself up on one elbow and
looked at the others, adding, 'It's most strange. Usually
I feel terrible after a jump, but I feel as though I could
fight an army.'

'Doc, the way I feel, that might be a good thing,'
Ryan commented wryly. 'But right now, let's just get
our shit together and secure the immediate area.'

He had seen nothing in the vague shapes lurking beyond the opaque armaglass of the chamber to suggest
that there was any kind of life in the redoubt. However,
triple red was the only way to approach evacuation.

When they were sufficiently recovered to make a move, they exited the chamber one by one, assuming positions of cover.

It was a futile exercise. The room beyond the anteroom was in semidarkness, where some of the fluorescent lighting had failed and the constantly blinking lights of the comp desks were all the life that appeared to exist.

Despite the fact that the air-conditioning and recycling plant should have kept a constant temperature, there was a distinct chill in the air, suggesting that it was more than just the lighting that was failing. The air itself was breathable, but carried a dank undertone, suggesting that areas of the redoubt might have been breached by outside elements. The one reassuring thing it did have, though, was that indefinable air of complete desolation. There seemed to be no human life here.

Still keeping their blasters to hand—instinct told them the redoubt was empty, but intellect still counseled caution—they left the chamber room.

The redoubt was in some disarray, not from any looting or ransacking from outside, but from the gradual breakdown of its own systems. At some time, probably during the immediate aftermath of the nukecaust, a breach had occurred in the walls of the structure. An earth movement strong enough to rupture the reinforced, thick concrete walls had caused enough damage to let outside elements creep in. Wherever this was located—and at present they couldn't be sure—it was beneath the local water table, as damp had suffused the very atmosphere. Great stretches of corridor were unlit where the lighting had shorted. The same could be said of sec doors that had started to close when the circuits shorted, but had been stayed by warps in the wall and were now jammed half open, half shut, a monument to the breach in supposedly safe defenses.

Rats had infiltrated the cracks, as had insect life. The winged insects buzzed around them, trying to bite. The red eyes of albino rats, almost twice the size of normal, glowered at them before the creatures scuttled for the safety of complete darkness. Here and there were small, stagnant pools where the damp had gathered enough to drip down the walls through the thin cracks that suffused the concrete. There were gatherings of moss and slime on the walls, delineating watermarks where there were occasional floods when the water table rose. Thankfully the mat-trans and anteroom had been just above this level.

As they rose higher, the signs of damage grew less, and there was less insect and rodent life hardy enough to brave the comparatively great distance from dank security. The electrical systems had still suffered, however, and some of the rooms were closed to them, sec doors failing to respond.

Eventually they reached a place where maps were displayed, revealing to them that they had landed on the Eastern Seaboard, beneath what had once been an area known as New Jersey.

'Not usual to have a redoubt so near a heavily populated area,' Krysty mused, indicating the above-ground map that revealed an expanse of predark urban growth.

'It was a heavy industrial area, probably one of the places they would have wanted to land some nukes first of all,' Mildred commented. 'I'd guess this redoubt was built so that they could have a base near to a big population, and near to some military factories that were located hereabouts. And you've got to say, it looks like it must have been hit really heavy up there for the damage that's come this far down. But then, there were a lot of nuke power plants along this coast—one not far from here, if my memory serves. You unleash a ton of nukes on top of that, and the only thing I'm surprised about is that this place is still here.'

'We've been along this coast before,' J.B. said, running his finger along the coastline. 'Remember? We got ourselves fouled up with that evil bitch captain…'

'Don't remind me.' Ryan shuddered, remembering the whaling queen who had looked like a man and had had designs on the one-eyed warrior. 'Fireblast, still gives me nightmares.'

'Nonetheless,' Doc mused, 'I see the point John Barrymore is making. Although we have not been in this particular spot before, we have been in the general area, and thus have some idea of the landscape we should encounter. We also know that the area is capable of supporting human life and it is likely that we will be able to come across some groups of survivors. Furthermore, if we find the area somewhat uncongenial, we will have an escape route of some kind planned. If all else fails, we should head for the coast.'

Krysty laughed. 'Doc, I don't know what's happened to you, but Ryan had better watch out. I can't remember the last time I saw you like this.'

'I shall take that as the compliment it appeared to be,' Doc said gravely, with a mock bow. 'I am, you might say, feeling myself again.'

'That's good to hear,' Ryan agreed. 'But instead of standing around telling each other how damn good we are, I suggest we see what there's worth plundering here and then get the hell out. It doesn't look like there's an immediate danger, but I don't feel comfortable underground when I know the mainframe's falling to pieces.'

Ryan had done little more than voice a concern that had been lurking at the backs of all their minds. When the support systems of a redoubt began to crumble they could take years to fail, or one short could start a chain reaction to close it down in minutes.

Time, then, was of the essence. The upper levels of the redoubt hadn't been damaged too badly by the earth movements. There were cracks in some of the walls, but nothing like the fissures on the lower level. The main problems were caused by the shorting of electrical circuits that had closed some sec doors and effectively sealed them by refusing to respond to the codes. Many of these were in areas where the companions would seek to plunder: the armory, the kitchens and food stores, and stores for clothing and footwear.

J.B.'s task was to open the doors without risking further damage to the potentially delicate balance of the redoubt. Under any other circumstances the task would have been simple—plas-ex applied to the points of balance, and then retire to a safe distance. But now he had to be careful about the amounts he used, much more so that usual.

Carefully, the Armorer weighed out the plas-ex and attached a detonator, making sure that, at all times, the companions would shelter from the blast in a position that would leave them on the right side of the explosion for the main exit should the need to flee arise.

In the eerie quiet of the deserted redoubt, the tension hung heavy over J.B. as he prepared each explosion.

The first two were small—more pops than blasts—but by his careful positioning the charges were enough to bend the doors, giving the companions the leverage they needed to open them manually.

The kitchen and clothing stores came easily. Despite his looks of apprehension at the roof overhead when the charges detonated, J.B.'s judgment proved sound. In the clothing stores they were able to kit themselves out in some fresh clothing, still packed in polyethylene, that replaced the tattered rags they had worn from the north.

Likewise, the kitchen stores hadn't been raided, although there was some evidence that rats and insects had been able to use the service ducts to get this far up the redoubt levels, driven onward by the scent of foodstuffs. As there was no knowing what may or may not have been contaminated, they stuck to self-heats and some foods where the packaging hadn't been tampered with in any way or was far from evidence of rats such as gnawing and droppings. The huge walk-in freezer compartments were still stocked and sealed. There were three, and although the power had failed in two, the third still contained some deep-frozen perishables that could safely be eaten when defrosted. They stocked up on as much as possible, preferring to keep the inedible self-heats for emergencies.

The third door J.B. had to open was the one that gave him most concern: the armory. Tricky enough to have to blow the door on an armory at the best of times, lest the explosive materials within be triggered by the explosion. But when they were up against a structure riddled with flaws that may give under such stress, it became a much harder task.

J.B. set the charge and looked nervously up at the ceiling before retiring to cover.

'If this fucks up, it's been interesting,' he said wryly in the moments before the small charge detonated. He closed his eyes and held his breath...nothing. Opening them again, he could see that the door had been blasted away from one side of the portal and that there appeared to be no residual damage within the room itself.

They advanced and opened up the room. It was exactly as it had been left before the nukecaust. At some point, there had to have been an evacuation, as there still lay in one corner an open crate and a clipboard and pen, as though the room had been deserted partway through an inventory of the ordnance.

Wasting little time, they equipped themselves with spare ammo, grens and plas-ex from the stores. J.B. regretfully looked at the crates of unopened and undisturbed blasters. There were rifles, SMGs and handblasters, any of which may have replaced their own favored arms, given time to test them in the ranges.

But time was one thing they couldn't allow. The redoubt may be fine for another century, or it may start to crumble at any moment.

Equipped, they left the armory—J.B. casting it a backward glance that was part wistful longing and part a hard-headed knowledge that they could have gleaned so much if given time—and headed toward the exit door.

The lighting was erratic along the stretch leading to the exit ramp, and all had cause to wonder what they might find beyond the final sec door. Had the circuits cut out because of the water damage in the lower levels or because there were other stresses operating out-side the walls on this upper level? Would the sec door open to reveal that they had been blocked in by a land-fall?

The latter was something that Ryan hoped wouldn't be the case. They needed to get out. The redoubt was too unsafe for them to stay and a jump would be too risky. Out was their only option.

'Here goes nothing,' he said to the others as he punched in the sec code, lifted the lever and leveled his Steyr. The chances of anyone lying in wait were next to nothing, but that wasn't zero.

The door raised slowly to reveal a landscape that was lush but strange. Everything was green, but low-level, as though it were made for small people. The grasses were close to the ground, plants were half size, the trees stunted. But it was a clear day and it was good to breathe fresh air untainted by sulfur as it swept into the musty tunnel mouth.

Ryan stepped cautiously out into a bright, sunny morning, with the sky clear but for a few fluffy white clouds. He looked around. The surrounding area was clear and there were no sounds of bird or animal life within earshot. He beckoned the others to join him.

'Gaia, it's like paradise compared to where we've just been,' Krysty said, breathing in deeply to savor the air.

'Yeah, even if it is a kind of half-pint paradise,' Mil-dred muttered.

'Not fucking cold.' Jak smiled.

'So far, so good,' J.B. agreed. 'What d'you think, Doc?'

It was when he turned to elicit the old man's opinion that J.B. was astounded to see Doc retreating backward into the redoubt, with the door closing on him, cutting him off seemingly at his own behest.

Chapter Four

Who am I? Is the real me the man who now posits these questions, or is the real me the man Jordan who they say I became for a short while? It does, does it not, raise many questions as to the nature of identity? Is all of this through which I move an artifice, the mere whim of my own imagination, or is it real? But then, what is reality?

Of all the things I remember, of all the things that have occurred within the confines of my own mind over the past few days, there is only the one constant: the search for some kind of truth. Whatever I am, and wherever I am, there is a part of my mind that is still active and still seeks to find an answer of some kind for what has happened, and what is continuing to happen. If I am to ascertain the truth, then I must follow that course through to the end. That quest is the only one which matters. Wherever that leads.

Am I in a padded cell? Am I here? Am I Theophilus Tanner? Am I Joseph Jordan? There is only the one way in which I can find an answer. I must follow my gut feeling. When the consciousness is confused, then intellect alone cannot be trusted. In order to find the answer, then I must follow what instinct tells me.

And yet what it tells me to do is something that I cannot share with the others. They would not want to go back to Fairbanks. Why should they? They lived that nightmare in a way that I cannot comprehend. By the same token, they could never comprehend the compulsion that drives me onward.

I have said nothing. I shall continue to say nothing. If I hang back in the tunnel, I can slip away while they walk out into the new lands. If I close the door behind me, then by the time they have noticed my absence, re-opened the redoubt and tried to find me, I will have traveled back.

Oh, I know only too well that the settings on the mat-trans are random, but that is the point. Whatever happens to me next will be a large part of the journey. If fate—or the workings of my own imagination masquerading as fate—decrees that I end up back in the frozen north, then it shall be nothing more than another sign that I have taken the right path.

These are not times for plans. Plans demand intellect; intellect is confused by the workings of insanity; the gut is the only true arbiter.

But I shall miss them. I dimly recall thinking of them as angels at one point in my madness. Perhaps they are, in a sense. Guardians of ideal qualities created by my mind, perhaps based on those I have known at some point. Or mayhap they are real, and this world is my reality. In that case, then they are angels of the best kind: firm friends in the face of adversity.

I salute them…

'WHAT THE HELL does he think he's doing?' Mildred yelled as she turned and ran toward the closing sec door, Doc now nothing more than a darkness in the shadows as he moved out of sight.

'Millie, wait,' J.B. yelled. He cast a glance at Ryan, wondering if his friend would want to follow Doc. The old man was still suffering from some kind of psychosis, and the last thing they needed—friend or not—was to become embroiled in more games.

But J.B. need not have wondered. Already, Ryan was catching up to Mildred and passing her on the way to the sec door.

'Bastard won't start to open until it's fully shut, even if you punch the code in,' he yelled breathlessly. 'We've got to get through it and get him, let the others wait.'

Mildred didn't bother to answer, saving her breath to try to keep pace with Ryan's longer stride. Particularly if she was going to make it under the door. They were now about twenty feet from the entrance and the door showed less than a foot of space. It was going to be incredibly tight.

Ryan was a crucial few feet ahead of her and he flung himself into the gap, flattening himself as much as possible and bracing for the impact as his flying body connected harshly with the floor of the tunnel. He winced in pain as his shoulder jarred, a tingling numbness momentarily shooting down to his fingers. He ignored it, concentrating on rolling so that he could get the hell out of Mildred's way as she came through.

Cursing loudly with her last desperate exhalation of breath, she took a flying leap at the ever-narrowing gap, feeling the edge of the door bite as it closed the gap uncomfortably. She threw herself with as much force and momentum as possible, the foot-long thickness of the tunnel almost catching and trapping the toes of her boots as she slid past, ironically just enough to kill her speed and insure that she didn't hit the floor as hard as Ryan.

The one-eyed man was already on his feet and headed down the tunnel as she picked herself up.

'That damn fool old buzzard. We should just leave the old bastard to do what the hell he wants,' she muttered darkly as she hauled herself to her feet and set off in pursuit.

They knew exactly where they were headed, and as they were stronger and faster than Doc, they might just have time to catch him before he entered the mat-trans unit. Once the chamber door closed, it would be impossible to open it until the process had been completed.

Neither of them wasted time looking to their rear. They knew that the others would follow as soon as they could get the sec door opened once more. It was more of an imperative to reach Doc.

Their choices were justified. As they thundered down the lower corridor, heavy footfalls echoing around the dank and scarred walls of the lowest levels, they knew Doc could hear them. But it didn't matter. Speed was more important than stealth. Something that was proved when they entered the comp room to find Doc about to grab the lever to the unit's door. He was almost crying with frustration as his shaking hands and trembling fingers, fraught with anxiety, seemingly refused to grasp the lever.

He looked up as they approached.

'Please. I did not want you to follow me. Allow me to do this.'

'To do what, Doc? To send yourself off into God knows where?' Mildred asked.

'It's something I must do,' he replied as firmly as he could.

'The hell it is,' Ryan snapped.

Doc looked at him, momentarily distracted. 'How the hell would you know?' he retorted angrily. 'You have no idea what I am trying to do, or why.'

'Then why don't you tell us?' Mildred questioned in as reasonable a tone as she could muster.

Doc sighed. 'It would take too long, and you would not want me to do it. I do not think you could understand—'

'Too stupid, is that it?' Mildred countered.

'No, it is not that. What's the point, you'll only stop me anyway,' he added with a resigned sigh, standing back from the door.

In the distance, they could hear the others approaching.

'C'mon, Doc, I really don't want to talk about it in here,' Ryan said softly. 'Let's go topside, and then you can explain. Mebbe we'll understand, after all.'

'I somehow doubt that that very much,' Doc murmured, 'but I suppose I should give you the chance.'

If nothing else, Mildred could treasure the confused looks on the faces of J.B. and Krysty when she, Doc and Ryan calmly walked out of the mat-trans anteroom. There was even a flicker of confusion crossing Jak's albino visage.

For the second time, they exited the redoubt and stood in the glorious morning. But there was little attention to be paid to the landscape or the blazing clear sky. The first thing was to try to sort out the problem with which Doc now presented them.

A few hundred yards from the entry to the redoubt was a small clump of trees, twisted and stunted with thick growth on their boles, but enough canopy to provide shelter from the heat and brightness of the sun.

They took refuge beneath these and Doc started to explain what had caused him to turn back.

It was a long, rambling tale. Sometimes he had to stop and go back on the story, as though there were parts that he even had to explain for himself. Which was no surprise, as what had made so much sense when mulled over within the confines of his own head now seemed to be disjointed and absurd when spilled out loud. He could see from the faces around him that they were having trouble understanding the questions he had to ask himself and the non sequitur answers that had caused him to take his instinct-led course of action.

He finished up weakly, shrugging and telling them that he didn't expect them to understand, but that it was something that he had to do.

'Doc,' Ryan said softly after a long silence, 'you weren't with us when that ville went up. Well, you were, but you were this other person. And then you were unconscious. You didn't see what happened to it. There was no way anyone could have got out of there. The whole tribe, except for mebbe those who stayed behind at the ville, were wiped out. There is no one for you to go back to, even supposing that, by some miracle, the mat-trans took you back to the right redoubt and you could find your way on foot from there without freezing. We only made it as a group because we could support one another. You'd have no one to lean on if you had to.'

'Yes, I understand completely what you're saying,' Doc stated, 'but can you not see that it makes no difference? This is not about being rational. This is about following an instinct because I cannot trust that which I see and hear around me. As far as I know—in an empirical sense—you may not even exist.'

'A what?' Krysty asked. 'Mother Sonja told me about some old ideas from before nukecaust, but that's a new one on me.'

'Doc,' Mildred said, deciding to try her luck, 'I've listened to what you've said, and although I can't totally understand, I ask you to trust me on one thing. As far as I'm concerned, I know I'm here. And knowing that, I trust my senses. And what they tell me, as a trained physician, is that you've been through an immense trauma from fever, followed by a concussion. From my perspective, this is real, and the things in your head that make you doubt yourself are the symptomatic results of a definite medical cause. It would be wrong of me as a doctor to let you follow your instinct at the risk of your own safety. I would recommend that we take you with us, even if we have to, at this stage, do it by force.'

Doc's face hardened as he looked around. He was met with features as determined as his own.

'I have no doubt that you would do that. I am out-numbered, and I have little choice but to acquiesce. Be warned, if I have the chance, I will try to get back to the redoubt and jump.'

'Mebbe so,' Krysty said softly. 'But consider this— mebbe part of your journey is to find another way back, and that is why we were allowed to catch up with you and stop you.'

Doc's face cracked into a wry grin. 'That's very good, my dear. In truth I have no answer to that. I am not allayed, but you have, nonetheless, set me a logical quandary that I must ponder.'

'That mean we get fuck out here?' Jak asked, dis-gruntled and a little lost.

J.B. rose, stretched and yawned. 'Soon as we find

which way's the best way, then, yeah, I guess so. Right, Ryan?'

Ryan shrugged. He felt uneasy that he hadn't quite grasped where Doc now stood, somehow angry with himself for not understanding; but action would force any issues that remained.

'Yeah. Sooner the better,' he growled.

USING HIS MINISEXTANT, J.B. got their bearings. A northwesterly path would take them toward the coast from their current position, and so they set out in formation. Ryan was at front, J.B. covering the rear of the line, with Jak in the middle, keeping close to Doc, and flanked by Mildred and Krysty. Doc seemed content enough to fall in with their plans, yet there was something that jarred. It wasn't like him to give in that easily. Nonetheless, there seemed little option for him at this time.

It was a strange territory in which they moved. The wide, stunted trees with their bizarre growths and sparse canopy were intermingled with sudden needles of tall, thin firlike trees that shot into the sky as though about to scratch the very surface of the heavens. There was no rhyme or reason to the placing of these particular trees. It was as though the mutated woodlands had produced mutations within the mutants. Clustered around the dwarf trees were spiky grasses of a brilliant color that were as tough as rope. The carpet of rough grass was interspersed with flora of an equally brilliant hue and of a wide variety of colors. Reds, blues and yellows splashed among the green of the woodland floor, their flowers showing as distended and distorted shapes among the grasses, leaves of differing sizes on the same bloom causing them to droop at bizarre angles, hideously enlarge stamen ready to spread pollen across the surface of the ground and into the air with puffball explosions.

It was inevitable that the blooms would have to spread their own pollen, for the one immediately noticeable thing about the terrain was that it had no wildlife: no animals, no birds, nor any insects. The only sounds that broke the silence, other than those made by the companions themselves, were the muted rustlings of the grasses and the leaves as the light breezes of the day caught them.

It was incredibly peaceful and after a short while the companions found themselves relaxing, their every instinct telling them that they were safe from any kind of attack. Yet, for all the ease that they could now feel, one question nagged. Why was there such a lack of fauna when both rats and insects had invaded the redoubt?

It was a question soon answered. After a couple of hours they broke stride briefly to rest. A small stream bubbled twenty yards from where they stood, and Jak made his way down to test the water. Hunkering, he let the cool stream run over his hand. As he did, something sent an involuntary spasm down his spine. Cupping his palm, he lifted a little of the water to his nose. There was a faint tang to it that set alarm bells ringing in his intuition. He flicked at his palm with his tongue, rapidly spitting out the few drops that caught on the flesh.

The water had a metallic taste and every sense told him that it would chill him to drink from the stream. He straightened and turned to see J.B. taking a bright orange fruit from one of the trees, holding it under his nose to sniff it. The Armorer turned, sensing that he was being watched. His eyes met Jak's and he nodded shortly. Prying the fruit open with both thumbs, he sniffed at it. A sweetness did little to overlay the sour stench that followed on the heels of the initial scent.

The others had observed this exchange, and each proceeded to test fruits, berries and leaves in a similar way. The results were completely inclusive: everything that grew or ran over the earth was toxic to the taste. The very ground itself had to have been heavily contaminated, either by the nukes or by something that had been let into the soil during the nukecaust. Given that this area had once lain close to heavily industrial and military suburbs, it should not have come as a shock. The mutie flora had adjusted to the soil from which it sprang, and any fauna had either perished or moved on.

It was, however, with a jolt that they realized that this gave them a problem. Not eating or drinking in the contaminated area would be simple enough; they had drinking water and self-heats, as well as some of the fresher food they had taken from the redoubt. But this wouldn't last forever, and from the complete silence surrounding them, the contaminated land obviously spread over a great distance. Would they be able to clear the area before they ran out of supplies?

'If we assume the place we started from is now about six miles back, and that the coastline hasn't changed too much from when that old map was made, I figure it's three days' march at most before we hit the ocean,' J.B. said as he double-checked their current position. 'This can't last all the way to the coast, 'cause we saw no sign of it before. And even if it does, then we just make a raft and risk it on the waves down the line of the coast itself,' he added with a shrug.

'Yeah, that sounds about the best of it,' Ryan agreed.

'Go triple cautious with the water, and we'll ration the food, try to keep those self-heats to a minimum. We should be okay,' he finished.

And it was true. They had enough for the distance J.B. estimated. But what if they had to change course? What if they were diverted before they hit the coast? Suddenly a simple route march had taken on a darker edge. They were used to facing practical matters head-on, and a nagging doubt at the corners of the mind was potentially more damaging to the group.

For two days they struck out toward the coast, eking out water and food. They made good progress as the only obstacles in their path were those created by the twisted and stunted boles of the trees, some a good yard across, and the patches of iron-hard grass that had to be avoided as they were too damaging even to the heavy boots worn by the walkers.

With no wildlife of any kind to impede them, it seemed certain that they would reach the coast easily before their supplies ran out. The cloud of possibility that they felt hanging over them began to dispel and they traveled at a greater pace, with more optimism around them.

The optimism increased, the pace decreasing, as they hit land that was less contaminated. The grasses and the trees became less warped and stunted, the going softer underfoot, and there were signs of life. Borne on the distant breezes were the sounds of birds in flight. The buzz of insect life became apparent, the flying creatures attempting to take bites from them. And in the undergrowth they could hear the rustle of movement. The smell of the woodlands changed from the sterility and sickly sweetness of the contaminated areas, the air now infused with the musk of living creatures, the woodlands in which they lived now stinking of life. It was at times an unpleasant odor, but one that bespoke life rather than the stasis of the contaminated area.

But the influx of life meant that they had to slow their pace. They had no real idea what shape that life may take. The sounds they had heard so far suggested that there was nothing particularly large or dangerous lurking in the shadows to leap out and chill them. Yet the smaller beasts could be just as dangerous; a bite could lead to an infection, or one well-placed claw could sever an artery. If there were packs, they could attack in numbers and prove difficult to repel.

So the only option was to slow the pace of their march. Jak scouted ahead. A natural-born hunter, his senses and instincts developed by years of practice, he was the perfect member of the group to recce ahead for any life and any danger it may represent. It was, after all, a function he had fulfilled many times before.

Despite the fact that they now had a possible danger with which to contend, they felt more at ease. This, at least, was a palpable threat, and one to which they were used; the unnameable fears that had lurked in each of their minds now began to subside.

The nature of the trees and grasses changed: softer and shorter underfoot, with boles and trunks that had a shape, height and width that was more like the kinds of growths they had seen in other areas.

'I figure the water and the fruits must be edible here,' Ryan mused. 'It keeps these damn insects going,' he added, batting away thirsty midges that dive-bombed his neck.

'We want to be careful about that,' Mildred cautioned. 'It's possible that whatever lives here has some kind of tolerance to whatever's in the soil. It can't be as bad as back there, as at least it does support life. But it might be too much for us.'

'In effect, my dear Doctor, we are in the same position—do not drink the water and stick to the interminable self-heats,' Doc mumbled. 'It is nothing more than the same thing all over. No change. Perhaps it would have been better if you'd let me go as I had wished—or perhaps had come with me.'

'Doc, don't start on that again.' Krysty sighed. 'It wouldn't have been any better if you'd got back to the north, and it could have been a whole lot worse. Who knows where you would have ended up.'

'Somewhere without a poisonous forest, perhaps,' Doc replied sharply.

'Dark night, will you stop going on about it, Doc,' J.B. muttered wearily. 'For the last two days, all you've done is moan. It's like you want to wear us down and make us admit we were wrong. But what the hell good would that do?'

'None,' Doc snapped bitterly. 'It would do none as it's too late to turn back. But don't think that I won't take another option if I can find it. With or without you.'

They hadn't heard him be this openly antagonistic before. It was as though the quietness of their progress over the past few days had done little for the old man except give him the time to brood on the wrong he thought they had wrought him. He had made no point to leave them and turn back, as though at least some part of him knew the futility of this; but at the same time there was little doubt that the thought of getting back to the people he considered his destiny was something that was looming larger still in his thoughts.

Which was something that could become a major problem if left unchecked. But for the moment, Ryan was thankful that it was all they had to be concerned about.

They continued for the best part of a day, their progress impeded by the need for caution. Most of the mammalian life in the woodlands was small: squirrels, rabbits, other rodents, some of which showed signs of the long-lasting toxic effects of the nearby ground by their mutations. None of the creatures were that big, and were misshapen, though not enough to stop them from surviving adequately in the woods. They were helped in this by the fact that nothing large seemed able to survive and prosper in the immediate environment. The birds, likewise, were all small. The flitted from tree to tree, always staying just enough out of sight to prevent themselves from becoming a target either to the companions or to the lower level life-forms.

The trees and plants were hung with a variety of fruits that differed from those in the contaminated area in as much as they were smaller, less hideously malformed and had duller colorings. They also showed signs of being eaten by the fauna of the woods.

Nonetheless, taking heed of what Mildred had said earlier, they refrained from partaking of the fruits, or hunting any of the small animals and birds, setting a fire to keep the rodents at bay as night fell, and relying on their dwindling supplies of food and water.

'By my reckoning, even though we've slowed down, we should be able to hit the coast by tomorrow night, the morning after at most,' J.B. told them after they had eaten. 'We just need to keep on this heading. Just as well we're past those shit strange mutie trees.'

It was an optimistic, contented group who settled for the night, Ryan taking first watch. Not that there was much to take note of. The birds had settled for the night and the only sounds were of some nocturnal rodents hunting in the undergrowth. Although nominally alert, Ryan allowed himself to relax slightly. There was nothing out there to disturb their rest or to impede their progress.

The following day, he felt, they would make good time.

WITHIN A FEW HOURS of breaking camp and setting off for the coast, he knew that his assumption of the night before had been incorrect. It wasn't something that could be put into words, but there were signs that a major change was ahead of them. Although the landscape around them remained the same—certainly showing no signs of deterioration into the contaminated state they had first encountered—the sounds and signs of life began to fade away. There were fewer birds and insects, less scuttling in the long grasses or flashes of fur as the smaller mammals turned away from the intruders in their land.

'Something's changed,' Ryan said softly. 'But what?'

Jak was doing a recon and he returned. Ryan repeated his question. The albino shrugged. 'Nothing. Trees same, ground same. But no animals, no birds. Something scaring them away, but not anything seen.'

'Fireblast, this is what I hate more than anything. Give me an enemy that you can see any fuckin' day. Triple red from now on,' he said, shrugging the Steyr from his shoulder and chambering a round.

'You want me to recce ahead?' Jak asked.

Ryan shook his head, his single ice-blue eye glittering as he surveyed the land around. 'No. This might not be something we can see that easily. If it can scare the wildlife away, then it might not be as simple as a single enemy we can see.'

'By the Three Kennedys, you're not suggesting that we may be up against some kind of supernatural agency?' Doc asked, his voice suspended uncertainly between fear and a desire to mock.

'Nothing as simple. Whatever's cleared this area has a wide sweep and has mebbe been doing it for a while. Notice the smell, anything else?' he asked.

'No spoor,' Jak said. 'No half-eaten fruit or plant. Been deserted a long time.'

'Yeah, that's what I figure. So we keep together, we keep going, hope we don't meet it—whatever it is—and we stay triple alert on this, okay?'

Blasters poised, they tightened formation and fell into line. It was hard, not knowing exactly what it was that they needed to protect themselves against: all they knew was that the danger was nearer than before, if less palpable. Their pace decreased, as well, so that it seemed they were making no progress at all.

So far, they had been blessed with excellent weather during their trek. The skies above the canopy had remained clear, the temperature almost humid. This now grated, as the sweat of concentration and fear began to gather upon them, running in slow rivulets down their skin, collecting in pools in the small of the back, under the arms, behind the knees. They were itchy and uncomfortable, the irritation adding to their mounting tetchiness.

It was therefore, perhaps, fortunate that they didn't have to wait long before the silence was broken. After only an hour's slow crawl, they became aware of something approaching them, head-on.

Jak caught first hearing and Krysty's mutie sense echoed his own acute senses, her hair coiling protectively and the dread rising in her. The enemy—whoever or whatever it may be—was approaching so quickly that it became audible to the others before either Jak or Krysty had a chance to verbalize their forebodings.

'What the hell is that?' Mildred whispered.

'I'd say there's at least a half dozen of whoever it is, and they haven't had much need to use stealth up to now,' J.B. commented wryly as the noise reached them.

'Take cover,' Ryan commanded. 'See how many of these sons of gaudys there are.'

The woodland provided ample cover. There were no paths as such that could be taken, rather a maze of gaps between the trees that could be utilized. None was suitable for more than two abreast, so it was a reasonable assumption that the oncoming force would have to split themselves in some manner to pass by where the companions were located. Jak shinnied rapidly up a tree to try to get a better look at the oncoming party while the others took advantage of the excellent cover the greenery presented.

From his vantage point, Jak could see that there were nine people in the party approaching. All were men aged from their early teens to their late twenties. There were no veterans among them—in fact, the age tended more toward the younger end of the scale—and this, allied to their seeming inability to use stealth, was a good sign. All the same, they still outnumbered the compan-

ions. The strangest thing about them was that they made
no attempt to camouflage themselves. In fact, their garb
was some of the strangest that Jak had seen from men
who were his opponents. They were all dressed in white
robes that were cut short, toga-style, rimmed in thick
red trim. Their legs were encased in leather thongs that
were crisscrossed and tied up to the knees. They carried daggers in sheaths and a variety of handblasters.
Jak thought he could pick out a Walther PPK, a Vortak
precision pistol and a Browning Hi-Power like the one
Dean had used before he'd gone missing. All good
blasters, but ones that needed a degree of skill. Looks
could be deceptive, but Jak doubted that these strangely
attired men had the skill to be effective—not if their
shooting echoed their stalking skills.

Jak scrambled down the tree and outlined the position to the companions beneath. Although secreted, they
were close enough to hear him as he rapidly gave them
the requisite information before taking cover himself.

All they had to do was to wait for the hunting party
to come upon them. Why they were in the woods was
a mystery. If they knew that the companions were
there—and how was another matter—then they were
making a poor task of concealing themselves. They
were easy to track as they closed on the area where the
companions were taking cover.

The nine men had spread themselves out among the
twisting gaps through the trees, making it hard to take
them all in one attack; and yet they were too close to
risk blasterfire once the companions engaged with
them. Too far apart to take out, too close to take out. It
was more luck than judgment, that much was clear, but
it was enough to make the companions' task harder.

Ryan signaled with a sharp whistle and the six friends shot from their hiding places as the strangely garbed hunting party passed them. It was a measure of how inexperienced the strangers were that they seemed to be completely unaware that they had the companions in their midst until they had already been attacked.

It was a swift and brutal battle. Unwilling to risk blasterfire that may hit their own people with stray shells, Ryan, Jak and J.B. had opted to use their blades. Mildred and Krysty used their bare hands. However, even in this they had the drop on their opponents, who had kept their daggers sheathed. The two men that the women chose to attack both fumbled for their blades rather than defend themselves, and both found themselves on the end of crushing blows. Krysty delivered a kick to the groin that was made more painful by the sharp silver point on her blue cowboy boots, whereas Mildred took out her man with a roundhouse punch that connected perfectly on the top of the jaw, just beneath the ear. The man's eyes rolled into his head as his skull snapped back.

Doc was the only one who held back. So many thoughts raced through his head, some of which he was obscurely ashamed of. Should he join the fray or see who won? What would benefit him in his long-term aim? But surely he should help his friends—ah, but had they been of any help to him, not allowing him to return to his destiny? All of this spun around his head, freezing him until the moment when he was actually attacked. A burly man with a blond beard to match his mop of curls snarled and thrust at Doc with his dagger. The old man smoothly withdrew the razored blade of Toledo steel from its cane sheath and parried the blow, countering with a thrust that swept across the man's chest, ripping his toga and drawing a line of blood from beneath.

At six on eight, the odds were already beginning to even up a little. They took another turn for the good when one man howled in agony, his arm sliced vertically by a blow from Ryan's panga. The flesh hung from his upper arm, blood splattering on the foliage around him. He was fortunate that it missed his artery, but nonetheless he recoiled and took no further part in the fray.

'It's not them…it's not them,' the cry was echoed around the hunting party, much to the confusion of the companions. They didn't stop fighting, but now found that instead of standing toe-to-toe they were driving their attackers back, as though the hunting party was deliberately retreating.

The strangely attired men pulled back enough to turn and flee. Jak was about to give chase when Ryan stayed him. Still the cry of 'not them…not them…' echoed from the retreating men.

As the sounds faded into the distance, the companions exchanged bemused glances. Who had the hunters thought they might be, and did that mean they weren't alone in the woodlands?

There was one way to find out. The man on whom Mildred had landed the perfect punch was still unconscious, sprawled on the ground.

Ryan strode over and pulled the man to his feet. The movement made him stir and his return to consciousness was aided by the open-palmed slaps Ryan delivered across his face. His eyes opened, bleary and unfocused.

'Wake up,' Ryan grated. 'You've got a lot to tell us, and you'd better do it quick.'

Chapter Five

His eyes opened, although they were not as yet focused, and they showed the naked fear that he felt in the midst of the group.

'Are you going to talk?' Ryan snarled. He had little time for those who attacked him without reason, and even less for those who showed the cowardice of this man. He looked as though he was about to defend himself.

'Don't even think about that,' the one-eyed man growled.

'I wouldn't give you the satisfaction,' the young man returned. Now that he was beginning to take in his surroundings, and that reason was returning to his muddled senses, he was growing in courage. He took in the half dozen people surrounding him. They weren't the ones his people had sought, although they had fought hard and were understandably angry. If he told them what they wanted to know, then perhaps he would be able to negotiate with them. After all, as he looked around he could see that there were no chilled bodies scattered around. They hadn't wantonly slaughtered the rest of the party.

His surreptitious glance didn't escape Ryan. 'I'll cut you a deal,' the one-eyed warrior stated. 'You tell me what I want to know, and you can go free.'

'You must think me a fool to agree to such a blatant untruth.' The young man spit.

Ryan allowed a grin to crease his weathered features. 'Fair point, but it works like this. We want to get through to the coast without being attacked. You come with us, to make sure that doesn't happen, and you're free to go. Your people obviously weren't attacking us—it was a mistake. Fireblasted stupe one, as it could have got us chilled, but this shit happens.'

The young man studied Ryan's face intently. In turn, the leader studied him. It was an open, soft face. The man was obviously just out of his teens, his long, dark hair and short beard showing the softness of youthful growth. His skin was clear and his eyes a blue almost as piercing as Ryan's single orb. There were traces of puppy fat still on him, suggesting he came from a ville that had plentiful supplies—which was worth knowing—and his bearing was strong. Despite the position in which he was held, and the fear that had temporarily assailed him on first coming around, he now held himself defiantly. It was probably a pose, but one he used to try to bluff his way past his fear.

Ryan couldn't help but like him. He had balls. Enough to not answer immediately, as though he truly had options to consider.

'Very well, I will answer your questions on the understanding that I will aid you with safe passage to the coast and insure that you aren't attacked by my people—however, I should add that it is still likely that you will be a target, particularly on the route that you wish to take, for my people aren't the only ones who are in this vicinity—'

'I kind of guessed that from the way you thought we

were someone else,' Ryan cut in. 'So why don't you start by telling us who you are?'

The young man looked around before speaking, then said, 'I have no objection to this, as such, but I feel I must point out that without a sentry of some kind, we may be putting ourselves at risk from those we were seeking.'

'If they were like your people, we'll hear them coming, all right,' J.B. commented wryly.

'Ah, but that's the problem,' the young man said, turning his earnest gaze on the Armorer. 'We're novices in the art of combat, and make no compunction in admitting such. It is one of the problems we seek to address in our quest for survival. But those we oppose—and who oppose us—are experts and masters in the dark arts of war.'

'Jeez, if you're gonna be this long-winded then you're gonna give Doc a run for his money,' Mildred said, sighing, 'in which case we really do need to set up a guard.'

Ryan laughed shortly. Mildred had a point. They withdrew to as secure a position as they could find, and Jak took watch while the young man hunkered down in the midst of the group.

'So what is it that you wish to know?' he asked simply.

'Who you are and where you're from would be a start, along with who you thought we were and why you tried to attack us,' Ryan answered.

The young man smiled and shook his head. 'A veritable avalanche of questions. Allow me to take them in the order in which they were posed. First, my name is Affinity, and I come from the ville of Memphis, which is eight miles from here, to the north and the west. We're a small ville, and all we want to do is to live in peace, which perhaps may surprise you in light of the way you encountered our sec patrol. But we have to be vigilant, for we're endangered simply because of our peaceful aims.'

'Why would that be?' Krysty prompted.

Affinity twinkled as he looked at the woman. 'I was about to explain, if but given the chance. We're a break-away ville, formed by those who have escaped from the larger ville of Atlantis. There, all are enslaved in the service of the greater cause. But there were those of us who didn't want to live beneath the whip and the chain. Though we have been brought up to believe in the cause of those who would come to claim us, we can't see the point of building and waiting to be taken to a better life that promises nothing but more oppression. So gradually we fled the sec maze that surrounds the ville and made our own homes...those of us who could make it through with our lives.

'And yet, you know, that somehow makes it all the sweeter that we have freedom, even if it be at the price of eternal vigilance.'

'This Atlantis—how far is it from your ville, Memphis?' J.B. questioned, trying to keep the young man focused before he lost the thread of his discourse. It was obvious that he was inclined to ramble, and time was of the essence.

'Atlantis is twenty miles to the south of Memphis, about fifteen from here, as the birds fly,' he answered with admirable brevity.

'And it's sec from that ville that you were looking for?' Krysty asked.

The young man nodded. 'They can often be found here, and they're our enemies.'

Doc leaned forward and tapped the young man on the knee. 'You must forgive a befuddled old man, and indulge him,' he began, 'but your discourse does not, in some regards, make much sense to me. You claim that these sec men are much better fighters than you, yet you were actively looking for them when you encountered us. Surely you can see that to an outsider this seems a strange attitude. To what purpose would you actively seek out conflict with those who could so easily best you in battle?'

It was obvious from the expression on Affinity's face that he was glad that Doc had spoken. Their similar modes of speech made him a much more receptive target for the young man's discourse.

'I would agree with you that, on the face of things, it seems folly for us to actively seek out and tackle with those who could so easily best us, but were life that simple. Although we've escaped the bondage of Atlantis, its ties are long and binding. There are those who would have it that none can escape the long arm of Atlantean law, and so they send out parties of Nightcrawlers, who seek to take back those who have transgressed by seeking refuge in our ville. We're new, and we have made our homes in the wreckage of an old, predark ville. We don't, as yet, have the security that Atlantis can boast, and so it is easy to breach our defenses.'

'What happens to those who are taken?' Doc asked simply.

'Public execution, as an example to those who may seek to follow,' Affinity said, a tightness creeping into his voice. 'I have seen it with my own eyes, before I risked escape.'

'And these Nightcrawlers, as you called them?' Ryan prompted.

Affinity looked at Ryan as though, for a second, he didn't comprehend what the one-eyed man had said to him, as though he were lost in some private hell, recalling what he had seen. Then he seemed to snap back to reality, answering concisely.

'They're what their name may suggest. They come mostly in the night, though not exclusively. They're painted in the colors of the forest, and they move with stealth and silence. This is also the way in which they strike. They are upon us before we have a chance to defend ourselves. They use knives and swords, mostly, but also they have blasters that some have the noise contained, so that they are almost silent.'

'Must be mostly handblasters or assault rifles. Few SMGs have silencer capability,' J.B. murmured. He noticed that Affinity was looking at him strangely. 'Just trying to figure out what we're up against,' he added.

The young man nodded briefly, then continued. 'We have little hope of catching them when we attack, and we have little in the way of fighting skills. Thus we seek to comb the forest before nightfall, perhaps hoping to keep them at bay by making it hard for them to approach Memphis unseen.'

'Seems a risky way to try to insure your safety,' Ryan pointed out.

Affinity shrugged. 'True enough, but there is little else we can do, and the attacks have less frequency since we first took these measures. It would seem that we have some success, if not, perhaps, enough. On which note I shall cease, for I think that I may have answered all your questions. Except for why we attacked you, but I think that is obvious—we mistakenly assumed you were Nightcrawlers, and attempted to withdraw when we discovered our mistake…at least, those of us who were able,' he added ruefully, fingering his jaw and looking askance at Mildred.

'Hey, what can I say? It had to be done,' she said, holding up her hands.

Affinity nodded. 'True enough, but you can't blame me for wishing that it had been one of my fellows and not myself who suffered at your hands.'

J.B. turned to Ryan. 'I don't get some of this. Unless my calculations are out, I don't remember any big ville being in that direction last time we were in this area.'

'True enough,' Ryan agreed, turning to Affinity. 'You're familiar with the whaling fleets along the coast, and the ville of Claggartville from where they come, right?'

The young man looked at him blankly and shook his head. 'I've never heard of this place, and we know nothing of what occurs along the coast. I should, perhaps, explain that Atlantis has kept itself secreted since the nukecaust, and deals as little as possible with outsiders. Most of the food and cloth is generated from within the ville, and other supplies are taken from the ancient ville of Trenton. This looms large in our legends from before the nukecaust, when those who knew what was coming prepared for the long winter of the soul. It's all we know, and is why we traveled along those old roads when we sought to build a home away from Atlantis.'

'So you're living in the ruins of Trenton, New Jersey, and Atlantis was built apart from that?' Mildred asked. When Affinity nodded, Ryan could see that Mildred was confused and he shot her a questioning glance. 'Hell, I don't know,' she said by way of reply. 'I don't remember Trenton being that close to the coast.'

'Could be the shape of the coastline has changed,' J.B. answered, 'or mebbe they think it's Trenton and it's not. Hell, we used to see signs that we thought gave us the name of an old ville then turned out to be a signpost all the time when we were traveling with Trader, right?' he directed to Ryan.

The one-eyed man nodded. 'Could be a whole lot of reasons,' he said to Mildred. 'Kind of irrelevant now. The fact that they're close together and warring with us in the middle is all we need to really know.'

'I would agree with you. I know not of the places of which you speak, but I do know that the night will soon be upon us, and to be out here in the unprotected forest would be a bad thing,' Affinity said softly.

Ryan looked up at the sky. The sun was beginning to sink and it wouldn't be long before twilight became dusk became night.

'Can we make it to your ville before the sun goes down? And if we did, would they welcome us?' he asked.

'As to the latter, I can assure you that the earlier conflict would be forgotten if you brought me home in one piece. It would be, as it were, an act of faith on your part, and accepted as such by my people. But as to the former, I'm not so sure. This is a dense forest and it is easy to lose direction.'

'So what are you saying?' Mildred asked. 'That we should make a camp here and wait for these Night-crawlers to sniff us out?'

'It's not, I agree, an ideal solution. It is, however, a

preferable one to roaming the forest at night. At least we can mount some kind of guard if we stay in the one spot,' Affinity answered.

'Seeing as we don't know exactly who we're dealing with, then that might be the best thing,' Ryan agreed.

He signaled to Jak, who appeared as if from nowhere. The albino had been up a tree, keeping a watch on the surrounding area, and had been able to pick out every word that had been spoken. Relieved that there was little need to fill in the details, Ryan selected a watch and, as usual, took the first for himself.

The companions made a small fire in as much of a clearing as they could muster in among the twisting growths. There was little space in which they could comfortably bed down together, yet it was important that they weren't split up. Their proximity to one another was vital for security.

As Ryan began to recce the darkening surrounding woods, Doc sidled up to Affinity.

'You interest me very much,' he began in an undertone. 'I find the names of your villes, and your name, of much interest. Also your garb. I suspect that there is some purpose to the coloring of your robe, which on the face of it would seem absurd to wear while on a hunt. The red and white combined are elements that ring distant bells in the recesses of my memory, and things begin to come back to me. I suspect that it ties on very well with the use of the names Atlantis and Memphis. I wonder, could it be possible that this construction on which you were once enslaved has something to do with the idea of being prepared for those who have been waiting to rise again?'

Affinity eyed the old man shrewdly. 'Are you seeking to play tricks upon me? I am sure that I mentioned the idea of the people from which I come waiting to be claimed—'

'Ah, yes, but you did not mention the idea of rising again…having once been of this land, and then sinking below before awaiting the moment when they can once more come to the surface and claim what is rightfully theirs.'

Affinity narrowed his gaze, as though seeking to peer inside Doc's mind. When he spoke, it was slowly, with every word measured carefully.

'You seem to know a lot about our old legends. I wonder how this could be, as we have always been taught that none outside of our closed community had ever heard them. Your mode of speech, and your seeming knowledge, what do you know of the lost continents and—'

Doc quieted him with a gesture. 'Not here and not now. Perhaps when we reach your ville on the morrow. There is much I would ask of you, and perhaps much I will be able to assist you with if you can but assist me in turn. But first we must have some privacy. There are things to which my companions are not privy.'

'I believe I understand you,' Affinity said carefully. 'I shall speak to you more of this when we are in Memphis.'

Doc smiled and left the young man alone. It left Affinity uneasy. He was in the middle of the forest with people he didn't know, one of whom appeared to be plotting against the others. And although he had seen at firsthand their fighting skills, he was still uneasy at spending the night outside of the safety of his ville. He knew the quality of the Nightcrawlers. There was a part of him that suspected he would never get the opportunity to find out just what it was exactly that the old man knew of the history of his people.

As Ryan kept watch, Affinity tried to settle to sleep. But try as he might, he couldn't. Instead he focused on the sounds of the one-eyed man who was their leader checking out the immediate area. Even though the forest was deathly quiet because of the lack of wildlife—the secret of which he was sure the old man had guessed—he could hear Ryan's movements only as the slightest echo of a whisper. He was good, there was no denying that.

But it was still enough. The Nightcrawlers made no sound.

And it was more than likely that they were out there right now, advancing toward where he lay with the unsuspecting others.

Chapter Six

First watch passed without incident, and the exhausted Ryan was only too glad to hand over second watch to Mildred and J.B. It was unusual to take a watch in pairs, but both had agreed that neither would rest that easy in the forest that night. Both were aware that they didn't share Krysty's and Jake's heightened senses. This being the case, both figured that doubling the watch would make detecting any intruders easier in a strange environment. The density of the woodlands and the maze-like nature of the paths that could be forged was a major concern.

Yet this seemed a concern that was a thousand miles away as they both prowled the silent forest. The night above was clear, the stars lighting up a sky that was further illuminated by a wan half-moon. Yet much of this light couldn't filter through the canopy of foliage cast by the forest, so that underneath, where the companions kept camp, it was a world of gray shrouded further by deepening shadows.

The lack of anything living—other than themselves—meant that the shadows were still and it should be easy to detect any movement within. The only sounds were the distant rustle of the foliage in night breezes.

Despite this, both J.B. and Mildred were on edge.

They had little doubt that Affinity had been serious and accurate in his description of the Nightcrawlers they had to guard against. Every slight rustle, every trick of the shadows that seemed to move or to deepen that little more, became something that made their nerve endings jangle.

For much of the watch they avoided each other, dividing the area around the camp into two 180-degree arcs that they would take individually. Each knew the other's footfall, the sound of each other's breathing and movement so well that they were able to filter out those sounds that they knew to emanate from the other.

It didn't make the watch any easier, and after nearly two hours, both felt that they were at breaking point. As their patrol arcs came close to each other, Mildred moved across into J.B.'s territory.

'What is it?' he demanded sharply as she approached. His voice was too low to carry farther than a few yards, but the fact that she was close enough to catch his words gave him cause for concern.

Something she was swift to allay.

'Chill, John. There isn't a problem. I'm just getting a little too strung out on my own. Kind of think that I'm going to be believing my own breathing is a freakin' Nightcrawler if I'm not careful.'

The Armorer gave a wry chuckle. 'Yeah, I know what you mean. I haven't felt this paranoid since I was left alone with a bunch of stickies on human fry night.'

Mildred gave him a bemused look. 'John, what the hell are you talking about?'

He shrugged. 'I don't know. I figure this is really getting to me, so that I don't really know what I'm saying. Have you thought that we might just be talking to reassure ourselves of the fact that we've actually got some company and aren't just here in the forest completely alone?'

'You mean that the total lack of anything else resembling a human being is getting to you, too, right?' she asked.

He nodded. 'It's too quiet. If they are out there, then we should be able to hear them. But if they're not, then…'

'The sooner morning comes the better, I figure,' Mildred muttered. 'This is playing hell on both our nerves.'

J.B. shook his head. 'You can say that again.'

THEY COULD HEAR someone in the forest. Someone who was other than those they sought. The runaways who had established the rogue ville of Memphis were too scared to be out in the forest at this time of night. And yet there were so rarely strangers who traversed these lands. Atlantis had deliberately been established so that it could hide from the prying eyes of intruders, far into the forest and near to the coast, where there were no major routes that would bring convoys and invite unwelcomed attention.

Whoever these people were, they had taken a lot of trouble to come this far. It was a shame that they couldn't take the extra trouble to be quiet and to protect themselves.

A vulpine grin crossed the face of the first warrior. This would be easy. They were making their position clear by their lack of concealment, and they would never hear a sec force as experienced in the sounds of the forest as the Crawlers. He turned and looked back, his night-adjusted eyes picking out the seven others in his pack. No one else would be able to spot them in this darkness, but he knew where they would be, was so used to the shadows that he could pick out the most infinitesimal change on depth and width of blackness, and had a sense of smell so highly attuned to the forest floor that he could even smell them.

Like his fellows, he was covered from head to foot in mud and paint, his tight-fitting tunic dyed to blend with his decorated skin. His hair was oiled and smoothed back to his scalp, and in his eyes he wore lenses that had been made by craftsmen. They were of a darkened glass, so that his eyes wouldn't reflect light. Each time he wore them they wore away at his eyeball a little more, so that he would have immense pain and blurred vision by the time that he was five years older. But it was worth it, to serve the greater cause in this way; and he would be rewarded, as all surviving Crawlers were rewarded. While others slaved at construction, the Crawlers were awarded a pension for the services they had offered to their people. The more recaptures and kills they had to their name, the greater the pension.

So far, his pension was good. That was why he was group leader, in charge of the operation. He had left it until the stiller watches of the night as he was aware of the juvenile efforts of the Memphis sec to keep his people at bay by mounting their ridiculous patrols. They offered no real threat, but a few Crawlers had been injured during skirmishes and the irritation they caused was something that the Crawlers could do without. They had stopped day attacks, but, as they were too scared to be in the forest at night, all they had achieved was to make their enemy concentrate on the time when they were at their most dangerous. In a sense, they had served the Crawlers well. Fools.

This contingent of Nightcrawlers had five men and three women. All were dressed identically, with camou robes, laced leather thongs dyed black and soled with rubber, body paint and dark lenses. All had their hair slicked back. Those whose natural hair color was lighter had dyed it dark, and those with long hair had it plaited. They were armed with blades. Blasters were too loud, and stealth was their watchword. Of course, carrying a blaster didn't mean that you had to use it. But in an extreme situation, the temptation may prove to be too strong, and subterfuge was paramount. So they carried Tekna and Wilkinson Sword hunting knives, as well as machetes and pangas. Each blade was sharpened and polished, with the resultant shine being dulled by the same kind of camou paint that they used on their bodies. The sheaths were oiled and tied to their bodies to prevent accidental collision and clanging of blades.

They moved independently of one another, hugging tree boles and moving at a crouch between the cover. They knew the forest well, and knew that—as there was no animal life to disturb it—the contours of the forest changed little with the seasons. In fall they had dry leaves underfoot, and this made it the hardest time of year to ply their trade; but now, with a canopy overhead adding to the dark, and little on the surface of the woods to make a sound beneath their footfalls, it was easy for them to move quickly.

They weren't totally silent. That was impossible for anything that took breath. But they were as quiet as it was possible to be. They were sure-footed on the ground, placing their feet where they would make the least noise on ground they knew almost as intimately as their own bodies. They avoided overhanging branches that would rustle if disturbed, and had no need to communicate with sound. Each Nightcrawler trained hard with the others so that they built up an almost preternatural degree of understanding with their fellows.

Eight pairs of ears identified the direction of J.B. and Mildred's conversation. Eight pairs of eyes focused in the almost pitch-black darkness on the area they had to cover. Even in this poor light, and with the strangers' earlier fire having been extinguished, they were able to discern different levels of dark as they saw the two move together, talk and then move apart.

The leader stopped grinning. Even his teeth would stand out in such absolute blackness. Nothing would break the shadow of his face, even though he was still smiling wolfishly on the inside as he began to move toward the companions, knowing without even looking back that his fellow Crawlers were on his tail.

These people wouldn't know what had hit them.

KRYSTY WAS HAVING a nightmare. Trapped in the tentacles of an octopus that was dragging her beneath the waves. She lashed out and it jetted a stream of dark ink into the water as it sought to protect itself from her blows. The darkness engulfed her in a swirl, the cold water becoming so dark that she no longer knew which way was up and which was down. But she knew that she was sinking into the dark.

She woke with a jolt and could feel her hair tight around her head and throat. It was more than the nightmare that was making her feel this way. There was a stirring in her bowels, a knot that only came when true danger beckoned. She sat up and looked around her. She could hear J.B. and Mildred talking in a low whisper and, as her eyes adjusted to the faint light, she could see them. They appeared to have everything under control, and yet...

Something had hit her right in her doomie sense; she didn't know what, but it was there.

And she wasn't alone. As she watched Mildred and J.B., she became aware that Jak had also stirred. She made to speak, but he stayed her with a gesture. His red eyes burned in the darkness, the faint light making his white, scarred face translucent and ageless as his brow furrowed in concentration.

'Stupe talking—cover all else,' he whispered shortly.

'Where are they?' Krysty asked, knowing already that the Nightcrawlers were out there, and guessing that Jak had caught wind of them.

'Circling Mildred and J.B.—can smell shit on their skin, make them dark. Almost can't hear them—nothing that quiet....'

Krysty was on her feet, although keeping low. 'Get Mildred and J.B. I'll wake the others,' she whispered. 'Triple fast. If you can hear them, you can bet your ass that they've already heard us moving.'

THE LEAD CRAWLER SAW two people rise from the group that lay beyond the two already standing. That made at least four. No matter. However many they had, they would be no match for his people.

Silently, and as one, they moved into attacking positions, each instinctively knowing where the others had gone. They quickened their pace and pulled their blades.

'I CAN SEE THEM!' J.B. yelled. 'In a line, right at three o'clock to six, coming quick.' He slipped the mini-Uzi into position and set it to rapid, firing off a burst into the dark. He had no idea if he had hit anyone, but the purpose of the blast was to try to delay the Night-crawlers, perhaps wake up the others. He needn't have worried. Ryan had already been awakened by Krysty, the sleep fog clearing rapidly from his brain as he took in the situation. He sprang to his feet, eschewing the Steyr and pulling the panga from its sheath. He understood J.B.'s motives, and also knew that in these conditions the use of blasters would be suicidal.

Doc and Affinity were also roused, while Jak was directing J.B. and Mildred to pull back into the central camp area.

'Dark night, we're sitting targets if we do that,' J.B. said, ignoring the irony of his curse.

'I think not,' Affinity said in a low tone. 'They never use blasters, only knives. And they always work in close. It's their trademark, if you will.'

They fell into silence, straining every fiber to catch the slightest sound made by their attackers. There was nothing. The Nightcrawlers had also fallen silent, as still as though they weren't there, waiting for their prey to crack first.

It was a war of nerves. The companions scanned the darkness, all but Jak able to detect nothing.

'Still where they were,' he whispered. 'Can smell them...but we move, then they, too.'

'Could try to fire on them again,' J.B. murmured. 'A quick burst of spray'n'pray might catch them before they can move.'

'Yeah, and in the noise and confusion they get to move out of position. At least this way we know where they are. Let them make the first move,' Ryan replied.

They stood still—as still as their opponents. The silence beyond the camp became oppressive and time slowed so that every breath seemed to take a day to draw.

Then it happened. The faintest of noises, and Jak yelled, 'They come!'

Before the companions had a chance to ready themselves, the Nightcrawlers were upon them. Their camou made them seem like indistinct shadows that moved across the lesser darkness, having no shape or form beyond an amorphous black mass that broke into pieces and reconstituted into different shapes when on the verge of the camp.

Jak had slipped knives to Krysty and Mildred, as they knew that their blasters would be ineffective. The razor-honed, leaf-bladed knives the albino youth used so well would still be deadly in the hands of the less-skilled women. J.B. had his Tekna, and Affinity and Doc had both unsheathed their blades.

The combat was silent. Even when the companions landed blows upon their enemies, they made no sound, as though they either controlled with a will of iron the reflex to shout, or they'd had their tongues ripped out by the root. It could have been either, but it had the same effect regardless. It was as though the companions were fighting phantoms that had no feelings and were invincible.

But definitely human. They stank of the body paint, and they were slippery with sweat and also with blood where the blades caught them. Slippery not just from their own blood. With the dark lenses over their eyes, they were almost impossible to pin down visually, and it was difficult to tell where their blows were coming from. Ryan winced as a blade sliced at his upper arm. Jak caught the point of one under the eye. He ignored it and struck home with a blow before his opponent had a chance to adjust balance, knowing that he had hit home when he heard an involuntary expellation of air. He was just thankful that the cut was under his eye. Above, and the running blood would have made vision difficult.

Krysty and Mildred were faring well. Although they couldn't see their opponents clearly, both women were wearing dark clothing that made their body movements harder to discern in the black of the night, and so were able to dodge the blades with ease. They also landed a few body blows that took a toll on their opponents.

Doc thrust and parried with his sword, grinning maniacally, as though enjoying the combat. Particularly when he felt one thrust penetrate into flesh deeply enough to stick. His opponent slumped noiselessly to the ground.

They had no idea how long they fought, or how well they were doing. It seemed as though their opponents were endless…and yet the Nightcrawlers were used to fighting opponents of a lesser mettle and were shocked at the skills of those they now tangled with—so much so that they began to withdraw. Because they were losing? Because they had suffered casualties? It was impossible to tell. The only thing for sure was that they melted into the darkness as smoothly as they had first materialized.

It was some time before the companions and Affinity could relax in any way. They expected the Night-crawlers to come at them as soon as they showed any sign of weakness. But as time crept on, it became apparent that their opponents had withdrawn from the fray. Comparing notes, they were sure that at least one of the Nightcrawlers had been badly wounded—the warrior skewered by Doc—and that two or three others had also taken heavy blows. For themselves, there were only a few cuts and bruises that Mildred could easily tend to when the sun came up.

Which was also when they expected to recover the wounded or chilled. And yet, when the light did break, there was no sign of any of their opponents. Doc was certain his opponent was chilled. If so, they had taken the corpse with them.

Apart from a few dark patches of blood on the floor of the camp, and some splashes on the nearest clumps of foliage, there was no sign of disturbance. Nothing to indicate that they had been attacked.

As though it had never happened.

Chapter Seven

The sec party stood back in cover when they heard the noises from the woods. There were four of them, and they were all dressed in the same white robes as Affinity. Using the dense woodlands as shelter, they stepped into shadow and waited as the sounds grew nearer.

'Mark, do you think that they are Nightcrawlers?' asked the youngest. Barely out of his teens, the clean-shaven Philo had only escaped from Atlantis a few months before and was keen to prove himself. Despite this, he could feel tremors on his right leg as the strangers approached.

'Idiot, have you ever heard a Crawler make so much noise, even when they thought there was nobody around to hear them? They know we have sec patrols now, and they would be ever more vigilant,' Mark snapped in a low whisper. He was nearing thirty and had been in Memphis for more than five years. He had several family members in his bid to escape, and was filled with a burning desire for revenge against the regime of Atlantis. That had driven him to rise rapidly to head of sec for Memphis. Not that there was a lot of competition. He sometimes felt—particularly at times like this—that he was almost fighting alone.

Philo stayed silent, although he felt slighted. What other explanation could there be other than that the approaching strangers were Crawlers? Those who had returned on the previous day had spoken of those they encountered as being strong fighters, but not garbed as was the norm for Crawlers. Perhaps this was a change in tactics by the men of Atlantis to counter the measures shown by Memphis. After all, who else could it be in these woodlands?

The sec party stayed silent, letting the strangers come to them. There was a low undertone of voices and the sounds of their progress were clearly audible. These Crawlers—if indeed they were—made no attempt to conceal themselves.

Mark showed himself to the others long enough to mutely direct his men into position for an ambush. He had determined the direction of the approaching party and wanted to make sure they were surrounded. Crawlers were tricky, slippery fighters. His men were probably outnumbered from the sound of it, and there was every chance that they would be outfought. But he was a great believer in the element of surprise.

He had little idea that in this instance it would be himself on the receiving end of such a shock.

As the four sec men adopted their new positions, and readied themselves for attack, Philo tried to calm himself by concentrating on picking out the words spoken by the approaching party. His guts were churning with fear and he supposed that to try to decipher their conversation would act as a distraction from his fear.

They were far enough away for the talk to be little more than a low buzz, but within a few seconds he had adjusted to the volume and could pick out a few words.

'...the methods of destruction, and the tactics involved, are sometimes schematic of an intelligence that is little more than misguided.'

'Doc, you talk such crap sometimes. The only thing you can ever think about is survival. That's the triple red priority.'

The first voice was rich and full. Male. Whereas the answering voice, although throaty and deep, was most definitely female.

The first man continued. 'My dear Dr. Wyeth, one must always consider beyond the knee-jerk reaction. It is the ability to think rationally and translate this into tactics that actually wins wars. Staying alive is one thing—'

'Can't win wars if buy farm,' a third voice, low and almost monotone, interjected.

'Exactly my point. I'm not saying that tactics are wrong—hell, if Ryan didn't give us some, then we'd long since have been chilled—but the numero uno priority is to keep moving and keep breathing.'

'I appreciate your willingness to enter into debate so freely,' a fourth voice added, 'but if you are to be moving on, I fail to see how it can be of any practical consideration.'

'A little learning never hurt anyone,' the woman's voice countered.

But the fourth voice, the mellifluous tone and the use of language… It couldn't be—he had been taken by the Crawlers the day before and was considered lost. It was Affinity, of that Philo had little doubt. The two men were friends, and the young man had been fired up by the apparent demise of his compatriot.

So these were the people the sec patrol had fought yesterday. And they hadn't chilled or taken Affinity. In fact, he seemed on friendly terms with them, and they were headed back toward Memphis.

This was most strange. Philo had no idea what it might mean, but he was sure that they should refrain from attack. He knew that Mark wouldn't have bothered trying to hear what was being said. The sec chief would be too busy psyching himself for combat. It was probable that only Philo was aware of what had been said between the approaching strangers.

He knew that he had to inform Mark straightaway and stop an attack that could be disastrous—unnecessarily so—for the sec party. The young man broke cover to seek out his chief.

Mark stepped from his own cover, grabbing the young man by the arm and pulling him into the shadow.

'What in the name of Minos do you think you're doing, you idiot?' he asked quietly. His tone, however, was anything but soft.

Rapidly, Philo gabbled everything he had heard, knowing that time was of the essence. When he had finished, Mark nodded briefly.

'You did right,' he affirmed. 'I'll halt the attack and we'll reveal ourselves.'

Philo allowed a smile of relief. It died on his lips on the silence following Mark's words. For silence was all there was. The advancing party had fallen quiet, as though aware of the ambush in wait for them.

RYAN HELD UP his hand to halt the party, but he needn't have bothered. The exchange of views dried to silence as an awareness that they were no longer alone swept through them—all except Affinity, whose puzzled expression was met with a gesture from Doc and an inclination of the head to the paths ahead.

Although seemingly relaxed, the companions had been acutely aware of their surroundings. They had tuned in to the silence around them, and although apparently paying no heed to the environment, had easily caught wind of the change. Ahead of them the foliage had moved in a manner that bespoke of more than the wind, and the rustling was underscored by something that could only be muffled and quieted human speech.

Ryan looked questioningly at Jak. The albino youth held up three, then four fingers with a slight shrug, indicating he couldn't be more exact about numbers. He then indicated the spread of the sounds.

Ryan nodded and gestured to J.B. and Jak to fan out and come around the source of the noise in a pincer movement. He further indicated that the remaining five move forward in a staggered line through the trees, with weapons to hand. For stealth, and because of the close yet shielded proximity, he further indicated that blades would be of more use than blasters.

Jak tossed a couple of leaf-bladed knives to Krysty and Mildred before he and J.B. headed off in separate directions, disappearing silently into the undergrowth.

The others began to move forward, now watching every step, keeping sound to a minimum. Affinity wondered at their ability, realizing that they were a match for any team of Nightcrawlers…and hoping that the opposition wasn't his own people's sec, if only for their sakes.

MARK GESTURED to Philo to move back into position, wincing at the relative noise the young man made as he went into cover. Mark knew that all his men were willing, but the fact was that they simply weren't of a comparable quality to their opposition. For all of the talk of Memphis mounting a raid on Atlantis to topple the ruling regime, he knew in his heart that talk was all it would remain, at least for a few years to come.

He slipped farther into shadows, then moved toward the source of the noise before it had ceased. In the time before he had run from the old ville, he had pretended; he had played the games and acted as though he'd wanted to become a Crawler, to become one of the elite. In truth, he was filled with loathing for them and the way in which they treated the people for whom they were supposed to be the sec force. But he knew that if he could learn a few of their tricks, then it would aid his escape.

It had. It also made him the best fighter in the breakaway ville of Memphis, and natural choice for sec chief. In many ways this was something that sat uneasily with him, as his natural inclination was not to lead. He loathed the concept of leaders and followers, as to his mind it led to the kind of situation that prevailed in Atlantis. So he tended to let his men have their heads. The only problem with that being that in a situation such as this, there were those who had no idea what to do.

Such was Philo. He was trying to keep his progress as noiseless as possible, but found it hard to tell as nothing seemed to be audible over the thumping of his own heart. He blundered forward, tongue licking over his lips, hoping that he would find the fighters with Affinity before they found him. If he could make himself known, it would prevent his being killed before recognition could be made with his friend.

The other two in the sec party, Paris and Jason, were still in position. They were frozen with fear, which would spell their certain demise under most combat conditions, but in this instance might just save them.

Mark was faced with a difficult choice. There was no way he could reach both of them and tell them of Philo's discovery. Partly because they had spread out in their initial formation, and partly because he had no idea where they had moved to, if at all. This was the problem with giving them their heads: he had no way of pinpointing their location. He didn't want them to blunder into the opposition, as he was sure they would be bested, perhaps killed. In these circumstances, a pointless waste of life.

His only certain way of insuring their safety was to reach the opposition and make himself known to Affinity, thus calling attention to who was out in the woods stalking whom: but even this had its problems, as he had to hope that they hadn't moved far from his estimate of their position.

How much easier it would have been if he had been alone, or if he'd had a better team of fighters. As it was, he could almost feel the weight of responsibility bearing down on his shoulders. It clouded his judgment, he was sure.

So much so that it took all his attention, and he was surprised when he felt the point of a blade nick the skin at the base of his neck when he stopped to take his bearings. He hadn't heard the owner of the blade drop from the tree above him, hadn't registered the sound until the cold metal was already pricking his skin, until he could feel the breath on his cheek.

'I don't want to cut you, but if you get jumpy you'll

have no spinal cord left. Drop your knife. Believe it or not, we're on your side.'

WHILE J.B. WAS OVERPOWERING Mark, Jak was taking care of Philo. The young man blundered through the undergrowth, making enough noise to be tracked by anyone. In point of fact, he was moving so fast and with such recklessness that the albino had to remove himself from the young man's path. If Philo had careered into Jak and lashed out in surprise and fear, then the albino would have been forced to act defensively, which could have entailed violence upon someone who was not actually an enemy. So, acting with a discretion that was far from his usual disposition, Jak sidestepped the oncoming Philo, then slipped into his wake as the young man passed.

A trip, a movement of the arm to flip him as he fell, and Philo was on his back staring up at the sky before he knew what had happened. And, before he even had time to take in this much, he found Jak descending on him, expertly pinning his arms and legs so that he was unable to move.

'Affinity says you shit fighters. Mebbe teach you otherwise if you stay calm now,' Jak said calmly.

Philo felt bile rise in his throat and choked it back as he nodded. He was so scared that he almost vomited. Jak wondered how he'd managed to stay alive thus far before letting him free, watching as the young man stayed hunkered down until he had, in fact, vomited away his fear. Having done that, he meekly followed when Jak indicated for him to rise and follow.

Paris and Jason had proved just as easy for Ryan and Krysty to overpower. Both had been rooted to the spot, wondering what to do next, when they were approached from the rear. Realizing that these opponents weren't Nightcrawlers—although being unaware of Affinity's association with them—they were merely grateful to be allowed to live.

Mildred and Doc felt a little slighted in the circumstances, if truth be told, with neither having the opportunity to engage with the Memphis sec. They stuck close to Affinity, and the three of them forged ahead, looking for any others who may, to the best of their knowledge, be lurking in the undergrowth.

With the dense cover, it was momentarily difficult for the companions to ascertain how successful their mission had been, but when J.B. and Jak moved back toward the centralized position of the group, it soon became apparent that the four-man sec force had been neutralized.

Mark was rueful and not inclined to be graceful at such an easy capture, although it soon became clear that he and Philo had been aware that the companions were no threat.

'Mebbe that explains why so crap,' Jak said, his matter-of-fact tone belying the bluntness of his words.

Mark shook his head. 'No, I reckon you would have had us anyway. Look at yesterday's mission. One lost, three wounded out of eight. Not the kind of ratio that speaks of success.'

'But I was not lost, Mark. I am alive, and I have possibly found us allies in our fight.'

Mark eyed the companions. 'They could teach us much. But you were, to all practical purpose, lost, Affinity. Can you not see that? To us, it was as though you had been killed by the Crawlers.'

'I see your point, friend,' Ryan said, adding the last word pointedly. 'Your people were in combat, and they didn't do as well as you feel they should. They returned without Affinity, here. If we had been these Night-crawlers you face, then the boy would be chilled meat.'

'Exactly. And we lose people every time they attack. We aren't that populous. The longer things continue, the more we face extinction. I think your help would be like a prayer to the old ones that has been answered.'

'You know, I'm getting a little tired about the way everyone sees us as some kind of holy sec force,' Ryan commented wryly. 'Long, long story, mebbe I'll tell you about it sometime,' he added on seeing the sec chief's puzzled expression. 'First thing we need to do is get back to your ville. Mebbe then we can settle and discuss things. We might be useful to you, and you might be to us. We'll see.'

With the Memphis people relieved to see Affinity still alive, and the companions glad that they didn't have to fight so soon after the previous night's battle, it was with a feeling of elation that the expanded party made its way to the ville. As they walked, Affinity explained to his people where the companions had come from and where they were originally headed.

'That is something that I find strange,' Mark commented when Affinity had finished. 'The fact that you came through the exclusion zone.'

'Exclusion zone?' Mildred questioned. It was a strange, old-fashioned phrase, the like of which she hadn't heard since before the nukecaust.

Mark nodded emphatically. 'Indeed. That area in which no animal life can exist has been called as such since before many generations. Part of the old legends say that our ancestors deliberately poisoned the earth in a belt surrounding the ville and the adjacent area when they knew that skydark was coming. It was intended to keep out any who may wish to intrude and take shelter or solace during the great darkness. To protect our people from outside interference. But I wonder… It is, after all, just as effective at keeping us in.'

'Surely there have been others before us who have come through there, people who, like us, have stumbled upon it by accident,' Krysty stated.

Mark eyed her shrewdly. 'There have been some traders who have made efforts to find new places to trade. But it takes an interesting kind of an accident to just—as you say—stumble upon it,' he said gently.

'Mebbe we just have a lot of accidents,' J.B. muttered dryly.

'No matter. This is something you can discuss with Lemur when you meet him. For even if you choose not to stay and help us, you'll still need guides to take you to the coast. The Crawlers are everywhere. They frighten us, and we stay because we have nowhere else to go. They frighten the birds and animals, and they leave, never to return. Perhaps that will give you measure of why guidance will be necessary—'

'It sure as hell explains a lot,' Mildred murmured.

Mark indicated agreement before continuing. 'Of course, if you choose to assist us, then perhaps you will perforce negate the need for guides.'

Ryan chuckled. 'You're not giving that one up easily. It'd be easier if you didn't all talk like Doc, too. Right, Doc?'

The old man looked up, his face blank, as though

distracted from a chain of thought. 'Hmm? Why yes, dear boy, of course,' he muttered before returning to his preoccupation.

Chapter Eight

Their journey to the ville of Memphis proceeded with little event and few words taking place after the initial exchange. On both sides, there was much to ponder, and the companions all, in their own ways, felt that silence would be the best path until they had a better grasp of what was going on in this isolated area.

As they approached, there were more sounds and the occasional bird or animal call to signify that there was, perhaps, a feeling of greater security surrounding the ville. Strange, given the fact that the sec chief felt his own people weren't up to the task of defending the ville. Among themselves, the companions wondered if the wildlife was really wild or captive and bred for food.

Memphis itself was made up of the ruins of a sub-urb. Mildred still maintained her feeling that it wasn't the Trenton of which Affinity had spoken, but as they emerged to the ruins of what had once been a freeway access, now overgrown apart from a desultory run of blacktop into nowhere, its progress broken by a shift in the earth that had swallowed whatever came before, she could see why he had made this assumption. Over the top of the desolated ribbon, hanging at an obtuse angle and obscured for the most part by creeping vines and the twisting branches of mutie trees that had climbed the rusting metal structure, there was the partial remains of a lane indicator sign. The only word that was visible through the grime, heat-blasted metal and rampant foliage was Trenton. As they were in New Jersey, it may have been an announcement that the suburb was the next exit, or it may have told the weary motorists of a time long forgotten that there was a certain distance until that destination was obtained. It was now impossible to tell. But to the people of Memphis, it was a landmark that defined where they lived.

As they left the overgrown forested area and entered the remains of the old suburb, the foliage began to recede. Yet, among the blasted and flattened two-story houses and rows of burned-out, razed shopfronts and minimalls that had once served the residents, there were many signs that a postnukecaust mutie nature had attempted to take back and remold the land. Where entire streets had fallen victim to fire, earth movement and heavy bombing, there was little sign that there had ever been anything remotely approaching civilization. The undergrowth and the strong, adapting and surviving trees had swept across the scorched earth, annexing the territory like an invading army and driving out all signs of a previous life. It could have looked this way for millennia, betrayed only by the occasional outposts of a ruined civilizations: houses and shops that had stayed upright, a strip of tar macadam road that had stubbornly resisted the forces beneath, and hadn't split asunder to reveal green life thrusting up from below as it had so easily with the paved sidewalks.

The farther they traveled into the suburb, the more that civilization began to win over nature, no matter how strong and mutated. After a quarter hour of walking, the sounds of life grew louder in the surrounding silence and the buildings became firmer, stronger and better preserved.

As they turned a corner, walking past an old shopfront that was now boarded and painted in white and red, covered with symbols that looked like some kind of pictogram, two men in robes stepped out from cover.

'Mark, what is occurring? Who are these people, and— By the sacred stars, it's Affinity!'

The sec man's questions were lost in a joyous greeting as he embraced the young man they had thought lost. Mark explained briefly what had occurred, and they passed on, leaving the two sec men to take cover once more.

'They will be partway through their watch, and pray to the old ones that it is a quiet one,' Mark commented.

'They just sit there, they don't patrol?' J.B. asked.

Mark allowed the briefest of smiles to cross his visage, as though the Armorer had joked with him. 'You have seen the Crawlers at work, and you have seen our men. They have the best of intentions, but what do you think would work best—to aimlessly wander and be ambushed or to take up a secure position and observe for movement?'

'True enough,' the Armorer replied after barely a moment's contemplation. 'So how far out do you place these sec posts?'

'As far out as cover will permit. Many of the buildings past that point—' he indicated the direction from which they had come '—are too broken, too derelict to be of much use. All the same, it is still a fair distance from where we maintain our population.'

Almost as if to illustrate his point, they kept walking for another four or five blocks, with little sign of life except the increasing noise. Seeing their puzzled expressions, he explained. 'We keep our ville as secure as possible. Atlantis is better trained in combat than we, and so it suits our purpose better. Of course, it could be argued that we have done naught except to exchange one jail for another, but at least it is a jail of our own design.'

His point was amply demonstrated as they turned another block to be confronted with a wall. One constructed of building rubble, old wags, pieces of sidewalk and roadway...anything that could have been used and taken from the surrounding ruins. It was poorly made, and constructed by people who hadn't the time or expertise to fashion their materials. From the top of the wall, which followed the line of the streets and so disappeared around corners and out of sight, there were poles obtruding from the junkyard construction. Between the poles were lengths of wire strung with metal strips and crudely fashioned bells. Anyone who attempted to climb the wall—which was only a few yards high at its peaks—would undoubtedly attract a lot of attention to themselves.

Mark grinned wryly as he caught their expressions. 'Crude but effective. In Atlantis we are taught to fashion and build slowly, and with care. Aesthetically, this jars with all of us, I think, and yet it serves its purpose, which is all we require when having to build quickly, with little manpower and only the materials that come to hand.'

Upon reflection, the veracity of this statement became more apparent. The wall was crude to look at, yet the detritus of the ruined suburb had been employed to fashion a construct that had a greater solidity than at first appeared. Each part of the junkyard defense had been slotted and placed so that the constituent elements interlocked into a fortress that had strength shot through its length.

Its hurried and seemingly slapdash construction was further belied by the sight that greeted them as they walked around another old suburban block. Set in the middle of the wall, with the junk flowing over the top in a smoothly interlocking design, was a gateway. This showed signs of having more time spent on it and gave truth to the training that the ville inhabitants had received before their voluntary exile from Atlantis. Slabs of masonry taken from the surrounding area had been fashioned into an arch that was rubbed smooth and engraved with pictograms similar to those the companions had seen on the painted sec post.

Within this arch had been set double doors of beaten metal, engraved and etched with another set of symbols. The stark design and simple beauty of the arch and the doors contrasted sharply with the visual clamor of the junkyard wall. And somehow they had to have a spy mechanism within them—unless somehow word had got back to the ville in another way, as the doors opened smoothly on their approach, and they were greeted by a group of men and women, all clad in the same white robes trimmed with red as those they had already met.

'I don't reckon much on their fashion sense,' Mildred remarked quietly to J.B.

'Must mean something…but what?' he replied.

She shrugged. 'Maybe we'll find out before too long.'

The companions and the accompanying sec party

were swept into the ville on a tide of goodwill, the doors being quickly closed behind them a reminder of the dangers that still lurked outside. Inside, however, was another matter.

The ville was well ordered and clean. As they were taken through the streets, the companions noticed that the buildings and streets were well-maintained and clean. The frontages had all been painted white with red trim, and there were white walls filled with red pictograms. The lack of any other color was noticeable. In other villes, even those that were well-maintained, there were vestiges of other colors, either from decoration or merely from the materials used to make the ville. But here it seemed as though every other color had been carefully and deliberately expunged, replaced with the white and red that dominated.

The streets were sparsely populated, suggesting that few were able to make an effective escape from the parent ville of Atlantis…and that the Nightcrawlers had been successful in snatching back some of those who were careless once free.

'This is an…interesting place,' Doc said carefully to Affinity as they walked through the streets. 'You seem to be extremely keen, as a people on the idea of everything being red and white.'

'Those are the only things we know,' the young man replied disingenuously. 'It is all we have been taught since first we were born. So it was only natural that we should wish to extend the motif once we found a place of our own.'

'Is that so?' Doc said, nodding blandly. In his mind he had reached a few conclusions of his own as to the meaning of the color scheme, tying up a few loose ends from the information he had elicited. There was purpose to this and he was certain that silence on his part right now would allow more information to drop with more ease than if he were to press matters.

By this time they had reached the center of the ville, and as they approached an old shopfront that had been carefully bricked over to turn it into a dwelling, a man and a woman came out to greet them. They were a little older than any that the companions had encountered so far, and this seniority was confirmed by the deference shown to them by the sec party and Affinity.

'These are the people we thought were the Nightcrawlers?' asked the man. He had tightly cropped, curly black hair, with a beard as neatly trimmed. He was short and stocky, but the way in which he held himself made him appear taller. The woman with him had long auburn hair tied back simply from a narrow-faced, almost milk-white-pale skin. Her eyes were focused on the companions and she had a gaze that suggested intensity of purpose. Together, they seemed a formidable team.

'That they are,' Affinity said excitedly. 'They say that they will help us—'

'Fireblast! Don't be so damn sure,' Ryan interjected heatedly. 'I said that we'd hear what you had to say. We have no fight with anyone unless they want it,' he added, eyeing Mark just to make sure that the sec chief, who shot him a glance, got the message.

'That seems fair,' the stocky man said, noticing the eye contact between the two men. 'Come, break bread with us, and I will tell you about our ville.'

'We've already heard something about who you are,' Ryan said carefully, 'but the offer of a meal will never go amiss.'

RYAN WANTED to know more of these people. If he was headed for the coast, and the ville of Atlantis had sec men who would make this simple objective difficult, he wanted to know their strengths and weaknesses. The inhabitants of Memphis could tell him this. It would also give his people a chance to rest up, clean up, and eat something a little better than the self-heats to which they were now reduced.

Thus it was that a few hours later the companions found themselves in the dining room of the building. It was painted in red and white throughout, with white sculptures as decoration on simple wooden tables that had, like the chairs, been stripped down to the natural grain after being carved. They were made of a variety of woods, which suggested that these people were adept at adjusting to their surroundings.

Despite the fact that he appeared to be what passed for baron in Memphis, their host helped in the preparation and serving of the meal, and those who would in other circumstances be servants sat at table and ate with them.

The food was simple: meats and vegetables pancooked in spices, with fruits preserved in spirit for dessert. They were given a choice of water or a thick, sweet wine to drink. Despite the fact that they lived in perpetual struggle, they were obviously able to farm to a certain degree. An impression reinforced when their host told them that he couldn't remember the last time an enterprising trade convoy had tried to make it through their territory.

When the meal was finished, their host asked them how they came to be in the territory. Ryan told him what

he had told Affinity and what Mark had gleaned: the
basic truth, glossing over the mat-trans and how they
managed to move across vast tracts of land. In this version of the story, as with so many others, recalcitrant
wags or beasts had left them on foot just before they
were discovered.

Leaving aside these details, their host seemed to believe Ryan. In fact, the one-eyed man got the distinct
impression that the man was looking on them as some
kind of answer to a problem. An impression reinforced
when he had finished and the man began to speak.

'Your story is an interesting one, friend Ryan. I call
you friend as you proved you were no enemy in your
treatment of Affinity. You obviously have some idea of
why we are here, and why there is danger in this local-
ity. But perhaps you do not grasp the full extent. Why
should you, this is not your land, and these are not your
people. But they are mine, by default.'

'I, Lemur, escaped from Atlantis many seasons ago.
More, now, than I can recall without difficulty. My wife,
Cyran, came with me—' he gestured to the woman who
sat beside him '—and we found this place. There has
always been a Memphis, as long as there has been an
Atlantis. For there are always people who cannot accept
the tyranny of Odyssey, no matter who he may be at any
given time.' He caught the bemused expressions of the
companions and smiled indulgently. 'I will explain in
due course, have no worry.

'I am now the leader of this ville, for no other reason than I have been here the longest, I have survived
and I am willing to shoulder the responsibility. That is
our way. Atlantis, however, has a hereditary leader who
always goes by the name Odyssey, and is trained from

birth to accept the cowl. Perhaps, because of this, we shouldn't be too harsh. For if I was in the same position, could I assure you that I would not be the same as the man who now bears the name Odyssey?

'No matter…to business. The ville of Atlantis was founded before the nukecaust by those who could see it was coming. They were told this by messengers from the lost lands of Atlantis, which had perished in a similar disaster many thousands of years before. Those who isolated themselves into the community of Atlantis did so knowing that this was the second coming. Those who survived would have the task of building ships in which the community who thrived after the nukecaust would be the chosen ones, taken up in these ships by the old ones, who first journeyed beyond the stars in the days before the first disaster, when the original Atlantis perished.

'Those who traveled beyond will send their descendants for those who wait. But in the meantime, those who wait have a hell on Earth. Odyssey makes them build bigger and bigger vessels, keeping the people beneath the thumb in thrall to his will. There is no freedom, no joy. The old ones are appeased in the hope that they will come soon with a series of rituals and sacrifices that are for their benefit. Many of us lost those we loved in such a way or were in such dangers ourselves.

'I ask you—is it possible that those who are our people would like us to immolate and sacrifice ourselves, or is not possible that that something has gone very wrong somewhere?

'To a greater or lesser degree, this is what we all feel, and why we have, over the years, fled to this alternative place. Those of us who believe are sure that our kindred would not forsake us because we wish to greet them in peace and freedom.

'In the meantime, the man who is now Odyssey is running ever more out of control. There was a time when Memphis was considered beneath Atlantis, and left in peace, albeit begrudgingly. But this Odyssey is obsessed. He wants to take us back and punish us. We are unskilled fighters, and need to learn quickly for our own defense. We also need to try to unseat him. It is kill or be killed. I am sure that there are many who would join us in Atlantis if they saw a glimmer of hope. We just need to be good enough to give them that.

'You have proved your mettle by traversing the exclusion zone, beating both our men and also Nightcrawlers, as I heard earlier. Your wish is to go on your way in peace. That is our wish. But I am sure that neither of us will have that wish unless we defeat Odyssey. I beseech you to join with us, teach us what you know, and insure your own ends as much as ours.'

Ryan reflected on what Lemur had said for a moment, then looked around the table at his people.

'Whatever we do, we're going to have to stand and fight, lover,' Krysty said when his eye met hers. He could see that she was speaking for all of them.

Ryan shrugged. 'Met enough bastards like this Odyssey before. If he's going to make it tough for us to go on our way, then I guess he's just asking for us to make it tough on him. You don't want much—no more than we do, in our way. Someone like Odyssey'll never understand that. Screw him. We'll stand with you. Might as well fight with friends at our backs as on our own.'

Ryan stood and reached across the table, extending

his hand. Lemur rose and took it in a firm grip. The one-eyed man had a growing liking for the stocky leader of Memphis, who seemed a man after his own heart, only wanting to live his own life with no hassle. How could they not back him?

Doc watched the two men grasp hands. He felt torn. On the one hand, he had sympathy with Memphis. Yet on the other he was fascinated by what he had just heard of Odyssey. What secrets this man held. Would it be possible to defeat him and grasp them, or would it be prudent to play a double game to insure that the secrets fell into the right grasp—that grasp being his?

He would have to bide his time....

Chapter Nine

'Dark night, there's something really weird about these folks,' J.B. intoned slowly as he broke bread into the thick soup that had been served for their meal.

'What's to know?' Ryan countered. 'They feed us, they put us up and they accept us training with them without a word of dissent. Friendly is what I'd call it.'

'That's just what I mean,' J.B. said softly. 'When was the last time anyone ever acted like that with us? Without first trying to blow our heads off?'

'John has got a point,' Mildred mused. 'It is kind of unusual the way that they've just let us become part of their community without any kind of test.'

Ryan pondered this point. In the few days since they had arrived with Mark and Affinity, they had been accepted into the ville without any reservations from the population. Lemur and Cyran had approved of their presence, and this seemed to be enough for the rest of the escapees from Atlantis. Certainly none of them had expected Memphis to be so open in its embrace of their presence.

Recognizing their worth as fighters, Mark had requested that he be allowed to let them train with the young men he was trying to mold into a sec force. Lemur had assented with a rapidity that suggested he was under no illusions as to how much help his sec men needed.

And that was plenty. During their first training session, it had been obvious that the young men picked by the sec chief were fit enough. They could run and lift with the best, yet they were hopeless at tactics and at close-in, hand-to-hand fighting. Which was exactly the kind of skill they needed to cultivate if they were to stand any kind of chance during an encounter with the Nightcrawlers.

For all that, they were well-organized and not short of courage. They were also eager to learn and extremely attentive whenever Ryan, J.B. or Jak wanted to show them something that would prevent them giving away their lives cheaply. It was just surprising that a force so tight in every other way should be so lacking in combat skills.

Remembering this, Ryan said, 'They need us. Mark knows it and Lemur knows it. Their people have seen what we can do, and they know its something they lack. So it makes sense that they would want us to teach them.'

'Yeah, but they're so trusting,' Mildred said with a sense of awe. 'It would be so easy for us to take complete advantage of the positions they put us in. Hell, we could be running this ville in a matter of hours.'

'Ah, but would we want to, my dear Doctor?' Doc interjected.

'Of course not, that would be really stupid,' Mildred replied with obvious irritation, 'but—'

'But nothing.' Doc cut across her words. 'We have no reason to take advantage, and they know this. Ergo, they can trust us in situations that other villes would not. They realize that we have no interest in their fight—' *Ah, but that is not true, is it, my friend? Best to keep this to yourself, however* '—and that we only wish to go on our way once we have righted a wrong. It is a simple equation, and they see things in these very clear, simple terms. As for their being organized and yet lacking in fighting skills, I would have thought that was obvious.'

Krysty looked at the old man. There was something about Doc that had been bugging her for a while—ever since they dragged him from the mat-trans chamber, in fact. He seemed to have accepted their argument and appeared to have resigned himself to not going back to the north. He hadn't mentioned it, and yet that was what was bugging her. Not even a casual mention or slip of the tongue. As though it had been expunged from his memory. But it couldn't have been. Nothing went that quickly and that completely. The only explanation that she could find was that Doc was deliberately keeping quiet about the matter. And such deliberation suggested that it was still on his mind. So did he have some kind of secret agenda? Was he burning with a desire to avenge himself upon them? Furthermore, was there something going on in his mind that could put them in danger?

Any cue she could glean from his gnomic utterances would help. Reassure her, or get more alarm bells ringing, it mattered little. Some kind of signifier, some kind of clue, was all she needed.

Unaware of what was running through her mind, Doc paused before answering, aware that the eyes of all were upon him. He was relishing the situation. The thought that he held some kind of power in the form of information was pleasing.

Yes, my friends, listen to me. Learn. As I learn. But I am faster...

'If you stop to consider where they have come from, and how they have ended up in this situation, then their apparently contrary attitudes become easily explained.'

'Yeah, keep easy, Doc. Want understand for once,' Jak muttered.

Doc continued as though he hadn't heard the albino's words.

'Everyone who is in Memphis—with the exception of our good selves—has escaped from Atlantis, where they were born and raised.'

'Doc, tell us something we don't know,' Ryan commented wryly.

'I do not have to,' Doc replied sharply. 'The key is in what you know, you have merely failed to apply that knowledge.'

Krysty frowned. The sharpness in Doc's tone worried her. It was something she had never heard from him before recently, and the fact that he would speak like this to the rest of them suggested he was psychologically separated from them. She looked quickly at the others. Mildred seemed taken aback at the venom in Doc's tone, but the men seemed to treat it as Doc being strange again, and nothing more.

But Krysty was sure that it was.

While that ran through her mind, Doc carried on, 'Consider the conditions within Atlantis, from what we have been told. It is run as a dictatorship by a ruthless baron who has a very definite set of aims that have been handed down to him for several generations. Along with these have been set practices for the way in which the affairs of the ville are conducted. To wit—the inhabitants are used as slave labor and are disciplined to work in this manner from the day they are born. Now, you may say that the people of Memphis are those who have rebelled against this system, and have made a conscious attempt to escape and find a new way of life.

'You would, of course, be correct in this premise. However, consider the fact that when Atlantis was founded it was with the deliberate aim of isolating it from anything that may be an outside influence. Thus, these people have no information of any kind other than that which they have known from birth.

'Therefore, it stands to reason that, when they have the chance to set up their own society, it will closely mirror that from which they ran. Think about it. What other way do they know? Of course they will use the model society that they are familiar with, albeit changed so that the elements from which they wished to escape are excised. They will take the colors, the discipline and organization, and they will use this. For change and freedom are dangerous and frightening things. To make a complete break with everything you know, even if it has been used to oppress you, is to take a step out into the darkness and the unknown that demands a particular kind of courage. A courage that it takes some time to amass when you have done little but follow orders from the day you were born.'

J.B. shrugged, dropping his spoon into the empty bowl, having continued to eat while Doc talked.

'Yeah, okay, so it all boils down to the fact that they've always been organized, so they just keep on being that way. I guess I can understand that, and if I can, then I can't see why any of the rest of us would have any trouble. But why so trusting, and why so crap at combat?'

Doc sighed. 'Again, my dear John Barrymore, a

question the answer to which you are already fully cognizant, if you did but stop and think.'

'J.B.'s not the only one who's had to think,' Krysty interrupted. 'If I follow on from your argument, then the answer to the second question is simple. In Atlantis only some people are selected for combat—those who make up the Nightcrawlers. They'd tend to be the kind of people who wouldn't want to escape, and so few if any of them would end up here. Everyone else in the ville is kept away from the concepts and skills of fighting, lest they form a threat to the established hierarchy. So these people know all about the discipline of living this way, but nothing about combat.'

Doc smiled warmly. 'It is gratifying, my dear, to know that someone else has been thinking about our situation.'

Yeah, Krysty mused silently, but I'm figuring that you've been thinking about a whole lot more than that. It's just that I haven't figured out quite what as yet. But she betrayed no sign of this as she accepted his words graciously before continuing.

'I've been thinking about why they trust us, as well,' she said. 'It's so obvious when you think about it, but it's just not something that would readily occur to us, with our knowledge of the world. They trust us because they don't know how to do anything else. They have no idea of outside duplicity. Everything is just so simple to them. We aren't part of the battle between Memphis and Atlantis, so we pose no threat to them. If we are not the enemy they know, then we are no enemy.'

'Exactly,' Doc concurred. 'They have been confined to such a narrow existence for so long that they have no conception of anything beyond the boundaries that they know. It would be easy to abuse their hospitality, as they would have no notion of what was occurring until it was far too late.'

'Yeah, but we're not going to do that, Doc,' Ryan said pointedly. There was something about Doc's manner during his discourse that caused Ryan some unease.

'I am not suggesting that we should. We should, however, be aware that this is how they are looking at things. It may be necessary at some point to explain to them concepts that we take for granted, and that they may find alien.'

'Tell you what else it means,' Mildred said carefully, with the air of someone who had been considering this point for some time. 'It means that if the people of Memphis are like this, then there's a good chance that they're like that in Atlantis, too. Mebbe even this Odyssey... He may rule with an iron hand, but he's only going to know the rules that have been handed down by the Odysseys before him.'

'That's a point that's got to be worth thinking about,' Ryan said slowly. 'It could be the key to breaking the ville open.'

'That would be good,' Doc said softly. 'Just think of all the secrets that we might find...'

'Not care about secrets. Just chill fucker and leave,' Jak commented dismissively.

'Jak's right,' Ryan said curtly. 'Secrets? Some old predark mumbo-jumbo shit that they've kept going. We've seen enough of that crap, and it's not our concern. We agreed to help Lemur off-load this Odyssey. Once that's done, we can just get the hell out of here and go somewhere where there are people we can understand.'

There was a murmur of agreement from the companions around the table. But Krysty kept her eyes firmly fixed on Doc and couldn't help but note his assent was a little less enthused than the others. She had a feeling he had a greater interest in the secrets of Atlantis than he was letting on.

DOC MIGHT HAVE BEEN concerned with the prospects of finding out more about the secrets that powered the myths of Atlantis, but for the others there were more prosaic and pressing concerns.

During the few days that they had been resident in Memphis, they had gleaned a reasonable impression of the ville. Walled in by the makeshift—though structurally solid—ring of rubble, the buildings within had little impression of the architectural and masonic skills of the inhabitants. Time had been at a premium, and so the buildings had been left relatively unchanged. However, some had been damaged and then made good by the skilled craftsmen who now inhabited them, and these alterations and repairs showed the kind of craft and attention to detail that was the hallmark of the people. These supposed repairs were simple and yet finished with a grace of line that marked them out from the weather-beaten and sometimes ornate and ugly buildings they made good. In this way, even though they hadn't had the time to make a ville of their own, the innate sensibilities of the Memphis people had impressed themselves upon their surroundings.

It wasn't just these running repairs. The decoration of the area within the walls separated the buildings inexorably from those on the outside. Within, everything was either painted in the red and white color scheme that had become so familiar, or was in the process of being painted in this manner. Members of the ville went about this task daily with a slow and steady hand, in no hurry to finish but determined to do a good job. Again, the attention to detail and the work ethic that had been ingrained in them from the day they were born had once more come to the fore.

Within the walls, the inhabitants seemed to feel relatively safe, yet the companions were aware of an undercurrent that ran through the ville. It was far from obvious as they went about their everyday tasks of farming, weaving and the manufacture and maintenance of the environment. On the surface, they seemed at ease in their new surroundings, even though they moved with a determination born of years of being driven, rather than relaxing into their new freedom. Yet it seemed to the companions as though they always had an eye cast over their shoulder and an ear cocked for their early-warning system. The Nightcrawlers had never come by day, yet even in the hours of light they seemed to walk in the shadow of fear. The years of living beneath the yolk of Odyssey's oppression still weighed heavily, even though they were now nominally free. They were, however, still slaves to their fears.

For those who were part of the sec force, these fears were channeled into a desire to learn how to fight back. Mark had started to learn some of those skills when he'd begun to train for the Nightcrawlers, yet there was little he was able to impart to those keen to learn.

As they watched him, it soon became obvious to Ryan, Jak and J.B. why this could be. The seriousness of their situation weighed heavily on the sec chief and made him impatient in dealing with his men. As the would-be soldiers lined up to practice on crudely made mannequins, as they fired at targets from standing and running positions, as they learned hand-to-hand with blunted knives and also unarmed, so it became apparent that Mark soon tired of their ineptitude. It was as though he despaired of their ability to learn the skills needed to become a competent sec force, and he hectored and bullied them so that they felt that they could do nothing right. The more he yelled, the less confident they became.

'Ryan, need talk him,' Jak said softly. 'Mebbe men always be shit, mebbe not. Not get ice inside with him shouting.'

Ryan knew what the albino youth meant. In combat, you made the fear work for you. No one ever went into a firefight feeling relaxed. Always you approached battle with that fear in your gut, your heart pounding and the adrenaline coursing through your system. But you didn't yield to it. You turned it in on itself so that you froze inside, became still, like ice on the surface of a river. Underneath, the current may be raging. On the surface, you were still, you were solid. You acted solely by instinct. That told you what you had to do and you rode into it smoothly, without wasting time on thought, without sparing the time to worry if you were making the right move. These men weren't getting the chance to hone that instinct. Instead, they were being undermined unintentionally on every move, so that the fear was always flowing outward, without channeling or direction.

Mark's own frustration with what he saw as a race against time was reflecting back off his own men, with the result that there would never be enough time for them to get it right.

J.B. watched Ryan as he observed the training, and could tell what was going through his head.

'They're keen. They look pretty strong. And they're not cowards, we know that for certain. If you talk to him, then me and Jak can start to work with the sec.'

They were standing on the edge of a fenced-in yard that stretched for over a thousand yards in width and around five thousand in length. At one time, before skydark, it had served as the parking lot for a Cineplex that had long since crumbled to the elements, its inability to exist as long as the concrete and brick buildings surrounding it a monument to the poor standards of late twentieth-century construction as much as the force of weather fluctuations postnukecaust. The neglected skeleton of the building threw shadows over the packed earth and traces of asphalt that now made up the sec training ground.

Ryan strode over to where Mark was addressing his men. A row of targets stood about seventy yards from where the group of eight were clustered, and the seven trainees were covered in dust and grime, scored by grazes and the welts of bruises that were starting to rise and color. The targets in the distance were splattered by blobs of paint and dye that were unevenly distributed.

As he approached, Ryan could hear the tail end of Mark's rant.

'...and you truly think that the Crawlers will stand there and raise their hands saying "Please, take your time, I'll just stand here and wait"? What kinds of fools are you if you truly think this? You must learn to adjust your aim and fire as you move, not stop dead and take vital seconds to sight the target. Great heavens, if you do this, then you will surely forfeit your lives. Not just yours, I may remind you—the lives of everyone in Memphis is dependant upon us and how well we fare when we come up against the enemy, and—'

'Mark,' Ryan barked, levering his way into the man's rant by force. 'Stop berating your boys for a second and tell me what's going on. Why are the targets covered in dye?'

Mark whirled. His face was a dark cloud of tension and anger that lifted slightly when he caught sight of the one-eyed man. 'Ryan, good to see you. Good to see someone who knows what he's doing when faced with an enemy that wouldn't hesitate to kill you on only half a sight.'

Ryan shook his head and kissed his teeth. 'Boys have got to learn to be men, Mark. It doesn't come overnight, it takes some time.'

'Time is something that we don't have,' Mark snapped in return.

'Mebbe,' Ryan acknowledged, 'but it seems to me that you don't have a choice. Boys have to train to be men, and that takes time. Meantime, you make the best of it. Can't fight things like that in the same way you can fight a stickie.'

'Fight a what?' Mark questioned, suddenly perplexed.

It hadn't occurred to Ryan that the sucker-fingered muties that populated the vast expanses of dead earth across the old U.S.A. wouldn't have penetrated into these areas, yet if convoys—with their wealth of old tech to help them—had only rarely traversed these lands, then it made sense that the muties would be an unknown quantity. Still, if nothing else, it had served a purpose by halting Mark's tirade.

'Tell you about it sometime,' Ryan answered with a dismissive gesture. 'Right now, we need to talk about a few things.' He put his arm around the sec chief's shoulders and led him away from his men. Jak and J.B. took this as their cue to move in.

While Ryan continued his discussion with the rapidly calming Mark, the two fighters stood in front of the sec detachment.

'Things not going great?' Jak asked them.

They shuffled their feet, looked embarrassed. Then one of them, rubbing idly at a graze that ran from elbow to wrist, spoke up.

'It's not easy. We've never had to do this before, and Mark expects perfection every time. I believe that we are all improving, but he makes us feel as though we are going backward. The targets have more hits—not in vital areas, it is true—than ever before, but it's hard. None of us ever fired a blaster before we fled from Atlantis, where Mark began to train as a Crawler. And these blasters—they're not like the ones we use when we scout and patrol. They feel completely different.'

The man shrugged as he held up a blunt-nosed blaster that didn't look like anything J.B. had ever seen before. The Armorer beckoned him to hand it over, and examined the strange weapon.

'Dark night! It's a paint ball gun. Next to useless,' J.B. muttered, shaking his head. 'These blasters have a completely different weight and balance to what you'll use in combat, and these little fuckers—' he squeezed the ball so hard that it burst, splattering dye over his hand, water running down his arm '—don't fly like any kind of ammo you'd use. How can you learn to fire straight with shit like this?'

'Mark figures that we might be shit, but at least we don't waste ammo this way.'

Jak spit on the ground in disgust. 'Stupe idea. You know fire these, but not real blaster…'

'If you use these to train, and then use your own blasters when you're up against an enemy, the balance and aim of the thing is going to be completely different,' J.B. explained to the trainees. 'Problem with that is that if you're not used to using blasters, as you people aren't, then you're not going to be able to make the adjustment in the heat of battle. And that's you buying the farm.'

'So what are we supposed to do about it?' asked another of the trainees. 'Mark makes the rules.'

J.B. looked over to where the sec chief was engrossed in conversation with Ryan.

'Mebbe we can do something about that,' he stated.

While Jak and J.B. had been talking to the sec men, Ryan had been trying to convince Mark that his men should train with live ammo.

'Listen to me,' Ryan said, winding up his argument. 'I know what it's like to be a leader. Everything comes down to you, and you're not just looking out for yourself but for everyone else. And it's hard, real hard. But right now all you're doing is making your men feel like they're shit. You've got to cut them some slack. Combat is won through guts, and guts comes with courage. They have to feel like they can come through. Bawling them out all the time isn't going to do that. And they're going to have problems with those chickenshit blasters being different weights and balances. You've got to train using the weapons they usually use…'

Mark shook his head. 'I know that makes sense, but—'

'But what?'

'But what about ammo? Our supplies are so limited.'

Ryan shrugged. 'How much do you need? Strikes me that—from what you say and from what we know—a lot of the combat is hand-to-hand and uses blades. That's the way the Nightcrawlers work. Mebbe you should be concentrating on that some more?'

'We do, but I want to put us in a position where we can kill them before they get close enough to engage in that manner. Rather than purely defensive, I want our strategy to be offensive.'

'Well, that sounds good to me, it makes a lot of sense,' Ryan acknowledged. 'But you can't run before you can walk. While you're working on your long-term strategy, then you're going to lose men in hand-to-hand. There's got to be some kind of balance.'

'You're right, I suppose,' Mark said slowly. 'It's just that… We're not equipped to look after ourselves as a community, not yet. And I have to—'

'Fireblast, man, you don't have to do anything,' Ryan said with emphasis. 'That's why we agreed to stay. We'll help you take that weight, make it easier to carry.'

Mark allowed himself a smile, the first time his grim visage had cracked in the short time that Ryan had known him.

'That's more like it.' Ryan grinned broadly and slapped him on the shoulder. 'Now let's do something about getting your men into shape on unarmed and knife fighting.'

Mark nodded decisively. 'But there's something I must do first,' he said, almost to himself.

While Ryan followed in his wake, he strode over to where his men were waiting, and he took the paint-ball blaster from J.B.'s hands, holding it out to his men.

'See this?' he asked. The trainees exchanged bemused glances, then nodded. Mark's smile broadened. 'This was a mistake. Forget it. We start over, and this time we learn properly.'

Pulling back his arm, he threw the blaster toward the standing row of targets. Ryan couldn't help but note that he had an excellent throwing arm; the blaster reached the level of the targets, smashing against one before falling in pieces to the ground.

'Okay, these people are going to show us how we should be fighting. I suggest that we take note of what they have to impart,' Mark continued. 'These may be the most important lessons we ever have to learn.'

'That's some build-up,' J.B. muttered to Ryan. 'Too bad Millie and Krysty can't be here to help.'

'Yeah,' Ryan mused, 'whatever they're doing now, I'd bet serious jack that they're not enjoying it.'

'I CAN'T BELIEVE THAT we're doing this,' Mildred muttered venomously as she began to stitch another tunic. 'We should be teaching these idiots how to fight, not learning how to sew.'

Krysty placed her tongue firmly in her cheek to prevent herself from laughing out loud. It would be impolite to their hosts, and would also probably make Mildred explode. Already, it seemed that she was on a short fuse that was burning ever closer to the detonator. However there was one thing she couldn't resist.

'So you never really learned to sew, then? Back in Harmony, it was one of the first things that Mother Sonja taught me.'

'Sweetie, I always wanted to be out playing baseball, and I never did all that well in home ec at high school,'

Mildred murmured darkly, her gaze smoldering as she looked around the room at the other women.

'I'll have to take your word for that, as some of it sounded like an alien language to me,' Krysty commented, having to concentrate extremely hard lest she howl with amusement.

'Don't make me explain,' Mildred whispered. Then she caught Krysty's eye and could see how hard the woman was trying to contain her mirth. 'Yeah, very funny…' Mildred forced through gritted teeth before the absurdity of the situation hit her, and she beat Krysty to the punch, her own frowning face cracking.

'It could be worse,' Krysty pointed out.

'Yeah? How?' Mildred countered.

From her perspective, it was easy to see how she could feel this way. It had soon become apparent that the roles of men and women in Memphis—which were, of course, defined by the learned behavior that they had brought with them from Atlantis—were rigidly defined and archaic in their structure.

Atlantis had been run very much as a patriarchy of the old type, almost classical in its design. Mildred had never been interested in history during her days in education, always being oriented more toward the sciences, as befitted her eventual calling as a physician. However, she knew enough of the ways of predark antiquity to know that whatever else lay underneath the philosophy of Atlantis, there was a strong strain of classical Greek contained within.

So it was that while the men farmed, engineered and fought, the women raised children, made clothes and cooked. Not that these women in Memphis were without accomplishment. There was artistry in the clothes they made, and many were responsible for the painted hieroglyphs and decorations on the murals that dotted the red-and-white landscape. Where there was intricate scrollwork on much of the building renovation, this, too, could be attributed to the women of the ville. Yet they weren't armed. They didn't take part in the heavy restoration and maintenance work. They didn't heal the sick.

This latter irritated Mildred intensely. Medicine was her territory, and yet when she had offered her services to Lemur and Cyran, they were politely declined. She had never been in a ville where they hadn't welcomed another pair of hands and a little more experience when it came to medical help, and it seemed to her that she had experienced nothing less than a slap in the face.

Yet when she had questioned why this was so, she had been met with nothing more than the assurance that the medical bay situation was in good hands...male hands. There was nothing more to be said, and this bland acceptance of gender roles irritated her in a way that the others couldn't comprehend. For Krysty as much as for the men, it was just one of those things. Every ville had its own ways, and you adjusted to these so as not to cause unnecessary conflict. For Mildred, however, it was something that went deeper. It was unthinkable that women should be anything other than equal. Of course there were times when men did things women couldn't, and vice versa. Size, strength, and even the individual all figured in that equation. But such a strict and arbitrary division, based on nothing more than an accident of birth, was the kind of thing she had spent her youth watching others fight for, and fighting against herself. So it was with an ill-concealed lack of grace that she watched the men go off to do real work, following Krysty as they were shown how the women of Memphis contributed to the running of the ville.

The first day or two had been spent baking and preparing food for sale and trade within the ville. With no system of jack, the people of Memphis operated a barter system whereby people exchanged services and good for others. So a meal could be purchased at the cost of a roof repair among the men; a toga for several days' child care among the women. It was a complex system, but one that the Memphis people operated almost as second nature.

After this, the two women were sent by Cyran to assist in the manufacture and repair of clothing. Again, only women worked in this trade, which was seen as a feminine preserve. They had been in this building for the past three days, and it was driving Mildred crazy. She had never enjoyed seam-work, and to be expected to keep up a high work rate on something in which she had neither real skill nor interest was something that was making her already short temper shorter by the minute.

'Another damn thing,' she added to Krysty after putting a needle through her finger yet again. 'If I'm not helping as a healer, then I'm going to be asking for a blood transfusion. I swear, I've been in firefights where I've had less injury than this.'

Krysty suppressed another smile. 'Come on, Mildred, we've got to go with what they do here. If the time comes to stand and fight, then we can forget all this. But if we're to be any good at all, we've got to meet them halfway.'

Mildred sighed. 'You're right. I know you're right.

But that isn't making it any easier. Besides which, I'm going to be ruining most of the clothes that come through here, dripping blood on them. So how's that going to go down?'

Krysty acknowledged that. 'Okay, mebbe we should have a word with Cyran or Lemur.'

'Have to be her, 'cause she's in charge of the women,' Mildred said with heavy irony. 'Still, it might make things a little better.' She put down the toga on which she'd been attempting to work and sat back, surveying the workroom around her. At benches and tables, women worked with their heads down, hardly talking or exchanging the briefest of words. 'You know something? When I was a kid I saw this thing on TV about sweatshop workers in the garment industry. All women, all heads down, working not talking…things don't really change, do they?'

'Don't they?' Krysty echoed. 'Mebbe not. I don't know about then, but I do know that people's fundamental drives don't alter. We're all driven by the same impulses, throughout history.'

'Damn, girl, you'd better watch it. You're starting to sound like Doc.' Mildred grinned mischievously. 'You don't want to make a habit of that.'

Krysty shook her head. No way did she want to be like Doc—not if she was right about what was going on in his head at the moment.

Chapter Ten

The secrets of power. The key to understanding what is happening, what has happened and what will happen. More importantly, the key to knowing why. If there is some reason why I feel compelled to do the things that I now do, some motivation that propels me ever onward, then perhaps it is here that I shall find it. If not in Memphis, then certainly in Atlantis. But how shall I get there? No matter. There will be time to worry about that later. First things first...

DOC HAD ENGINEERED his fate so that he was able to escape both the sec training and having to accompany Mildred and Krysty. Actually manipulating matters so that he had a free hand was simple enough. A murmured word to Lemur and Mark about his recent injuries ensured that he wasn't considered fit to train at present. Another word in the ear of Cyran and he assured her that he wouldn't wish to transgress gender barriers and offend tradition by accompanying the women. It was simple. Doc understood the exiled Atlanteans perfectly. In social mores and manners they more closely resembled the genteel classes of his own age than anyone that the rest of the companions—even Mildred—would have ever encountered. Playing them was easy.

Not so easy was escaping the notice of Ryan and the

others. This couldn't be achieved with subterfuge. Obviously they would notice his absence, so it became politic to make a small speech, carefully worded.

'You know that I am unable to fight effectively until my wounds have healed—no, Doctor, there is nothing to concern you, I assure you, but my recovery time is greater than for any other one of you. I would not wish to hamper your training by exacerbating my injuries at an inopportune moment—' the blank looks from Jak and J.B. had told him at that point that his ploy of using arcane language for simple concepts was working well '—and it would be an insult to our guests to accompany the women. No, I feel I could make a greater contribution to our cause if I were to go my own way, and ask a few questions. The key to everything lies in what these people have known from their earliest days. They do not know this because it has always been there. Therefore, it behoves me to uncover this.'

Ryan—after picking his way through the minefield of Doc's carefully chosen obtuse language—had agreed.

Of course he had. In many ways their agendas coincided. It was important for the companions to know what made Atlantis tick if they were to devise a way of defeating Odyssey. It was important for Doc to know what made Atlantis tick if he were to annex the secrets of the ville and use them for his own ends. Under the guise of fulfilling one brief, he could achieve both.

There was an old saying he had heard used during his brief time in the late twentieth century. The whitecoats and the men in suits who had been their enforcers had used it in conversations that he was not supposed to overhear. What had it been? Ah, yes...

Hide in plain sight.

'I WONDER, young man, if you would take the time to spare me a few words. I have some curiosity about the ways of your society and the history that lay beneath.' Doc tilted his head and tipped his hat as he spoke, in a reinforced gesture of deference.

Affinity lay down the chisel with which he had been smoothing a concrete block, making the gray rubble into a perfect corner stone, and wiped the dust and sweat from his brow.

'I can assure you, sir, as one of those who saved me from being taken back to Atlantis, I am in your debt.'

It occurred to Doc that the only reason they had saved Affinity from this fate was because he had been captured by them—rendered unconscious, in fact—during an earlier skirmish. Yet the young man hadn't figured that out. The youth was keen, but not perhaps as intelligent as some, and Doc felt sure he would be perfect for eliciting information.

The old man looked around at the interior of the room. Once an old shopfront, it now served as a workshop for stone masons engaged in hacking the remains of the old suburb into something that could be used for maintenance. The room was heated—almost unbearably so—by a kiln in the far corner that made bricks from the clay soil. The air hung heavy with the heat and with the dust from a dozen masons hewing blocks of concrete, stone or blocks of brick. The air was filled with the sharp squeal and clang of chisel and hammer on stone and the muttered under-tones of conferring masons as they followed the plans of builders who were engaged on the task of renovation.

'Wait for a second, Dr. Tanner. I must first make sure that I do not transgress.'

Affinity left Doc and went to the far corner of the room, where one of the masons stood over a three-foot-square block of stone, taken from the cornice of a crumbling building. He was gesturing over it and speaking rapidly to a builder whose sole concern seemed to center on arguing the opposite point of view to whatever was said. Because of this, it took Affinity some time before he was able to interject. A few brief words, a glance at Doc from the master mason, and a brief incline of the head insured that the young man was able to leave his post and join Tanner.

They left the stone-cutting workshop and began to walk along the street outside. A light drizzle filled the air and a cool breeze blew. Affinity lifted his head up to the sky, letting the damp, cool air fall on him, and sighed.

'You have no idea how good that feels. I enjoy my work—as much as any man can—and I like the fact that I am contributing to the greater good of Memphis, yet, at the same time, I feel that I have no time to stop and enjoy the fact that I am now free, and no longer under the yolk of Atlantean oppression.'

'I'm so glad you decided to mention that,' Doc said smoothly. 'There are some questions that I would like to ask you. It seems to me that the philosophies on which Odyssey runs Atlantis are similar in some ways to old ideas that I have encountered during our travels. That very similarity suggests to me that if I can but find an Achilles' heel—'

'You are familiar with the concept?' Affinity questioned excitedly.

'But of course,' Doc continued as smoothly as before. 'There are many ideas that have permeated from the days before the nukecaust. Naturally, many of them have become distorted over the ensuing years. Yet there are elements that are common enough to suggest that these ideas have staying powers that could not have been dreamed of. I feel that if I can ally my knowledge to that of, say, yourself, concerning the specifics of Atlantean lore, then it is possible that we may yet find a way to bring down the tyrant.'

'I hope so,' Affinity affirmed, his eyes gleaming with expectation. 'Just tell me what you wish to know…'

'DOC, JUST WHAT HAVE you been doing the last few days?' J.B. asked.

The old man shrugged. 'This and that. A little information here, a little there…'

'And does this add up to something that's worth knowing, or is it just a whole lot of nothing?' Ryan queried.

'That rather depends on how you view the matter,' Doc answered with a sly grin. 'First, why not tell me what you know so far?'

'Not much,' Ryan admitted. 'There was some stuff Affinity told us in the forest, and then what Lemur said a few nights back. But it doesn't make much sense to me.'

'I don't know,' Mildred mused, 'there are bits of it that make sense.'

'Then tell me what you think, my good Doctor, and I shall attempt to fill in the gaps.'

Krysty viewed this with some distaste. There was still something nagging at her concerning Doc's behavior. There were things that didn't add up, and this underlying feeling that he was taunting them in some way.

She was sure that he had an agenda of his own, but she just couldn't make out what it was that he wanted.

Meantime, Mildred was gathering her knowledge.

'Okay, Doc, let me run this one by you. Atlantis was an island that was supposed to be the seat of all civilization. It was technologically and socially in advance of everything else on the planet, and then it got swept away in some kind of disaster. Except that there's no proof that it really existed. The way I remember it, it came through myths from the Greeks and Romans, so I'm guessing it must have been from before then. Mebbe it was some kind of allegory—a model of what should have been but never was.

'Thing is, a lot of people took it literally and believed that it had really existed. A lot of time and money was spent by rich cranks looking for it, that I do remember. And it seems like whoever founded this Atlantis took it real serious…and they must have been into that Greek thing, as well, because all the names we've come across are derived from Greek myth and history. Actually, that isn't strictly true, because I don't know what the hell kind of name Lemur is. Some kind of little animal, as far as I recall.

'The Greek thing must be big for them, and must tie in to old Atlantis myths. Otherwise how would you explain the way they dress. That's very classical Greek, so their own myth must have a strong vein of that in it. White and red is a weird one, though. When I was a kid all the things we had from ancient Greece were white—statues and the like—so we assumed that they only ever dressed in white. But that was because all the old paintings, and all the decoration on the statues, had worn away over the centuries. Their paints didn't last in the way that they did in later years. So if the founders of this Atlantis had some half-baked ideas they cobbled together, that explains the white. But the red?

'And then there's the UFO thing. I can understand that, because in the last half century leading up to skydark there was this real big thing about unidentified flying objects. It seemed that the more technology there was, the more people were frightened that little green or gray men from outer space were going to invade and attack. Either that or they were going to come down and save the chosen few who believed in them.

'Hell, I always thought aliens were a bunch of crap, but that was before I woke up to find myself here, so I don't want to dismiss anything out of hand anymore. Don't find it likely, though. There was one school of thought that the idea of aliens was about man feeling insecure in an environment where machines could take over and render him useless. Psychologists figured that man liked feeling bigger than everything, and UFOs were a projection of those fears of being reduced. If you look at what they did with their tech, and maybe the psychologists had a point. It certainly grew in proportion to how much closer we got to annihilation. But how that ties up with Atlantis and with the Greeks, I don't know.'

She came to a halt, looking around her at the others. Doc had a smug grin on his face. The others registered varying degrees of confusion and comprehension. Why not? There were a lot of ideas tied up in this ville that would be unlike anything they had encountered thus far.

Doc took his cue. 'I trust you are all with myself and the good doctor so far? What she has told you, in as far as she knows, constitutes a good basis for understanding how this concept of Atlantis works. Allow me now to join a few dots, so that the picture begins to take on a more recognizable shape.

'What she has said about the old legends of Atlantis I can do little more than confirm, except to say that when I was a young man there were some ideas about a race of supermen who lived in the center of the earth and had a greater knowledge and power than those on the surface. They had continued to develop at a rapid rate since leaving the face of the earth, and although there were many names for them, and for their societies—Bulwer-Lytton called them the Vrill, and some attributed them the ancient Asian name of Shamballa—there were those that believed they were the survivors of Atlantis.

'I believe I can explain the appearance of red among the white in the predominant colors of our current hosts if I follow this line of argument. Many of these beliefs and underworld societies had strong occult connections. They were not so much against the then-predominant Christian religions as coming from a completely different and much older tradition. In this sense, they tied in with the paganism that characterized the old Greek religions, and the many ideas of magic—that is to say, breaking the laws of science and bending the world as we know it to the will of the few.

'In my day, these views were gaining strength. From what I know of the days before skydark, they were still growing in strength. The idea of witchcraft, powers greater than those known by humans... Are they so different from the idea that there are those on the outside of the earth with a greater power? Is not the idea of a superior alien race nothing more than an old pagan god explained by increased technology?

'Ideas of an advanced society living on a surviving Atlantis, deep in the earth, crossed over with ideas that these were in fact superbeings from another world who became stranded here, or who had the power to go beyond our world. Of course, you may ask why they stayed in the center of the earth, or allowed themselves to sink in the first place, if they had such powers, but belief systems rarely cover all the angles.

'The traditional colors of magic, the occult hues that carry power, have always been red, white and black. The lack of black here is a little perplexing in light of this, but I suspect that either something has been a little lost in the passing down of the traditions postnukecaust, or else there is black in Atlantis if not here.'

He paused, waiting to see if his words had made any kind of sense or had been little more than gibberish to their ears. From their expressions, he realized that he had given them a lot to digest. Time to wrap it up and see what they had to say.

'The only thing left, I think, is how the idea of Greece, Atlantis and the UFOs tie together. In a sense I have already answered this in outlining the significance of color. I believe that the ideas concerning superior races, the occult, and some kind of supermen from outer space have somehow become mixed—'

'That's it,' Mildred interrupted. 'I knew that it made some kind of sense somewhere—right at the back of my mind, buried. I remember when I was ill, just before the shit hit the fan and I hit the freezer. When I was a kid, we used to have my cousin Martin stay with us, and we used to sneak watching the TV late night…so many bad old sci-fi and horror movies. Anyway, when I was ill, Marty gave me this book for when I was in hospital. I guess he just picked it up and thought it was about old movies. It was, in a way, but it was some kind of crank book about how the government was feeding us information about UFOs through bad movies, to get us ready for when it was revealed the little green men were real... It was a crock-of-shit book that contradicted itself all over the place, but there was one bit that really caught my eye. The writer kept referring to how much red, black and white was used in color sci-fi movies, and explained the occult history of the colors.

'God, you don't think the first Atlanteans based their society on some crank book. C'mon, that's just too...'

Mildred lapsed into silence, shaking her head in disbelief.

Ryan sighed heavily. 'I don't know. I'm not sure if I've even followed half of what the hell you two have been talking about, but I do know one thing. I've seen a ville base the way it lives on a whole lot less than that. Anyway, it doesn't matter what it's based on, only that we know. Mebbe now we can understand why they think and act like they do. And mebbe it can give us some kind of insight into how we can help them bring down Odyssey.'

'I agree with you. The veracity of the source is unimportant,' Doc mused. 'What it may highlight is that, if Odyssey and his predecessors have been serious about reaching other planets—particularly those who founded the ville—then we may be up against some extremely hazardous old tech, and we need to tread carefully.'

'Doc's right,' J.B. said thoughtfully. 'If they've got old shit we haven't seen before, there's no knowing what it could do to us.'

'Triple red, then,' Ryan said. 'Until we know exactly

what we're up against, we don't make any rash moves.'
Looking around the group for agreement, he gained
their assent one by one, finishing with Doc.

We?

Chapter Eleven

From the outside, no sound could penetrate the inches-thick layers of brick and stone that constituted his inner sanctum. It had been one of the first edifices constructed after the nuclear winter of skydark, and had stayed erect and proud as a monument to the power of the dynasty of Odyssey. Seven men of that name had lived within its walls, each preparing for the day when they would be saved.

He sat, brooding, over the reports. The people of Memphis—particularly those fools Cyran and Mark—thought they had achieved autonomy and escaped from the father empire. How wrong they were. There would always be dissidents, and they would always seek to escape. The secret of leadership wasn't in forcing them to stay, perhaps spreading unrest within, but in letting them out on a leash, like an overexcited dog, so that they thought they had freedom but could be jerked back when they stretched too far.

It suited Odyssey's end to let these dissidents set themselves up as another ville. To foster the illusion of autonomy, and to keep the numbers low, he would send sec parties out to catch some, bring them back for ritual slaughter—a culling of the dissenters, and a lesson to those who stayed and worked. Ultimately, however, he had them exactly where he wanted them. On the outside, they could pretend they were free without disturbing the running of Atlantis. Yet they were still under close observation and monitoring, so that any root sign of a problem could be crushed underfoot before it had a chance to grow and become a choking weed, a thorn in his side.

Odyssey looked at the stunted tree, in an earthenware pot, that stood on the corner of the room. It disgusted him: a symbol in its weakness of what this world had become. Perhaps that was why he thought of Memphis in such metaphors. They, too, were weak, stunted and caused him a sense of disgust.

A sense that grew stronger as he considered the reports. It was one of the drawbacks to allowing these people a taste of freedom to dispose of them. They truly believed they were free, and acted as such. He had no real provenance over them other than in a covert manner, and so—unlike the people of Atlantis, whom he could rein in with ease—he found himself frustrated by his inability to crush them. Easy as it would be in real terms, the fact that there was an outside colony acted as a device to siphon off the small but continuous stream of dissenters. Take this away, and disorder could fester within the ville.

So, much as he would like to detail teams of Nightcrawlers to simply take out the problem at source, he had to play a waiting game. And there was nothing worse than that when you were a man accustomed to flexing the fist and obtaining immediate results.

There was little doubt in his mind that the current reports spelled danger: a danger that could grow if not checked. The problem was how he did this without upsetting the delicate balance he had established between his domain and the satellite of Memphis.

He felt the need to speak of this: yet, to who? The name and rank of Odyssey, all that it entailed, was handed down, and with it came an absolute power that meant absolute isolation. To discuss a course of action was to show weakness, and that could never be done. Yet he still desired to mull over his course of action. The only way to do this was to find a subordinate and talk at—rather than to—him. It meant that being the supreme commander and leader of the chosen people was a lonely place. Yet he had been raised for this end, and knew what to expect.

Sometimes, that knowledge didn't make it any easier.

The reports were written in black ink on a red woven paper edged in white. They were prepared by the agents he had placed within the ville of Memphis, who posed as dissidents, but used their position to monitor events within the ville and report back via rendezvous with Nightcrawlers. It was a simple system, aided by the incompetence of the Memphis sec. Should they gain a degree of skill in their task, then he would be forced to consider another course of action. That, however, had looked far from likely.

Until now…

He glanced at the hieroglyphs that covered the red surface. They told him a story that made him ill at ease. Strangers rarely made it this far past the desolation that curbed their territory. Strangers who wished to stay for a while were rarer still. Rarest of all were those who appeared to have knowledge and combat skill.

Up until now, he had remained calm. Now the cold fury that had been building within him erupted into a white heat of passion. Snarling, he took the reports and ripped them up, throwing the pieces to the far corners of the room. Some of them landed in the earthenware pot, which made some kind of sense to him.

Breathing heavily, he forced himself to calm down. He couldn't be seen to exude any kind of emotion other than a serene reassurance that all was going to plan. That, too, was part of his training. Except that things weren't: the new vessel for the journey was behind schedule. The phases of the moon and stars would soon come into alignment once more, and if this time the travelers didn't return to retrieve those left behind, then it would not happen in his lifetime. The next alignment was many seasons away.

From history, from his own childhood—the last time there had been an alignment and the travelers hadn't come—he knew that for a phase to pass with no action resulted in unrest, and a testing time for the incumbent Odyssey. The problem with the prophecy—the thing that the people didn't understand—was that the travelers hadn't specified a date for their return, only an alignment that would be in the night skies. This wasn't the fault of the leader. All any man with the name Odyssey could do was prepare a vessel for transport and hope that now was the time. But the disappointment and frustration of the people was vented on the leader.

It was inevitable… But didn't they realize that the leader felt that frustration, too? And now there was this obscure threat, coming at a time when he should be preparing for the final push toward the time of alignment.

Odyssey looked around him, at the walls of his inner sanctum. The only light was cast by flickering lamps and torches mounted on the stone walls, as he was in the center of the building, with no windows, and corridors and anterooms surrounding him on all four sides. Each room, each corridor, sealed by a lock that could only be opened by those who knew the combination. Part of him wondered if this was to keep the people out or to keep him caged in. No matter.

The walls were hung with tapestries in red, black and white. In pictographs, they depicted the history of Atlantis, from the earliest days when the island continent had flourished, through the sinking of the original lands and its rebirth in this location. Hardwood chairs, a simple table covered in papers and the remnants of a meal, and a long chaise covered in white cushions were the only furniture, with additional decoration supplied only by the stunted tree and a few weak plants in smaller pots. Sculptures of old Greek gods filled one corner, but they weren't decoration: a shrine to those who had come before the revelation from space, who were no longer godheads but were still revered as prophets.

The room was twenty feet high, forty wide, yet it seemed like a casket, burying him within it at this moment. The cool air that circulated from ducts built into the structure of the temple now seemed dank and rancid, as though he were breathing in his own despair.

Enough of these thoughts that rattled around in his head without reaching any kind of resolution! To think only made them louder, resounding inside his skull until they blotted out the capacity to think. He had to voice them, and in so doing find some resolution of action.

Leaving the fragments scattered across the floor, he strode to the doorway and twisted the red, white and black combination lock until it released the door. As he left, the guard stationed outside snapped to attention.

'Where is Xerxes?' Odyssey snapped.

'Master, he will be on vessel site, master. It is inspection time,' the guard stammered nervously, having accurately judged his leader's black mood.

'He'd better be,' Odyssey muttered savagely before walking away and leaving the guard relieved that he hadn't been arbitrarily punished. It wasn't far from the bounds of possibility that Odyssey would have had him killed merely because he was in a bad mood.

Releasing himself from the self-imposed prison of his inner sanctum, hitting the combinations and scowling at guards as he passed, Odyssey silently exited the building and came out onto the streets of Atlantis. To his rear, a flank of guards fell silently and unobtrusively into place.

Once beyond the thick stone walls, the noise became overwhelming. Atlantis was a carefully ordered society, with the rule of law imposed by Crawlers who trained as sec guards from birth. Everyone was selected for their tasks from birth, decided for them on heredity. Most followed in the footsteps of their parents, while some were specially selected from outstanding parents to progress to the next social level. The decision was always made by the leader, and for successive generations he had to keep a close watch on the development of his people.

Guards followed guards, masons followed masons, bakers followed bakers. It was a rigidly maintained social order, and for the most part the people were happy with it. This was, of course, because they knew nothing different. However, very few had ever questioned. Most accepted that to be ready for the day when they—or their descendants—would finally take the journey to a better place, they had to fulfil their allotted tasks.

Which was why the day was filled with the clamor of activity. People went about their everyday tasks with a renewed vigor as the days of alignment approached. There was work to be done, and they were happy to do it in the build up to the joyous time.

The streets of Atlantis were clean, the buildings painted white, red and black. Most had been erected just before the nukecaust, and any damage that had been incurred during the time of skydark had long since been repaired in a manner to make it seem as though it had never occurred. The designs were classical in structure, with fluted columns supporting porticoes over paved walkways. Square and rectangular buildings of clean line and little outward decoration lined the streets, which were themselves precisely divided into blocks of rectangular or square design.

The streets were populated by men and women in robes, all of whom seemed happy enough, but none of whom stayed still long enough to stop and talk beyond a few brief greetings or matters of business. There was always too much work to be done, and not enough time; furthermore, as Odyssey passed, a darkly brooding presence, those citizens nearest to him fell silent and parted swiftly to cleave a clear path for him.

His destination was obvious. There was only one site within the city that was under construction. As the population rose with each generation, so a larger vessel, taller and wider, was needed for the journey. The original temple, built at the same time as the rest of the city, had long since been made obsolete, torn down and rebuilt larger with succeeding generations. It was a constant battle against time, from generation to succeeding generation, to prepare the new vessel in time for the time of alignment.

Which was why the temple construction site was where he would find Xerxes, his sec chief and the only man he could talk to. They had an understanding, forever unspoken, that Odyssey's thoughts bounced against the sec chief would be open to a liberal interpretation. It went against all the conventions of Atlantis, but Odyssey had an implicit trust in his sec chief and in his ability to know his job better than anyone.

Xerxes was on the seventh level of scaffolding that surrounded the outside of the construction. The shell of the building had been erected, all that remained on the outer workings were the decorations and the placing of the roof. The interior was still being constructed, although all load-bearing walls were in place. Still there were chambers allocated to professions to be walled off, and doors fitted, according to required capacity.

Odyssey was glad to catch his sec chief before he attended to the close inspection of the inside. On the outer work, there was less to do, and his inspection was more routine. As sec chief, he had to insure that the work was carried out well, and that the workers didn't slack in any way. Security was about prevention of problems as much as killing those who transgressed. It was a view that Xerxes had brought to his job that had been alien to his predecessors. Yet Odyssey had given him his head, as it had yielded results in the shape of greater productivity.

The downside to catching him on the outside inspection was having to climb seven levels of scaffolding. This was still three below the roof level, for the new temple towered above the surrounding buildings, which were only four storys at most. Three below, but still high enough for a man with an uneasiness about heights. An uneasiness that Odyssey had to keep disguised. He had been taught from an early age that a leader should never show fear, for it was a sign of weakness.

Taking a deep breath, he scaled the scaffolding until he was level with his sec chief.

'Odyssey, master. What brings you out to see me when I am about my humble tasks?' Xerxes asked with deference.

'I have received word from our people in Memphis, and I wish to tell you of it and of my plans. Somewhere where we will not be overheard,' Odyssey replied. While the notion that there were Atlantis spies in Memphis was something that was kept from the majority of the people, there was little chance of their being overheard this far up. It would, however, get him inside and away from the edge of scaffold and sky, which loomed too large for comfort.

Xerxes indicated that the leader follow him through the nearest portal, which gave onto an open plan room, currently being marked for division by masons. As they entered, a stranger would have assumed that Xerxes, with his tall, thin frame, long aristocratic nose and thick head of curls, was the natural leader. Certainly there was authority in the way he dismissed the masons and indicated that the guards stay outside on the scaffold. By contrast, Odyssey shuffled in his wake, shorter and stockier, his dark brown hair thinning at the crown, bent over by his worries and concerns.

The room was large, but the manner of construction meant that the sound was dampened within, rather than magnified and echoed, as would have been expected.

'So, master, you have had word?' Xerxes said softly, halting in the center of the room.

Odyssey nodded. 'Your Nightcrawlers were correct. There are strangers in Memphis, and they do seem to have arrived on foot. This is most strange, as I can but wonder how they managed to journey so far without transport of some kind. However, there is little point in such speculation. They are here, and that is all there is to it.'

'But from your tone, master, I can deduce that they are no normal interlopers.'

'Whether anyone who could arrive at this point on foot—or would wish to—could be described as "normal" is an interesting question,' Odyssey replied sharply. 'The fact that they are here should be neither by nor by. Yet there are things about them that are of the utmost concern. They number six, and my reports say that they seem to know much of the faiths that underpin our society. They have been spied upon while in private discussion and two of them—an old man and a black woman—seem to have a knowledge that could either be useful or dangerous.'

'Dependent upon whether they are for or against us?'

Odyssey nodded. 'Exactly. I would like to know more of them. And of the party, which numbers six, there is one other of interest—the rest are mere drones. There is a woman who speaks of calling upon the powers of the earth to assist her in times of great need.'

'A practitioner of occult arts?' Xerxes mused.

'It could very well be. I would like to learn more of her—if she truly has ways of tapping the hidden powers on the outside of this dimension, then her secrets would please the travelers when they return.'

'You wish that I organize her capture?'

'That would be satisfactory. Furthermore, I need the old man and the black woman. I want to know from whence their knowledge springs. If they are dangerous. If there is anything they can tell us that would add to our own understanding. It is possible that they may have arrived at this time as messengers, we are so close to alignment.'

'So you would wish me to arrange their capture without harming them?' Xerxes pressed.

Odyssey paused, then shook his head. 'I said only that they may be messengers. They are equally likely to be an enemy. We should take no chances. The prime objective is to get them away from Memphis. If they prove too much of a problem, then it will be safer to kill them.'

Chapter Twelve

Affinity hadn't seen any of his new friends since the first evening. Not until Doc had taken him to one side and questioned him about the nature of the beliefs held by the people of Memphis and Atlantis. Although the young man had been glad to answer him, and found something in the old man with which he could feel a kind of kinship, there was something about Doc's manner that made him uneasy. It wasn't a thing that he could easily pin down, less a concrete cause than a nebulous feeling of unease, as though behind the easy manner of Tanner there lay something dark that was waiting for the chance to surface.

This feeling of unease grew within him and the next day he sought out Cyran. The tall, willowy wife of the ville leader had known Affinity before his escape, and they shared a common bond. Both had been born to families that had rank within the rigid hierarchy of Atlantis, and both had led life of comparative luxury before opting to risk an escape to freedom. There were those in Memphis who couldn't understand why they should give up such privilege for the hardships of living in Memphis.

Had those who had risked their lives for freedom done so only because they were at the bottom of the chain? If they had been born into a life of privilege, would they have stayed? Affinity doubted that. Memphis was a small enough ville for most to know the others. There were none he could think of who would have preferred to stay beneath the oppression of Odyssey, even with comparative comforts. But some perhaps doubted their own motivations more than Affinity, and he was aware of a residual wariness among some of the others.

Cyran, once Lemur had made her his wife, was even more open to these suspicions, and the two had spoken of that often. It was a small community, and those who had escaped from privilege were smaller still in number. It was natural to seek support. And in so doing, Affinity felt that he could share his concerns with her.

He went to her building after finishing in the mason's shop. His lack of guile and fighting ability in allowing himself to be captured by the companions had led to his being ejected from the sec force by Mark. There was a rapid turnover of sec men coming and going, as only a core small in numbers showed themselves to be even partially able. To be ejected was no shame as such, but nonetheless he still felt a twinge of regret as he entered the building, which also housed those bodies that ran the ville—the sec and Lemur's council—as well as being the dwelling for the leader and his spouse.

Cyran was painting when Affinity was shown into her chambers by a sec guard. There were always three on watch over Lemur and Cyran, and although she was used to their presence, Affinity found it a little disturbing. He was none too sure if he felt at ease to speak freely.

Cyran left her painting and greeted Affinity. His response was stilted and nervous, making it obvious that he was preoccupied.

'What concerns you so that you lose all familiarity in my presence?' she asked, leading him to a long table and seating him before pouring wine for them.

'There are many things,' he began after a pause, then, shaking his head, 'No, not many. Two, specifically. First, I feel uneasy at speaking on matters that demand confidentiality when there are ears around us. Second, the matter on which I wish to speak is one that is, perhaps, delicate to broach.'

She chewed on her lip thoughtfully before answering. 'For the first matter of your concern, I can only say that the men who guard Lemur and myself know their duty. They are not to report on, or talk of, anything they may see or hear within this building lest it be contrary to the greater good. I have never been aware of anything that has been said that shouldn't have been.'

Affinity frowned. 'This is all well and good if they are true to their word, but sometimes it seems as though Atlantis knows of what we feel and think as soon as we do ourselves.'

'You think they may have agents that move among us, gathering intelligence?'

'It is sometimes spoken of, and events lend credence to such an idea.'

She looked at him askance. 'What a strange idea. I cannot say it is one which I have often encountered myself. Where, I wonder, would it emanate?'

Affinity looked flustered, stammered as he searched for words. 'I-I know not what you imply, but I feel I am being judged harshly for half-suspicions that should not, perhaps, have even been voiced. It was only a passing notion, and one that is taking us away from the matter I really wish to discuss.'

'Very well,' she said gently, 'we shall say no more about it. But you have my word that whatever you say shall not reach beyond this chamber. Now do, by all means, continue.'

Hesitatingly, haltingly, Affinity began to voice his concerns about Doc and the way in which he had probed the young man for information. He couldn't say, exactly, why it so unnerved him, but hoped that he was able to voice his concern, no matter how nebulous it may be. When he finished, he looked at Cyran imploringly.

'I cannot say why this worries you so,' she said after some consideration. 'I would have thought it was an obvious course of action for our allies to wish to know more about us. Such knowledge could only assist in their understanding of our plight.'

'But why did they not ask openly? Why send Dr. Tanner to question me, a humble mason? Why did their leader, Ryan, not ask these things of Lemur or yourself?'

'Perhaps to openly question in such a way could be construed as rudeness or hostility in their etiquette,' she mused. 'After all, as they know little of our ways, so do we, correspondingly, know little of theirs. Perhaps they saw that Tanner and yourself had forged an acquaintanceship, and it wouldn't be such an imposition, under their way, for him to ask these things of you.'

Affinity considered that, nodding gently, but still something irked him. 'I see, but even so there was something about the manner of the man that suggested that there were things that were important to him in a manner far more personal than that of the group.'

'But why would this be?' she asked in soothing

tones. 'I feel sure that you are worrying for no reason. Perhaps you have overlooked the fact that, no matter how well you seem to understand Doc Tanner, he is still from the outside, with different ways that may seem alien and unnerving to us, when in fact they have no import at all.'

Affinity brightened. 'Of course. That would explain it, and it is logical. I should, perhaps, have considered this before even coming to see you. I fear that I may have wasted your time.'

She smiled. 'Dear child, you could never waste mine, nor anyone's, time when you have a genuine concern for the safety of your compatriots. Calm your fears, and go about your business now.'

Affinity left her company feeling reassured. That vague worry was still there, but now he felt that he could explain its origins, and was able to calm it with more ease.

He was so wrapped up in his own sense of relief that he didn't notice that the sec guard watched him leave with interest, nor that the guard hadn't been patrolling the corridors, in which instance he should now be on the other side of the building, but seemed to be in the same location as when he had shown Affinity into Cyran's chamber.

For her own part, Cyran was nowhere near as unconcerned as she had led Affinity to believe. His words had left a deep impression on her. She believed that his initial impression had been correct. The old man had wanted the information for more than reference to his group. There was an underlying motive. Whatever it was, it could be disruptive, and that was information that it was invaluable for her to possess.

Knowledge informed power, in many ways was power. It just depended on how a person chose to use it.

THE NIGHT WAS CLOUDLESS, balmy, and the woodlands were silent. With a surfeit of silver light from the three-quarter moon, it seemed as though it would be an easy night for the chosen sec patrol. Especially as they felt more confident, sharper after their short bout of training with the companions. They felt looser, more alert, and more at ease with their weapons.

Yet the line between confidence and overconfidence is narrow, especially for those who have no experience on which to base judgment.

The sec patrol worked its way through the densely packed wood in a loose line. Even with the canopy above and the shadows cast by the trunks, it was still easy for them to keep at least two of their companions in sight at any given time. Not that it mattered. They had a shared feeling that nothing could go wrong this night.

Jason had been with Mark on the expedition when they had encountered the companions. Since then, he felt that he had learned so much from the strangers. He held his blade loosely in his palm, and he was calm. The nervousness that had eaten at him before, every time that he had stepped foot into the woodlands on a sec patrol, was no longer with him. Whatever he had learned in terms of combat skill, he hadn't grasped that it was using the fear, not losing it, that was important.

Although he would be better able to defend himself in combat, he had first to be in a position to engage. And as he looked up at the clear skies through the darkened canopy overhead, he felt secure. Nothing could disturb his world. There was complete silence. No signs of movement.

But then, he wasn't really giving it his full attention. He knew how skilled the Nightcrawlers were in their chosen arts, and so should have been on triple red. But so confident was he in his newly won ability that he no longer had the sensitivity that fear had given him.

His hand stayed slack on his blade, even as the muscular arm snaked around his neck, hand clamping over his mouth. Even as the blade slipped under his ribs, the pain like a white-hot needle in him, first numb and then so intense that it propelled him beyond the capacity to scream. His vision closed into a tunnel of blackness that grew tighter, light receding into the distance as though he were traveling backward at immense speed. The faintest scent of oil and sweat, sweet and rank at the same time, reached into his brain before it began to shut down, his kidneys ripped by the knife, massive internal hemorrhaging flooding his lungs.

Jason had bought the farm before the Nightcrawler even let his body slip to the woodland floor. The Crawler looked down, prodded him idly with her toe, then gave a short nod of satisfaction before slithering back into the shadows in search of additional prey.

It was an eight-man sec party and the orders to the Nightcrawlers were clear. One among the party was a traitor, who would arrange for their access to the walled ville. If possible, they were to leave the sec alive, so that it wouldn't look suspicious for the insider to be left standing. But some had to be killed, to make the attack seem authentic.

Jason had drawn the short straw. His only mistake—other than lack of awareness—was to be on one end of the strung-out sec line. At the other end, a man named Homer was also being eliminated, a Crawler dropping on him from a tree, landing with a gentle thump astride his shoulders, pulling back his head and running a razor-sharp blade across his throat as the downward momentum forced him forward and into the turf. The gargling of his death rattle was muted by the moss and grass into which his face was pressed, the earth around now made mud with his lifeblood.

Along the line, Crawlers watched the sec patrol go by. The fact that two of their number had dropped out of sight should have alerted them to the possibility of attack. The Crawlers responsible for the killing avoided this by moving between cover, making it hard to distinguish their exact outline, making themselves visible as little more than a shadow in the night. It was enough to make the sec party believe that their numbers were at full strength.

As they moved, so their pace was controlled by the thickness of the foliage they had to pass, and so they began to move out of phase. It became harder to keep sight of one another the deeper and darker the woodland became.

Time for the Crawlers to take advantage. The sec party was two down. Another two were put out of action, though not killed. Slipping from the shadows without making a sound, two Nightcrawlers came upon sec men and downed them with swift blows. No blades were used, only the iron-hard sides of trained hands, which efficiently hit nerves and blacked out the unaware sec men before they had a chance to react.

Four down. Four left standing. Three were to be left alone, ignorantly blundering their way through the patrol. One was waiting.

'I thought you were never going to arrive,' snarled the sec man as a Nightcrawler appeared at his side, making him start violently.

'Shut up. Go,' the Crawler said softly. In the quiet of the woodlands, any words were amplified out of all proportion. The Crawler was aware of this, even if the sec spy wasn't, and had no wish for the remaining sec to be alerted.

The sec man was around five seven and thick set. By contrast, the dark figure beside him was more than six feet and almost invisible in the darkness. Even if the remaining sec men had seen their traitorous companion standing in the woods, he would have seemed to be alone unless they were so close that the Crawler would have a chance to dispose of them. Sound, not vision, would be the only thing to give them away now.

Stelos, the sec man who had kept allegiance to Atlantis, squared up to the Crawler. He was doing a dangerous job, risking a slow kill if his treachery were to be discovered, and the last thing he wanted was some outsider telling him what to do. His task was simple: he was to lead the Nightcrawlers back to Memphis and gain admission for them without raising the alarm. It was simple, yes, but a major task. His sense of his own importance wouldn't allow him to be treated in this manner.

The Crawler sighed inwardly. For the mission to proceed smoothly, it required cooperation. But the spies within Memphis had grown slack and were no longer the disciplined force from whence they had sprung. It would give him no greater pleasure than to dispatch this idiot to the hereafter. But no, there was a greater job to do.

The two men stood for a moment, eyeballing each other. With the dark lenses, it was hard for Stelos to tell what the Crawler was thinking. One thing was for sure, though, he was feeling more unnerved by the second.

'All right, all right, let's go,' he mumbled.

As the two men moved back toward the ville, the other Crawlers in the party melted from the shadows and joined them. They kept in a tight formation behind the rogue sec man, far enough back so that they could melt right back into shadow if he was approached.

As he had planned, there was neither opposition nor obstruction to their progress. The sec party were still in the depths of the woods, and there was only the sec on the main gate to deal with.

Stelos had planned it that way. They moved through the ruins with ease. The few sec posts that were scattered within the old suburb were far flung, and it was easy for someone with knowledge to pilot a path through them. To try to tackle them would risk blaster-fire, alerting others to the Nightcrawlers's presence. It would be pleasing for the Atlantis warriors to send some more of the Memphis scum to the hereafter, but right now that was not their task. It was about stealth and achieving an objective that dictated getting inside the walls.

To attempt getting over would be pointless. The sec system was crude but effective, and to counter it would take too much time, risking being seen. The only way was to get past the gates. And that could only be done with Stelos's help.

As they approached the gates, the traitorous sec man beckoned the Nightcrawlers into cover.

'Two men on,' he said, breathing hard through exertion and fear. 'I'll give the code, when the gate begins to open, come through hard on my heels. I'll take out one man, but you'll have to deal with the other.'

'Already done. Just go,' the tall Crawler snapped.

Stelos jogged toward the gates, pausing to gather himself before delivering a coded knock. It was an emergency signal that all sec personnel knew, to enable them to alert the gate guard if they should arrive detached from their patrol.

There was a silence of almost brain-numbing intensity before the gate began to open. This was when Stelos felt an adrenaline rush and knew that the childishly simple plan—which was, perhaps, its strength—couldn't fail.

An armed sec man appeared in the widening gap, blaster raised. 'Stelos?' he murmured, confusion written across his features. 'The others? Where are—'

'No time to explain,' the treacherous man said quickly, indicating that the sec man join him. 'You need to see this.'

Stelos was relying on the fact that, despite the training from Jak, J.B. and Ryan, the sec force of Memphis was still shot through with ingenuousness. His instinct didn't let him down. Without wondering why Stelos was alone, or questioning why he would wish to take another outside the walls, he stepped forward.

'What? What is it?' he asked, nerves making his voice shake.

'This,' Stelos whispered, showing the man the blade he had cupped in his palm. He looked the sec man in the eye, noting the confusion as he tightened his grip on the knife before bringing it up smoothly so that it pierced the sec man's stomach and ripped across his intestine, resisting slightly against the wall of muscle before rupturing it and letting his intestines spill out. The light of confusion in the other man's eyes faded into blankness as his life spilled out over Stelos's hand.

The sec man had barely the time to moan before his life was extinguished, but it would have been enough to alert his partner on the other side of the gates if not for the fact that party of Nightcrawlers had already swarmed from the shadows. Even as Stelos guided the sec man to his doom, the Crawlers were level with the traitor and past him, making the open gate.

Surprise was always the greatest weapon. The reactions of Memphis sec men were slow, not yet honed by training, never sharpened by combat. By contrast, the Crawlers were like a visceral machine, ready to move fluid and fast whenever it was required.

Before the startled sec man had a chance to raise his blaster and even begin to tighten his finger on the trigger, he bought the farm. The Crawlers swarmed over him, one ripping his hand away from the heavy handblaster, a remade 9 mm Walther PPK that had been his pride. His pride, yet never fired in anger; and destined never to be.

A second Crawler pulled him back by his long, curling blond hair, slicing across his windpipe in one smooth motion, the blade opening his throat at the same time as it ripped his carotid artery, his blood arcing out in a spume in front of his own startled vision. Few have the opportunity to see their own lives drain away in front of them. He wanted to yell, but nothing emerged but a bubbling, hideous gargle.

Before he was even killed, the Crawlers had left him in the dust, his body contorting in death throes, spreading his own blood around the asphalt. He was still thrashing when Stelos entered the ville, sweating as he tackled the heavy gate alone. The Crawlers were already on their way to their intended target, and the traitor had to work hard to catch up with them. The intelligence fed to them in Atlantis had told them where their target was housed. In fact, Odyssey had a full road and house plan of Memphis, and could pick his targets at will. The presence of Stelos wasn't necessary, but the traitor wanted to be in at the end of the chase. His main duty was to insure that the gates stayed clear for evacuation before joining the sec patrol in the woods as though nothing had occurred. However, his pride dictated that he not let himself be marginalized.

He headed for the house where the companions reposed, his heart thumping as much from exertion as from stress. He had been away from Atlantis too long and had lost his edge of fitness. If he didn't hurry, the action would be over before he arrived.

JAK JOLTED AWAKE from a dreamless sleep. It wasn't often that his rest was free from the personal demons that stalked his nightmares, and he relished such moments. So his mood was darker than the night outside as he sat up, breathing slow and shallow to cut out extraneous noise. Something had disturbed him, but he wasn't sure what.

Memphis was a true son of Atlantis. The people lived to a rigid schematic, rising early and working hard before retiring early to a long and much-needed rest. In many ways, they lived just as they had in Atlantis. If Jak could be bothered to think about it, he would reflect on how freedom was such a nebulous concept. They did exactly the same in so many ways, yet were happy with this as they were free, and not forced to act in the way that, paradoxically, they opted to choose.

But Jak was no philosopher. Instead he was glad that there were no bars and no gaudys, no fights and loud noises to keep him awake into the night. At least here he was able to rest, and it was quiet.

At least, usually it was quiet. Not now. The sounds were small, but they were enough to disturb him in this silence. They were out of character, out of place and that made them a possible danger.

Now that his attention was focused, he could hear them clearly. Still a few streets away, but approaching rapidly. He could hear people, moving fast and with some care. They were attempting subterfuge, and would have succeeded in another ville than this. Muddled so that he couldn't make out how many at first, he soon narrowed it down to seven or eight people. Farther back, there was another: less stealth, more noise. Not one of them. Was he following or chasing?

Nightcrawlers. It had to be. There were no others they had encountered in this region who moved with that degree of practiced stealth. And a sec man bringing up the rear. Another enemy if he had aided their egress, or an ally who would soon be in need of assistance.

Another thing. They moved with assurance: they knew where they were going. And from the way in which they were changing direction, they were headed for this house.

Jak sprang to his feet and moved across the room to where Ryan lay. Without ceremony, Jak shook him once and began to speak before Ryan's eye had even opened.

'Enemy. Headed here. Seven, eight. Mebbe Night-crawlers.'

'Fireblast, wake the others,' Ryan snapped.

As Ryan hauled himself to his feet and shook the last remnants of sleep from his head, so Jak had moved to J.B., repeating his message. The Armorer rose from his rest faster than Ryan and woke Mildred, who lay beside him.

While Jak moved across to wake Doc, who was already mumbling, disturbed by the noises in the room, Ryan bent over Krysty. She had been sleeping apart from him ås her rest had been uneasy, turning and waking constantly.

'Hey, mebbe you were right to feel shit,' he whispered as he gently but firmly woke her. 'Mebbe we've got incoming.'

She woke instantly, her eyes burning bright, boring into him. 'You know, lover, you could be right,' she said huskily, feeling her sentient hair protectively crawl around her scalp and neck.

Within thirty seconds of Jak's initial warning, the companions were awake and mobile. Although the house in which they had been billeted boasted more than one room that could be used for bedding, they had opted to share a large room under the suggestion of Ryan. The one-eyed man had felt that things were too quiet, too easy in Memphis, exactly the kind of conditions in which fighters were caught out and chilled.

His gut instinct had proved right once again.

Speech had been kept to a minimum as they rose, but still Ryan raised a hand to indicate complete silence. No speech, no movement, nothing that would block outside sound.

The Crawlers were only a few hundred yards away, and closing fast. The companions were using a ground-floor room at the front of the house, and Ryan cursed himself for not choosing somewhere that gave them a better defensive position: upstairs, or at the rear. No matter now.

It was also plain to hear the man lumbering at back of the Crawlers. Friend or foe? Could they risk catching him in cross fire?

Ryan gestured to J.B. and Jak to move into the hall and cover the main door. Doc and Mildred he directed to the shuttered window in the room. The shutters were closed, and were on the outside. He cursed to himself. If they had been open, they would have given a perfect view and a perfect opening shot on the enemy.

Gesturing to Krysty, he indicated that they should move toward the stairwell in the main hall. It would be an advantage to get above their enemy as they entered, but it would risk exposure as the well was open. It was a few yards back, and would leave them out of cover as they made for it. Jak and J.B. could provide cover from their positions, but still…

Krysty understood and joined him as he made for the hall. But then something happened that stopped them in their tracks. The sounds outside changed. The Crawlers split into two groups, one stopping short of the house. That was the only way to explain the way in which the number of footfalls seemed to decrease. Furthermore, those that continued went past the house before stopping suddenly a few yards farther on.

J.B. turned to Ryan with a puzzled expression. Then his face cracked as realization dawned on him.

'They're not coming in the front,' he said urgently, 'they're coming over the top from each side.'

Ryan swore under his breath. If they entered the top floors of the house and came down, they would either trap the companions or force them into the open street. Furthermore, to do this they had to be entering adjoining property, as this old street was comprised of attached housing. So what were they doing to the inhabitants within? But what did that matter? A few more chilled Memphis dwellers would be a small price if they could eradicate a major threat. Ryan hadn't known of any covert activity within the ville before, but it was obvious. Why else single out this building?

If they got out of this alive, they had to tell Lemur he had at least one traitor in his midst. Probably the sec man running behind the Nightcrawlers. Fuck him; Ryan would personally chill him for this.

Meantime, they had a building to defend. Leaving J.B. and Jak in the hall, Ryan beckoned to Mildred and Doc to join him and Krysty as they took the stairs. A passage leading off on either side stood at the head of the well, and the risk was in the Crawlers reaching that before them, leaving them exposed.

Taking the lead, with Krysty close on his tail, Ryan took the stairs three at a time, SIG-Sauer in his right hand, the panga in his left. In five strides he was at the head, and he risked a look along the length of the passage. Two doors on each side of the stairs, both closed. Krysty was at his back, breathing in his ear.

'Well?'

'Clear,' he whispered. 'We'll take this side. Mildred and Doc the right,' he added, indicating his left. 'A door each. Attack, don't wait for them.'

Ryan and Mildred took the far door on each side of

the stairwell, moving swiftly across the nearest while Doc and Krysty covered them. When they were in position, Doc and Krysty took up their own positions. Breathing heavily, pausing to gather themselves, they each listened for any sign of movement within the rooms.

There was nothing. Could it be that the Crawlers hadn't yet gained access? If so, then it would be simpler for them: secure the room and take out their targets as they tried to enter.

On a signal from Ryan, they made their move. In unison, four doors were kicked in and they entered the rooms, fingers taut on triggers.

Entered the rooms to find the Nightcrawlers were waiting for them. One in each room. As they entered, they found themselves face-to-face with the enemy. Each Crawler stood silent and still, the lenses removed from their eyes, the whites of which were exaggerated in the darkness of their camou-disguised faces.

They wanted to fire. It was a simple, natural reaction that they had carried out many times before in the process of combat. Yet each of them found that their fingers were numb and unresponsive, and that their capacity to think was growing more sluggish with each second.

Growing more sluggish as a weight seemed to descend, crushing them, forcing them down into some kind of dark pit.

Ryan tried to lift the SIG-Sauer, which had tipped downward as his grip loosened. It felt like it was a lead weight and he fumbled with it. If he couldn't defend himself, then he was easy meat. Yet the Nightcrawler stood there, fixing him with an unblinking stare.

The whites of his eyes. The hazel and the jet-black pupil, boring into him…

All he could see before it went black.

'RYAN, RYAN, wake up, man. What the hell happened?'

The voice came from a distance, the words stretching and taking forever to form, then growing in volume until they resounded around his skull. Ryan opened his eye to see Lemur standing over him, with Mark at his shoulder. Both men were grim-faced.

He was alive? As he began to gather his thoughts, Ryan was more than a little surprised that he hadn't bought the farm. Why had the Crawler let him live when he'd had him at his mercy? The one-eyed man sat up, groaned, then fell back before lifting himself again, this time more slowly to avoid the sickening spinning in his skull. He felt like a man who had taken too much jolt, drunk too much brew. Yet all that had happened was… What had happened?

'Lemur—the others—are they…?'

Mark answered. 'Doc and Krysty are gone. The others are like you. Like they'd been knocked out somehow, but with no bumps, no blood, no sign of struggle. They were in and out of here with no noise. Each side, people just like you. They killed two guards to get in, and there's a sec party out there unaccounted for, but otherwise…'

'How the fuck did they do it?' Ryan asked, tentatively shaking his head to clear it. It only succeeded in making him feel nauseous.

'Why is a better question,' Lemur answered.

'No, I want to know how first,' Ryan insisted. 'I was facing the bastard, ready to blast him out the window, and then I couldn't. All I could do was see his eyes.'

'Specially trained Crawlers,' Mark said coldly. 'Got to be. Odyssey has the power to cloud minds, to make you yield to his will. There is no way on this world that he would let others have that secret, but perhaps just a little. Enough to knock you out without a fight, without making any noises that would wake Memphis. In killing, you risk noise, risk raising the alarm. That's why they only took out the gate sec. In here, they could pass unnoticed if they kept noise to a minimum.'

'But they could have just slit my throat as I lay here,' Ryan murmured. 'Why not do that, erase me—all of us—from the picture?'

'Why waste time when they have a specific purpose? Besides, they're Nightcrawlers, they have every confidence that they could best you in combat any time they came up against you. You represent no threat at all to them.'

'Then why take Doc and Krysty?'

'That, I don't understand,' Mark admitted.

Lemur spoke. His voice suggested that he had given the matter some thought. 'Krysty is unusual. I know not how, but there is something that marks her apart. That would make her of interest to Odyssey. As for Doc, I know that he has been asking questions, that you have been attempting to find out more about us and about Atlantis.'

'There was no deception,' Ryan began, but the Memphis leader cut him off with a gesture.

'That is immaterial. What matters is that Doc seems to have some understanding of our beliefs. That much has been apparent to those he has questioned. This knowledge from an outsider would be as of much interest to Odyssey as Krysty.'

Ryan's head was still muzzy, but he was sharp enough to figure out the implications.

'You know what you're saying, don't you?'

Lemur assented. 'I am well aware.'

Ryan continued. 'If this was a definite plan to sneak in, snatch Doc and Krysty, and take them back for Odyssey's use, then the bastard knew they were here, he knew what made them of interest, and he knew how to get past your sec patrol and into the ville. He knew exactly where we were. There's only one way he could have known all that.'

'Spies,' Mark said. 'Wretches who claim to want freedom but are nothing more than dogs.'

'More than that,' Ryan murmured. 'Who are they? Who can you trust now? You, Mark, you trained as a Crawler and you knew nothing of spies?'

The sec chief glared at Ryan. 'If I thought you doubted me… No, I didn't, whether you choose to believe me or not. I trained only briefly, at the most basic level, before making my escape. There is little to which you are privy until you climb high in Atlantis.'

Ryan fixed him with a stare. Mark returned it, unblinking. Finally, Ryan nodded. 'You know, I figure that I believe you. You've put too much in here to be a traitor. But someone is, and if they know about us, then they know about everything you do.

'If we're going to get my people back, and get this asshole off your back, then we're going to have to move fast, before the intelligence has a chance to find its way back to Atlantis.'

He pulled himself to his feet. 'Are you ready for this?'

Lemur shook his head. 'No, but we have no choice.'

Chapter Thirteen

A land beyond all time and space, where everything exists at the same instant. All experiences are registered as nothing more than a rush of impulses that occur instantaneously in a moment that last less than the blink of an eye, and longer than forever. That, it is said, is what happens when you step outside of space-time as we know it—if, indeed, we can ever be said to know such a thing, and into a fourth dimension, although there are said to be an infinite number by some, and no more than three by others—where you can look down upon all human history...all history period...and see it as nothing more than a single jumbled, knotted ball of events that happens simultaneously.

If you could detach yourself in this way, in this manner, and then come back to the entropic flow that we know as time—pastpresentfuture—what decisions would you change? At what junctions in your life would you stop, step back and choose the alternative to your initial choice? If, as some say, there are an infinite number of branching realities where at each juncture another is formed, the one through which you move, and an alternative through which there moves an alternative you, then which has made the right choices. Which would be you, and which would you choose to be if given that luxury?

I know that I would not have left the Inuit. I would have stayed in my identity as Joseph Jordan. I felt secure. The fact that it may have been a figment of my imaginings rather than something that was real—a genuine manifestation of the phenomena of soul transmigration—is irrelevant. What matters is that I felt at home with that persona. I had purpose, I had meaning. Things that have long since been denied to Theophilus Tanner.

Was it my destiny? In the sense of a greater purpose from a divine being guiding me, then no, perhaps not... In the sense of finding a purpose for myself, in searching out a meaning for my continuing existence, then yes. Whether I am still in a padded room, whether I am in the nineteenth, twentieth, twenty-first, or, indeed, beyond, century, it does not matter. The truth is that the notion of reality in that concrete sense has become a cat's cradle of perhaps, maybe and possibly. I cannot say for certain. The only reality I can trust in any real sense is that which unfolds in front of me. If I stick with that, then I have a method in which to give my being a sense of purpose, a sense of worth, whether it lives in an outside, concrete reality; or whether it merely lives within the confines of my own skull, and the limitless plains of my own mind.

Whatever happens next, I have to find my own redemption.

If I can work out what that should be...

DOC OPENED HIS EYES. His head was whirling with thoughts that were chasing their own tails. Momentarily he thought that he may, after all, have made the mattrans chamber and returned to the frozen wastes of the north, that the last few days were nothing more than a fevered mat-trans dream.

No. That couldn't be the case. First, he didn't feel as though his body had been bolted back together on the wrong order. He had no headache and no nausea. These were so much a part of a jump that he almost didn't notice that they weren't there; the assumption was so strong. But they weren't. He felt clear-headed, his stomach settled. In point of fact, he felt better than he had for some time, as though he had been able to rest more fully than at any time in the past few years.

Blinking, he also noted that wherever he may have landed, it was no mat-trans chamber. There were no wisps of fading mist, no faintly pulsing disks in the floor, and no armaglass walls of any opaque color you cared to mention—he had seen them all, over the years.

Instead of the hard floor he had expected beneath him, he found that he was reclining on a chaise covered with a red brocade and plush wrap that extended the length of the piece of furniture. As he was more than six feet, and lay full-length without either legs or head dangling from the side, he judged that it had to be closer to seven feet than six in length. With a medium-hard cushion beneath his head, to support it, no less.

Someone had taken great care to make sure that he would be comfortable. Doc raised himself up into a sitting position, carefully at first lest the initial impression be deceptive and he found his head spinning with sudden movement. But no, he was fine.

The room was lit by oil lamps and tallow candles. Soft and muted, but bright enough for the surrounding room to be clearly visible into every corner. Which took some doing, as it was quite a large room. Stone: walls, ceiling and floor, although there were patches of plasterwork that had been simply decorated with the kind of pictogram he had seen in Memphis.

Was it day or night? He couldn't tell, as there were no windows. Hence the array of lamps and candles, for all hours. A cell, then? He doubted if a cell would have such lighting or such decoration and furniture. For the rest of the room was sparse, but had pieces that bespoke of quality. There was a table and three straight wooden chairs that were carved with grace and simplicity. A stunted tree stood in an earthenware pot in the corner of the room. Hangings on the wall in red, black and white carried hieroglyph messages and stories.

Black. Not Memphis then. His eye traveled past the hangings until he noticed this. Dragging his vision back, looking closer, he could see all decoration in the room carried black as well as the white and red he associated with Memphis.

This had to be Atlantis.

But why?

There was another chaise in the room, its raised back to him. Only one. Assuming it had an occupant, that would mean that either the rest of the companions had been taken elsewhere or that a maximum of two had been snatched.

Doc stood and flexed his limbs. It was truly remarkable how fit he felt. And not just in his body, which seemed to have a whole new surge of energy flowing through it. He felt sharper in the mind, as though a whole weight of doubt, fear and confusion had been lifted from him.

Time to see who—if anyone—was on the chaise. He strode across the room with renewed vigor and peered over the raised back. He was—surprised? No, perhaps just bemused, to see Krysty laying there. As he loomed over her, he saw her eyelids flicker as she began to rise to the surface of consciousness.

'Good… Well, I cannot say if it is morning or evening. Or indeed afternoon, for I do not know. But welcome back to the land of the living.'

'You sure about that, Doc?' Krysty asked sleepily, rubbing at her eyes. 'I feel like someone in one of those old fables Mother Sonja used to tell me when I was a child. Some woman who slept for a hundred years.'

'Rip Van Winkle slept for a hundred years, although he was not, as far as I am aware, a woman. Perhaps your guardian was speaking of Sleeping Beauty. It's heartening to know that stories such as that survived even the rigors of skydark. Nonetheless, I feel I should point out that in all probability it is far more likely to be merely a few hours that we have rested.'

'Yeah, but what a rest,' she replied as she hauled herself upright. 'I feel great.'

'Refreshed, full of vigor? Greater strength and clearness of mind than for some considerable time?' Doc queried.

'You, too, eh? Remind me to thank whoever took us and imprisoned us for such a beneficial method of capture.'

Doc smiled, despite the circumstances. 'How pleasant to know that your renewed energy has only sharpened your tongue. You may yet attain the heights of the sainted Dr. Wyeth.'

'Thanks for the compliment…I think,' she said, taking a good look around. 'Does it strike you that this isn't too much like a prison?'

'I must confess that the thought had occurred to me. I suspect that the lack of an outside view is determined more by architecture than a desire to keep us incarcerated. It would also be absurd to have such fine hangings and furniture in a cell designed to keep us as demoralized prisoners. I assume, by the by, that you have realized that we are in Atlantis?'

Krysty was casting a searching eye around the room for the first time. 'It seemed unlikely that we were anywhere in Memphis, but what makes you sure?'

Doc pointed out the use of black in the designs. 'The third occult color. I assume that in Memphis it isn't used as a way of disowning the past—casting out the darkness in the magic, if you like. It is a trifle simplistic but, commonly, black was bad magic, white good.'

'So just the two of us?' she added with an acknowledgment to Doc's explanation.

'It would appear that way, unless the others are being kept elsewhere.'

'Figures. But why would they do that?'

'Why would they take us and leave the others? Only if they had some knowledge of our presence and decided that—'

'Trouble in paradise, right? Some of the escapees didn't exactly escape. If that was so, then I can understand them taking you. It must be common knowledge that you have an understanding of their religion that is just plain weird for an outsider. But why me?'

'You have some uncommonly beautiful features,' Doc said softly, indicating her hair. 'To someone who has little or no experience of mutation, then it could appear—'

'Magic,' she finished. 'Great. So we're in Atlantis, and have no idea where the others are or even—'

'—if they are still alive. Can you remember anything about how we were taken? All I have are a few impressions. Footfalls, preparing defense, then…'

'Eyes,' Krysty said firmly. 'I remember eyes that bore into me, sapped all my will. Hypnosis.'

'Undoubtedly,' Doc affirmed. 'We were singled out. The fact that we are now alone… I think that, until we have evidence to the contrary, we have to assume that the others have been chilled.'

It was something that had been in both their minds since discovering they were alone, but for Doc to finally voice it made it seem just a little more possible.

'Just us, then,' Krysty said in a small voice. 'We owe them something. To try…'

'I agree with you, my dear,' Doc said, briefly laying a hand on her shoulder before looking away, unable to meet her gaze. 'Now, let us see if we can find some way of getting out of here.'

There was only one point of exit. That much was obvious. The doorway was ostentatiously covered with plaster carved into spirals, decorated with hieroglyphs. The Atlanteans weren't overly concerned with decoration, but when they decided to decorate, they did it with some panache. And there, in the middle of the portico on the left-hand side of the door, was an inset combination lock.

Krysty experimentally pushed at the door, which was solid and unyielding. 'I didn't think we'd get that lucky,' she said quietly.

'Perhaps we will,' Doc said softly, examining the lock. It was comprised of three rows of stones, four abreast. They were red, white and black, set in an indeterminate pattern, and as he moved them he saw that they worked as a tumbler, moving each way, with no two colors occurring recurrently. 'An interesting little puzzle. Obviously a color code combination.'

Krysty watched him fiddle with the tumbler. 'Yeah, but how many combinations can there be in there before you hit the right one?' she mused.

Doc looked up at her and grinned, showing his unusual bright white teeth. 'Chance is an interesting thing, my dear girl. And frankly, there is very little else occurring right now to take up our time, is there?'

'TIME. IT'S THE ONE THING we need, and the one thing we don't have,' Ryan said through gritted teeth.

'When's it ever been any different?' replied a laconic J.B.

'True. Don't make it any the easier, though,' Mildred added.

The four of them were in Lemur and Cyran's main room, seated around the long table. The ville leader and his wife were also here, as well as the sec chief, Mark. Outside in the corridor were the sec men who had been with Lemur and Mark when they had discovered the companions. They were waiting, under guard from a phalanx of sec men in whom Mark had an implicit trust. It didn't insure their complete fidelity, but Ryan trusted Mark enough to place an equal trust in his judgment. There was little else he could do.

'We shall have to bring all our plans forward and make our attack now,' the stocky Memphis leader said in an agitated tone, mirrored by the manner in which he was pacing the floor.

'That assumes that we have something that can actually be defined as a plan,' Mark pointed out. 'As far as I am aware, it's been little more than an aim that has receded further into the distance with each setback we have encountered in trying to train a halfway competent force. Indeed, even now I would be loathe to lay claim to our ability to mount a successful operation.'

'Is this true?' Ryan questioned, fixing the Memphis leader with a steely glare. 'Stop pacing and answer me. Is there a plan?'

Lemur stopped, sighed heavily and shook his head. 'Mark is right. We have this aim, but without having a force worthy of the title, there was little point in making concrete plans. How difficult can it be? Fighting is fighting.'

'Chilling is chilling, buying farm is buying farm.' Jak spit. 'Not just fighting. Not done this, always man working without weapons, only tools, yeah?'

'I was a clerk, drawing plans for the vessel, accounting for stone delivery and transportation from origins to building site,' Lemur said.

'So you haven't thought about the fact that winning a battle isn't just about who can hit harder, who has the bigger blaster. Just how did you think you were going to get into Atlantis in the first place?' Ryan asked.

'I had trust in Mark,' Lemur said in a small voice.

'And I assumed you had a game plan,' the sec chief said bitterly. 'How stupid does that make me?'

'It makes you someone who had trust in your leader,' Ryan said softly. 'That's something you're supposed to have. Sitting here bitching and fighting over it isn't going to help us now. We need to get our asses moving if we're to stand any chance of saving Doc and Krysty.'

'And if we have spies in our midst, then we won't be safe until they're expunged. And as that would take some time, the only other option is to try to eradicate their reason for spying,' Mark said grimly.

'Damn right,' Mildred agreed. 'There's no point in any long-term planning if it could be leaked. And if Odyssey gets anything at all from Doc and Krysty, then he's going to want to wipe the rest of us out. And shit, he can't repeat the same trick, because we'll be wise to it.'

'I still don't know how the Nightcrawlers managed to get the gate guard to open up, but the sec party on patrol did encounter them on the way,' Mark added. 'Two of them were killed, two more rendered unconscious, and four returned unharmed.'

'Then that's how they gained access,' Mildred asserted. 'You've got a spy in that sec party.'

'How can that be?' Cyran queried, a frown wrinkling her otherwise smooth forehead. 'Two were killed, two more attacked.'

'Dark night, it's obvious.' J.B. sighed, as though addressing a slow child. 'Why were two only knocked out? Why not chill them like the other two? If they were able to get past them without four even seeing them, then why bother even wasting time chilling those two? They didn't chill anyone unnecessarily while they were within the ville walls, did they?'

Mark screwed up his face in frustration and slapped his palm against his forehead. 'I do not deserve my position,' he said slowly, the frustration showing in his strained tones. 'How could I be so stupid? Kill two, render two unconscious, then it is no surprise if one or the other goes missing during the course of the patrol. The one who leads them to the gates, lures out the guard, and then furthermore leads them to where they can find you.'

'One of the sec party is a spy. A spy with the blood of their fellows—four this night alone—on their hands,' Cyran intoned.

'Got there in the end,' Mildred muttered. 'You people don't think like fighters, do you?'

'Madam, is it such a surprise?' Lemur pleaded. 'We are not, by teaching. Only those who become sec in Atlantis are ever taught such skills. To teach the general populace such things would only invite rebellion from those of us who wished to escape.'

'Okay, okay,' Ryan said firmly, standing and gesturing to each of them to calm down. 'Too many recriminations, not enough action. Mistakes have been made, but screw that. It doesn't matter now, not after what's happened. What's important is that we start—right now—getting it right.'

Mark nodded. 'Then we must try to insure that no word can escape from Memphis on this night.'

'How the hell can we insure that?' J.B. asked. 'They've been damn good at sneaking it out up until now.'

Mark allowed himself the ghost of a bleak smile. 'Because we have not been aware of them. Words exchanged within the walls, one on the sec who is not what it seems, a rendezvous or dropping point for a written exposition…it isn't that hard if you have the security of knowing you have been working undetected. But it may be if we seal the ville.'

'I get you,' Mildred said, slamming her hand onto the table. 'Anyone who tries to get over the walls alerts us via the alarm system, so you sew up the only way in which they can get out undetected. Completely reliable gate guards.'

'Precisely.' Mark nodded. 'That will have to be some of your people, Ryan. I must stay and liase with yourself and the leader in planning an attack, and I can no longer take as fact that my own people are reliable.'

The one-eyed man nodded slowly. 'Yeah, I see what you mean. Jak and Mildred would be best. J.B. is my right hand when it comes to planning a firefight. Jak can patrol the walls, Mildred can take the gate. You okay with that?' he added, turning to the people in question.

'You're the boss, Ryan,' Mildred replied with a wry grin. 'Gotta go with your call.'

Jak didn't bother to waste words, merely nodding briefly.

'Good,' Ryan murmured. 'Get going, seal this bastard tight. When we're ready to roll, I'll fill you in on the game plan.'

As the two companions left to take up their position, Ryan turned to Lemur and Mark. Cyran drifted away from them, knowing that she wasn't necessary to the task.

'J.B.'ll need to know exactly what's in your armory. We also need to know what kind of manpower you can muster, and what we're facing. Think you can do that quickly?'

Mark looked up at the ceiling. 'I can tell you all of that without needing to ascertain detail.'

Ryan gave the sec chief a crooked grin. 'Then start talking. Every second counts.'

MILDRED TOOK UP position by the gates. The two sec men who had replaced those the Nightcrawlers had chilled were nervous, and raised their blasters as she approached, even though they knew who she was. It wasn't the most encouraging sign she could have wished for. If they were this jumpy right now, what the hell would they be like when they went into combat? She calmed them and explained her orders. None was to leave, and they themselves were not to open or step outside the gates. She didn't explain why this decision had been reached. If they were spies, then she didn't want to alert them; if they weren't, then she didn't want to start a panic. However, their baffled expressions and bemused questions were open, and told her instinctively that these men weren't among the traitors.

It was a start, but as she settled into watch on the gates and the road leading into the silent city, she wondered how many there were like them within the walls, and how many like the scumsucker who had chilled their workmates and allowed the Nightcrawlers to take Doc and Krysty.

Not knowing was the worst of it. Unless you knew upon whom you could rely, then how could you go into combat knowing that you could devote your full attention to the enemy ahead when, lurking at the back of your mind, was the knowledge that you may have to be watching your back?

She looked at the two sec men who were on watch with her. Come to that, how could you rely on these poor, nervous, inexperienced fools?

Shit, she really hoped that Ryan and J.B. had a good plan.

JAK PROWLED the streets of Memphis, cradling his .357 Magnum Colt Python. He trusted Ryan to find a way that would minimize risks, but, like Mildred, he was unhappy with the caliber of fighter he would have to stand beside. These were good people, who only wanted to be free. But they couldn't fight for that freedom, and flinging them into combat was little short of sending them off to buy the farm. Which was okay if it was their choice and they were the only ones involved. But their ineptitude could get the companions chilled; perhaps even more relevant in the current circumstances, it could stop them getting to Krysty and Doc, getting them out in one piece if they were still alive.

And the latter was Jak's primary concern. Sure, he would follow Ryan's orders, but ultimately he had no interest in these people. Their choices were theirs alone. They had to be the ones to fight for their liberty, whether it took the shape of weeding out the scum who were spying against their own people, or whether it took the shape of going into a head-on firefight with the forces of Atlantis, risking all to insure their final freedom.

The streets were deserted as he circled the walls of the ville. No birds or mammals from outside the walls to scent the air, rustle and disturb the peace. Without that scent or sound, Jak felt lost and alone. His entire existence had been spent as a hunter, and to walk along the line where his honed senses could delineate between where there was life—inside—and where there wasn't—outside—was disorienting. He couldn't understand how these people could live in such a sterile landscape. Even the frozen lands of the north they had recently escaped carried more life, despite the harsh climate.

Memory of which made him wonder: Doc. Even at the best of times Doc seemed crazy to him. But he'd been triple crazy when they were in the icy wastes, and still the same when they'd first made the jump. Every-

one seemed to think that he'd got back to normal, but
Jak wasn't so sure. There was a kind of feral cunning
about him now, as though he were keeping his madness
to himself, wrapping it up within him until he felt safe
enough to let it out again. And if that happened, then
there was no knowing what could occur. Doc was a
loose cannon at the best of times. Separated from the
others, who knew what he was thinking?

Fighting with fools was one thing. Against sec as
good as the Nightcrawlers was another. But throw in a
random factor like a triple crazy Doc, and anything was
possible.

All the while this had been going through his mind,
Jak continued his patrol. The empty streets, silent and
still under the moon, seemed to mock the concerns that
raced through his mind.

He hoped that Ryan had a plan. A good one…

'THIS IS HOPELESS. We need some kind of plan.' Krysty
sighed, watching as Doc tried yet another combination,
pulling and pushing at a door that refused to yield.

'There is little point in having a plan if we cannot
even get past the door,' Doc snapped waspishly. He had
been working at the lock for what seemed like hours,
and his own patience was also wearing a little thin.

While he had been doing this, Krysty had been examining the rest of the room, to see if there was any
other possible route of escape. An interior room with
no obvious ventilation had to have air ducts. But when
she found them, she was disappointed—if not surprised—to find that they were far too narrow for any
kind of egress.

The one thing she had learned was that this wasn't

a common cell or even regular room. On closer inspection, the furnishings were too fine to be anything other than intended for one of high rank, and on the table were a number of scrolls with hieroglyphs that, even though she could not affect a translation, had an air of some importance around them.

She concluded that the lock was as much to keep people out as to keep them in. Which was curious. It was almost as though they were guests rather than prisoners.

'Doc, I think we should forget the lock and think about what we're going to do when our host arrives. That's what I mean by a plan. He may be our quickest route out of this room, and we need to know what to do next.'

'"He"?' Doc asked acidly. 'You mean that you have an inkling of who may be our captor?'

'If I knew what the fuck an inkling was, I might say yes,' she snapped back. 'And I could do without sarcasm. You know as well as I do that Odyssey has us, if we're in Atlantis. But I said host, not captor. I think these are his own quarters, and he's not going to be treating us as prisoners.'

Doc said nothing. If she was correct, then Odyssey would not wish to drag information from them with interrogation and torture; he would seek to ingratiate and to form an alliance. This is something that would suit Doc's purposes very well. If it were so, then he would have little wish to escape. He could strike a bargain...though he was sure Krysty would not feel the same way, hence her insistence on a plan of escape.

He would have to play the both of them along if he was to get what he wanted. And so the last thing he would want is what happened at that moment.

Idly, as these thoughts ran through his mind, he had still been spinning the combination lock. To his sudden horror he heard a sound that he would have wanted only scant seconds before. The tumblers hit the right combination and he heard a soft click within the portal as the lock disengaged.

Cursing to himself, and hoping that Krysty hadn't heard, he flicked one of the red squares out of sequence, springing the lock back into place. He looked around. Krysty was on the other side of the room, poring over one of the scrolls, trying to make sense of the pictograms. Racking his memory to remember the sequence from which he had started, Doc flicked the combination back, insuring that the lock was exactly as he found it: but not before noting the correct sequence. It might come in useful.

To Krysty, as she looked up at Doc, muttering to himself, it seemed as though Doc were still toiling on unlocking the door. She smiled to herself and gave a gentle shake of the head, little realizing the deception.

'Give it up, Doc,' she said gently. 'Come and see if you can make any sense of this.'

'Very well, if you insist,' Doc replied, trying to mask the relief in his voice.

They were still absorbed by the scroll some half an hour later, when the lock gently snicked back and the door opened. Odyssey stood in the open portal, flanked by two sec men armed with handblasters. He took in what they were doing, then indicated that the sec men should wait outside. He entered and closed the door behind him, leaving it unlocked. His entry had been without ceremony; so much so that he was halfway across the room before Krysty and Doc looked up to see him approach.

Although his squat frame didn't have the majestic bearing they would expect from such an exalted leader, there could be no doubts as to his identity. Only a man like Odyssey would approach them alone and unarmed, such was his innate assurance.

'My dear sir, how charming it is to meet you at last. We have heard so much about you. Although I must say, it was a trifle dramatic of you to bring us here in such a fashion,' Doc added with a chuckle as he walked around the table and grasped Odyssey firmly by the hand, pumping his arm. Doc continued. 'There's so much that you can tell us, and so much, indeed, that I would wish to learn from you. Really, all you had to do was ask.'

With which Doc led a momentarily stunned Odyssey toward the portal, asking him about the hieroglyphs, while Krysty looked on, openmouthed. Whatever you thought about Doc, and however many kinds of crazy you called him, he never ceased to surprise you. And maybe—just maybe—this approach would yield some kind of result. Krysty knew that she was looking for a way out. She kind of figured that Doc was after that, too, but to be truthful she couldn't be certain.

Following in their wake, she reached them just as Doc had finished discussing the artistry on the portal and had smoothly moved on to his next subject.

'Now, my dear sir, I am sure that you have us here because you have heard of Krysty's abilities, and you have heard that I—a stranger, no less—appear to have some knowledge of your society even though you live in relative isolation, and I have never encountered you before. I daresay that would interest you, and we will, of course, reveal all in due course. I am, by the way, as-

suming that you have somehow infiltrated Memphis.
The fact that you have not crushed them, but allowed
them to flower, shows a certain tactical cunning that I
find intriguing. But please, permit me to ask of you
this—before we open our own secrets to you, please tell
us how your splendid city came into being.'

Doc finished with a smile that he intended to be
warm and winning, but came out as unctuous.

Odyssey, waiting for the next outpouring, was silent
for a moment. Then, when he realized that Doc was
waiting for him to speak, he allowed himself a wry grin
and finally spoke.

'I shall tell you all you wish, in return for which I
expect a fair exchange of knowledge. But first, we shall
have a less formal atmosphere...'

Odyssey turned to the door, issuing orders as he
opened it to the waiting sec men. Within a few minutes,
food and wine was brought into the room and musicians
entered to play while they ate. The music was played
on stringed and wind instruments that resembled a lyre
and panpipes. It sounded ancient, with strange scales
that were almost atonal, yet at the same time soothing.
Although he said nothing about this, Doc suspected it
was an attempt by the founders of the ville, prior to skydark, to approximate ancient music. It was, in truth, as
genuine as the cracked philosophy on which the ville
was based.

'Our society is based upon ancient ways. The original inhabitants of Atlantis, who were either forced underground or left for the astral skies, sowed the seeds
from which all subsequent civilizations reaped. Our
ancestors...'

As Odyssey began to tell them of the origins of the

society over which he now held sway, Doc began to tune out. It was almost exactly the same thing he had heard from Affinity and had pieced together from speaking to Lemur and Cyran, among others. The litany of Atlantean history was something that, it seemed, every inhabitant learned like breathing, indoctrinated into them from the day they were born. The difference between this version and that he had heard in Memphis being, Doc mused, that Odyssey waxed at great length about how people were happy in their place and glad to serve the greater good, taking their place in society, no matter what that might be. Easy for a man born into the role of leader, waited on hand and foot, to say… However, despite that fact that Doc found him a bore, he couldn't doubt that there was no insincerity to the man. Odyssey firmly believed in the concept of Atlantis.

While Doc waited impatiently for the man to spill any secrets about old tech that may have survived, much of the information was new to Krysty and, added to the baffling discussion between Mildred and Doc in Memphis, things began to take shape and finally make sense.

However, it didn't need her doomie sense to start screaming at her when Odyssey looked directly into her eyes as he said, 'At each conjunction of the stars, when alignment is right for the return of the travelers, we gather in the vessel. They haven't come, and that is our failing. We have not mustered enough power for them. There are rituals that we can perform to give them a sign, to add to our power. Mostly these are simple, but there is one that requires a woman who is able to harness great occult power. We have never had such a woman in our midst, but I have heard things that suggest…'

He trailed off with a gesture toward her, as though he expected her to confirm his suspicions. Krysty felt no inclination to do anything except rip his heart out, regardless of the gathered servants and sec that could chill her. Better that way than anything Odyssey may have in mind.

It was Doc, too impatient now to notice what was happening between Krysty and Odyssey, who broke the mood.

'These rituals—you have a separate temple for them?'

'Hmm?' Odyssey looked blankly at Doc, taking a moment to shift focus and assimilate what the old man asked. 'Yes…yes, there is a specific temple room dedicated to the old ones in this very building.'

'I would like to see it,' Doc snapped.

He was lucky. From the attitude of the servants and sec, it was clear that at any other time such a lack of respect would elicit a harsh punishment. Yet Doc was so strange, so disarming, that he was able to beat the odds. Furthermore, Odyssey was besotted with Krysty, and to show her the temple where his magic ritual would take place was something that was pleasing to him.

'Yes, you shall see it. And you,' he added, looking into Krysty's eyes. 'While we are there, you can tell me much about your power and about your knowledge. I have fulfilled my side of the bargain. Now it is time for you to fulfil yours. Yes,' he mused, 'I feel it would benefit us all to see the temple of the old ones.'

Krysty looked across at Doc. Gaia, old man, what have you set us up for? she thought, consoling herself with the notion that once they were out of this chamber, there would at least be more options to effect an escape.

Trouble was, it was starting to look as though escape was the last thing on Doc's mind.

Chapter Fourteen

By daybreak, the attack was planned. To take a large force would be to risk two things: a mass wipe-out by the Nightcrawlers and the risk of a traitor sabotaging the assault. A better option was to take a small force, led by Mark and augmented by the companions. Focused, with their game plan to infiltrate hard and fast, heading for the main temple, Ryan figured they had a chance. A small, highly mobile force could dodge patrols, could keep track of one another with much more clarity in the confusion of a firefight, and left a greater force back in the defense of the home ville.

Memphis was smaller than Atlantis, and its fighters, man for man, no match for Atlantis sec. However, Ryan reasoned that it wouldn't take a complete overthrow to plunge Atlantis into confusion. The ville was so tightly run, the people so oppressed, and the rule so absolute that only one clear strike was necessary: take out Odyssey. With him removed from the game, then Atlantis would be at the mercy of any opposing factions that may wish to assume command, and the uprising of those who hadn't previously thought it possible to self-determine. In this kind of confusion, it would be easier for them to rescue Krysty and Doc—Ryan's prime objective, if not that of Lemur—and effect an escape. As attack was so near, Ryan had recalled Jak and Mildred for the final stages of planning, reasoning that any spies making a break for Atlantis wouldn't have time to deliver a message before the Memphis attack had commenced. Things were running as smoothly as he could hope for in the circumstances.

There was only one obstruction: the insistence of Lemur in joining them.

'Sir, with the best will in the world, you aren't a fighter. Nor have you ever been,' Mark pleaded with him.

'I know,' the ville leader agreed, choosing his words carefully. 'This is true. I realize it is a great risk to myself, and more importantly that it means you are carrying someone who is not supreme in combat. But this is about more than merely fighting. How can I lead my people if I stay skulking in the shadows while I send others to their doom? Surely I cannot claim to love freedom, and to wisely lead those who also seek it, if I'm not prepared to lay myself on the line for the sake of my beliefs. If I go with you, then Memphis will be united in this cause. But if I do not, many will ask themselves about the wisdom of this decision.'

'You realize that I cannot guarantee your safety, any more than I can guarantee the safety of any of us,' Mark said.

'I would not have it any other way. Although I am nominally leader as someone has to head the chain of administration, yet this is a democratic ville. I wouldn't expect preference.'

'It's not only you,' Cyran said, coming forward. 'I will join you. I cannot let you go alone, my husband. We are a team, and we stand and fall together.'

J.B. pulled Ryan to one side. 'What's going on

here?' he whispered urgently. 'We can't let them join us. It's going to be a difficult enough mission as it is, without—'

Ryan shook his head, interrupting. 'We don't have a say, here. Most of the personnel are theirs, and if they want to do it, then we can't stop them.'

'Yeah? And we can't let them buy the farm, either. If they get chilled, and we come back with Doc and Krysty, then we're in big trouble.'

'We've faced worse,' Ryan said with a resigned air.

'Mebbe,' J.B. snapped, 'but we won't be in any kind of state to stand and fight again after—if—we get back from Atlantis.'

While Mark and Lemur discussed the leader's role in the action, Mildred and Jak had joined the furiously debating Ryan and J.B., catching the end of the argument.

'John's right,' Mildred agreed, 'but the fact remains that he's not going to be moved on this, so we've got to go with it.'

'We think about watching backs for them,' Jak said in low tones. 'Mark good sec, but men not up to task. Have to be us.'

'Jak's right.' Ryan sighed. 'It's something we could do without, but we have to keep those two alive as much as get Krysty and Doc.'

'Great, make it easy.' J.B. moaned. 'Anything else you want while we're at it?'

Unaware that this had been going on, the Memphis people had finished their affirmations of togetherness and were now waiting for the companions to rejoin them.

'Everything is well, I trust?' Lemur said as they approached the table once more.

'Fine,' Ryan lied. 'We just need to finalize the plan of attack.' There was little point in regaling the Memphis leader with their concerns. The decision had been made, and they would just have to work with it.

Lemur spread out a map on the table. It was a beautifully drawn plan of the two villes of Atlantis and Memphis and the land between.

'As you can see, the space between us is comprised of woodland much as that you have already encountered. The dangers here are Nightcrawlers. It is unlikely that we will encounter much resistance from them during daylight hours, even though they have, of late, made sorties during sunlight.'

'I don't think we can bank on that,' Ryan said, shaking his head. 'Odyssey's no fool. He's snatched two of my people. He'll know us by them, and he'll know that we'll be coming for them sooner rather than later. His intelligence will have told him what we can do. He'll have people in wait.'

'Can we skirt them?' Mark asked. His apprehensive tone, however, betrayed his concern.

'You already know that one. They're more likely to spot us than we are them.' Ryan grinned coldly. 'We'll just have to be ready for them.'

'No doubt,' Lemur remarked. 'But I fear that, even if we should encounter them, they will not be our main problem.'

'If they aren't, then who or what is?' Ryan questioned.

'The maze,' Mark replied softly. 'The great unknown.'

'You've mentioned this before,' Mildred murmured. 'What's so difficult about it? A maze is a maze, and you

said that some of your people have escaped through it—
so why don't we just take them with us, to negotiate it?'

Mark sighed. 'If only it were that simple. If it was a fixed maze, then of course anyone who had managed to find their way through it would have no problem on their return. But alas, it is far from that easy.'

On seeing the quizzical glances from the companions, Lemur took up explanation. He knew more about the maze than anyone, for in his previous existence in Atlantis he had worked on the project in his work capacity.

One of the men named Odyssey, several generations before the current incumbent, had devised the maze as way of keeping out intruders and keeping in those dissenting workers who sought escape. The idea of surrounding the city with a wall or moat wasn't defense enough. It would neither keep out—or indeed, keep in—the determined. So the leader decided to surround his domain with something that had a degree more security. He would build a maze around his city, a puzzle that would kill those who couldn't solve its mystery.

It was based on something that had come down to them in legend. The Cretan maze of Minos, with the centaur at its heart, had been the inspiration. The walls of the complex puzzle were constructed of stone, and instead of one beast at its heart, it had a series of traps that were manned by wild beasts bred to be vicious and kept in a semistarved state, ravenous for anything or anyone that might stray into their path. The hidden beast traps and the labyrinthine nature of the walls made them difficult enough for the unwary escapee to negotiate; Odyssey had another trick to make it almost impossible. The walls themselves were movable, by a remarkable feat of pivot engineering that required no driven machinery.

This meant that the dead ends and open passages could be changed whenever the ruler so decreed. To insure that no one worker or sec man overseeing the operation would know the new layout of the maze, as planned by Odyssey, each team of movers and sec who worked on each section of the maze had plans that told them only what they were to do in their given sector, and they were dispatched at different times to insure that no two or more teams could liaise to build a better picture of the new maze.

As he told them this, Lemur indicated the maze area on the map in front of them. It was surrounded by a dotted line, the maze walls delineated only by a series of horizontal and vertical lines that formed a grid.

'So you're telling me that we're going into something that we have no idea how to get through?' Ryan asked.

Lemur shook his head reluctantly. 'I wish I could tell you otherwise, but that wouldn't be the truth.'

Ryan whistled. 'You really don't want to make this easy for us, do you?'

'It isn't easy for us, either, if it comes to that,' Mark pointed out.

Ryan nodded slowly. It was a fair point. 'Okay,' he said at length, 'if that's the way it's got to be, then that's the way it's got to be. Get your sec force together. It's daybreak now, and before too long the sun will have risen enough for good light. We head straight out, try to catch them before they have a chance to marshal their forces.' He added to himself, Because if they do, then we don't have too much of a chance…

WHEN ODYSSEY HAD OFFERED them the chance to view the temple dedicated to the old ones, Doc and Krysty had no idea that they would be privy to such a treasure trove of preskydark artifacts. Neither did they expect that those items would reflect such a skewed version of prenuke society.

The temple room was lit by scented candles—incense, rose and a sweet blend of herbs and spices that Krysty couldn't identify, but that reminded Doc of something from another lifetime, something he had once smelled when in the southern swamps, taken by a colleague in pursuit of voodoo ceremonies. In the dim light, it was possible to see that a stone alter was surrounded by tapestries that depicted the sinking of the old island, and also saucers arriving from outer space. There were old paintings in dusty glass that they could identify, on close inspection, as being framed movies posters for 1950s, 60s and 70s movies about the coming of aliens. *Earth Vs Flying Saucers, Invasion of the Saucer Men* and *Close Encounters of the Third Kind* were those whose titles could be easily read. With others, the ravages of time and the elements, despite the reverence in which they were obviously held, had crept beneath the glass and made the print illegible, leaving only the lurid images of men from space and their craft.

An old TV and video recorder stood on the altar, powered by a generator that looked as though it had ceased to be supplied with fuel many generations before. A thick layer of dust covered the screen and the carefully arranged pile of tape boxes beside it. They were all movies and documentaries about occult and

UFO phenomena. Krysty and Doc could tell this from a perusal of the titles and the pictures on the boxes.

The walls of the stone room were lined with shelving. On these shelves were hard-backed books still in their dust jackets, crumbling paperbacks whose cheaper paper and bindings had succumbed to time, and bound magazines and journals. Alongside them were stacked box files and folders bulging with papers. A personal computer stood idle and now dead to one side.

'Can you use the old tech anymore?' Doc asked, looking at the comp, which was primitive by the standards of those both he and Krysty had used in redoubts.

Odyssey sighed. 'Alas for myself and those who come after me, the tech was powered by that generator—' which he indicated '—and I regret to say that the fuel ran out several generations back. Despite the efforts of my men, not many traders come anywhere near Atlantis. That which is our natural defense is also our enemy at times. At times it frustrates me. I can read what is written in the books and in the files of those who founded our ville, but only with difficulty. Reading is something we do not, on the whole, use. The old ways of the hieroglyph were instituted, even though the history of our people and the ideas that led us to this place were written and compiled by those who used the common word and language. To see old tape of our ancestors and those who supported them, those who recorded the history, would be good.' He swept his hand over the tapes, the TV and the comp.

Doc and Krysty exchanged glances. She knew enough of the predark histories, had seen enough of the old cultures, to know that the books were the work of cranks, and the films were made-up stories, not the recordings of true history that Odyssey seemed to believe.

Doc, who was now studying the shelves, was frustrated. He had believed that it was possible that Odyssey was housing a wealth of predark tech and power. But this? An old TV and simple comp with a generator that had been so long without fuel that it would probably fall apart if ever fired up again? A few pieces of entertainment that were passed off as great and profound legend?

And these books. Some were paranoid conspiracy theories about the old U.S. government. Others were paranoid conspiracy theories about the existence of extraterrestrial life. There were books about secret government programmes—ironically, nothing about the kind of evil empire that had led Doc to this place—and there were also books about technology that came from beyond the stars. Books and magazines about so-called UFO sightings stood next to tomes about other strange and anomalous phenomena.

These were the frippery. Delve beneath and there was something a little more substantial—if it could be called as such. The Shaver theories about races from the center of the earth stood next to books about the search for the ancient site of Atlantis. Tomes from the nineteenth and twentieth centuries about the races beneath the earth nestled next to those from a similar sweep about ancient Greece and Egypt, and about Phoenician and Macedonian society. With these were books about the Golden Dawn and the secret masters of Shamballa.

Everything was as Mildred and Doc had worked out—not so hard, perhaps, but somehow disheartening to see that their supposition was correct. What had seemed to be a society based on possible revelatory theories, corrupted by the passage of time and distortion of those very theories, was now revealed to be nothing more than the wide-eyed and raving paranoia of people deranged by the insanity of late-twentieth-century living, terrified for their future in a world that seemed on the brink of annihilation.

At least they had been right about that, Doc mused bitterly. Everything had collapsed. But their way hadn't been the answer.

Despite the evidence to the contrary, he still harbored hopes that the old tech he had sought, that he had made himself believe, was hidden in Atlantis may yet exist. Perhaps this generator was starved of fuel because it was being saved for something bigger. Even as the thought flashed through his mind, he knew he was grasping at straws so slight that they weren't even real.

He realized that he had been more than hoping—he had been taking as a fact that this mythic ville would have the facilities and power to help him fulfill his destiny. Whether that meant the Inuit and the identity of Joseph Jordan, or whether it meant taking these people forward and trying to forge a new way of thinking—so new that he had not as yet felt it take shape within him—that would sweep across the land, he wouldn't find the means to further that ambition here.

He realized that this feeble construct was all that was holding him together. The fragmentation that he had been feeling since their arrival in the frozen wastes hadn't gone away; it had not been unified into the new aim that he now held. Rather, that aim was an attempt to paper over the cracks in his psyche, to weld the shards of himself together into a strange, angular, ill-fitting construction that would give him purpose and drive, would stop him from crumbling into the gibbering wreck that he feared most of all. For, without any kind of purpose, what did all the hardship and torture that he had endured mean? What purpose had it served?

When Doc turned to face Krysty and Odyssey, the woman shuddered at the glint in Doc's eye. It was desperate and unhinged, and ran completely contrary to the soft tone of his voice.

'My dear sir, you have no idea how interesting this is to me. I see that you have amassed a fine degree of ancient knowledge. I can help you make sense of this, add my store of knowledge to your own. I can help you make sense of Atlantis's place in history, and help you to attain the greatness that your heritage warrants.

'But first, if this is to happen, you must tell me if there is anything else that you hold, beyond this temple. Anything that remains from the old times must be shown to me if I am to help.'

'Doc...' Krysty said hesitantly.

The old man held up his hand impatiently. 'No.'

Odyssey scanned Doc's face. It was a shrewd survey and took him some time as he searched Doc's visage for any sign of duplicity. Finally he nodded, almost to himself.

'There are some things. Their meaning and use is long since lost. But this is partly why I wanted you both here. I need you, and I was sure I could help. Come, I will show you.'

With a sudden bustling energy that spoke a renewed determination, Odyssey led them from the chamber and past the sec guard who fell in to their rear.

Krysty looked uneasily over her shoulder. Whatever it was Odyssey needed them both for, it set alarm bells ringing in her skull. But no more so than Doc's attitude. It was as though, when faced with the evidence of pre-dark times, something seemed to snap in his mind once more. Now she had no idea what he was thinking. And a wild card Doc was a dangerous thing.

Odyssey set a fast pace, his footfalls ringing in the stone corridors. At each sec door he spun the colored stones to free the combination lock with a practiced ease and speed. Krysty tried to see over his shoulder, so that she could crack the code, but each time, it seemed as though Doc was deliberately blocking her.

More alarm bells.

Whatever their intended fate, it was delayed when a tall, muscular man came through a sec door from the opposite direction, followed by two Nightcrawlers.

'Xerxes, what is it? You should be at the vessel—'

'I'm sorry to interrupt you,' Xerxes panted breathlessly, 'I wouldn't do it except in the direst circumstances. Word has just reached me—' He stopped, looking questioningly at Doc and Krysty.

'You can speak freely, they're going nowhere,' Odyssey remarked in an offhand manner that sent a chill down Krysty's spine.

'Very well. A force of warriors has left Memphis, headed in this direction. I have sent Nightcrawlers out to block their path.'

'Then the matter is settled. Their people are no match for ours.'

'Perhaps. The other outlanders are with them. They are an unknown quantity to a large degree, but the one thing I do know is that they are strong warriors. I think we should take measures.'

'You are, possibly correct. I concur.' He turned to the

sec men with him. 'Take these back to my chamber until
I can deal with them.'

Without another word, he turned back and left Doc
and Krysty at the mercy of the sec men. Their handblasters and blades were poised, and the two companions were left with no option but to go with them while
Odyssey strode away with Xerxes and the Crawlers.

Being pushed into Odyssey's chamber, and hearing
the lock click softly into place, felt like being back at
the beginning, with no progress made. If anything,
Krysty felt that matters had deteriorated.

Ryan and the others were on the way, yet she and
Doc were frustrated and unable to do anything to assist
them.

That's if Doc, in his present state, actually wanted to
lend aid. And, as she looked at him, she could no longer
be sure.

As THEY PASSED the old building painted in the red and
white colors of Memphis, Ryan noted that it was empty.

'They all are,' Mark replied to his questioning
glance. 'I pulled all my men back within the walls after
the discovery of your comrades's abduction last night.
As soon as it became apparent that we had spies within
our midst, I felt it was incumbent upon me to insure that
all personnel were within the boundaries of the wall, to
prevent any further leaks of information. I am sure that
there was no way in which news of our operation could
have leaked out.'

'Good,' Ryan said simply. 'It was the right thing to
do.'

The war party was on its way out of the old suburbs
surrounding Memphis, passing those buildings that

were dotted around the ruined city and that formed the ring of outer sentry posts, once populated by two-man sentry teams. It was uneerily quiet as they passed, the area now deserted of all life.

Ryan knew that Mark had made the right decision. As it was, they would need every break they could get if this was going to work, and to get as far as the maze before having to enter into a firefight would be a positive addition to their chances.

The party was sixteen strong. Ryan, Jak, J.B. and Mildred were each in command of a group of four Memphis sec, who were answerable to them. These included Mark, Lemur and Cyran, and the young man Affinity, who had volunteered before Mark even had a chance to ask him. The young man had an implicit trust in Ryan's people and their potential to rid Memphis of the shadow of Atlantean oppression that still hung over them. The Memphis leader and his wife had readily agreed to be subservient to the companions, as had sec leader Mark, as they readily acknowledged the superior combat skills of Ryan and his fellow warriors.

· They knew enough of the sec, handpicked by Mark as his best and most trustworthy fighters, to know that they could rely on them to battle strong and never give up when it came to combat. But Ryan was still uncomfortable at carrying Lemur and Cyran. It reduced their effectiveness, gave them two less in real manpower terms, and added an extra responsibility—that of watching the backs of the leader and his wife—that Ryan was aware was a burden on his people. But the leader had remained adamant and couldn't be swayed.

Ryan admired the courage of them both, but doubted

their judgment. Unfortunately, it had never been his call.

Nonetheless, he had done his damnedest to weight things in favor of the Memphis party. By splitting into groups he had allowed lesser fighters to be aided by those of greater combat skill. Now, as they progressed through the suburbs and hit the edges of the woodlands, they weren't in a line, strung out as those parties he would usually lead. Instead they were operating in clusters, each within eye contact of another. The cluster consisted of either Ryan, Jak, Mildred or J.B. at the head, with the most experienced Memphis sec man bringing up the rear, keeping the slighter fighters in the center. It was a variation of the line formation, which Ryan always used to protect those on his own group who may be carrying injuries.

As they split into these groups and moved into the densely wooded areas, Jak and Mark formed the defense in the cluster that had Lemur and Cyran at center. The sec chief had been insistent that he stay with his leader, and Ryan had agreed, knowing the sec chief to be the best Memphis fighter. For a similar reason, he had detailed Jak to head the cluster.

Mildred was in a cluster that included Affinity, and as they headed into the cover of the woods, the young man murmured, 'I confess, I feel like turning and running back to the safety of my own bed.'

'Sweetie, you wouldn't be human if you didn't feel your guts churning, and you know that if we don't do this, then that bed isn't ever gonna be safe,' Mildred replied. Affinity acknowledged that, and said no more.

Ryan looked up at the early morning sun as it sparkled through the canopy of foliage above. It was going to be a clear morning. That was good: the more light that penetrated the canopy, the easier it would be to see any Crawlers if they were out there. And, although he was sure that Mark had been correct in assuming that no word could escape Memphis of their plans, he was equally sure that a leader as astute as Odyssey would insure that roaming patrols would be out to either act as early warning in case of mass invasion, or to mop up smaller parties of resistance.

The companions set a fast pace for the clusters to move toward Atlantis. Speed was of the essence if they were to strike effectively. The Memphis sec used to patrolling these areas were able to assist them in direction, for even though they had studied the map before leaving, once out in the dense forestation, detours were sometimes required. To negotiate these and also keep the other parties in sight was easier in daylight, but still difficult at times as the tangled limbs, roots and trunks of the stunted trees drove them in opposite directions.

It was when they were at their most strung out and distant that the first party of Nightcrawlers chanced upon them.

XERXES'S ORDERS had been simple. As soon as his people had returned with Doc and Krysty, he had assumed that a retaliatory attack would be mounted. To that end, he had sent out three parties of Nightcrawlers, each consisting of six people. They were to take three delineated areas of the lands between Memphis and Atlantis, and run regular patrols. For each party there was a runner to act as liaison, so that if one party should locate an enemy group, the others could be alerted. These three groups had been out since before dawn and had scoured the lands thoroughly, working a system that led them out from the maze and then back to the start once more.

They were on their third route when the first party scented trouble.

Still camouflaged in their dark paint, despite the fact that the sun was now up and their dark tones made them stand out against the day, they were sweeping the woodlands when one Crawler held up her hand. The highly trained troop halted, heads up, every sense straining for the signs that had alerted their comrade. To their right, ahead of them by about five hundred yards, they could hear the slight sounds of foliage being disturbed. There was movement, and it was toward them. They knew that it had to include the strangers: Memphis sec couldn't move that silently when left to their own provenance.

One of the Crawlers peeled off and headed in the direction of the adjoining sector, in search of another party. Backup, and an alert. The five left standing realigned their direction and began to move toward the source of the sound, prepared for combat.

JAK CAUGHT WIND of something strange. There was really little secret to his seemingly preternatural powers. He had honed his senses by hunting since he was a small child, pitting his wits against wildlife that had such highly developed senses that he was forced to train his to stand any chance of catching game.

Now it had become a second nature to him, and without even thinking what he was doing he had worked out the rhythms in which the different clusters were moving; their breathing, when audible, and their footfalls. Some had a light tread, others heavy. Some took three steps to another's two. Some were heavier on one foot than another, while others distributed weight equally. Together, these sounds constituted a complex symphony of rhythm that he could understand. Even the rustling of the disturbed trees, grasses and plants was discernible, dictated as it was by the rhythm of those moving through it.

So when something intruded on that symphony, it was like a discord that came from nowhere, immediately noticeable to those who understood the notation.

Jak, whose cluster was surrounded on both sides by another, as part of Ryan's plan to afford Lemur and Cyran as much protection as possible, indicated to Mildred, who was across the line, visible through a thick and twisted clump of gnarled wood. He swiftly pointed the direction of the intrusive sound and the numbers as far as he could tell. Mildred, having spent so long in combat situations with the albino youth, was immediately familiar with his meaning, and while those around her seemed confused, she was already scanning for Ryan, signaling to him as he appeared in a gap in the cover. Meantime, Jak had turned his attention to J.B., repeating his signal.

The clusters realigned themselves so that they would meet the incoming enemy head-on. They were still moving forward, albeit at a twenty-degree angle to their intended destination, and they were now prepared.

The two forces moved toward each other, the Crawlers fanning out, having worked out by sound that they were outnumbered more than two to one. But they had confidence in their abilities, knowing that they outclassed the Memphis sec. Besides, their runner was swift and would soon bring reinforcements.

Despite the confidence of the Nightcrawlers, it was Jak who took first sight of the enemy. Although his red eyes were better suited to darker conditions, he knew where he should be looking, and his other sense augmented his albino sight. All it took was the slightest creak of fern and branch underfoot, the slightest footfall, and the scent of the oily paint in which the Crawlers covered themselves. This, allied to a movement in the distance, changing the pattern of light that fell through the canopy for only a moment, and Jak knew enough to identify the enemy.

It wasn't close fighting, and there were no comrades in the line, so he took his .357 Magnum Colt Python and loosed a round in the direction of the disturbance. The boom of the discharge was magnified in the silence around, the echo carrying the whine of a ricochet as it chipped a tree trunk.

Although it didn't hit its intended target, it was a galvanizing moment. Any pretence at concealment was lost as the Nightcrawlers realized they had been seen. Now their objective was to reach their target without being fired upon, and engage in hand-to-hand combat. In this, they knew they had the skills to balance the numbers, perhaps even best them if their compatriots arrived.

The shot did more than just set these two opponents in motion. It echoed through the woods and alerted the other Nightcrawler parties that there was a firefight. The runner from the engaging party had reached his target, but the third group, over in the far sector of the woodlands, was now alerted. With their trained senses, it was simple for them to ascertain the direction of the shot and to proceed to aid their comrades and engage in combat.

The four cluster groups were unaware of the other parties, approaching them from differing locations, and were concentrated on their primary objective. Taking cover, J.B. and Ryan directed their groups—who they had adjudged to be the weakest of the sec—to spread across in a line, backing and covering for the groups of Mildred and Jak, who would now move into more offensive positions.

Mark gestured to Lemur and Cyran to take cover and not to join himself and Jak. The Memphis leader shot his sec chief a glance that betrayed both an anger and frustration that he couldn't join the offensive, and yet at the same time a relief tinged with shame, as he knew he would be more of a liability in this situation.

Six warriors headed toward the source of the enemy approach. Stilling their own breathing, treading with an extreme caution, they tried to silence their own movements, so that they could pick up any from their enemy. But the Nightcrawlers were far more experienced, and for Mildred there was a split second of shock when a Crawler stepped out in front of her, blade raised to hack at her.

It was fortunate that the Crawler had chosen to meet her head-on rather than risk the wait until she had passed. If she had been taken from the rear, she would have bought the farm. Even if the Crawler had elected to hold the knife low and sweep at her guts, she would have had trouble defending herself. But the enemy had chosen to use a downward blow that would pitch the blade into her chest.

It was a lazy option, taken because—ultimately—the Crawlers were used to Memphis sec who couldn't adequately defend themselves. It gave Mildred just the edge she needed. She was shocked, yes, but her recovery time was swift. As the Crawler's arm descended, she reacted just quick enough to block the blow, deflecting the knife arm so that the blade skidded off the shoulder of her padded jacket. It ripped the material, but didn't bite deep enough to penetrate to the flesh beneath.

The sweep of the Crawler's arm left his body open. The fact that he was almost naked, covered only in paint, meant that he had no padding to soften the blow Mildred delivered. Straight-armed, knuckles bent to form a ridge, she drove her hand into the man's rib cage, delivering a hammer blow under his heart. It expelled the air from his lungs with a startled gasp and he tried desperately to suck in air and move his numbed body, the shock of the blow resounding around his nervous system.

Mildred didn't give him the chance. Another blow to the head, striking him by the temple, felled him, the knife falling from nerveless fingers. As he fell, she went down with him. Grasping his head and twisting savagely, she heard his neck snap. The light of understanding flared briefly, as he knew his life was over, before fading.

Quickly she scrambled to her feet, taking the knife. It was a good, strong blade, slightly longer than a hunting knife but not quite a panga. Now she had a blade, she was on even terms for close fighting...although she hadn't, so far, found it to be a problem.

'One less,' she muttered tersely to herself as she scanned the surrounding area to take in what was happening.

The Nightcrawlers were finding themselves outnumbered and outclassed as the Memphis sec put into operation the lessons learned from training with the companions. Close-up knife fighting was something they had always found impossible, but with the training they had received, and the greater numbers, they were repelling the attacks from the Crawlers. Indeed, in many cases they were able to turn the tables and force their opponents onto the back foot, driving the Crawlers back as they attempted to gain an upper hand but found themselves forced into defensive measures. Some of the sec sustained injuries, blood flowing from superficial wounds where they hadn't been quick enough to avoid a blow. But these were instances that would, in the recent past, have seen them succumb to a sucker punch and fall. Now they were able to recover and keep fighting.

The sec force drove the Nightcrawlers back, not heeding the direction they were headed. The Crawlers may have been losing the battle, but they were at least succeeding in pulling their opponents off course. J.B. was aware of that, and yelled above the melee for the sec to try to finish off the Crawlers, or to make them run. And if they succeeded in this, to let them flee rather than pursue and lose time.

It didn't matter if some of their opponents retreated alive. The greater priority was to press on for Atlantis.

The sounds of combat were louder than the silence that had preceded them, but were unbroken by blasterfire following Jak's initial shot. This was close-in fighting, with blades safer than bullets lest you inadvertently take out your own side. So there was little enough background noise for Jak to catch a break in the rhythms and another set of sounds assailing his ears.

'East, west, come fast,' he yelled over the sounds of clashing steel and screaming men.

J.B. and Ryan were on it. There were no Memphis sec in these directions, so no need to be careful. While their backs were protected by their fellows, who now had the direct opposition on the run, both men took positions and listened. Over the general hubbub it was hard to pick out sounds that didn't fit; but the wildly differing directions made it easier once they were able to assume positions that allowed them to detach themselves from the fighting at their backs. Exchanging glances, both opted to take higher ground.

The stunted trees didn't add much height, but it was enough to give them a better view of the surrounding area. Added to this, the thick, gnarled and mutated trunks, with their twisting boles, gave the two men easy foot- and handholds, so they were able to shin up them rapidly.

Once in the cover of the branches, they were able to settle themselves and to watch for incoming. They didn't have long to wait. Although the canopy of leaves obscured their own views as much as it provided cover for the two companions, there was still enough space to spot the dark Crawlers, whose camou was now becoming counterproductive; and even if they kept in the obscurity of the cover provided, their movements still sent small ripples across the surrounding area.

Ryan had the Steyr settled comfortably into his shoulder and was scanning the territory to the east. J.B. had opted for the mini-Uzi, set to rapid fire, and was surveying the west. It was only a matter of time before they located their targets and were able to open fire.

Ryan faced a greater task than the Armorer. The

Steyr was an excellent target rifle, but to pick off his prey he had to make every shot count.

J.B., on the other hand, knew that the mini-Uzi wasn't a precision target weapon. However, that didn't matter, as his tactic would be different. Simply, he would size an arc that covered the Crawlers he could see, or movement that would indicate their position, and then he would tap the trigger and open fire in a spray'n'pray arc that would echo his initial assessment. There was a good chance that he would hit an opponent each time he fired, and even if that wasn't the case it was likely that such an action would pin them down or drive them back, nullifying their effectiveness.

The two men watched and waited for their chance. The woodlands were so still beyond the battleground beneath that it was simple to pick out any movement. And any movement could only mean one thing: the approaching Nightcrawlers.

Ryan allowed himself a cold grin as the tall figure of a Crawler hove into view, making his way between points of cover and exposing himself for a fraction of a second. It was enough. With his torso and head presenting a clear shot, Ryan sighted and squeezed. The sharp crack of the rifle's report echoed around the woods, sounding over the battle beneath. He saw the Crawler drop from view, a splash of crimson in the dark paint indicating that he had been hit in the thorax.

The sound of the Steyr signaled a flurry of activity across the east and west approaches to the scene of battle. The foliage moved violently as the Crawlers sought cover. But for those who came under J.B.'s province, the flurry of foliage did little more than give him a clear arc to mark out and fire. Selecting his start and end points, he tapped the trigger and brought the SMG around in a smooth arc, the constant rounds of fire chopping up trees and pulping leaves and branches. It also caught several of the Crawlers who were in the line of fire. Some dropped without his being able to see, either chilled or too incapacitated by their wounds to be able to move, and others staggered into the open before dropping, pain making them forget all caution. These he was able to pick off with ease, switching to single shot.

Over in Ryan's target area, the burst of fire from the mini-Uzi had reaped a positive result for the one-eyed man. Thinking that they were to be hit with a similar spray'n'pray attack, the Crawlers he was firing on began to move rapidly, separating to deflect a clear arc and leaving trails of disturbance to mark their path. Although he couldn't see them clearly, he was able to estimate where they would be in the moving foliage, and so pick a shot. The cessation of movement was testimony to his accuracy with such a chance maneuver.

The attack from east and west had been repelled. Those who hadn't fallen began to move in an opposite direction. The survivors weren't cowards, but they were true fighters, and realists. They had figured out that to stay and be picked off would achieve nothing. To hit at the Memphis attack force, they would have to retreat, return to their ville and inform their sec chief and Odyssey of what had occurred, so that a contingency plan could be put into place.

Ryan and J.B. watched them go from their vantage points. There were less than half the number remaining, and the farther they retreated, the harder they would be to pick off. Was it worth trying to hit them, or should they let them go? If they were able to pick them all off, it would prevent word reaching Atlantis that an attack was under way. However, Ryan figured that if there were Crawler patrols out here, then Odyssey was already assuming such a course of action. Added to which, runners may have been sent back to the ville before these parties had initially advanced. Those who had survived the blasterfire actually had no idea how strong the raiding party was. Given the way they had been scattered, and that they were unused to any real competition, it was likely that they would overestimate.

Ryan was undecided if this would be a good thing. It would mean a greater sec force against them, but conversely it would be easier to slip past any sec parties if they were geared to hunting a greater number.

But none of this would mean shit if they didn't get past the maze. And that would count for nothing if they didn't move out fast from this position.

The noise below was lessening, and as Ryan shinned down the tree he could immediately see that none of the Crawlers had been left standing.

'Others?' Jak asked.

'Either chilled or on the run,' Ryan said swiftly. 'We need to get back on course and get moving. They'll be expecting us, but they don't know how many. If we're on their tails, then they won't have time to add any more defences to the maze. And getting past that bastard is my main concern.'

'Okay,' Mark grunted, turning to his fellow Memphis people. 'Shape up into the same formations as before. Wounded?' A couple of fighters raised their hands, but claimed—with a hint of pride, Ryan noted wryly—that they were merely superficial wounds. Confidence was high. They had bested their enemy for the first time, and also perhaps for the first time they truly believed that they could fulfill this mission.

'Let's do this,' Mark said to Ryan. The one-eyed man nodded and directed the reformed clusters to move out in the direction of Atlantis.

The only members of the party not to feel elation at their progress and victory were Lemur and Cyran. The Memphis leader was, in truth, a little alarmed by what he now saw as bloodlust in his people. Were they no better than those he hoped to overthrow? If this was so, did it mean that the loss of one despot could only give rise, ultimately, to the birth of another?

He didn't doubt that they should fight, but it did worry him that they may forget what exactly they were fighting for.

Chapter Fifteen

With no opposition to impede their progress, and buoyed by the sense of victory that the Memphis sec felt after the battle, they made swift progress toward the outer edge of Atlantis. The clusters began to move closer together without realization, as the increasing gaps between the trees allowed for more room to move.

As the density of the woodland began to decrease, and there was more light seeping through the lessening canopy above them, Mark indicated that they should slow.

'We are within a few minutes of coming upon the maze. There is a patch of open ground that circles this defense.'

'So before we hit it, we're out in the open,' J.B. muttered. 'That's just great.'

Mark admonished him. 'It isn't, generally, defended by any sec men. And it isn't, in itself, a trap. As I understand it, the land surrounding the maze has been poisoned by the toxins that are used in some of the interior traps, that have escaped and seeped into the earth. There is a similar stretch of land on the far side of the maze that is also useless for building or farming.'

Ryan stopped dead. 'Wait! Why didn't you mention this when we were making our plans?'

Mark gave him a baffled glance and answered with

a disingenuousness that could only be genuine. 'I did not consider it would be that important—there is a fear of the land, and the Nightcrawlers are loathe to stand upon it for any length of time. It isn't patrolled, so—'

Ryan had trouble controlling his anger. 'So that doesn't matter so much this side of the fucking maze, but once we get through—if we all do—then we're going to be tired, and mebbe running on empty. Last thing we need is to be clear targets, out in the open.'

'But I said—'

Ryan cut the sec chief short. 'Fireblast and fuck it, man. Mebbe it wouldn't matter normally, but they know we're coming, don't they? They're not just going to stand around waiting for us to come knocking, are they?'

Mark grimaced. 'I suppose that is a fair point,' he conceded reluctantly.

Lemur cut in. 'This is no time for disagreement. It was an oversight, nothing more. Even the best of us are not used to such conditions of war, and things that you, with your skills, could pinpoint as being important, may not seem of significance to us.'

Ryan couldn't resist a wry grin. It was obvious why Lemur had risen to become Memphis leader. No pride would be wounded on either side by pointing out such a fact, and it smoothed tempers enough for a solution to be sought without recourse to recriminations.

'Okay, let's leave it at that. It does give us a little problem, though.'

The teams of fighters had now stopped, and Ryan sent Jak to scout ahead and report on the gap between the maze and the end of the woodlands that provided their cover.

'It's not that I don't trust your word, it's just that…
It's like Lemur says, mebbe Jak will be able to see
things you don't notice,' he explained to Mark. The sec
chief nodded his agreement. Ryan appreciated that.
Some in his position would have seen this as a put-down
coming from strangers. Maybe that was part of the reason Ryan had taken to the men of Memphis: they put
the needs of the many above their own petty pride and
jealousy. Things the one-eyed man had been forced to
swallow many times during his life.

While Jak scouted ahead, Ryan and Mark went over
tactics with the group once more. Given that the maze
was interchangeable, there was no way they could pre-
arrange a route. Each cluster had yarn that they had been
given before departure. Each ball of yarn was a different color. One white; one red; one gray; one pink, made
by washing out dye from a red ball. The clusters would
set off at intervals and mark their path by yarn. It was
something Mildred had suggested, inspired by a legend
she remembered from grade school. Minos had inspired
the Atlantean labyrinth, and so the legend of slaying the
beast in the original maze had given her the idea of
marking their paths by yarn. The differing colors would
mark which party had left the trail, and so if one hit a
dead end, they may be able to retrace and find the
marker of another party that had forged ahead with—
perhaps—greater success.

The tactics were simple. By necessity, they could be
little else. Each cluster would set off for the entrance to
the maze, spaced thirty seconds apart. Only the last
party would have to risk the trip across open space without cover, although Mark was adamant that wouldn't be
necessary. Once inside, the cluster teams would mark

their paths with the yarn, and stay triple red for the traps and for the beasts that were allowed to roam within. Mark was unsure whether they were kept penned or tethered, used as part of a man-trap or used separately. They would have to stay frosty and assume that anything was possible.

Once on the other side, they were to wait for the other teams, no more than five minutes at the most. Even this length of time may not be possible, for they may come under attack from the Nightcrawlers, particularly if the far side of the maze left them as exposed as now seemed the case.

When the teams—or as many as made it through—were assembled, then they would set off for Odyssey's temple, using the ex-Atlanteans's knowledge of the ville to keep in cover as much as possible. They would be actively pursued, but their small number dictated they try to keep cover…something that the very lack of numbers should make easier to insure.

Ryan and Mark had only just finished their briefing when Jak arrived back; his absence had not concerned Ryan, as Jak had already been told the extent of the plans and was not likely to forget. Of all of them, he had a mind that was as safe as a steel trap for such matters. Besides which, his information and reconnaissance was far more important.

'Not bad like expected,' he said, starting without preamble. 'Cover drops to nothing at fifty yards, but enough conceal. No sign sec this side. Mebbe beyond. Open space about a hundred yards. No cover at all—earth hard, no grass. Good footing run fast.'

Ryan nodded shortly. It sounded as though there was little to fear as long as they could cover the ground swiftly. Any offensive would be mounted on the far side of the maze.

'Okay, let's do it. No point in wasting any more time.'

'One thing,' Jak said, staying him with a hand before they set off. 'Smells bad—like end of a good hunt. Smell fear and chilling. We need be triple careful in there.'

'I wouldn't have it any other way,' Ryan replied. 'Just got to ignore that and be ready to shoot shit out of anything that gets in our way.'

'That's what call plan.' Jak grinned.

They covered the remaining ground at a fast pace, eating up the distance, assured that they would encounter nothing this side of the maze. But still it paid to be cautious, so they pulled up as the foliage began to grow more and more sparse, taking what little cover there was as the woodlands gave way to the poisoned earth.

Ryan had determined that his cluster would be the last to make the run for the head of the maze. It was his responsibility to provide cover for his people until the last. He would send Jak's cluster in second, with Lemur and Cyran protected by the albino and Mark. Which just left him with the choice of J.B. or Mildred to go in first.

It had to be the Armorer. J.B. wasn't used to being point man, but overall he had the strongest team of fighters. Ryan had been able to observe and assess their part in the earlier fight while he and J.B. were taking their places in the treetops. Mildred had a weak link in Affinity. The young man had heart, but he was a clumsy mover and perhaps not suited to being a fighter. He would try, but his technique was poor, and if Ryan had to bet jack on anyone buying the farm in a battle, it would be the lanky youth.

Ryan gave them the order of action, and J.B. prepared to lead his men across the empty space. A hundred yards now loomed like a hundred miles, such was the lack of cover. The sun beat down on the parched earth like a spotlight, waiting for them to step into it and become easy targets.

'Check blasters,' J.B. ordered. His three-man team was carrying remade Brownings and Lugers—heavy handblasters—and they checked they had full clips and a round was chambered. Satisfied that his men were ready, he gave a short nod. 'On three, go… One… two…three…'

The Armorer barked the last number in a throaty tone, flinging himself forward, eyes flickering side-to-side as he ran in an irregular pattern across the empty space. The three Memphis men followed on his heels, distancing themselves enough to make a spread target, also varying their line, keeping low and always keeping their target in sight.

The walls of the maze loomed ahead of the Armorer. From a distance, it hadn't seemed that much, but as he approached the huge white slab of stone, which on closer view revealed itself to be a wall constructed of seamlessly joined smaller blocks, grew in stature, so that it seemed to fill his field of vision and impose itself as some kind of crushing monolith, a forbidding presence through which no man could pass.

J.B. slammed up against the wall, back to the stone that was cold even in the heat of the late-morning sun. He was blowing hard, sweat spangling his brow and trickling from under the rim of his fedora. He clutched the mini-Uzi across his chest and watched the horizon as his three men came hot on his heels.

They, too, were blowing hard when they hit the wall, backing against it. Up close, the white stone betrayed signs of weathering. There was some erosion from the acid rains, and the toxins in the parched earth beneath had discolored the stone, brown and black stains creeping up in tendrils.

There was one entrance, about four yards to J.B.'s right. Otherwise, the wall was blank for the entire length. He guessed that there may be an entrance on each side, similarly placed. You could access the maze from any direction because unless you knew exactly how it was laid out on the inside, chances were that you wouldn't make it all the way through. And it was up to him to try to buck the odds.

'Dark night, I guess no one said it was going to be easy,' he murmured to himself. 'Got the yarn?' he asked in a louder voice to one of his men. A weather-beaten man with scarred hands produced the ball and nodded. Mouth too dry to speak, J.B. figured. He didn't blame him. 'Let's do it,' he said out loud.

As the Armorer edged toward the entrance, mini-Uzi now at a perpendicular angle to his body, the smell hit him. It was cold, dank and reeked of buying the farm. The gap beyond the entrance yawned darkly. The movable walls were housed within a roofed structure. Whoever planned this knew what they were doing: darkness, danger, no light to see and the claustrophobia and disorientation of not being able to direct by the sun or stars above. It would be all too easy to lose a sense of direction, double back on yourself, become confused.

He cursed the mind that had conceived this pesthole, then took a deep breath and plunged into the unknown.

JAK TOOK HIS TEAM across the open space even as J.B. was entering the labyrinthine abyss. The albino focused on moving fast, casting glances over his shoulder to check that Lemur and Cyran were following close behind. Although his wife was surprisingly fast for someone who had shown little if any sign of physical aptitude before insisting on accompanying them, it was the Memphis leader who was having a little trouble. He was a heavyset man, and although he had shown stamina, speed wasn't his forte. He was starting to lag, and Mark dropped back to cover him, even moving close and taking his arm to guide and encourage him to greater speed.

Jak looked back with concern when he reached the wall. Cyran was already joining him, but the other two had dropped back so far that Mildred's team had already started their run. Cursing inwardly, Jak indicated to Cyran that they should enter.

'Not without my husband,' she said sharply. 'He'll be fine once we're in the maze.'

Jak shrugged. His allotted task was to cover their backs, not argue. But he felt sure that this would cause problems later if another burst of speed was needed. What if they should need to move fast when negotiating the scorched earth on the far side of the maze? It was just something that he would have to deal with if and when. First they had to get through here.

Mark and Lemur had arrived. The Memphis leader was red-faced, sweating, blowing hard, breath coming in rasps. 'Not…used to…running,' he gasped. 'Better…at the stealth thing,' he added in a wheezing breath.

'Mebbe what we'll need,' Jak commented, wasting

no time in leading them into the labyrinth, noting the direction of J.B.'s white yarn.

MILDRED AND AFFINITY easily outdistanced the other two members of their team, hitting the wall at the same time.

'Boy, you've got some speed,' she gasped.

'Truly, it is amazing what fear can do,' the lanky youth said with a wry grin.

Mildred knew that he wasn't the best fighter in her team, but she had warmed to the young man. He was a born trier, but he also knew his limitations, and wisely let them work for him rather than push against them. This would make him a calm head in a crisis, and she was sure there would be a few of those before they had reached the end of the day.

The other two fighters reached the wall, gasping for breath.

'I'll fight any man or beast, but I doubt if I could do that again for some time,' panted one of them, a stocky man with heavy upper body development and a jagged scar running down his right cheek. He wasn't an athlete, so it was little surprise that this part of the assault had proved the most difficult for him. His companion, taller and slighter, but with more of a gut from an easier life, clapped him on the shoulder.

'I agree,' he gasped, 'whatever dangers we may face in the maze, at least we know they are there. Running without knowing if a shot or a blade may come out of nowhere. That is worse.'

'Boys, I'd save that judgment until we're on the inside,' Mildred said, producing her ball of yarn. 'Now what do you say we get with it before boss man Ryan's up our ass wondering why we're still standing here like half-wits.'

Affinity gave her an askance look. 'I don't understand how you can travel with someone like Dr. Tanner, who is so comprehensible, and yet be so baffling?'

''Cause Doc's as crazy as they come, and I'm just trying to keep it real.' Mildred grinned, noting on seeing his confused reaction, 'Don't worry about it. Let's just get this thing going.'

RYAN HAD NOTED with no little satisfaction that the three teams had made it across the open ground with no hint of opposing fire; nothing, in fact, to suggest that they were being overlooked in any way. Although he had been ready with the Steyr to provide covering fire, the rest of his team poised with their heavy handblasters, there had been no need for him to click out of standby mode.

Without even referring to his wrist chron, he had mentally counted off thirty seconds since Mildred's team had begun its dash across open ground. They were now about to enter the maze, following the first two teams, who had successfully negotiated stage one.

Time to move. Ryan shouldered the Steyr and turned to the three men whose faces were writ with a mixture of fear and adrenaline-pumped excitement.

'Let's go,' he said simply. 'Keep low, keep triple fast, and remember that we've got no one covering our asses.' Fireblast, if that doesn't make them move, nothing will, he added to himself.

Ryan counted off and led the charge. Breathing hard and deep, he could feel the blood pumping as his feet hit the ground in a loping, lazy stride. He had always been a good runner, which was about more than fitness; it was about having a sense of balance that enabled you to adjust to changes in the terrain without breaking stride and losing rhythm. For the few seconds that he was in the open, he forgot about everything except the flow of energy through his frame, powering from his midriff down his thighs and calves, driving his lower body while his upper moved with economy, keeping his center of gravity as low as possible.

Before he even had time to think, he was at the wall. Turning, he could see that his team had done well; they were only a few strides behind him.

'Okay, people, let's not waste time,' he said without a hint of the effort expended.

Insuring that that their yarn marker was ready to pay out, and noting the three lines left by the other teams, Ryan took a deep breath and ventured into the darkness.

'WE CAN'T JUST SIT around here doing nothing, waiting for whatever that creep has lined up for us,' Krysty ranted, pacing the floor. 'I don't think that we're on our own anymore. They're alive, and they're coming straight into a trap. And what are we doing? Nothing…just waiting for whatever Odyssey has in store for us.'

'So you keep repeating.' Doc sighed. 'But in truth, I have no idea what you think we can do about this.'

'We could try to get out,' she said, walking over to the door and examining the lock. 'I was trying to get a look at Odyssey when he was using them, but you kept getting in the way. Sometimes I wonder what you're thinking,' she added.

'I apologize for any inconvenience I may have

caused,' Doc replied archly. 'However, if you feel I am up to the task, I could always try to open the locks for you. I was close last time.'

'Close isn't enough, but I guess it's all we've got.'

Doc stood and joined her by the door, bending over the lock. In truth, he had long since cracked the code. For a time it had made no sense, but it was one of those things that, once discovered, seemed so astoundingly easy that you wonder why you didn't guess it sooner. Certainly, Doc felt that way, having realized that the combinations on each door that they had passed through differed slightly and were incrementally increased binary and tertiary codes based on lines of color. This particular lock, being the one he had chanced to crack himself, had been the key. Like Krysty, he had been observing Odyssey as he locked and unlocked each door they passed through. Unlike Krysty, he had caught the codes and knew how they would work, and—by extension—how he could operate those locks they had yet to encounter. In truth, he hadn't wanted Krysty to see the combinations. For he was unsure if he wanted them to escape.

Thoughts ran wild, emotion rampant and confused in Doc's mind. The timing of the raid on Atlantis couldn't have been worse from his point of view. Odyssey had been on the brink of offering up some great secret. Would that have been the kind of secret Doc was hoping to be revealed to him? Or would it be another let-down? He had no idea what form it took, but if Odyssey was the man he had been hoping, then the revelation could have been the very thing he sought.

Now it had been snatched from him before he'd even had the chance to find out. If only he could find some way to take it back…

Yet, at the same time, he was heartened to realize that his companions may not have bought the farm. He could see in Krysty's flashing eyes and agitated state how much this meant to her. It was a meaning that was echoed within him. There was a very large part of him that wanted to effect an escape so that he and his companion could join with them once more and fight.

He had to find balance within himself. The conflicting impulses were making his temples pound, his forehead throb. It was as though they were battering at his skull, punching behind his eyes with a force that flashed lights in front of him. It was all he could do to not let this raging torrent of clashing emotion show.

If only he could make some kind of compromise, both in the situation and within himself. To try to effect escape and yet at the same time trust to fate, and hope that Odyssey would return to take them to whatever it was that he had first intended, before he'd been distracted by his sec chief.

It was something that would make no sense to anyone other than a man drowning in contradiction, grasping at the straw of compromise. To appease one half of him while at the same time allowing fate all the opportunity it could require.

Doc began to unlock the door. He spun the colored stones, sometimes hitting one line correctly, but delaying the soft click of the bolts by spinning another out of sync. He was careful, making every move seem as though it was carefully considered, even though he had no doubts about each and every action.

Krysty was looking over his shoulder. He could feel her breath hot on his neck, could smell her sweetness.

How could he betray her? But was it betrayal when he would, eventually, release the lock?

'Come on, Doc, you're almost there,' she whispered in his ear, encouraging him.

He felt more confused and weak than ever. How could he even consider doing this to her? Yet part of him screamed that he should stop right now, walk away and wait for Odyssey to return.

It was a course of action that he couldn't take. He spun the last two rows of stones until they formed the coded pattern that he had previously established. There was a soft and satisfying click as the stone bolts slid back.

'Gaia, you've done it, Doc,' Krysty breathed wondrously. 'You've cracked it. Think they all have the same combination?'

'I very much doubt it,' he said carefully, 'however, I would wager that they all operate on a similar pattern to the cryptograph I have just stumbled upon.'

She clapped him on the back. 'That's all I need to hear, Doc. Come on, we've got a hell of a way to go until we're out of here.'

'Indeed, we have,' Doc echoed, trying to keep the doubt and confusion from his voice as he followed her cautiously into the corridor beyond.

Chapter Sixteen

Mildred had to hand it to whichever of the Odysseys had built this hellhole. If his aim had been to produce a rancid, dark, nerve-tearing puzzle with possibly fatal danger lurking around each corner, then he had more than successfully achieved that aim. She could feel the sweat pouring off her, despite the fact that the thick stone walls kept the enclosed space cooler than the outside.

She wasn't alone in her estimation. Affinity whispered in her ear, 'I would rather face a battalion of Nightcrawlers unarmed than ever have to do this again.'

Mildred turned on him, trying to stop her heart from racing. 'Boy, you ever do that again and you won't have to worry about doing anything ever again,' she whispered.

The look of surprise in the youth's eyes, and the way in which his jaw sagged at this sudden display of anger showed that he had no idea that she would be so tense and that he would surprise her in such a manner.

'Don't look like that, son. You'll catch some real nasty insects in here. Maybe I shouldn't have reacted like that, but hell, don't ever sneak up on someone who's expecting trouble. Didn't anyone ever tell you that?'

'They have now,' he muttered, almost to himself.

Mildred allowed herself the flicker of a grin as she

turned away. In truth, Affinity had inadvertently done the right thing. She had been a little too uptight up to this point, and perhaps resultantly a little too quick to overreact; something that could be as dangerous as not reacting quickly enough. But the atmosphere in the maze was getting to her.

Enclosing the movable sections within a structure that, in effect, formed an above-ground tunnel around the ville, with only one—maybe four if there were similar doorways on each side—small egress, had converted this into an oppressive hole. There was no way that air could circulate freely, so that contained within was barely breathable in the more enclosed sections, where the walls formed tight dead ends and cul-de-sacs. Foul air, stagnant and also tainted with the musk of the animals that lurked within the labyrinth. More than that, with the charnel house stink of those who hadn't made it through the maze in one piece, and had either fallen prey to the animals or had been left to rot in the traps that had chilled them.

The walls and floor of the labyrinth were slick to the touch, layers of grease, sweat and blood mingling with the rising fungus that had been birthed in the tainted earth and rancid air. The air was filled with the sounds of their own breathing and the distant baying of the beasts that awaited those who stepped out of line. The sounds were desperate and faint, but with walls this thick and the strange echoing effects of the long passages, they could be on the other side of the maze, or just around the corner.

You would only know when you walked into one.

As for what kind of beast it might be, none of the companions had been able to get a straight answer.

Those who had truly known were those chilled in the labyrinth, and those who had survived and made it through knew only by guess or rumor. The most likely candidates were wild dogs and foxes, made feral, taunted and half starved. Possibly there were others. Rumors had always existed about mutie animals bred from the remnants of a predark suburban zoo, a few creatures surviving the years of rad damage and inbreeding to become meaner and madder than anything else.

Mildred doubted that anything from such a small gene pool—let alone one so rad-blasted—would have made it this far, but some of the high, keening yowls that floated through the labyrinth made her wonder if she was right. A primal fear of the unknown rose within her, and even though she fought to quell the rising gorge, it still lurked at the edge of her mind.

At least they had light, unlike those poor souls who had made this journey in reverse. All the companions had flashlights, raided from a past redoubt, and all had checked that they had working batteries before setting off from Memphis. Mark and Lemur had been fascinated by these pieces of old tech that were completely new to them, and this alone had given their confidence a small boost in setting out on the raid. However, while Mildred was glad of the light, she could only hope that the batteries would last and that they wouldn't give out at an inopportune moment.

Which could be any moment. The yarn was being payed out by Mithos, the young sec man at the rear of the party, and that rate of drop was lessening with every yard. They were slowing, as it became harder to judge which was the right passage to take. At every junction, Mildred found herself pausing longer and longer, trying to decide which was the best to take. Was there a through draft of any kind, suggesting that this way didn't terminate in a dead end? Were there animal noises coming from this direction, suggesting they take an alternate route to skirt around any traps? As for pit traps, hidden blades, or any other kind of snare, how the hell did she decide whether there were any of those lurking?

They had long since lost track of the other yarn tracks, having taken an alternate passage some time back. She wondered how the others were doing. It was impossible to tell if there was one route through, or more than one. Maybe she was heading in the right direction and they weren't; maybe it was the other way around.

Were they progressing forward, going sideways or moving backward? In the darkness, with the amount of turns they had taken, it was almost impossible to orient themselves.

Still, there was one good thing: they had avoided any dangers so far.

She wondered if that were true of the other parties.

J.B. MOVED SWIFTLY AND SURELY. There was something in the Armorer's nature, enhanced and honed by years of practice, that made it easy for him to decide on direction. It was almost as though he had an internal compass that enabled him to define direction.

His three sec men were content to let him lead. They knew he had the greater experience and the greater skill in such techniques, and despite their own dread at entering the maze they had an implicit trust in him.

It was no accident that Ryan had sent J.B. ahead. If

anyone could use his skills to pilot a safe passage through the labyrinth, then it would be J. B. Dix. And he had set a strong pace, using his sense of direction to keep forging ahead, and the other skills he had learned in the noble art of staying alive to choose the passages they would traverse.

But even so, J.B. was finding it hard. He could hear the baying of the trapped animals and the charnel house atmosphere was strong enough in this section of the labyrinth to make him feel like puking, even after all the things he had seen, heard and smelled over the years. The dark seemed to do little more than intensify the pungent stench, so much so that it threatened to overwhelm the raiding party.

'Dark night, how many have never made it out of here?' he asked quietly.

'Too many,' came the unbidden reply. 'Those of us who did get through know this smell all too well. You are doing well to hold on to your stomach,' the sec man added wryly. 'Certainly better than those of us who were born to Memphis and had never—thankfully—experienced this before.'

As if to emphasize the point, J.B. could hear one of the men retching behind him, bringing up what was left of his last meal. He was the second to have succumbed, and it was a matter of pride with J.B. that he not join them. For, if nothing else, he had more important matters on which to concentrate.

'If we go right here, I figure that we run into something living and real pissed off,' he commented, catching the wail of a starving animal drift toward him. 'But left doesn't feel right. It takes us straight ahead, angling back toward a straight path through to the other side.'

'And it's not going to do that for the purpose of assisting us,' mused the sec man at his shoulder. 'To be that enticing, it must house a trap of some kind.'

'It's be triple stupe not to assume otherwise,' J.B. agreed. 'But what kind?'

The sec man paused for a second before answering. 'The only kind of traps that I know of for sure are those that are covered pits, staked at the bottom, and have swinging blades. I don't know how they are triggered—trip wire or something hidden in the floor, perhaps—but they let loose a circular blade that swings across the tunnel walls.'

'Shit, that sounds real nasty,' J.B. commented.

The sec man gave a lazy smile. 'Ah, but it isn't the fastest of weapons, and if you're quick enough—and scared enough—you can duck beneath.'

J.B. flashed a returning grin. 'That sounds like experience talking.'

'I'm still here,' the sec man replied, 'although I nearly lost the top of my skull. Beware, there is no indication until the blade begins to swing.'

'Flashlight may help, may catch the blade and give a quicker warning,' J.B. mused. Then he shrugged. 'Fuck it, what else can we do? To the left, and keep alert.'

The Armorer took a deep breath of fetid air and began to walk slowly down the straight passage, the flashlight beam casting a narrow arc some ten feet in front of him. A small part of the smell was explained by the rotted corpse that lay ahead. There was no way of telling how it bought the farm—or even if it was male or female—as it had been ground into the floor of the maze when the walls were rearranged, and half of it was now obscured by a stone wall that cut diagonally from chest to hip. That which remained had little recognizable flesh left on the crushed bones.

J.B., even as familiar as he was with such carnage, had to swallow hard as he walked over the remains. Perhaps it was this that disturbed his concentration, diverted his attention for just one second, but one second was enough. A few feet past the corpse and he realized too late that one of the reasons it had been left there was to act as a diversion.

As his right foot hit the ground, it yielded beneath him, crumbling and giving way to a yawning gap. The flashlight beam swung around in a wild arc across the wall and floor, for a moment lighting up the drop beneath him. Six by four, the width of the passage, it seemed to run under the wall of each side—perhaps the pit was dug to an incredible width so that any passage was prey to its charms. No matter now. The most important thing was that it was more than six feet deep, and three of those were populated by wooden stakes sharpened to a point. The bones gathered beneath, briefly illuminated by the flashing beam, held testimony to how many had tumbled and rotted away on those deadly sentinels, stakes to which J.B. was now headed with the gathering momentum of a falling object.

Somehow, despite it all, he kept hold of the flashlight. If nothing else, if he was going to buy the farm, he wanted to see how. But before he could view his own demise, he found himself jolting to a halt, suspended in midair. The sole of one foot still had the barest of contact with the edge of the pit, but he could feel the solid, tightly packed dead earth becoming less tightly packed with each passing moment. He could also feel the pull of his belt and waistband, the only things that stopped him from plunging downward.

'Hang on...' His rescuer's voice was strained with effort and he could feel the man's grip tremble as his aching muscles protested. 'Quick...' he heard the man implore.

Another hand grabbed his belt and hauled back. If the leather didn't cut into the band of muscle around his stomach, then the muscle would rip the leather unless they gained another handhold.

A third set of hands grabbed at his jacket, reaching out and clutching the leather, snatching at it to try to get a grip. J.B. felt completely helpless, suspended over the pit, with only his clothing keeping him from plummeting downward. He had to hope that it could take the strain. He was light enough in himself, but as ever he was laden down with his armament supplies, which was enough to add considerable weight to his small frame.

Thankfully, inch by inch, they clawed him back upright, the seams and material of his clothes protesting all the while, before they were able to get a stronger grip and right him. He poked and probed backward with his floating foot, trying to find a foothold. The movement was too much for the soil edge on which his grounded foot was resting, and with a sudden jerk the earth beneath his heel gave way. With a sickening lurch he plummeted back down again, this time feet first, his calves scoring tracks in the earthen sides of the pit.

His groin seared red hot with pain and his guts felt as though they would fall out of his ass, but his sudden downward progress was halted by the straining arms of the three Memphis sec men. Now seemingly taking such matters in their stride, they hauled up the Armorer until he was seated on the edge of the pit. Shuffling backward, he scrambled to his feet.

'Thanks,' he said, as calmly as he could muster, to the sec man who had saved him. It occurred to J.B., as he put out his hand, that he didn't even know his name.

'Demis,' he murmured, as though he could read J.B.'s mind. 'I knew there'd be something along here, but I would have put money on a swinging blade.'

'You might be a lousy gambler, but I'm thankful you've got good reflexes,' J.B. countered. He shone the flashlight—still in his hand and in a paralyzed fear grip that would probably take some time to loosen—over the edge of the pit, and then as far over the other side as it would reach. The gap was too far for them to risk jumping, and there was no way they could get around the pit, seeing it extended beneath the walls on each side.

'Looks like we're going to have to track back and take the right-hand passage after all,' Demis said softly.

'Unless you want to go back to the junction before and try that one,' J.B. replied.

'It might be better to do that, particularly if you can get us back on track again,' the sec man mused.

J.B. gave him a wry grin. 'Listen, I've nearly just lost my guts to a bunch of spikes. Rather than risk losing them to some mutie bastard, I'd say I could get us back on track.'

'Then let's do that. You can have too much excitement in one day,' Demis said without a trace of irony in his voice.

'TOO MUCH EXCITEMENT in one day. Couldn't get better, could it?' Ryan said with bitter irony as his party reached the dead end of another cul-de-sac. 'Fireblast and fuck it, is anything going to go right in this pesthole?'

Like Mildred's party, Ryan and his sec men had lost track of the initial yarn trail left by J.B. some time back. One wrong turning and a length of yarn lost in shadow was all it took. Now they had no idea where they were, and although they hadn't as yet encountered any obstacles, they had managed to hit three dead ends in as many choices. Ryan could see them following their trail back to junction after junction until they found themselves back at the entrance once more. At least they'd still be alive—but how far behind the others would they be? And how long would it take them to make up that time, even if they could get it right starting over?

Ryan punched at the wall in frustration. If he had a trap to respond to, a beast to fight, then he would be able to act, but the sense of helplessness at getting nowhere was the worst of all possible worlds for him.

'Ryan, I know it's not much help, but if we've hit all these cul-de-sacs, then at least we know where they are and we've just got to make progress on our next choice,' the sec man with the yarn said as he began to retrace their steps.

Ryan wanted to yell at the man, but managed to prevent himself from exploding. The Memphis man was right, and he was only trying to show support to his team leader. 'Yeah, guess you're right,' Ryan gritted, hoping it didn't sound too strained.

They arrived at a junction. The yarn stopped, indi-

cating one of two alternate passages. 'We've been up
there, I'm sure,' he said.

'Why?' Ryan questioned him.

The man grinned and directed Ryan to use the flashlight to illuminate a section of wall. A symbol was
scratched into a sweep of black mould on the stone.
'Can't do it at every junction, but where there's this
black stuff, I've scratched that in with my blade, as an
extra little reminder.'

Ryan clapped him on the back. 'Good thinking.
That's going to save us a little time.'

Mebbe the tide was turning, the one-eyed man
thought as they set off down the only passage they
hadn't yet traversed.

The beam of the flashlight, narrowed as he concentrated it on the areas directly in front of them, sweeping floor, ceiling and roof, was the only relief from the
almost pitch-black that surrounded them. Although they
couldn't see the roof, they could feel it above them, almost seeming to lower with every step, as though this
in itself were part of a trap, descending to crush them.
They could feel its oppressive weight above them,
poised to seal them in this stone tomb.

As if that weren't enough, the distant sounds and the
full-on smells were enough to fray the already ragged
ends of their nerves. Ryan was keeping calm. The fact
was, he'd faced much worse than this before now, and
was he chilled yet? But the other three weren't as experienced and he could feel the tension coming off
them, hitting him in the back with an almost physical
force.

They would be more of a danger to themselves than
anything else in here, if they didn't control and use the fear.

Ryan carefully put one foot in front of the other, testing the ground ahead for solidity before trusting it with his full weight. He had ordered the others to do the same, and from the sounds of their shuffling, he knew that they were calm enough to remember that. But how would they be able to detect any traps that might spring from the walls or ceiling? The long stone slabs that constituted the passage walls were joined in sections, and in these divides there was the possibility of a hidden weapon. Yet that was too obvious. Surely a weapon would be better concealed than in such an obvious break? Besides which, Ryan figured that these fissures were where the plates comprising the wall structures could be moved, to change the layout of the labyrinth.

So they were looking for something that, by design, wouldn't be visible.

Well, that makes it so much easier, he thought bitterly.

Another thing that bothered him was how they used the beasts within the labyrinth. Short of putting them down a pit or tethering them, he could see no way that they could contain the creatures so that they couldn't just wander their way out of the labyrinth eventually. If they were in a pit, then you just had to watch the floors. If they were tethered, then you just backed up and kept a distance.

There had to be something else, but what?

He could have cursed his question. It was as though he had tempted the fates by thinking this right now.

The flash hadn't picked up the wire. It had to have been covered with grease or mold, deliberately disguised by those Crawlers who operated the labyrinth. The first he knew about it was when he felt it pluck at his hairline. He thought it was a spider of some kind, on a thread, and he swatted at it. When he felt the tension of the wire against his hand, he knew he had made a wrong move. A very wrong move.

'Watch—' he started to yell, turning back to his men. But it wasn't the fact that they were at his back that made him turn; he realized that his reflex had been triggered by the grinding sound of stone on stone. He directed the flash beam and could see that one section of the wall was moving on a pivot, turning to cut off the passage to their rear.

If it was doing this, then it could only mean that the danger lay ahead.

'Back, before it shuts,' he yelled as he whirled and started to run toward the closing slabs of stone. The sec men, faces caught in the wildly swinging beam, were confused, half turned and frozen in indecision. Ryan ran for the slab, reaching out to try to halt its progress. He grabbed at the stone, slippery with mold, failing to find a grip. He dug his heels in and cursed through gritted teeth, but no matter how hard he pulled he couldn't stop the inexorable progress of the slab. By this time, the sec team had realized what was happening and was attempting to aid him. Yet it was impossible for all of them to gain a hold as the gap between the stationary and moving slabs grew more and more narrow.

'For fuck's sake, get through,' Ryan ground out. There was enough space for one of them at least to get on the other side of the slab; yet they were so thrown by what had happened that none of the three caught on to his meaning, and so the opportunity was lost. The gap was now too narrow to squeeze through, and Ryan let it drop, cursing heavily as the slab closed with a squealing, grinding finality on its stationary companion.

Breathing heavily from the effort, Ryan directed the beam of the flash back in the direction from which they had just come. As he had feared, there was more movement up ahead. The sounds of moving slabs from the far end of the passage had been initially masked by those they now stood near, but he could see that the shape of the passage was changing. Another slab moved across to block the passage less than 150 yards ahead. But, rather than boxing them in by moving in the same manner as the slab at their back, by moving from the right, this one moved from the left wall, blocked the way ahead while revealing a new opening in the newly formed space to their left.

There was a rank, musky smell that came from the new opening, traveling even that short distance in but a moment. It was the stench of animal feces, old blood and rotten meat, mixed with the warm smell of a live predator. A low growl came from the darkness, and as Ryan edged closer to the gap, drawing his SIG-Sauer, he could almost swear that some of the shadow was a swirling darkness deeper than the rest.

He figured that the open cavity was a pen, and that was how they kept the animals caged without having to leash them. Clever system: the animal would get you nine times out of ten, and if it didn't, then you had to work out how the hell to get out of the enclosure.

First things first. He had the advantage. The animal might have been hidden in darkness, but he had a blaster. Furthermore, it could only come at him from the one direction. As long as he didn't take his eye off the target… He watched the moving shadows keenly, gesturing with his free hand for the sec team to keep back, the flash beam sweeping across the roof of the passage in time with his movements.

He could have used the flash to find the creature in the darkness, but he preferred to let it come in its own time. The cavity probably wasn't that deep, but what if the flash didn't cover all the territory? The last thing he wanted was to drive the creature back into shadow, prolong the tension. Conversely, he had no wish to catch the creature full in the beam and make it react wildly and in shock. That way, there was no way of knowing what it would do. This way, it would act as all wild creatures: it would size up its enemy and make its attack.

And he would be ready.

Within the darkness, the differing shades of black moved, swirled and coalesced into shapes…into one shape. A shape that moved toward him at speed, snarling as it sprang up from the floor of the labyrinth.

Ryan tensed, following its line of flight with the arc of his arm. As it moved from the depths of its lair and into the ambient light cast by the beam of the flash, diffused as he held it away from the opening, so its shape became apparent.

It was a cat of some kind. Not the feral, scrawny creatures that hung around the edges of villes, scavenging in packs. This had more in common with the kind of larger wild cats that he had seen in the areas around the Rockies. It was larger than a big dog and far more muscled. Despite the fact that its ribs were visible, and it was obviously half-starved, it still had an impressive musculature gathered at shoulder and haunch, testimony to the power that nature had imbued in its legs. Power it showed by the force of its spring, and the size of paws that reached out to him, broken but lethally sharp claws extended. Its amber eyes were jaundiced and staring wide, the teeth yellowing and the breath so hot and fetid that he could smell it even at this distance.

Never taking his eye off the creature, Ryan squeezed the trigger of the SIG-Sauer three times. In the enclosed space that had been made for them, the rounds echoed off the walls, reverberating so that they felt powerful enough to burst the eardrums of all four men.

The big cat was deflected in its flight by the power of the three rounds as they ripped into its underbelly, scoring through the soft flesh and spilling intestines in midflight. The exit wounds spun the beast, bone shards deflecting the flight so that the spent rounds came out through the spine and the rib cage.

Ryan flattened himself to the far wall. Despite the shots chilling the creature, despite the look of dumb surprise in its eyes as they dulled and died, and despite the fact that the line of flight had been interrupted, the momentum of the leap was enough to carry the chilled cat forward so that it almost landed on Ryan, flattening him.

With a dull whump, the chilled flesh that the cat had now become landed heavily at his feet.

'Thank fuck for that,' he breathed as he trained the flash on it. 'I thought—'

For a vital second he had been distracted. It hadn't occurred to him that the pen might have contained more than one big cat. Why should it? He had assumed that any such pen containing two half-starved creatures would lead to their trying to tear each other apart. As, indeed, it might have if they weren't a mating couple.

Hindsight was a wonderful thing. Given a chance to indulge in it, Ryan would have reflected that the Atlanteans had to breed more of these bastard animals somehow. But at that moment, it was the last thing on his mind and, with his ears still ringing from the triple discharge, he didn't hear the second creature howl at the death of its mate and launch itself from where it had been waiting in the darkness.

Ryan felt the air move, saw a flicker of movement, heard nothing but tinnitus, but nonetheless was aware that under the ringing was a deeper, angrier tone. The flash caught the female cat in flight, ears flattened against her head. There was no time to fire, so he dropped to his right, hitting the floor badly so that his shoulder jarred and the SIG-Sauer dropped from a momentarily numb grasp as he tried to roll away from immediate danger. The female cat hit the wall, where he had been standing scant moments before, with a squeal of agony. His only hope was that she had stunned herself too much to recover before he had a chance to gain his feet.

He wasn't going to get that lucky. His arm still numbed from impact, he hauled himself awkwardly upright. The flash was now rolling on the floor some two or three yards from him, the light directed toward him and the she-cat, casting dramatic shadows against the wall behind them. To survive, he'd have to drag his panga from its thigh sheath. But it was on the wrong side for him to grasp easily, the arm he usually used being the damaged one. And now the she-cat was up, shaking herself and snarling, circling to locate him, there was no time for fumbling.

Around his neck, Ryan still had his scarf. He hardly had cause to use it. It was a relatively ineffective weapon unless close-quarters stealth or a concealed weapon became a necessity. But now it was the only thing to hand, and with little time he had to make this count.

Using his good arm, he unraveled it from around his neck and wrapped it around the flat of his hand with a deft flick. In the ends were metal weights that, if used with a slingshot action and a matching accuracy, could stun an opponent. No way would it chill this fury-spitting hell-cat, but it may just stun her enough to buy him some extra time.

Stumbling as he adjusted to the imbalance caused by his useless arm, he started to twirl the scarf as the cat leaped at him. He had only the one chance. With a flick of his wrist, and a whispered prayer to whatever long-forgotten deity he could bring himself to believe in, he snapped the scarf so that the weights, carried by momentum, cannoned against the head of the leaping beast, striking her just above the snout and between the eyes. The creature let out a yelp of pain and landed to one side of him, rolling and tumbling as the sudden pain distracted her, shaking her head to clear the fog caused by the agony of the sharp blow.

'Fireblast, where are you?' Ryan bellowed as he backed away as fast as he could. It was a reasonable question. He'd been battling these beasts alone, when in truth he should have had at least some assistance from his team by now.

The three men were frozen not by fear but by shock and surprise. They had written him off because they would have been easily chilled by the first cat, let alone the second. The fact that he was still alive only added to their shock, and it took his words to snap them from their reverie.

All had handblasters: two carried heavy Lugers, the

third a Browning. Suddenly snapped into action, they drew the weapons. The cat was rolling to her feet in the glare of the discarded flash, and was an easy target.

The air filled with the roar of blasterfire. Round upon round, each man firing at least twice, overlapping so that Ryan couldn't tell how many shells ripped into the beast. However many, it was more than enough to chill her. Her snout disappeared in a shower of blood and bone, her jaw hanging loose. Any sound was literally ripped from her throat as her chest and neck were opened up by blasterfire. Her carcass jerked as other rounds pounded her flanks, gouging open the flesh— not that she could feel it, as she had bought the farm with the first few hits.

It was more than just the deafening roar. The air was also filled with the stink of cordite, blotting out and overpowering the stench of death and the charnel house atmosphere that had previously prevailed.

'Enough,' Ryan bellowed, over and over again until the firing ceased. 'Fireblast,' he yelled into the sudden silence, unable to judge his own voice over the deafening ringing in his ears, 'save some ammo. It's chilled. Better late than never, I guess.'

He bent and retrieved the flash, which was casting a crimson glow from the gore splattered across the glass. He wiped it off and walked to the far wall, by the big cats' now deserted pen. If he could open this some-how—and it had to, as he knew it was on a pivot sys-tem to close—then they could progress in the right direction. He ignored the smell from the pen and the pools of blood gathering around his feet.

'Don't just stand there, you stupe bastards,' he yelled over his shoulder, 'come and help me find some way of opening this. Otherwise we're going to be stuck here until the Nightcrawlers come for us, and there's no telling how long that would take.'

JAK HELD UP A HAND to halt his party. They could hear distant blasterfire echoing through the passages.

'Someone's found the wildlife,' Mark said with some concern.

'Ryan,' Jak answered. 'Sound like SIG.'

'Hope they get past the obstruction in one piece,' Mark added.

There was a second round of fire, much more intense.

'It chilled now,' Jak said wryly. 'Mebbe should look for own instead listen them.'

'You lead the way,' Mark suggested. 'You've got a better eye for these paths than I.'

Something that was literally, as well as metaphorically, true. Jak's red, pigmentless albino eyes gave him a faded vision in the outside world, allowing as they did a less filtered light to reach his retina. But in the darkness, they came into his own. The sensitivity that had to be compensated by his smell, taste and hearing in normal daylight now allowed him to differentiate objects with a much smaller degree of ambient light to guide him. What appeared to the others to be nothing more than a continuing stretch of darkness was filled with shape and contour, the low levels of light seeping beyond the beam of the flash allowing Jak to see twists and turns in the passages that were invisible to the other three members of the party.

But it was more than that. Jak had an instinct for direction and a feeling for danger. He was taking them in the right direction, and at a pace that wasn't as quick as J.B.'s, but didn't leave them far behind. His experience enabled him to sniff out the direction in which the animal traps were laid and to skirt around them. They couldn't follow J.B.'s route completely as the lines of yarn left by the Armorer and Mildred had become, at one point, intertwined, knotted and pulled so tight that they had broken, something that the parties ahead couldn't know.

Nonetheless, Jak was leading them past the beasts, and his sense of imminent danger meant that they had so far avoided three traps: one was set in the wall and was triggered by a raised step in the floor. It was only slightly raised, just enough for the impact of a foot to trigger an air release that shot razor-sharp darts across the width of the passage, from ankle level to the roof. Jak saw it as a raised bump, and triggered it with a pebble that he tossed with practiced ease after staying them with a gesture. The raised step was on a hair trigger, to allow for even the slightest chance contact from whoever may pass, and the darts shot across from concealed holes with a hiss of air pressure, striking the far wall with a dull clang before clattering to the floor.

The second had been a pit trap like the one that had almost claimed J.B.'s life. Jak couldn't have told the others how he knew it was there, only that there was something inside him that screamed for him to stop. Flattening to his belly, he had crawled ahead, testing the ground in front of him with an outstretched arm until he had reached a point where the ground had been softer, more malleable beneath his fingertips. Further probing had left the layer of topsoil, suspended on a flimsy film of material, giving way beneath his probing, triggering a reaction that led to the whole surface of the passage floor falling in for six feet in front of him.

Mark, Lemur and Cyran had peered into the abyss, the flash lighting the sharpened stakes pointing up to them, the remains of less fortunate travelers scattered on the pit floor.

'Twice we should have perished without you,' Lemur said softly to Jak as he stood upright and dusted himself down. The albino youth said nothing, but Mark pondered on how fortunate they had been when Ryan had assigned Jak to them. Twice, the albino had made him understand why: it was important that the Memphis leader and his wife be kept as safe as possible. The sec chief doubted that any of the other strangers would be able to insure this as well as Jak Lauren.

The third time bore this out. They had been within sight of a junction, the flash beam showing that they were about to reach a T-junction in the labyrinth, when Jak had pulled them up short.

'What?' the Memphis leader had asked, adding disbelievingly, 'There's no room for anything this close to the end of a passage, surely?'

'Good job you not in lead,' Jak said dryly, pointing the flash toward the floor. Barely visible on the stone-pitted dead earth was a wire, covered with dirt but just raised enough to catch his trained and better-adjusted eye. 'Watch carefully,' he said, edging toward the wire and extending the toe of his boot. It was something he didn't particularly wish to do, but there was little other option. He had to trigger the trap somehow, and it was pointless to wish for something long with which to prod at the wire when there was nothing to hand.

On the plus side, it wasn't likely that it was explosive, so he should escape with his foot intact...

As he felt the tension on the wire give at his gentle but insistent pressure, he tried to work out what kind of trap it could be. As Lemur had said, they were close to the end of a passage, and he had noticed that all traps came near the center of slabs, rather than the end. It made sense. The closer to an end, the greater the chance of the slab splitting when the trap was put in place. So what would this be, and how would it work?

It seemed to take an eternity for the wire to give, but when it did, the result was instantaneous. A blade swung from the ceiling, swooping down in an arc that would have cut through the skull of anyone who was in its path. It was scimitar-shaped, and as sharp, for the sound of it slicing the air was high and keening. As it hit the wall slab, bouncing back, it left a deep mark in the stone.

'Above, below, and from each side. Is there nowhere that can be counted as safe?' Lemur murmured.

'Not think anything safe—stay alive longer,' Jak said, examining the blade. He looked up at the ceiling. It had been concealed in a groove covered with earth to look like mold. The wire had been secured in the earth and run around the end of the slab, at the junction, so that it would not show on the wall. Jak felt the blade, admiring its honed edge, and wondered if he could somehow detach it. If he could, there was no doubt that it would be useful.

It was then that, inexplicably, Cyran reacted to a sudden animal cry. Giving a small scream, she bolted around the corner of the junction, headed to the left.

'Come back,' Lemur shouted, making to give chase. He was stayed by the hand of Mark.

'No. If we go, we go together.'

Jak joined them and followed her with the flash. What the hell was she doing? She had been incredibly calm and collected so far. It just didn't fit.

What made it all the stranger was that she seemed to be heading toward the animal cry, rather than away....

Chapter Seventeen

How much longer can I continue to walk this fine line, this silken thread that is like that which connects my id and ego to the real world—or, at least, that which I call real. Truth is a subjective thing so much more than it is objective. It depends upon perspective, mood, attitude and intellect. What do you see and how do you see it? When you explain, are you accurate in detail, do you sin by omission, or do you mislead through nothing less nor more than inarticulacy?

Questions such as this are the things that concern me the most, especially at a time like this. Of course, it would be but a matter of moments to plow through these childishly simple locks now that I have divined the code through which the combinations are obtained. It is all a matter of going through...through life, through truth, through the means by which I can justify to myself my own actions. For I am a foul and wretched creature, torn between serving my own needs and sacrificing those for the good of those that I call my friends. For even if I have doubts about my own friendship, then there is lit- tle doubt that this is what they are to me. How many times have they drawn me from the fire when it seemed that I would be consumed by the flames?

She waits at my shoulder as I appear to labor over a task that I make arduous, yet could be over in an in-

stant. I am compromising at this juncture. We could easily make our escape, seek out our friends, join in the fight. Yet the more I delay, the more likely that Odyssey will return and show me the secrets that, despite the need within me to fight, I still feel will show me the means of ultimate salvation.

I do not say no to either option. Instead, I take the cowardly way out and wait for chance and fate to force my hand. If I make a show of one thing while waiting for another, then the gods of fate will smile upon me and make for me a decision that will be right, whether I know it or not.

This accursed lock is too simple. She watches over my shoulder now, and yet she has not, yet, divined the cipher for herself. She is not fool enough to be unable to work it out—if she did, that would force my hand. But because she trusts me, she does not think twice.

'Doc, why are you looking at me like that?' Krysty asked, bewildered. 'Just keep working on the lock.'

The old man shook his head and returned to his task. For a moment, he had been unaware that his meandering mind had caused him to leave the lock and stare at her. As he returned to finding the right combination of red, black and white squares to trigger the lock, his mind raced once more. They had taken more than a quarter of an hour to get past three doors, and at this rate they could be anything up to an hour getting out of the inner temple. By rights, his rate of progress should have increased, as he should have learned more about these locks from each one he cracked. Even playing for time as much as he had, there was no way he could keep it up without her becoming suspicious.

If nothing else, as his mind wandered, his fingers slipped into automatic and the lock was soon released.

'By the Three Kennedys!' he exclaimed, as surprised as Krysty that the door was yielding, 'I may be getting the hang of this, after all.'

If there was a hint of regret in his tone, it escaped her as she clapped him on the back.

'Carry on like this, and we'll be out of here in no time,' she said as they hurried through the open door and along a corridor lit by flickering torches before coming to a split.

'Which way?' Doc asked.

Krysty frowned. 'Left has a slight incline. I'm guessing we weren't at ground level when we started, so we need to go down.'

'Whatever makes you say that?' Doc asked, puzzled and for a moment forgetting his dilemma.

Krysty frowned, shook her head. 'I don't know for sure. It's just that I think it's that there were no vibrations beneath us. Stone floors would carry them up from the ground. If we were at the center of a ville, and we were on a stone floor like that, when we were left in silence we'd pick up something of what was going on outside. We do all the time, I guess it's just that we don't notice it. But whatever there may have been was killed off, and the only way that could happen—'

'Was if we were, perhaps, raised in some way. A good point, my dear girl, but what if there was nothing because there were cellars beneath us—what if that is where we are heading?'

'Then we head up again. If we keep going up from this point, then we're stuck on the roof of this damn place,' she added with a humorless laugh.

'Very well, down it is,' Doc proclaimed, leading the way.

The corridor ahead was clear, and shortly they came to another locked door.

'Think you can crack this one quicker?' she asked.

Doc gave her a grin. 'My dear girl, the secret is all in the cipher, and I do believe I have defined the code on which it is based. Only a theory, but time to test it.'

He stood in front of the jumble of red, black and white stones that made up the grid, and theatrically cracked his knuckles. There had always been a little of the ham actor in Theophilus Tanner, and even now it was a hard habit to break.

Slowly, he maneuvered the grid, explaining his theory of binary and tertiary codes as he moved each line. Within a matter of seconds, the lock mechanism had smoothly slid back.

'Gaia, it was really that easy?' Krysty breathed.

Doc laughed, shook his head. 'Things are always "that easy" when you finally work them out,' he murmured, opening the door.

Odyssey stood on the other side. He looked as though he had been expecting them and failed to hide his amusement at the expressions on their faces.

'Oh, do not be too surprised,' he said mockingly. 'I have had to withdraw my guards to divert the manpower to the labyrinth. We are, as you know, under attack. The size of the force is unknown, but I have my men waiting. Anyone who can make it through the labyrinth will walk—stumble, perhaps—into the waiting arms of my Nightcrawlers.

'Of course, this means that the inner temple has been left unguarded. I suspected that Dr. Tanner would be able to solve the puzzle of the locks eventually, but I did not reckon on his speed. I was returning to attend to you when I heard the movement behind this door. They are thick stones, but not so thick as to preclude all sounds, particularly when the rest of temple is deserted. I thought it would be interesting to wait, to see how long it took for you to work the individual combination for this door. Not very long at all. I am impressed.'

He clapped mockingly.

'So glad that we've entertained you,' Krysty said, acid dripping in her tones 'but we really can't stand around here all day listening to you tell us how clever we are—or how you are, come to that. We've got things to do.'

'You have, you have,' Odyssey agreed, nodding vigorously. 'It's just that they may not be the things that you were expecting.'

'And you mean what by that, exactly?' she asked.

'You'll come with me now,' Odyssey answered, ignoring her question. He turned his back on them and began to walk away.

Krysty sighed. 'I didn't have you down as a triple stupe. You don't have your sec to back you up now. You're a stocky guy, but I don't figure you do much fighting. You don't look like you've got a blaster on you. Okay, so we haven't, but there are two of us. And even if you could match Doc, there was no way you could match me.'

Odyssey turned to face them, a slow smile spreading across his features. 'I really didn't have you down as either that bombastic or that stupid yourself,' he said gently. 'Do you really think that I need physical prowess to make you do as I wish? If that were the case, I could have had you put in chains from the moment that you arrived, so that there was no chance of your effecting any effort at escape.

'I'm also disappointed that you think so little of me as to assume that I would fall for such a ridiculous and obvious loophole in my plans. Perhaps you are not the people I took you for. But no matter, it is too late for that now.'

Krysty snorted and shook her head. 'Words. I've had enough of them from you. We've got people who need us.'

The woman began to move toward Odyssey, slowly but with a body language that spoke of an intent to harm. Doc followed her, but something made him hold back. Why would Odyssey be so sure? They could easily best him, unless...

'Krysty, don't look at him,' Doc yelled.

But it was too late. Her eyes were fixed on the figure ahead, sizing up his own stance and posture, so that she could take him out. She was only a few hundred feet away when she began, and the distance was covered in a matter of seconds.

Yet it seemed to grow greater as her limbs became leaden and her head fogged. Sizing him up, she had caught his eyeline, and now found that she couldn't tear her vision away from him. However hard she tried, her eyes were locked on to his, and they became like burning coals that burned into her brain, cauterizing the cortex and rendering her unable to act.

She realized too late why Doc had suddenly implored her to look away. If only she had caught on a few seconds earlier herself, then this wouldn't have happened. She cursed herself as a veil of blackness started to descend.

As Krysty collapsed, Doc stood paralyzed. Perhaps if he tried to rush Odyssey, then the Atlantean leader would divert his attention and the woman would be able to recover. But then he would fall prey to the man's powers. And if both he and Krysty were rendered inactive...

'You cannot make up your mind what to do?' Odyssey asked him, without taking his eyes from Krysty. 'That wouldn't be the first time, would it? You think I don't know, from the questions you ask, that you want to know more? You think that I don't know, from my intelligence sources, that you have other priorities to those of your traveling companions? You think that I don't know you have been faking the amount of time it has taken you to unlock these doors? By the souls of the travelers, man, it is a simple code for one such as yourself, that you knew as soon as you were through the first door. Indeed, I believe you knew it the first time that I saw you. You think that I wasn't aware on letting myself into my own chamber that the lock had been tampered with and left just one color out of place?

'You want to join with me. You want to know more.'

Doc felt his anger rise, sweeping over the impotence that had stayed him.

'No,' he yelled, 'I am not alone. And I do not act alone.'

He made to run at Odyssey, but had left it too late. Krysty had slumped unconscious to the floor, and as Doc put his first foot forward, he found his eyes drawn inexorably to those of the Atlantean leader.

'THIS IS THE PLACE I wanted you to see earlier. It is quite splendid, is it not? I always thought that this would be where I would really know for sure if I was the chosen one, or just another in the long line of those who have to wait for the time when we will be returned to our rightful home.'

Odyssey's honeyed tones lulled Doc from the deep black of his sleep. It was uncommonly rare for the old man not be troubled in his rest, and as his head started to clear and the voice filled his ears, the mellifluous tones beginning to make sense, he realized that it was highly unlikely that he had been doing anything as simple as taking a nap.

Of course, Doc reasoned, it was beginning to become clear now. If the way in which he and Krysty had been abducted without the other companions buying the farm in the event was to make any kind of sense, the idea of hypnosis had to be involved. That much had already been obvious. However, it did beg the question of how the Nightcrawlers learned the art. If they possessed it, then it put them in a position of great power, particularly if they were able to practice it with such ease. The position of each generation's Odyssey would have been, to say the least, precarious...unless, of course, they had been taught it by a master, and that master happened to be the leader of the ville himself.

Doc knew a little of the art of hypnotism. Mesmerism, it had been back in the days when he had first heard of it, long before these series of nightmares had begun. But no, he couldn't let his mind stray in any way; he had to keep focused. So: hypnotism. The ability to cloud minds and bend them to one's will. It wasn't a simple skill to develop to a degree where you had anything that could be called mastery; and there were schools of thought that stated it was impossible to make a person do something that—deep within—was against his or her will.

Perhaps that would be true if the hypnotist was a normal man or woman. But what if there was some kind of mutie strain that ran through the ville of Atlantis, making it possible for them to practice these arts to a hitherto unseen degree? Certainly, it would explain the power with which Odyssey had been able to subdue both himself and Krysty.

Furthermore, such a mutie strain, and the power it bestowed, would certainly account for the man's bombastic pomposity and his ridiculous sense of grandeur.

Well, who would have thought. all it took to knock some sense into Doc was to brainwash him with a quick fix of hypnotism. He couldn't believe it. Whatever problems may now beset him, the voices in his head, the conflicts, had now all vanished.

Doc flexed his limbs experimentally. He couldn't feel them. They weren't just numbed, or bound, it was as though they no longer existed. He tried to twist his head, but it wouldn't respond. He knew that he was breathing, but when he took deeply from the air, he could feel it in his sinuses, but nothing from the neck down.

This was truly alarming. He had either been drugged, or a powerful posthypnotic suggestion had been implanted that wouldn't allow him to move in any way. He opened his mouth to speak, but although he was aware of his jaw moving, there was no sound issuing forth. His vocal cords, like everything else, were paralyzed.

'Come now, my dear Doctor—you didn't think that I would allow you the luxury of speech to rant at me and shout over what I have to tell you, did you?' Odyssey

purred, with an infuriating self-satisfaction. He had to
be watching Doc and to have seen his jaw move use-
lessly. The Atlantean continued. 'Please, I know you are
now awake, and as aware as you will ever be. Do not
delay the inevitable or attempt to play games with me.
Open your eyes, for sight is all you have now.'

Although he wanted to know what was going on, it
galled Doc to open his eyes then, as it would be taken by
Odyssey as a sign of obedience. Nonetheless, he felt
compelled to see what trouble they had got themselves
into.

Doc opened his eyes, blinking at the light. He was
able to move his eyes, if not his skull, and so could take
in much of the chamber in which he and Krysty now
found themselves. It was a stone room much like the
others, except that it was decorated in colors other than
the red, white and black he had come to expect. On the
walls were hangings in crimson, purple and a rich, deep
blue. They were embroidered with scenes of Tantric sex
magic and human sacrifice. Other hangings in greens
and yellows depicted the cycle of nature and showed old
Pagan gods.

Something for everyone, and an indication of the
haphazard way in which the founders of this ville had
cobbled together their philosophies.

More importantly, Odyssey was in Doc's eyeline,
standing in front of a stone slab. There was someone laying on it, and from the flash of Titian hair at one end, he
could tell that it was Krysty. She was as immobile as himself, and he guessed that whatever had been done to him
had also been inflicted on her. She was covered with a
long white tunic similar to the ones worn by the women
of Memphis, and she wasn't bound in any manner.

Odyssey watched as Doc's eyes flickered around the chamber, taking in the hangings, the slab and its occupant. A smile played around his mouth.

'This is what I wanted you to see,' he said simply. 'It reveals the inner truth of our society, and I felt that you would be possibly the only man I have ever—or would ever—meet who would be able to understand the import of what this means.

'You have already seen the temple to the elders that houses so much of the material from which our history is made. That is the history that everyone in Atlantis is taught from their birth until their death. But it isn't all.

'Every society is built upon those things that are seen and known, and those that are hidden. The real secrets of power. I promised you that I would make you privy to these, and so I shall. For here is where the real truths lay. The lost continent of Atlantis endured—not just in those who were taken into the skies, and not just in those who stayed beneath the earth. Neither in their descendants who founded this ville. No, the lost continent endured in its ideas and thoughts, which informed the occult lore and philosophies of all humankind. Our home, and our people who shall be saved when those who have traveled arrive to take us onward with them, we are the end result of those ideas, and we encompass them all. We are the final result of humankind, the ones for whom everything that has come before has been nothing more than a rehearsal. Even this physical shell we inhabit is nothing more than a shabby anteroom to a glorious palace. That which is the place to which we shall go.

'None but my predecessors—and now you—have known that the ideas that our people are taught to reject are, in fact, a part of ourselves. They are simple, and wouldn't comprehend the totality of such things.'

Doc winced. It wasn't the first time that the notion of a people misunderstanding a totality had been put to him; and, like then, this was about keeping people in the dark to give the few power over them. Odyssey's braying lecture was beginning to irritate him, but as he was paralyzed, he had no choice but to keep listening.

'All things are as one. All knowledge and occult power is gathered within this place. The time of alignment is near, and to be sent one with the knowledge, and one with the power, is a sign that I am to be the Odyssey who will lead my people to the promised lands beyond the stars. The new vessel is almost complete, and the people will gather to be taken by the travelers, in their vessel of light. In order to boost our power, our signal to them that we are ready, I will send them a sign.'

If Doc had been able to speak, it wouldn't have mattered. He would have been rendered speechless by the realization of what was going on. The secrets that he had hoped—had put faith in and betrayed his companions for—were nothing more than a bunch of old occult superstitions and spurious gods, realized only on some tatty pieces of predark cloth and the ludicrous ideas that had been fed to this megalomaniac from birth. And if he wasn't wrong, then the madman proposed to sacrifice Krysty in some sort of absurd magic ceremony to hasten the mass slaughter of the people of Atlantis.

For this was the only thing Doc could make of his rambling speech. The population would assemble in a newly built temple and await annihilation from a energy beam that would vaporize them, and so take their souls rather than their corporeal form to another place. It was nothing less than another manifestation of the kind of absurd UFO cults that had claimed so many suicides in the years before skydark, but one that had lived on and festered rather than prospered in the ensuing decades.

It was for this that Doc had given away that which was most precious to him. For no man was an island, and in his madness he had tried to act like one: to be the sole savior of a people and of his own soul. Wandering through his mind not being able to pick out what was real and what was illusion because he was looking in all the time, rather than outward to those who were around him. His identity and meaning lay in their reaction to him as much as in himself.

And he had placed Krysty in this position through his own selfishness. If he could do anything to atone, he would. If he could move, he would have ripped Odyssey limb from limb, regardless of whatever wounds the Atlantean may inflict upon him. He would have done anything to save Krysty from what was about to happen to her, even at the expense of his own life. It was the least he could do. But the most he could in his current situation was nothing.

He listened helplessly while Odyssey continued.

'Your people, and those from Memphis, will soon be through the maze. They have no real chance against my Nightcrawlers, but I have a notion that it wouldn't be the first time that your compatriots have been in such a position and emerged triumphant. I cannot take chances. Not for my people. I do not have the right to take such a chance. I must begin the ceremony now.'

Odyssey lit cones of incense and began to chant in

a language that Doc recognized as a bastard mix of old Greek, Latin and English. He circled the altar, anointing Krysty with oils.

Chapter Eighteen

'Where did she go?'

Lemur's tone was questioning and fearful. His wife had seemingly vanished after taking flight. He, Jak and Mark had arrived at a dead end, after following the trail of yarn she had left in her flight. Jak had to hand it to her: she'd been a lot faster, and a lot less noisy than he would have reckoned, and it had been difficult to track her movements, especially as he had to keep the other two men in sight. Thankfully, she had inadvertently left this trail, which now seemed to vanish beneath the stone wall in front of them.

'She cannot simply have walked through a stone wall,' Mark said in a puzzled voice, placing his hands on the stone slab as though he would find it was less substantial than it seemed.

'Mebbe not.' Jak shrugged. 'Look like, though.' He joined Mark at the face of the slab, probing at the solid stone similarly to the sec chief. 'Must be mechanism, trigger open.'

'Just as there must have been to cut it off,' Mark mused. 'But would that have been this side, or on the other?'

'They move these?' Jak asked.

Lemur answered for them. 'That is what we told you, and that is how it is. To insure that the labyrinth has no set pattern, and so cannot be easily solved by those who enter, the walls are capable of realignments to change the pattern of the passages.'

'Lot words to say yes,' Jak mumbled.

Mark suppressed a grin, saying, 'Are you, perhaps, thinking that if the slabs are adjustable, there must be triggers to set them off from all sides?'

Jak looked at him. 'How else work all time?'

The two men set to searching across the surface of the slab and down the walls on each side. There was no need for further explanations, although Lemur, as he stood holding the flash on them, may have wished for one.

'Clean,' Jak said as they both finished. 'Mebbe step trigger?'

Mark assented. 'Not sure how we could miss that on the way through, but—'

Jak shook his head. 'Only work once from side when down, but if can find it, then can lever up, reverse action...mebbe.'

'But what if—'

'No point what-if,' Jak warned the sec chief, indicating the watching Lemur.

Mark knew that he was right and could have bitten his tongue for speaking without thought. If the wall was part of a trap, then there was no telling if Cyran was alive on the far side. It wasn't something that they wanted the Memphis leader to consider.

The two men sank to their knees, indicating that Lemur train the beam on the hard-packed and stony soil surface. Backing up, covering every inch of the ground with painstaking care, they had backtracked by five feet before Mark held up a hand.

'Jak, I think I've found it.'

The albino youth crawled over to where Mark was smoothing the dirt covering from what seemed, at first glance, to be nothing more than a patch of bare ground. However, as he took a closer look, he could see the outline of a hexagonal shape imprinted in the dirt. Faint lines appeared where the finer particles of dust fell down the slight gap between the step trigger and the surrounding earth.

'That's it, all right,' Mark whispered, 'but how are we supposed to release it?'

'Pressure make drop, so pressure bring back up,' Jak said simply, palming one of his leaf-bladed knives so smoothly that Mark was taken aback by the glint of the blade suddenly appearing in Jak's fist. Without further comment, the albino youth slid the blade down the slight gap and began to work at the step and the earth around. If he could just loosen it enough to gain some purchase on the buried sides of the step, then he may be able to lever it up.

It was a slow process—too slow for his liking, but he had little option but to continue. To leave Cyran behind, or to trust to her finding her own way out by blind luck, was something that couldn't be contemplated. So he continued to work at the soil, wearing it away so that he could lever the blade down, try to make it bite into the stone of the step, perhaps even underneath, and lever it up.

Jak cursed suddenly and jumped back in surprise as the mechanism gave and his knife slipped. The blade flew up as though from a spring, the tension released as the stone step parted company with the mechanism beneath, spinning out of its hole and across the ground.

The albino beckoned Lemur to bring the flash closer, and as the beam spread down into the gap in the ground, he was able to see the locked spring mechanism. The stone step had been a covering, and had been easier to pry loose that he thought. But it still hadn't released the mechanism. At least now he could actually see what was going on down there: the trigger locked into a wheel-and-cog system that drove the slab pivots. For all these mechanisms to work however the walls were arranged, the dead soil had to be littered with a tiny tunnel system.

No matter now. He could see how it worked, and the gap left by the broken step was large enough for him to get his hand down. Squeezing in up to the wrist, his supple fingers were soon able to release the spring. He cursed again as the mechanism cut his hand on release, but he was rewarded for this by the sound of the slab beginning to move.

Quickly starting to bind his hand, he rose to his feet to join Lemur and Mark, and was greeted by the sight of Cyran, huddled against another dead end, ten yards in front of them, the ball of yarn at her feet.

Jak furrowed his brow. There appeared to be no trap in the boxed enclosure. Mebbe the space was so small that the intent was to leave the trespasser to slowly suffocate as they used all the air? That seemed to be too subtle, not bloodthirsty enough. It seemed that Odyssey liked to make certain of a chill.

None of these thoughts went through Lemur's mind. He was just overjoyed to see his wife again. With a cry of joy he pushed past Jak and Mark, running toward where she hunkered down.

No, there had to be another trap, Jak was sure of it.

And it had to be darts or a blade. Without a thought he set off after the Memphis chief, knowing that whatever happened he would have just fractions of a second in which to make a difference.

Lemur ran flat-footed, slowly. It was easy for Jak to gain on him, to be on his heels, to catch just a sense of something wrong. It was a dull click, perhaps; a footfall that looked awkward, mebbe. Whatever it was, it told Jak that the Memphis chief had inadvertently triggered a trap of some kind. To try to pull him back would have meant altering balance for both of them, wasting precious time. There was only one course of action. Jak sprang off his toes, launching himself into the small of Lemur's back, powering the man forward and down, momentum lifting them both from the ground before they thudded down again.

Jak had been right about the trap. Darts flew out of concealed holes in the slab to their right, an expellation of air like a sigh signaling their release. As Jak's flight carried himself and Lemur past the flight of the weapons, it was a matter of the time it took to take one breath that prevented the albino taking the full force of the darts in his body. As it was, two of them plucked at his heavy combat boots as his feet passed their path, the sharpened points embedding themselves in the heel and sole of his left boot, the force of their impact knocking his legs to one side so that he landed awkwardly, feeling his ribs jar, his elbows and skull cannon against the man underneath him. The impact made his head reverberate, cutting out the sound of the darts clattering against the far wall before falling harmlessly to the ground.

Mark rushed up to them, saying something that Jak

couldn't quite take in as he shook his head to clear it. Then it dawned on him that the sec chief was thanking him for saving Lemur.

'Okay, okay, cut crap and move,' Jak said dismissively, waving the sec chief away as he climbed unsteadily to his feet , then pausing to pull the darts from his boot. As he did, he watched the others. Mark was making a great play of seeing if his leader was all right. As he should. Lemur, for his part, was a little dazed, but his relief at seeing his wife alive took away all thoughts of his own brush with danger.

Cyran was the hardest to understand. Perhaps it was the shock, but she seemed distant from everything, as though she couldn't understand what had happened. She seemed oblivious to almost everything going on around her, and almost dismissive of her husband's release. Instead, she merely looked disoriented.

Mebbe it was just shock; even so, Jak couldn't work out how, short of blind luck, she had managed to avoid triggering the trap.

It was something that nagged at the back of his brain, tugging insistently. Like why she had just taken flight. He shook his head. There was no time to worry about that now. They had lost valuable time and ground. It was imperative they start trying to get out of this labyrinth; try to rendezvous with the others. That was assuming, of course, that anyone else managed to get out of here alive.

STRATEGY. THAT WAS THE KEY. If any of the four teams were to make it through the labyrinth, let alone all of them, then there had to be a plan. Mildred's idea of using the yarn to mark their path had been simple. Those who were forging a clear path could mark for those that came after. And if you should take a wrong turn and need to backtrack, the yarn would enable you to retrace your steps without risking the possibility of taking another wrong turn upon another, compounding your confusion.

For confusion was one of the most powerful weapons the labyrinth had in its armory. There may have been weapons, traps and wild animals lying in wait for those who tried to get through, but the worst thing of all would be to wander endlessly, unable to find a way that led to the outside world, until you either bought the farm from exhaustion, or you were so disoriented that you blundered into traps for which you were initially alert.

The truth was that no one in Memphis had been able to even tell the companions if there was only the one entrance and exit to the maze. The way in from the inside was similar in every description, yet it seemed that different escapees had approached the maze from different sectors of the ville. As for exits, the only thing that could be agreed upon was that there was only one exit in the wall. When questioned further, those who offered an opinion couldn't say for sure whether they had emerged into the same sector of woodlands as their fellows.

With no time to recce the area, Ryan and J.B. had thought it best to assume that there may be an entrance and exit built into each of the four sides of the maze. This would give the planners of the maze a much greater option in rebuilding and realigning the interior. If they so wished, they could leave only one, or all four, or any combination in-between, open.

If this was the case, then the four teams wanted to insure, as much as possible, that they would be able to make their way through the labyrinth and emerge together at the same spot. To be split up and break surface at different areas would be disastrous.

This was another reason for the use of the yarn. It was perhaps too simple: easy to break the line, to get it tangled or confused. But short of time and short of inspiration, it was the best they could do. If they all followed each other's trails, then wherever they ended up, at least it would be in the same place, and they could take the mission from there.

Strategy: so simple to plan, so simple to discuss when you were standing around a table. It was, however, something that was far from simple when you were in the middle of a dark, fetid pesthole, unsure as to which way was forward and which was back, not knowing which was left or right in relation to your intended destination, and where the other groups had reached.

The truth of the matter was that now they were in the labyrinth, it was proving harder than any had imagined to follow the trails of yarn, to keep at least a semblance of contact with each other. The yarns knotted, got pulled tight and broken; they were dropped, kicked to one side where flash beams couldn't catch them under layers of freshly turned dirt; sometimes they went off into conflicting passages where the latter had occurred and the sec team had mistakenly taken the wrong route.

It had reached a point where all four teams were now acting almost independently of one another. And yet, in some sense, the system had worked well enough to keep them on track. J.B.'s innate sense of direction and Jak's ability to sniff out danger and direction like a hunting dog had enabled these two teams to keep on track, despite the delay engendered by Cyran bolting from her fellows. Mildred had been careful to insure that Mithos had payed out his line with care, so that even if they lost the trail of the others, they wouldn't double back on themselves. And Ryan had used a sense of direction mixed with the care to insure his line was laid to keep his own track sound.

They were moving toward their target. What would be beyond the exit was one thing: what was certain was that they would be able to tackle it as a whole unit.

J.B. SNIFFED THE AIR experimentally.

'Dark night, I think we're almost at the end,' he said softly.

'I can but hope,' Demis said, at his elbow. 'I know I, for one, will be glad to escape this hellhole, but that will be nothing compared to the relief of our fellows. Too much longer in here and I fear that their nerves will crack.'

J.B. looked back over his shoulder at the two young sec men who comprised the other half of the team. They were following on his heels, assiduously sticking to their task with care. But it was easy to see, even in the dulled and refracted beam of the flash that Demis was now carrying in front of them and playing on the walls, that their faces were taut with tension, grim lines etched on faces that were far too young to show such concern.

All the more reason to reach the open: J.B. pressed ahead to the next junction. Even before he reached it, he knew the adjacent passage to theirs led to the outside. Some ambient light bled through and onto the soil in front of the gaping maw. The air was fresher and carried the hint of a breeze.

'Okay, we're nearly there,' he said, turning to the men at his rear. 'Triple red. I know you want out of here more than I do, but we need to recce to see what's on the outside.'

The two sec men nodded, their set expressions unchanging.

'Want me to take a look?' Demis asked the Armorer.

J.B. shook his head. 'Should be me. I'm head of this unit, and one of the privileges of that is getting to take all the risk.'

Demis's mouth quirked into a wry grin. 'The responsibility of leadership, eh? Sometimes it's just as well to be a humble foot soldier.'

'Tell me about it,' J.B. replied, indicating that the party should halt. 'Looks like we're the first to get here. Let's hope we're not the only ones. Meantime, I'm going to risk a look around the entry. Stay here.'

The Armorer shrugged the mini-Uzi from his shoulder and set it to fire short bursts. It would enable him to cover himself should he be fired on, but he hoped that wouldn't be the case. The last thing they needed was to get this far and then be pinned down at their only point of exit…short of finding another way around the labyrinth.

J.B. edged toward the corner of the exit passage. He knew that there would be a stretch of dead earth between the portal and the first buildings of Atlantis. No-man's-land. Would he be able to see anything across the distance? He was sure that there would be Nightcrawler teams posted opposite any exit, waiting for them. A lone face in an exposed portal would be easy meat. The problem was how to recce the outside without alerting any observers of his presence.

He reached the point of no return. Still in shadow, he could see the opposite wall of the exit tunnel. Angling his head, it became clear that the tunnel was about ten yards long, ending in a stone portal much the same as the one through which they had entered the labyrinth.

J.B. decided a little experiment would be in order. Taking the fedora from his head, and giving it a little wistful look before acting, he threw it into the open passage. He was half expecting a barrage of blasterfire to greet its appearance.

There was nothing. That could mean that whoever was mounting guard had a steady nerve and wouldn't fire on impulse or it could mean that the entrance wasn't as closely watched as he thought.

In truth, it told him nothing. It did, though, give him the incentive and reinforce his resolve to step out and recce.

As he edged around the corner, feeling the sweat stream down his brow and dapple his chest and back, sticking his shirt to him, he was aware of the pulse pounding in his throat—suddenly dry, as opposed to his now slick skin—and thumping in his chest; it felt as though his heart would break through his rib cage before he had a chance to recce.

Psyched-up and ready for just about anything they could throw at him, J.B. stepped into the light, the mini-Uzi in front of him, ready to lay down covering fire. Ahead of him, the corridor seemed to stretch for miles instead of the few yards that it was in actuality. Every step seemed to take him backward, partly because he perceived no progress, and partly because he was perpetually ready to throw himself toward the dark passages to his rear.

Yet nothing happened. As he got closer to the portal leading out into the wasteland, the angle of his view increased to take in a greater section of the ville in front of him.

Eventually, he stood in the portal, to one side, shoulder resting against the right-hand wall, the blaster still poised, but his vision taken up by the oddity that lay beyond.

If the companions had considered the haphazard design of Memphis bizarre, then the layout of Atlantis was beyond this. It was like nothing the Armorer had ever seen before, and for a second he was transfixed. For Atlantis took the strangest parts of Memphis and discarded those elements that had been familiar to the outsiders.

All traces of the suburban ruins that had been woven between the newer constructions of Memphis had been eradicated from this area, and it was only those strange erections that remained. Presumably because the ville had been founded, and initial work commenced, before skydark the ground in this area had been raised of all previous building to start from a level field. There was no wall past the patch of poisoned earth, only the straight lines of roads that weren't paved, sidewalks that had no curbs and buildings that were constructed of bleached stone and brick, with squat designs that were square or rhomboid, roofs and porticoes supported by immaculately carved pillars.

It looked like a model of Ancient Greece, though to the Armorer it just looked strange. There were only two buildings that climbed above a two-story level, and both appeared to be situated in the center of the ville. One was five storys and looked to have been extant for as long as the rest of the ville. The other was much taller, and was still under construction. Flimsy scaffolding circled it, and workers milled like insects over the face of the building. Closer to the maze and parched earth surround, Atlanteans dressed in red, black and predominantly white went about their business, sparing not a thought or glance for the maze and the opening in which J.B. stood surveying them.

It crossed his mind that those who were content to live under Odyssey's regime, or who were too scared to risk making a break, were so secure in the impenetrability of the labyrinth that it had never occurred to them that they might be watched from its entrances. At the same time, the fact that they were blithely going about their business suggested that they were unaware of an attack being mounted.

J.B.'s mind raced, weighing up possibilities. Could it be that none of the Nightcrawlers had reached Atlantis and reported to Odyssey? He found that impossible. Nonetheless, there had been no sec to pick him off as soon as he appeared, and it seemed as though the populace had been unaware of any imminent arrivals. Could it also be that Odyssey was so confident in the impregnability of his maze that he was unconcerned about any of the attacking party making it through?

J.B. allowed himself an indulgent grin; now that really was a stupe thought. Best option as far as he could see it was this: the Crawlers had reported back, but they had no idea of the real size of the Memphis force. It may have been just the party they encountered, or it may have been a vanguard. In which case, Atlantis needed to be on an all-out war footing. Looking at the people going about their business unaware of him, he had to say that it didn't look too much like a war footing to him. It was all second guessing, but he would assume that the Nightcrawlers were on full guard, waiting to move as soon as any offensive was taken, meanwhile keeping a low profile so as not to concern the general populace. Certainly, everyone was busy, and it didn't look as though Odyssey was about to let them stop.

J.B. wasn't to know that Odyssey would never commit a full populace to battle while the vessel was still under construction; not with the alignment so close. But even without this knowledge, it was a more that reasonable assessment.

The Armorer couldn't tell for sure whether or not he'd been seen; all he knew for certain was that no cold-heart had attempted to chill him. But it was a fair bet that they could, if they were triple careful, get across the wasteland and into the body of the ville before the fighting would start. And he knew enough about his own people to know that this would put them on a level field of battle, no matter the size of the force they may face.

J.B. edged back into the shadows, feeling a little more assured than when he had started out.

Attaining his previous position, he was more than pleased to see Ryan and Mildred's sec crews waiting for his return.

'What took you so long?' he asked dryly.

'You know what it's like,' Mildred replied, 'you think you know your way, and then it turns out that you've made a left instead of a right...'

A brief exchange between the three companions established that they had managed to find their way to this spot despite each other's trail's petering out along the way. The fact that they had made it here independently suggested that there may, indeed, be only one way in and out of the labyrinth.

'That's the case, then all the Crawlers are going to be concentrated on this area, right?' Mildred asked the Armorer.

J.B. scratched his head and placed the fedora—retrieved on his retreat—on the back of his skull before outlining the seemingly unaware landscape he had surveyed. When he had finished, Ryan whistled.

'Fireblast, never come up against someone like this Odyssey before. What the fuck are his tactics? Can't plan against someone you can't fathom…'

'Makes it all the more dangerous for us, right?' Demis questioned.

J.B. nodded. 'It's hard to prepare a defense when you can't figure out their attack options.'

'Well,' the sec man said slowly, 'instead of trying to do that, why don't you ask us what's going on?'

J.B. looked at him blankly for a second, before a slow grin spread across his face. 'What a stupe. I'm sorry, I should have realized…' He gave a short laugh, turning to Ryan. 'Demis, here, is an escapee from Atlantis. Unlike some of our sec, he knows the ville. I'm going for another recce, take him with me.'

Ryan agreed. 'Good idea. If it gives us some kind of insight…'

So while the rest of the war party waited, the two men edged toward the exit passage once more. There was still a need for caution, but J.B. was able to make quicker progress this time, and as the two men stood as much in shadow as possible and surveyed the vista in front of them, Demis explained the significance of the building work and the timing involved.

'Let's get back. I think you need to tell everyone this,' J.B. commented, pulling them back to the safety of the labyrinth.

Once back, Demis repeated his story to the assembled party. Ryan assimilated the information into the strategy forming in his mind.

'That's good,' he said when Demis had finished, clapping the Memphis man on the back. 'You have no idea how helpful that's been.' He turned to the assembled party. 'We leave here the same way that we entered. In clusters, my group moving first and establishing a safe position. We then cover the next group. Once we're in, we move towards Odyssey's temple—shit, it's not hard to find, right?—and we recce then attack.

'That's our position. Against us is the fact that the Crawlers will be all over the ville, and they'll be waiting for us. Those of you who know the layout of Atlantis will lead us to the temple, and also tell us where we should recce for ambush or hidden traps.

'What we've got going for us is that most Atlanteans don't know how to fight, and in all probability will bolt. Even those that stand—no matter what we may think of them as an oppressed people—have to be fought. Mebbe we'll have to chill a few to help free the many. Hell, if they've got any sense they'll leave it to the Crawlers, and it'll be a pleasure to chill those cold-hearted bastards.

'With a little luck on our side, we should be able to reach the temple without too much of a firefight. Remember we have blasters, and we know how to use them. They use blades, and will want close combat.

This makes it more likely they'll try to ambush. Shoot on sight, people. It's possible that they'll hold back a little as they don't know if we're the advance party or the whole deal. Let's hope they do…but don't expect it.

'Okay,' he finished with a mirthless grin. 'Let's do this.'

'What about Jak?' Mildred asked as Ryan turned to leave. 'He's got Lemur and Cyran. What about them?'

Her question stirred up some response from the Memphis sec, who had been wondering something similar. To go into battle without their leader, to leave him behind it was unthinkable.

When Ryan turned back to answer, she could see it had weighed heavily on him. For a fraction of a second, as he began to answer, it seemed that his shoulders slumped.

'We can't go back to look for them. That's taking too big a risk that we get lost ourselves. We've made it this far, and Jak's party entered before mine. There's nothing else we can assume other than they just haven't…that something's happened.' He couldn't bring himself to suggest that they had bought the farm, and this realization momentarily cast a pall over the gathered fighters. Ryan sighed, gathered himself up. 'Fuck these assholes and their stupe games. Let's go get this idiot Odyssey before he fucks over any more people.'

It was hard for J.B., Mildred and Ryan to dismiss the notion that they may never see Jak again; equally so for the Memphis sec to think the same of their leader and his wife. But the hard kernel of anger that it left in their gut was something to spur them on.

Ryan could feel this as he and his party made their way to the portal. Little did he know that it was an anger that would prove unnecessary.

Chapter Nineteen

'We must hurry. They may think us deceased in the labyrinth,' Mark muttered to Jak as the albino led his party through the maze. Jak shot the sec chief a withering glance. Mark held up his hands. 'I know, I know. I shouldn't have said it. It is stating the blindingly obvious, but…'

'We have no way of knowing if any of the others have made it through,' Cyran blurted. There was an edge of panic to her voice that had been with her since they had recovered her from the trap. 'They may all have perished.'

Jak looked at her, his red orbs piercing in the gloom. 'They okay. Would know, feel.'

He didn't have to finish. There was something in his tone that would brook no argument. Cyran looked away, seemingly ashamed to have even suggested such a thing.

They reached another junction. Jak halted and gestured for them to be still. In the ensuing quiet he listened for even the slightest sound that could give them a clue. They had lost track of all other trails, and even their own had become obliterated in the effort to recover Cyran after her flight. They were filthy, exhausted and at least two of them were terrified. The leader and his wife were proving to be the liability Jak had suspected—he was slow and out of condition, and she was seemingly a hysteric—while Mark seemed to be on edge. Jak could smell the tension coming off him. He knew that the Memphis sec chief was no coward, but wondered if the added burden of having to baby-sit Lemur and Cyran was proving too much.

One thing for sure: if they were to keep it together, then Jak had to get them out of here, and triple fast.

Jak strained every sense. If ever he had needed to call on his years of hunting—human or animal prey—then it was now. The scent of a charnel house hung so heavily over the maze that it was difficult to pick out anything else. He couldn't pick out his friends' individual scents, not at such a distance, but he could tell the warm musk of human scent from that of a wild beast, and he knew that they were still in the game. There were enough of them to make a sizable olfactory dent in the stench of the labyrinth, and if he could just match their musk with the direction in which the air drifted...

Then he could ally this to the sounds he faintly registered above the distant howls of hungry wild beasts. Human sounds. Faint fragments of discussion, the padding of footfalls, the sound of a body of men gathered, ready to move.

Jak was sure that the other three parties had found one another and, that being the case, had also found the way out of this pesthole. Now that he had found direction, it was just a matter of guiding his party there without falling prey to any traps; there would be no dead ends, not now he could follow scent and direction.

He turned back to his party with a rare grin breaking across his usually somber white visage. 'This way... quick,' was all he needed to say.

He led the party in the direction indicated, a fresh sense of purpose to their actions.

RYAN CAWDOR HEADED for the squat, white stone building that stood at a thirty-degree angle from the exit portal. It was closest in terms of distance and seemingly empty. Certainly, the people that moved around the streets of Atlantis were farther into the built-up area, and less likely to register bodies in the otherwise-deserted area of parched earth if they were headed away from them.

Despite this, it was a nerve-shredding and naked run across the flat ground, the Steyr held across his chest as he ran, keeping low. He was half expecting a Nightcrawler to step from nowhere and engage with him. Okay, so he was being covered from the portal; that wouldn't matter if J.B. couldn't get a clear shot. And even if he did, blasterfire would let loose all hell.

Ryan's breath escaped from him in a gasp of relief as he made cover without being fired upon or attacked in any way. His orders to the next runner were to wait until he signaled. Unlike their entry to the maze, where they knew there was no opposition to immediately attack, on the exit run he wanted to check the chosen building for signs of life before risking the life of a fellow soldier.

Checking the Steyr, Ryan counted five to psyche himself before checking out the building. The wall he had thrown himself against had no window and the side to his left was a porch supported by pillars. Two windows and a doorway broke the length. Swiftly and efficiently, as he had so often with buildings of different style but similar layout, Ryan checked for occupancy.

A quick glance to see if anyone was passing, and he was into the building, checking the rooms.

They were in luck. There had been no one near the building as it was currently unoccupied, the rooms bereft of furnishing. Swiftly, he passed through every room, confirming its safehouse status. Within a minute he was out again, signaling for the next member of his party to make the run.

The evacuation from the labyrinth proceeded at pace, with each successive runner entering the deserted building while Ryan maintained cover. The fact that no Nightcrawlers seemed to be waiting for them, or had as yet made themselves known, played on his mind.

What were their tactics? Were they waiting to see how many emerged? Would they then attack the safehouse? On this assumption, Ryan had detailed the arriving sec to mount guard within. If they were to wait until the entire party headed for the temple, how then would they attack? Despite the fact that he had laid out a simple plan of action when in the labyrinth, Ryan was still wondering if there were any angles he had missed, something that would surprise his troops, endangering them.

However, the surprise coming his way would be most unexpected.

'JAK, WHERE THE HELL have you been?' J.B. yelled exultantly as the albino youth appeared at his shoulder. 'No—no time to explain now. Listen…' With which the Armorer filled in Jak's group on Ryan's plan. Jak and Mark stood and listened intently, but Demis, standing to one side, waiting for his chance to make the run to Atlantis, couldn't help but notice the contrasting attitudes of Lemur and Cyran.

To the Memphis sec man, who took the time to watch them carefully despite the controlled chaos going on around him, it appeared that his leader was distracted and nervous, whereas his wife seemed detached, almost as though she weren't really here, and would any minute awake from a nightmare.

He figured to himself that he should mention that to J.B., see if it was worth bringing up with Ryan, when something happened that shocked him and made him reassess what he had just seen.

Cyran had appeared to be diffident all the while that J.B. and Jak were conversing. She was standing a little apart from the group, and wasn't noticed. But when Jak turned to ask if Lemur and Cyran had taken in all that had just been said, her demeanor changed. In the blinking of an eye, her manner became suddenly cowed and nervous, so that she resembled a shrinking baby animal. When she answered Jak's request, it even seemed as though her voice trembled with the rest of her.

Demis didn't know what to make of this sudden change in manner. Was it another manifestation of her fear? Or was she, for some reason he couldn't fathom, playing a part? If so, why?

He would definitely have to raise her behavior with the hardened fighters. Something was very wrong, and the fact that he couldn't put his finger on the exact reason was all the more worrying. But he wouldn't be able to do that right now. While he had been watching Cyran with growing unease, the evacuation had been progressing and there was now only himself, J.B. and the newly acquired sec group left to make the run.

As Demis made his way swiftly across the open space, his mind raced faster than his feet. He had to speak to Ryan or J.B., but what exactly could he tell them—that he had seen Cyran act in a strange way that unnerved him in a manner he could not define? It would be hard to know where to start.

Wherever it may be, it wouldn't be at that point where he arrived at the white stone building.

'Ryan, I have something to tell you,' he began breathlessly, only to be cut short by the one-eyed man, whose face was split by a broad grin, staring over the sec man's shoulder.

'I know, I can see,' he said, relief and exultation in his voice as it had been in J.B.'s. He added, 'Get in cover man, hurry.'

Demis looked over his shoulder as he turned the corner of the building. Ryan's delight had been caused by the sight of Jak making his run from the maze. The moment to mention Cyran's bizarre behaviour had passed, yet he had to make sure it came around again. And soon.

BUT TIME WAS SLIPPING away from the anxious sec man. Now that they were in the ville, things were to move at a faster pace.

J.B. was last man to make the run, and as soon as he was clear, Ryan followed him into the house, where he found that Mildred was jubilant at the return of Jak, while the Memphis people had similar emotions over the appearance of the leader they thought lost. Realizing that there was no time for this, Ryan called them to order and reiterated his plan, for the benefit of Jak's party and also to focus the minds of the others. He didn't notice the sec man who lurked at the back, seemingly apprehensive and searching for the right moment to raise his voice.

Even if he had, Ryan would have assumed it was nothing more than a case of combat fright, and tried to talk him up rather than listen. So they left the deserted building on the edge of Atlantis with Demis's fears and concerns unspoken. There were more pressing matters, or so it seemed.

Even though they were now in the streets of a ville, rather than the woodlands, they adopted a similar formation. Once more they clustered into their original groups, stringing out into a line of clusters, with Ryan at the head and J.B. at the rear. This way they could keep some distance between the groupings to make firing on them harder, and within the clusters they could once more shelter the weaker fighters.

It was now a strange kind of combat. Mildred had once, in history classes when she was at high school, heard the phrase "phony war." It had been applied to the beginning of the Second World War, when Britain had declared war on Nazi Germany, and long before the U.S.A. became involved. She remembered that she had been taught that there had been a period of several months in which, although both sides were at war, there had been hardly any activity. Both sides had been waiting for the other to make a move, with the emphasis being—in a sense—on which side would crack first. A war of nerves.

That was exactly what this march felt like. They were making progress through the ville, toward their intended target. But there was no opposition, or so it seemed. There was, however, a growing sense of tension and dread that an attack would come at any moment. A tension so great that it could cause some of the fighters to snap, making them easy to mop up. Hell, she could feel it herself; like a watch wound so tight that the mechanism was about to break. And she was used to this kind of action. How, then, were the less experienced Memphis sec feeling?

The streets of Atlantis were virtually deserted. True, many seemed to be working on the new building, swarming like ants on the scaffolding as the time of alignment drew nearer. Yet even so, there should have been more people going about their daily business. Those few that they did encounter were of no threat. From a distance, it was almost as though they had wandered into the line of the Memphis party by mistake or accident, as though they weren't supposed to be there. One look—fear crossing their faces, writ large even at such a distance—and they would scuttle for cover before there was any opportunity to engage.

It was as if they had been told to stay clear of the area, to keep out of the path of the oncoming force.

Of course: Ryan realized what was occurring. The Nightcrawlers were assessing the size of the force they were up against. They had cleared the path they knew the enemy would take, after all, there was only one direct route to Odyssey's temple, and the Crawlers knew that the Memphis sec would direct them thus. Now they were observing, taking note of size and potential.

For the one-eyed man, the fog of indecision and the taut air of tension that had weighed them down was now lifted. As they moved nearer to the center of the ville, and the twin constructions that dominated the skyline, he knew that the point of contact would have to come soon. There was no way that the Nightcrawlers could allow them to enter the midsection of the ville, where there would be, of necessity, a dense population.

'Heads up, people,' he yelled, 'we're getting near the center. They can't keep us isolated any longer. Incoming!'

A self-fulfilling prophecy. Although the point of contact would have to come soon, Ryan was calling them out by declaring that their tactics had been rumbled. At the same time, it enabled him to break the tension with his own people and snap them into combat mode.

Not a moment too soon.

Silently, and without seeming to come from anywhere, the first of the Crawlers appeared on the road in front of them, as though assembling from the very air. With their darkly painted bodies and their black lenses, they appeared as demons of legend rather than flesh-and-blood fighters. An impression that was emphasized when Ryan drew his SIG-Sauer and directed a 2-round blast at one of them that seemed to go right through the Crawler without affecting him.

For a second, the one-eyed warrior was dumbfounded, reactions dulled enough by the shock to allow a Crawler to close on him. It was only as one man descended on him with a blade and the Crawler he had fired on seemed to dissolve back into the air in the manner he had arrived that Ryan realized what was happening.

The Nightcrawlers had appeared from the air and seemed to be phantoms, for the simple reason that they had the powers of hypnotism to which his people had fallen prey back in Memphis. The ability to cloud minds and distort the truth had enabled them to seemingly appear from nowhere and to cast living shadows of themselves to distract fire.

Ryan now realized that blasters would be useless.

Chances were that they would be firing at phantoms. If any chilling was to be done, it would have to be hand-to-hand.

The Crawler leaped at him. From previous combat, Ryan knew that their body camou made them oily and slick to grapple with. Rather than engage, he side-stepped and chopped at the man, using an outstretched foot to take away the Crawler's leading foot. The enemy's own momentum, aided by the blow at the back of his neck, carried him forward and down onto the dirt road, allowing Ryan enough time to smoothly holster the SIG-Sauer and unsheathe the panga, in almost one flowing motion. By the time the Crawler had rolled with his fall and come back up to his feet, Ryan was the one advancing on him.

A thrust and a parry erupted from the Crawler, followed by an open-fist blow that was intended to hit Ryan on the temple, stunning him momentarily and making him easier to finish. But the one-eyed man was too quick, and before the blow even had a chance to land he had slipped inside the Crawler's defense and delivered a savage blow with the panga to his opponent's open chest. The blade slipped between two ribs, and Ryan felt the suction as he tried to extract the blade, twisting both to aid extraction and to cause more damage. It was strange to see the man's face contort in pain while his lens-shielded eyes remained blank. Almost as though he truly were as supernatural as the Crawlers's sudden appearance had suggested.

Nothing was supernatural, however, about the manner in which he slumped to the ground when Ryan had freed him of the panga's deadly support.

One man down, but all around him was the clamor

of battle. No tension now, all was in earnest. And not just in the manner that Ryan would have expected.

Mildred appeared to be fighting thin air, throwing and closing on an opponent that wasn't there, at the same time leaving herself open to an attack from a female Crawler who was approaching her from behind. Ryan didn't even have the time to wonder what the hell she was doing. He had to act fast. In a few strides he was on the Crawler, hauling her back by the throat. Mildred was still fighting a phantom, and it took him yelling her name to suddenly make her snap out of what she was doing and to realize that she was fighting thin air. She whirled and took out the attacker Ryan was holding, a jab over the heart stilling the woman, making her drop her blade; a blade Mildred snatched up and used to chill her.

She cast a quick glance back to the empty space she had just been fighting.

'It seemed so real,' she muttered.

'Fucking hypnotism—watch for it,' Ryan barked, aware as he spoke of how difficult was such a task. They both knew how easy it was to be deceived. How could you watch for something you may not even know was there?

But the Crawlers and their phantoms weren't the only problems that the war party faced. Mithos and another of the Memphis sec men in the group were attacking their own.

Mithos headed straight for Lemur. The bulky Memphis leader was slower than anyone else and was finding the combat difficult. He was ill-equipped to deal with such matters, and was proving the liability that Ryan had feared. As such, he stood transfixed as his own man closed on him.

'For the glory of Atlantis,' Mithos yelled as he raised a blade. Lemur was frozen: a simple target. More confusing for him yet when the young sec man's head dissolved into jelly, blood and splinters, spattering the leader and the surrounding area.

'Watch your back, man. I can't do everything,' Mark yelled at Lemur. 'Snap out of it.'

The Memphis leader's stunned gaze moved around to see his sec chief, Luger still raised, facing in his direction. He had been unable to defend himself, but his loyal sec chief had been there in the most dire moment.

At the expense of his own life. Lemur opened his mouth to warn Mark, but it was too late. In firing on Mithos, Mark had turned away from an approaching Crawler. He was about to get a knife in the back that would surely buy him the farm. Lemur fumbled with his blaster, torn between warning his protector and firing on the enemy. He could do neither. Mark screamed, high and keening, as the enemy blade ripped into his kidney.

Something hardened with the Memphis chief. Seeing the man who had saved his life be chilled because he couldn't return the favor focused Lemur: he might be too late to save Mark, but he could avenge him. He raised his Browning and fired two rapid shells that jerked the Crawler, hitting high in the chest each time and pulping the organs within.

'The gods blast you all,' Lemur muttered savagely, looking for another target, now strangely calm.

Not so far away, in the melee, Demis was engaged in a fight with a Crawler and a sec man he had thought of as a friend, but who had been a traitor in their midst. Despite the fact that he was outnumbered, he had prevented them inflicting anything other than the most superficial of wounds. But he hadn't the strength or skill to kill either of them, and he knew that he was only holding them at bay. To prevent his own death, he would need assistance.

So it was with relief that he felt rather than saw someone move in beside him to join the fight.

'Thank the gods for their mercy,' he gritted.

'You shall have your chance soon enough,' a familiar voice whispered in his ear. His eyes widened in shock as he felt the blade slip between his ribs and he turned to face his traitorous aggressor. 'You see too much. Time for your eyes to be dimmed,' the voice added as Demis slipped to the ground, life ebbing from him.

Meanwhile, Ryan was taking count as best he could. He could see that he would have to marshal his troops, and soon. Although all the companions were holding out well, there were two traitors who had turned on their own—one of whom had been chilled—and there were three others who had bought the farm. Even as he took stock, another Memphis sec man took a chilling blow from a Nightcrawler.

Bastard would pay for that. Ryan took him out with a shell from the SIG-Sauer. The Crawler's back dribbled red from the entry wound, his stomach spread by the wider exit wound, spilling his innards onto his still warm victim.

He would have to regroup his people right now or there wouldn't be any left to regroup.

'THEY ARE very strong fighters. It is a shame that they couldn't be persuaded to our cause,' the Crawler leader

said calmly. He was unmoved by the deaths of his own
people. The Nightcrawlers lived to die: that was part of
their task, to sacrifice their lives for the greater good.

'I agree. It is a shame that they will not be able to
join with us. I believe we could learn much from them,'
Xerxes mused, taking the telescope from his eye. The
two men were standing on the scaffolding around the
vessel, ignoring the work going on around them and
concentrating their attention on the battle below. A battle so small and localized that many in Atlantis did not
realize that it was as yet taking place.

The Crawler leader pondered his sec chief's words.
'True. We will have to kill them. They are not many, but
if even one should make it to Odyssey's temple…' the
Crawler leader shrugged '…he is alone with the other
two outsiders. All our men—'

'I know,' Xerxes said, cutting him short. 'What I
cannot understand is why so few. Unless the one with
a single orb believed that many of those in Memphis
would be killed without result, and it would be easier
to mount a small raid on one target.'

'Hence their direction,' the Crawler leader said flatly.

'Exactly. Strike at the heart of Atlantis…'

'While our other Nightcrawlers wait for an attack
that does not come. Sir, they must be—'

'I will decide what must be done,' Xerxes cut across
his words with a smile playing at the corners of his
mouth. 'And I think it is time that something was done
for the greater good of Atlantis. The time is near, and
we cannot be led by such a fool as this Odyssey. When
the travelers come, they don't want to see the bloated
idiocy that he has become. They want to see a ville
waiting for redemption.'

'Led by you?'

Xerxes shook his head. 'Led by no one. The fat fool has no heir. We must start again. I don't want the task, but we must find someone who is equal to it. And it starts now. We shall let them have what they want. It will do them little good. Pull back your men, let them attain the temple. Once they are inside, we have them—and Odyssey and their friends—at our mercy.'

'This is treason.' The Nightcrawler leader spoke in hushed tones, not wanting them to be overheard.

'Perhaps,' Xerxes agreed. 'But is that idiot satisfying his moronic interests with those two outlanders at the expense of his real work—the vessel—any the less treasonous?'

The Nightcrawler leader didn't answer.

'I suspected not. And there are many who will feel the same. We act, as always, for the greater good. Now go.'

He didn't look around. He knew that the Crawler had already departed. With a self-satisfied nod, Xerxes returned to watching the combat through the telescope.

THEY DIDN'T UNDERSTAND how it had happened. They only knew that it had. Where they had one moment been fighting a battle that they were slowly losing, despite their best efforts, now they were standing alone on the deserted street. The Nightcrawlers had vanished as mysteriously as they had arrived: one second a solid presence, the next a phantom that dissipated on the winds.

Ryan looked around and took stock. It wasn't good. As the Crawlers had departed, their parting shot had been to chill most of the Memphis sec left standing.

Now the contingent numbered only three: Lemur, Cyran and the youth Affinity. All the companions were left alive.

'Dark night, what was that about?' J.B. questioned.

Ryan shook his head. 'I don't know, but I don't like it. The bastards are playing games with us. Why have they left us alive when it would have been simple for them to keep fighting? They would have overwhelmed us in the end. And why us?'

'What do you mean?' Affinity asked.

'It's obvious, son,' Mildred said quietly. 'You, Lemur and Cyran. The only ones left out of your people. Leader and wife, sure. Not sure about you,' she added, eyeing him speculatively. 'But there's all of us. Like there was a reason to trim the fat, leave only those they wanted.'

'Fuck it, we'll be walking into a trap when we reach the temple,' Ryan gritted. 'For what purpose, who knows? But we can't turn back. Shit, hardly likely they'll let us...' he added with a mirthless grin.

'Then let's go,' Jak said simply. 'Sooner spring trap, sooner see hunter.'

Chapter Twenty

'Too bastard easy,' Ryan murmured as they entered the temple.

'Don't knock it, boss man,' Mildred answered in a voice that was harsh, stretched tight by tension and exertion. 'Least if we don't have to fight yet, we're saving it for when we do.'

The Nightcrawlers had done their job well. On being withdrawn by their commander, a team had been dispatched to the temple to spring the locks on all the heavy stone doors that lay between the Memphis war party and Odyssey. The Crawler leader had understood Xerxes clearly: the war party were to be the puppets who disposed of the Atlantean leader before being eradicated themselves by an avenging force. Trapped as they would be within the temple, this would be a simple task.

So it had to be insured that they would be able to reach Odyssey quickly. The coded red, white and black locks, although simple once you knew the key, would be alien to the intruders. It had taken the clever ones captured and held in the temple long enough to work them out. By contrast, these intruders were seen as the foot soldiers, the ones who fought, not thought. The Crawler leader sent his men through the temple, unlocking the doors as they went, bleeding out into the outside world without being noticed. Xerxes couldn't trust his regular sec for this task—they were loyal to Odyssey, as his personal guard, and wouldn't countenance such a move.

So it was that the war party—now consisting of just seven personnel—made their way into, and through, the temple, constantly expecting to come under attack, little realizing that they were being left alone for reasons that they couldn't know.

'Dark night, I hate places like these,' J.B. muttered as they progressed upward. 'Give me some kind of pesthole like the maze any day. At least you know where the hell you are with something like that.'

'There is some truth in what you say,' Affinity murmured in reply. 'Dangers are more real in a situation such as that.'

'Danger real everywhere,' Jak snapped. 'Shut up.'

There was an overall mood of darkness that pervaded their party. In some sense, it was possible that they had a instinct that they were now no longer the masters of their own destiny. Their aims had been definite, but now it seemed as though these aims were subsumed beneath those of someone who wielded greater power. They were being used, directed for some purpose that they couldn't define.

But there was little they could do but go with the current and hope that it would become clear as they proceeded farther into the temple.

'The place is deserted,' Mildred said, her voice strained after they had passed through yet another unlocked door. They had encountered empty chambers, each carefully recced and secured before proceeding, and were moving ever upward. It seemed as though it would not be too long before they came out at the summit of the temple, having found nothing.

'Are you sure that they wouldn't have evacuated, left it completely empty?' she asked Lemur.

But it was Affinity who answered. 'Odyssey rarely sets foot outside the temple. There is nowhere else that he would be, or where your friends would be held. Atlantis doesn't take prisoners. No, they are here, and so is he…but where are the guards?'

'They should be here. It is their duty to protect him,' Cyran said softly, an edge to her voice that made Lemur look at her strangely.

There was, however, no time for him to question her on this, as Jak stayed them with a gesture and a harshly whispered, 'Stop—someone in chamber.' He indicated the closed door about twenty feet away and to their left. At first it was hard to detect the sound, as the closed door was of thick stone, and it seemed that that silence stretched along the endless, torch-lit corridor, with nothing more than the fluttering of the tapestries in the through breeze to disturb the peace. But as they focused, they were able to pick out the slightest of sounds. It was the muted chanting of one man, rhythmic and with a keening edge.

'What the hell is he doing?' Mildred asked.

'More to the point, how come we can only hear one—where are Doc and Krysty?' J.B. asked.

Ryan's sole blue orb glittered hard as he spoke. 'Only one way to find out.' Without pause, he strode forward the few yards to the stone door and could see that the lock had been set in a pattern he had come to recognize. This door, too, was unlocked, so either Odyssey wanted them to enter, or someone else re-

quested the pleasure. Either way, Ryan was in no mood
to deny them.

The entire war party carried their handblasters—
apart from J.B., who as ever eschewed a smaller weapon
in favor of the mini-Uzi—and Ryan indicated that they
should be ready to use them. Mentally counting to three,
he took the door and then stopped dead. He found it
hard to believe what he could see in front of him. At his
back, the others, entering the room, also found themselves stunned to momentary inaction. They had been
expecting sec men, a firefight, the sound of one man to
conceal others in wait: the trap that they thought had
been laid for them.

Perhaps now they were beginning to realize that a
trap had been prepared, but it wasn't merely for them.

'Fireblast and fuck. What's going on?' Ryan asked
rhetorically—for it was plain to see what was occurring,
if not to understand why.

The sight that greeted them was one that, in any circumstances, would seem bizarre: Krysty, in a white
robe that was slashed open down to her waist, lay on a
slab. Her face was impassive, her eyes blank, and she
was silent. To one side, amid the hangings and decorations depicting ancient rituals, Doc was squatting, hunkered down. He was immobile and as silent as Krysty.

And overseeing the scene was the potbellied figure
of Odyssey, chanting a prayer to ancient gods as he pu-
rified an ornate, curved knife in a flame on the altar.
Clearly, Krysty was about to be sacrificed.

There was very little that could still the reflexes of
the companions. Endless combat situations had prepared them for most things. But this was something so
bizarre that they were all momentarily frozen in inac-

tion. It was the Memphis people who were the first to recover their wits.

'You defiler,' Lemur yelled angrily, brushing past Ryan and stepping up to the slab, pushing the Atlantean leader away from Krysty. Odyssey fell from the altar, crashing to the floor.

'You poltroon,' he yelled, suddenly coming out of the trance into which he had placed himself for the ceremony.

'Is it not enough that you have perverted and ruined the ideals on which this city was built?' Lemur rasped, striding around the slab so that he was standing over the prone Atlantean leader, his blaster a few feet away from the terrified Odyssey's face.

It occurred to Ryan that Odyssey was only following in a long line of fellow oppressors, but he thought it politic not to mention this to Lemur. The Memphis leader was angry and taking direct action. He had the Atlantean right where they wanted him. Still keeping his eye firmly on the scene in front of him, he indicated that J.B. and Mildred should attend to Krysty, while Jak saw to Doc.

Lemur continued, unnoticing. 'To build a vessel with which we are reunited with those who have gone before us, that is a noble aim. Not to treat those who should be reunited as though they were nothing more than disposable slaves.'

'It is for the greater good of the cause,' Odyssey yelled.

'This? This sacrifice?' Lemur shouted in reply. 'I recognize none of these things—' with which he waved his blaster around the chamber before bringing it back to rest on Odyssey '—with which you do little more than justify sating your own twisted beliefs. I should kill you now and end this, I—'

A shot rang out around the chamber, freezing everyone where they stood. It came from behind Ryan and he could almost feel the hot blast against the back of his head.

Lemur dropped his blaster and pitched forward, landing on Odyssey as the Atlanetan desperately struggled to escape the falling corpse. A head shot had spread the majority of the Memphis man's skull over an old pagan hanging of a green man in congress with a goat. The decoration seemed somehow appropriate.

But Ryan hardly noticed that. It had to be Affinity who fired the blast. Unless… In a sense, he was less than surprised when Cyran stepped past him, turning so that she had the rest of the chamber covered.

'Good, I thought you would never fire on that madman,' Odyssey said without the slightest trace of irony as he hauled himself to his feet and stood beside her, brushing himself off. 'And that will not be necessary,' he added in an offhand manner, gesturing to her blaster and then sweeping a gaze around the room.

Ryan realized what he was doing a fraction of a second too late. He could see J.B. had the same idea, as he stopped with the mini-Uzi half off his shoulder, where he had slung it while trying to help Mildred lift the prone Krysty from the slab. For his own part, Ryan had the SIG-Sauer half directed, but couldn't move muscles immobilized by one hypnotic glance. It had to be some kind of mutie in-bred ability handed down genetically to the leaders. There was no other explanation. Not that this thought was of any comfort right now.

'You realize that I could have been killed if you had

delayed any longer? No matter, you did as you had to in the end,' Odyssey purred. He looked over the frozen group. 'Not many of you, although I feel you must have done tremendously well to get this far. I shall have to have words with Xerxes, as there should have been a better guard to stop you intruding on my ceremony. I must admit, I am a little surprised to see my little Cyran here…' He turned to the woman and touched her cheek. She kept her eyes, and her blaster, firmly on the group and away from Odyssey.

He, on the other hand, now seemed to be back in control.

'A little conceit of mine, to have the wife of the opposition leader as my chief spy in the camp. She was mine before she was his, of course—that was the reason for her searching him out. And after all, even though they all knew there were spies, who would suspect the faithful wife, the one who seemed to be so against my regime. Convenient. She could send back reports and do my work. Memphis has long been a thorn in my side, and in truth they are so inept that it would be easy to crush them if I could be bothered to devote the manpower to such a task. But the time it would take, and men better employed on the vessel. The time of alignment was too close, and I needed to keep them occupied with their own follies.

'But you had to come along and alter that. I curse you, even though you gave me the woman with powers that would help me in the ceremony. Because even with that, you had to interfere before I could conclude. No matter. You cannot move. You shall watch me as I conclude the ceremony. It is unfortunate that one so beautiful must be sacrificed upon this altar, but the time is almost nigh and the deed must be done."

Odyssey took the frozen Krysty from the equally powerless grip of J.B. and Mildred, pulling her back onto the altar.

'That should be me.' Cyran's voice was harsh, grating in the silence. Odyssey turned to her, amusement writ large on his face.

'You? You would dare to tell me what I should do?'

'Yes,' she replied, almost unable to keep the tremor from her voice. 'I was the one who loved you, who believed in you. You think that Xerxes does? You think that there were no guards on your temple by accident? He has been waiting for a long time to depose you. Yet still he underestimates you. He knew of my status as a spy, but not that I loved you. I wanted to be the one who partook of the ritual with you, who sacrificed all for you, not this bitch from the outside world.'

'Xerxes is a fool, and he will pay. You will have your reward. But this woman has gifts that you cannot even imagine. She is special. You? You are just one of many.'

'Get away from her.' Cyran leveled her blaster at Odyssey. His mouth quirked in a cynical grin.

'You think I am afraid of you? I know how you feel—you killed your husband for me. I have nothing to fear from you.'

'You're wrong,' she replied, her voice suddenly cold and low. 'I killed him because he was about to kill you, yes. But not for the reason that you may think. I killed him because you have betrayed me, and I wanted the pleasure of taking you out for myself.'

Odyssey gave a guttural, barking laugh. 'You couldn't do that. I wouldn't let you—' With which he focused his gaze upon her.

From his vantage point across the room, Ryan could

almost see the muscles in Cyran's body tighten as the hypnotic glare of Odyssey hit her. But there was something, a willpower born of anger, a last rage of defiance. Almost as he could see the paralysis grip her, he could see the impulse to squeeze the trigger travel down her arm, just that fraction of a second ahead of the hypnosis..

The shot reverberated around the chamber. As with her first, it seemed to fill the whole room.

Odyssey looked down in surprise rather than pain and anger. There was a neat hole in the middle of his chest, with just a trickle of blood surrounding it. A larger wound had been torn in his back by the exit hole, although he couldn't see the ripped flesh that disfigured his noble being. He could, however, feel that he was drowning in his own blood as his shattered lungs filled with arterial blood and his ruptured heart, bombarded by bone splinters, pumped one—twice—erratically before finally giving out.

The once leader of Atlantis fell backward, off the stone altar and onto the hard ground. He was beyond feeling any impact.

As he bought the farm, so he reached out, with the willpower of a dying man who wished revenge, and triggered a mechanism in the side of the stone altar. The door to the chamber shut, the lock smoothly falling into place, just a fraction too soon for Ryan to reach it, his limbs still like jelly as the hypnotic effect wore off.

Another round of blasterfire, higher and of a different caliber, exploded in the room and Cyran was thrown backward, chilled by a shell between the eyes.

'Bitch. I trusted you. We all did,' Affinity said into the silence behind the roar.

Ryan tried the door, not looking back until he had ascertained, with loud cursing, that it was locked. Everyone in the room still living was beginning to move. Krysty hugged the tunic to her body, awkward and unsure what to do, not knowing where to begin in putting together what had happened to her.

'Affinity, what the fuck's going on here?' Ryan barked.

The young man tore his eyes away from his handiwork. 'Ah, self-destruct. Odyssey had many triggers built into the temple. I worked on some of them myself,' he said quickly, his mind racing. 'The doors are sealed for those who don't know the code. Then the foundations are undermined by a series of old explosives that were kept from predark for just such purposes. We have about ten minutes before the complete mechanism runs its course.'

'Fireblast,' Ryan yelled, punching the wall. 'The bastard can't win now. Do you know the code?'

Affinity shook his head. 'Only Odyssey and temple sec know how the codes work.'

'I know,' Doc interrupted in a shaky voice. 'I worked it out. I can get us out.'

'Then why—' Ryan began, before shaking his head. 'No matter. Let's get the fuck out of here.'

With shaking hands, Doc fumbled the stones until they were in position, and the lock sprang back.

'Come on. J.B., help Mildred with Krysty. Jak, come ahead with Doc and me. Affinity, cover our asses.'

Ryan moved out, pulling the stumbling Doc with him, Jak at their side. He had to hand it to the old man. He was shaken, and had every right to be in a state of shock, yet when it came to each lock he was completely focused. Gibbering slightly and trembling as they traversed the passageways between doors, when he came to the locks Doc managed to control his shaking fingers and hit the combinations of stones with a surprising fluency.

There was no opposition on the way out. Their only enemy seemed to be the building itself, which began to tremble as the old explosives went off with a muffled thud in the bowels of the temple. Disturbed stone moved against disturbed stone, and it seemed that the building was poised to tumble around their ears.

They were moving downward as fast as was possible, but would that be fast enough?

Chapter Twenty-One

'Hurry, Doc. I don't think we've got a lot of time left...'
Ryan muttered the second half of the sentence, speaking almost to himself as another rumble started in the bowels of the building. The entire structure began to move slowly, as though the balance of the entire edifice was shifting slightly. Dust and particles of stone, chipped by the coming together of the blocks, fell on them in a silent, dry rain.

Doc ignored Ryan, his fingers feverishly twisting the colored stones to release the lock. He was only too well aware of the urgency of the situation. There were two main considerations. First, he had to get them out before the whole temple came crashing down on their heads. Second, he had to get them out before the shifting of the temple walls jammed the stone doors, rendering any attempt to release the locks as useless. The first was a precursor to the second, and if nothing else he was determined that he would do his damnedest to fulfil his function.

He didn't turn to look at those behind him. He had to focus on his task.

The stones formed a pattern, the lock released, inaudible over the grinding and moaning of the shifting stonework. Doc pushed at the door and it opened. He went through while Ryan hustled the remainder of the party through without delay before joining Doc at the vanguard once more.

'We might just do it, Doc,' he said grimly, trying to keep the old man's spirits raised but being betrayed by his tone.

Doc didn't reply. It took all his concentration to keep moving. His body was racked by fits of shaking, and it was only by a supreme effort of will that he could control his fingers when dealing with the locks. Otherwise, it was all he could do to put one foot in front of another.

'How far down are we now?' Ryan yelled at Affinity, having lost track of where they were in the interminable corridors. They were sloping down as they moved, but that was all the bearing he could find in these long, winding stone passages with no windows, and little else to mark their differences now that the shuddering building had thrown the hangings, lamps and candles from the walls. In some parts, the corridors had been plunged into darkness and the companions were forced to use their precious flashlights. It was only with some reservations that they did: better if they could preserve the batteries for renegotiating the maze.

Affinity stopped momentarily, as though this would help him better to get his bearings, before answering.

'Near the entrance. One door more before the exit. The corridors start to curve differently as you approach the exit passage.'

The last thing Ryan had time for was an appraisal of the architectural values of the temple, so he took the young man's word on trust. Though, on reflection, it did seem as though the passages in this last section of the temple took them longer to traverse.

Even with the building beginning to fall around their

ears, Ryan knew that they would have to exercise caution as they neared the exit. Whatever plan the Nightcrawlers had been putting into operation by allowing them to enter the temple unhindered, it had to have hinged on attacking them at some point. Either when they were inside or when they attempted to leave. The fact that they had encountered no opposition thus far, and that the building was about to crumble, left the enemy with little option other than to attack on their exit.

So they would have to tackle the seemingly contradictory task of getting out quickly with exercising the caution needed to avoid being caught in an ambush.

Ryan cursed as he dodged a sharpened sliver of stone that sheered off a ceiling block and dropped down as the stones clashed, bowing under the pressure of the walls closing on them in another shift. The floor was becoming uneven as stones were thrust upward, potential hazards to trip and injure them.

How could he successfully evacuate his people and also avoid the ambush he knew must be waiting? The only way he could see this happening was if he took an immense risk upon himself. He would have to blindly charge, hoping he could draw any fire while J.B. and Jak assessed the opposition forces. They had no time for anything else.

A noble sacrifice? A triple stupe one at any other time, but right now he had to play the odds. And the odds were that better one chilled and the others have a chance of escape than everyone buy the farm under several tons of rubble.

Doc was only a couple of paces behind the one-eyed man as they hit the final sec door before the exit. The old man looked up at the bowing ceiling, the stones grumbling and protesting under the pressure. He took a deep breath and started to manipulate the lock, twisting the red, black and white stones until they were in the right coded combination. He held that breath while he listened for the mechanism, almost inaudible under the noise that was growing around them. To his immense relief, he could pick out the sliding of the lock mechanism. It was hesitant, but it went all the way. With the distortion of the shape of the walls and ceiling that resulted from the shaking foundations, he had feared that the lock mechanism would jam.

The closer they came to ground level and the final exit door, the more likely such an occurrence became: the closer to the explosives beneath the foundations, the more likely for the shock to have taken effect. So far they had been lucky. He only hoped that their luck would hold for the exit door to the outside world.

Behind them, Jak and J.B. had already worked out that there was a strong chance of an ambush, and were wondering what Ryan's plans might be for such a contingency. They were ready for any eventuality, but with two of their party being virtual passengers, and another concerned with tending to one of those passengers, they weren't left with a lot of options.

Affinity and Krysty were those passengers. The young man was terrified. He had never experienced anything like this, and it was only the adrenaline rush of fear and excitement combined that were keeping him going. He had no idea what he was doing, hoping that the others would tell him. Blind terror had erased all capacity for rational thought. It was his desire to stay alive that was keeping him on his feet and still running.

Paradoxically, part of him just wished that the world would fall in and kill him, ending this dreadful misery and gnawing of terror in his guts.

Krysty wasn't thinking. Not much. And that which did pass through her brain, she wanted to blot out. She had been in physical danger before, but she had never been so completely at the mercy of someone as she had been with Odyssey. She had never been so aware of what was happening to her and yet so physically helpless to halt it, no matter how her mind cried out for her to act. It kept playing over and over in her mind, like a loop. It couldn't change, no matter how much she wished it to, and the knowledge of that was driving her mad.

As mad as Doc? He had no problems with the coded locks now, and it was likely that he had known how to operate them all along. Yet his duplicity—for whatever reason she couldn't guess—had led to Odyssey's control of her. She wanted to break Doc's stupe scrawny neck, yet at the same time she knew that whatever his aim, it hadn't been what had actually happened. She could see that from the way that he had reacted when they had been rescued; from the determination he was now showing to get them out of here, even though his body wanted to shut down.

Doc had been mad, and this experience seemed to have snapped him back to sanity—or, at least, as near to sanity as he ever came. His desire to get them out showed that he wanted to make amends. The way he had looked at her showed that he felt guilt to the core of his being. Whatever had powered him to act as he did was gone, and he was the Doc that they had last known before they'd reached the icy wastes of the Alaskan tundra.

But was it too little, too late?

They reached the end of the final passage. The last stretch to the exit sec door was longer, straighter, than any other they had encountered. It had a slightly steeper incline to lift it to the mezzanine level they had just left. It had a door of a different shape and size at the end. There was no mistaking it.

It also had a series of hurdles thrown up by displaced floor slabs that had risen in the disturbance of the explosions beneath. This would require some nimble footing to traverse, particularly for Doc. The old man had shown immense determination to get this far, and to keep up with Ryan at the vanguard, let alone the rest of the party. But could he carry his weakened and trembling body over the slabs, which stood eighteen inches high in places? Relatively simple for Ryan, but for Doc?

Only too well aware of the movement in the stones surrounding them, Ryan slowed his pace to help Doc over the obstacles. J.B. and Jak caught up with them, the former showing no desire to guard the rear of the party anymore. The time for that had passed. They were alone in the temple, and if he didn't lend assistance, then they would be the only ones buried beneath its remains.

The three men almost bodily lifted Doc over the slabs, while Affinity helped Mildred with Krysty. The red-haired woman was in better physical shape than Doc, but still had poor coordination as the deep hypnosis she had endured hadn't completely left her. Try as she might, her limbs failed to respond quite how she wanted.

Even with the assistance of Jak and J.B., Ryan felt as though they had slowed to a crawl, and he felt the precious seconds tick away faster than ever. As they

took the last slab, and placed Doc down for the final few
yards to the exit door, Ryan quickly outlined his plan—
such as it was—to the other two.

'Triple stupe, Ryan,' Jak replied. 'Let me—faster,
smaller, got more chance—'

'No. I give most of the orders in this outfit, so I have
to take the big chances. Goes with the territory.'

Before either Jak or J.B. had a chance to contradict
him, Doc's voice sounded from where he stood, bent
over the lock, twisting the stones.

'It may not be necessary for any of us to take such a
chance.'

'Doc, they've got to be waiting out there. Why else
would they—'

'They may have intended that, but I doubt very much
whether they are thinking of their plans right now,' Doc
replied without looking up from the lock. His voice
was halting, his concentration focused on the combination he keyed in. 'Have you, perchance, noticed that
there are recurring rumbles of explosive noise, and yet
they seem to be distant? If they are so numerous, why
have they not yet reduced us to rubble? And if they are
beneath us alone, then why do they sound so distant?'

'It couldn't be,' Ryan whispered, pausing to listen to
the distant rumbles. 'That mad bastard didn't just have
his temple booby-trapped.'

'No, indeed,' Doc agreed, twisting at the stones and
hoping that the door would respond. 'Such was the
man's megalomania that he extended the explosives to
undermining the entirety of Atlantis. "Après moi, le
deluge," indeed.'

'What?' J.B. queried.

'"After me, the flood," my dear John Barrymore.

One of those interminable French monarchs said it, just before the revolution. I can never remember which one of the Louises it was—not that it matters now. I am sorry, I am rambling. But you see, the notion of mega-lomania is something with which I'm all too familiar with. I may explain one day. Suffice to say that when I was in the company of those whitecoats, oh so long ago in so many ways, I learned more about such things—and not just from their high-handed behavior. Perhaps Dr. Wyeth may care to back me up on this, but I recall hearing of a man named Hitler, who was the cause of the greatest war before skydark. Such was this man's overweaning ego that when his country fell in war, he destroyed all—land, people—before the enemy's path rather than let them take it, before falling on his own sword. It seems to me that this Odyssey was such a man—small in intellect and heart, but large in ego.

'If such is the case, then—curse these bastard stones—it would not be beyond him to wish to destroy the ville if he should also be destroyed. If he was not the one to fulfil the destiny of Atlantis, then no one should have the opportunity. Ah, at last.'

The door began to grind painfully as the lock was re-leased. Unlike the internal doors, the lock on the exte-rior door worked on a pivot system, so that as soon as it was released, the door began to open. Usually smoothly, but with the distortion of the portal caused by the gradual collapse of the temple this became a halt-ing, jerking progression.

'Perhaps we shall find that the danger we face is not from an ambush,' Doc said over his shoulder.

Whatever they may face, Ryan knew that they had to get out of the temple as quickly as was possible. The shuddering and crumbling of the stones incrementally increased with every minute, the previous shock wave from beneath hitting the apex and returning to base, where it met another wave on the way up. Down here, at ground zero, he found that he was adjusting his weight and balance to ride with the motion of the floor.

Whatever the Nightcrawlers had waiting for them outside, it had to be better than staying in here and being crushed when the force of the waves grew too great for the structure and collapsed it upon them.

'Fireblast.' Ryan wanted to say more, but his tongue was stilled by the sight that greeted them as the door finally gave out onto the ville beyond.

There was no ambush. There couldn't be, not in an environment where it was impossible for any to hide. Even if the Nightcrawlers had been resolute in any original intent, and tried to wait in hiding, the events around them would have made combat almost impossible.

For Atlantis was in chaos.

The streets were alive with people. In contrast to the sedate, ordered populace that was the norm in Atlantis, and to which the companions had grown accustomed through their knowledge of the Memphis exiles, the streets were now filled with people who were in the throes of panic. They ran without direction, some screaming in panic and terror, others mute with shock. They ran into one another, either ignoring the collision or starting a fight as a result, with no leeway in between. Men and women who would normally be the very models of polite civilization were now howling as they rained blows on one another. Domestic animals ran between them, headed in directions only they knew, but with a sense of purpose that was directly counter to the humans around them.

There were Crawlers visible, but they were taking little notice of the entrance to the temple. They, and other armed men who could only be members of the temple guard, were attempting to quell the population as it escalated from panic to full-scale riot. But they had little experience of a populace that didn't respond, and their heavy-handed attempts only led to groups of outraged and terrified citizenry turning on them, swamping individuals beneath packs of howling men and women.

There were indications of the other booby traps going off beneath the ville. Some of the older roadways on which the ville had originally been built were showing damage, where the blasts had forced old asphalt and packed dirt to split asunder. Cracks from these fissures spread across the ground and under buildings.

It was the buildings that were showing the most signs of damage, and it was this that had undoubtedly triggered the panic among the populace. The squat houses and public buildings had been closer to the impact, and so had started to fall as their foundations were undermined. Porticoes and columns had tumbled, frontages showing signs of damage as plaster and stone began to crumble under the stresses. Doors had popped out of their lintels, and in some buildings these shifts had caused roofs and ceilings to collapse. Dust filled the air, and it was already possible to see some bodies trapped in wreckage. These were the occurrences that had undoubtedly driven the people into the streets, only to be greeted by a sight that was sure to drive them into a further frenzy.

The vessel: that which was to be the vehicle of their salvation. If Odyssey's temple was shaking like jelly dumped haphazardly from a mold, then the vessel was like a vicious caricature of the smaller building. The tremors from the land underlying the building had set up a series of vibrations that had the towering edifice rocking and spinning like a top. It was a testament to the skills of the masons who had worked on the vessel that it was still virtually intact. However, at the first sign of shock waves, the scaffolding had collapsed, throwing those who were standing upon it onto the ground beneath. One of the first to be chilled, and to be tossed like a rag doll from the vessel, was sec chief Xerxes. His sudden demise was why the companions found no direct opposition at the head of the temple. It was also a bitter irony that his plan to cause the demise of Odyssey had been directly responsible for his own premature end. Not that this mattered for anything. All that mattered to those alive was that they stay that way.

As Ryan looked up at the vessel, spinning with a visibly increasing momentum that was beginning to throw loose slabs and stones from the upper levels, he could tell that it would soon come tumbling down—and they were directly in the path of any debris that may fall. Even as he watched, those stones flung loose rained on the streets below, some falling harmlessly with a crash on the houses and sidewalks, some hitting Atlanteans who were fleeing in blind panic.

They couldn't stay where they were. The temple was close to collapse, let alone the rain of debris that would follow the collapse of the vessel. They had to move, yet in so doing they would be engaging with a terrified populace and those Nightcrawlers and sec who were attempting to control them.

It wasn't quite the rock-and-a-hard-place situation that Ryan had imagined, but it was still perilous.

Particularly as Doc and Krysty were still unsteady on their feet.

'Head for the maze, shortest possible route,' he barked over the noise of falling masonry and voices crying out in terror and pain.

'I can do that,' Affinity said promptly. 'I can take us the shortest route, and find a way past any blockages.'

Ryan looked at the young man. He was obviously terrified, but Ryan could see a determination in his eyes that was intent on overcoming the fear. He clapped him on the shoulder. 'Good man,' he said shortly. 'I'll take point with you, keep us covered. Jak, J.B., take defensive positions, and Mildred—you take good care of Krysty and Doc.'

'No problem.' Mildred grinned. 'Falling buildings, collapsing streets, mad fuckers out for blood. Just another day, Ryan.'

Whatever else they may face, Ryan was sure that they still had the group spirit to see this through to the bitter end. Without another word, he moved out into the chaos, taking Affinity with him.

The young man was as good as his word, soon deviating from the path that they had taken when entering the ville, taking them away from the main streets and into side alleys that were narrow, but less populated with the scared citizens. They ran the risk of the buildings crumbling and falling on them, but this was nothing next to the time and risk in stopping to fight their way through the ordinary citizens, temple sec and Nightcrawlers.

One good thing, Ryan considered as he ran: the Nightcrawlers were too concerned with trying to keep their own people in order to worry about the party of outlanders.

There were other, more pressing concerns; one of which announced itself with a loud groan and the sound of rendering stone as the vessel succumbed to the forces of gravity that had been plucking at its coattails. The fleeing war party paused for a second and turned as one: the sound of a dream collapsing was something that couldn't be ignored.

Many of the citizens of Atlantis had gravitated toward the vessel as it spun, some trying to force their way inside. The Crawlers and temple sec tried to stop them, but for many the catastrophe befalling the ville and the movement of the vessel weren't about the destruction of the ville. Rather, they were indications that all was in alignment, and the time of the travelers's return had come. They had to enter the vessel as they were about to be collected and taken on the journey. They were the chosen ones.

'Sweet heaven, could it really be true?' Affinity whispered, for one moment wondering if his doubts about Odyssey and the purpose of Atlantis had been wrong. Doubts that he knew were right as the vessel spun one last time before seeming to stop, frozen for one brief moment before starting to fall. Blocks of stone seemed to turn to dust, and those between either shot out in an arc or tumbled downward into the empty spaces that now existed beneath them.

With a slow, almost infinite majesty, the vessel imploded on itself, leaving nothing but an outline in dust proscribed in empty air that had been occupied just a moment before. An outline that disappeared in a cloud of stone dust that spewed out and up across the ville as the giant structure hit ground.

'Dark night! Cover up!' J.B. yelled, turning away from the scene of destruction.

The ground beneath them shook with the massive shock wave that followed the collapse of the vessel, the earth seeming to jump up at them in ripples as the dust cloud obscured all around, covering them with its choking thickness. The companions and Affinity had hit the ground, riding the shock, and covering their mouths, noses and eyes as best as they could to stop the dust clogging, stinging and stopping their breath. Despite their best efforts, it still choked them, but they were able to wait out the worst of the cloud.

As it began to lift, and they clambered to their feet, there was a relative silence that hung like a pall over the ville. A few scattered shouts, screams and cries broke this silence, but for the most part it was a heavy presence after the pandemonium they had just witnessed.

'Shit, what the fuck is going on here?' Ryan whispered as he turned to look at the empty space where the vessel had once stood. There was no telling how many Atlanteans had perished either in the collapsing building or under the spewing wreckage, but it seemed as though the ville was now deserted.

For as long as there would be a ville. There were still rumblings underneath the ground. The explosions had ceased, but other sounds spoke of incredible movements beneath their feet.

'Come on, let's move. Move it!' Ryan yelled, rallying his stunned and bemused troops into action. Affinity looked at the space in the sky where the vessel had stood, then back at Ryan.

'All over...all over,' he said softly, before seeming to snap out of his trance. 'No matter, we must get out quickly.'

With which, and without waiting for the others, he

set off toward the end of the narrow road on which they
stood. The companions followed him, Doc now able to
walk without the shakes affecting him too much, Krysty
still slow and stumbling but making good progress with
Mildred's support. They reached the junction when
Affinity suddenly jumped back, colliding with Ryan.

'What the—' the one-eyed man began, before cursing softly when he saw over the young man's shoulder
what had caused him to halt so startlingly. The road in
front of them began to dissolve in front of his eyes, the
old asphalt seeming to melt into a hole that appeared in
the center, spreading out in all directions, sucking in the
substance of the road until it suddenly ceased, leaving a
gaping maw with jagged edges where they would have
been standing if Affinity's reactions hadn't been so
sharp.

'Now I understand,' Affinity breathed softly. 'The old
ville on which Atlantis was originally built was riddled
with tunnels and sewers from the days long before skydark. Odyssey had mined them all, so that when his
temple went, all of Atlantis would follow. The whole of
the land around us will slowly fall into such holes.'

'Then not talking. Show way out,' Jak snapped.

Affinity nodded, changing direction without a word
and taking them on another path that would lead around
the newly formed pit. They had to backtrack, and as
they emerged briefly onto a main road, Ryan caught
sight of some of the remaining inhabitants of the ville—
civilians, Crawlers and temple guards—moving toward
the wreck of the vessel. Whether they thought that they
had missed the moment of truth, or whether they were
in shock that the dream had ended, he couldn't tell.
Only that they seemed in a kind of shocked trance, fall-

ing to their knees. Some were walking up to fissures that opened in the earth, kneeling and waiting for the ground to swallow them up, as though there were nothing left to live for, and all they could countenance was sacrificing themselves to die with their ville, with their dreams.

But there were others who thought differently. Affinity led them through another tangle of streets, avoiding opening fissures and throughways blocked by falling masonry, forced by circumstance to take a circuitous route back toward the maze. It was on rounding another corner that seemed to take them backward that they walked into trouble.

Three Crawlers faced them. Flanking the dark-painted warriors were two temple guards with hand-blasters. Although the Crawlers had only blades, they stood their ground, not advancing immediately for hand-to-hand combat.

The temple guards fired off three rounds each, causing the companions to dive for cover. Ryan, Affinity and Doc ended up on one side of the road, sheltering in the shattered open front of a store. Mildred, Jak, J.B. and Krysty were on the far side, covered by the end wall of a house that had otherwise collapsed. Krysty had been slow to react, and in pulling her clear Mildred had taken one of the rounds high up in the arm.

It was a flesh wound, and the slug had passed clean through, but the sudden agony was like a red-hot poker pushed through her bicep. The arm was pouring blood, and was momentarily useless. With her useable arm, she clawed at her coat, reaching for the dressings she kept squirreled away within. The old vacuum-packed dressings were medicated, and if she could just staunch the wound for now and dress it, then she could attend to it properly when there was more time and greater safety.

Tears pricked at her eyes and she swore loudly as she pulled the pack open with her teeth. Krysty watched her and, despite her own state of lethargy, seeing Mildred in trouble seemed to stir something within her. Shaking off the hesitancy that had marked her demeanor since they had found her, she moved across to Mildred and, without a word, helped her to dress the wound.

J.B. watched. Mildred was out of action, and Krysty was next to useless right now. If they stayed where they were, in cover, that was okay. It left Jak and himself on this side, with Ryan, Doc and Affinity on the far side of the road. Doc seemed to be almost back to his old self, and had shown his usual grit in tackling the temple locks. Affinity had also borne up better than the Armorer had feared when they had started out.

That made five on five. Good odds. But they'd better get this firefight started or else the whole damn ville would fall in beneath their feet, and it would all be for nothing.

Setting the mini-Uzi to rapid fire, J.B. poked the nose of the SMG around the corner of the wall, firing off a covering burst. Easing his finger on the trigger, he risked a look. He was greeted with a sight that caused him to exclaim out loud.

'Dark night! Where have all the rad-blasted fuckers gone?'

Chapter Twenty-Two

Ryan heard J.B.'s exclamation and turned to Doc and Affinity. 'Back entry, now,' he snapped, moving to the rear of the old store, indicating that the two men flank the rear entry.

If the road outside was empty, then the enemy was planning to attack from the rear. Given the mesmeric powers of the Nightcrawlers, Ryan couldn't allow them to sneak up or to gain the upper hand. To do so would be to voluntarily buy the farm.

While Doc and Affinity flanked the door, Ryan scaled the staircase on the left-hand side of the store. It was open to the rest of the room, which was good. The last thing he wanted was to try to tackle it blind, coming face-to-face with the enemy.

All the while, they could feel the ground shifting beneath them as the old tunnels and sewers began to collapse under the surface. No time to think about that; only time to focus on what was going on aboveground, not beneath.

Ryan took the stairs three at a time, the Steyr off his shoulder. If he was lucky, then he would reach the upper floor before the Crawlers or temple sec. If not, then... He didn't want to think about that as an option.

The upper floor was deserted, with no place to hide. It was an open plan, as the ground floor, and used as a storeroom, with sacks of flour, dried fruits and dried meats piled on the floor space. The room smelled sweet and sour, the air dry. It was also empty.

Two windows to the rear, about fifteen feet apart. Which one should he take? Better to stay back, keep both covered. He knew that the Crawlers were silent runners, and over the noise coming from outside there was no way that he would be able to hear them. Wait for the first sight. He would only have problems if they appeared in both spaces at the same time.

Ryan cursed out loud as that very thing happened. He should have known his luck wouldn't hold. A Crawler to the left and a sec man to the right, the latter blowing hard from trying to keep pace with the considerably fitter comrade. Balance against this the fact that the Crawler only had a blade, while the sec man carried a blaster.

Weighing the odds in less time than it would take him to verbalize them, Ryan opted for the sec man first. A shell from the Steyr took off the top of the man's skull, sending him pitching back to the street below. A rapid adjustment to his aim and another shot snatched off at the Crawler.

A yelp of surprise and pain escaped him as a blade plucked at his arm. It sliced through material and took off the top layer of skin, but no more. Enough, though, for his shot to fly wide and the Steyr to drop from his grasp. Enough for the Crawler to be through the window, headed for him.

Ryan fumbled for the panga, momentarily off balance. He knew even as his fingers found the hilt that he wouldn't be quick enough, and braced himself for attack.

A deafening roar came from behind him and the Nightcrawler looked down in surprise to see a ragged red hole torn in his body paint as a full shot load from Doc's LeMat ripped through him, pulping his internal organs and splintering his rib cage. He hardly had the time to register his shock before the life drained from him.

Ryan turned to see Doc standing on the top stair, a determined look on his face. 'I told you to stay down there,' Ryan yelled.

Doc shook his head. 'I could not. You may not understand why yet, but I have much to atone for. This is a start.'

Ryan was puzzled by the old man's words, but there was no time for explanation. Without answering, he scrambled to his feet, grabbed the Steyr and ushered Doc down into the main body of the store. Affinity was still guarding the rear entry. He greeted them with a questioning glance.

'Two down. Anything out there?' Ryan snapped. Affinity shook his head. 'Right, only one way to find out,' Ryan said, flexing his wounded arm and unholstering the SIG-Sauer. Blood ran down his sleeve, his arm was stinging from the flesh wound, and his patience was exhausted. They had to get out of this ville before it fell into the ground, and there was no way that he was going to waste any more time than was necessary.

Using the pain and anger to fuel his actions, Ryan strode up to the rear door and raised his left leg. One strong kick and it was open. There was no immediate response, so he took a roll into the alleyway, coming up against the far wall, sweeping the blaster from side to side.

The only body in the throughway was the chilled corpse of the sec man.

'Fuck it, the other three must be after J.B.'s team,' he snapped at Doc and Affinity, who were still within the store. Doc had an eye on the front.

'No sign of them,' he mused. 'Perhaps they always believe in attacking from the rear. Many have found it the safest, I suppose.'

NO SOONER had J.B.'s exclamation escaped his lips than he had fallen back into the gap between the buildings where they were holed up. He exchanged glances with Jak and started to move toward the far end of the wall. There was a hole halfway down, where falling masonry had punched a gap in the remaining structure. Jak paused before crossing. It would give him a good view of any incoming, but would also leave him exposed as a target.

He risked a brief look around the cracked stone edge, receiving a face full of dust and stone chips for his effort, kicked up by a ricochet from the sec guard's blaster. Nonetheless, it had told him just what he wanted to know—the sec man was in the main body of the ruined building, and Jak had also caught sight of one Crawler in the wreckage. Two where he could get them. He wasn't going to wait for them to come to him, like some wide-eyed creature caught in a wag's headlights, ready to be roadkill.

Jak rolled over the lip of the gap, ignoring the dust kicked up around him by off-target shooting. There was enough cover for him here, and as he came up onto his haunches he already had the Colt Python in his grasp. One sight was all he required. He snapped off a shot that took out the sec man. But there was no sight of the Crawler.

Jak allowed himself a humorless grin. This would be an interesting battle of stealth skills.

In the throughway beyond, J.B. was alarmed to see Jak disappear into the building. He swore softly, realizing that there was nothing he could now do to help the albino. Instead he had to concentrate on the throughway. He checked the mini-Uzi, which was still on rapid fire. Any bastard who appeared in the alleyway would be chopped in two. But could he risk Jak suddenly appearing through the gap and getting cut down by friendly fire?

He shouldn't have thought about it. His attention distracted for just a second, he was astounded when he looked up to see a Crawler bearing down on him. In the distance he could hear the roar of Doc's LeMat, but found he couldn't summon the will to squeeze the trigger and fire at the oncoming Crawler. The mesmeric glance had him before he even had a chance to look away.

Krysty appeared at his side. She had her Smith & Wesson Model 640 grasped in both hands to steady her shaking grasp. From the corner of his eye, he could see that she was looking to one side, to avoid the gaze of the Crawler. Quickly, before she felt compelled to look, she squeezed off three quick blasts.

J.B. felt the movement tingle back into his limbs. The Crawler had been hit by one of the shots, thrown backward as the .38 slug took a chunk from his left shoulder. It was enough to break the spell. J.B. finished the job with a quick blast of fire that stitched the Crawler from crotch to neck.

Jak heard the firing, figured it was time to bring this farce to a conclusion. He had been prowling the ruins, listening for the Crawler, who he could hear circling him. He wondered if the Crawler knew he could hear him. Probably not. It was unlikely it would occur to him that anyone could have the same capabilities.

Jak gambled on this. Knowing the Crawler only had a blade, he stood upright, inviting attack, knowing that he was facing his enemy. The blade flew toward him. Under any other circumstance, it would be a certain chill for the Crawler. At any other time, if it took Jak by surprise, it would be hard for him to escape injury or fatality. But this was different. He had been expecting it, and had marshaled all the concentration he could muster.

Jak slowed his breathing and the world around him seemed to slow with it. Everything around him except the blade ceased to exist. It came at him in a tunnel of light, slowing as it moved so that he could pick the exact moment at which to pluck it out of the air.

Pluck it out of the air, spin it in his fingers, and return it from whence it came, using its own momentum to speed it on its way.

Before the astonished Crawler had a chance to move, the blade buried itself in his breastbone. He fell backward. Before he even hit the rubble beneath him, Jak was standing over him, the Colt Python directed at his adversary's skull. Fractionally, as the dying man tried to save his own life, Jak felt something clutch at his consciousness, directing him not to fire.

The Nightcrawlers had never had to use their powers on the Memphis dwellers, and only felt fit to use them when up against a superior enemy. Now it was too late even for that. Jak ignored the feeble clutches, and fired.

Game over.

THE TWO GROUPS EMERGED into the main street, too cautious to assume that the other had completely disposed of the threat, yet driven by the need to move quickly.

'All in one piece, more or less,' Ryan said with some humor, showing his own wound to Mildred as he noted her dressing. 'Let's keep it that way.'

The route back to the maze became more labyrinthine as they tried to progress: more of the roadway was falling into the earth. That which was still intact was often covered with debris from buildings that had been toppled by similar cave-ins. There was little sign of any life, now. The only Atlanteans they could see were those who had already bought the farm, or those who had been injured in the land and building collapses and were close to death. Certainly no one who could oppose them. Their only enemies now were time and the perilous state of the ville.

Ryan was thankful that they had Affinity with them. The young man was sure-footed, and when they hit a dead end he was able to backtrack and find an alternative with little pause for thought. They were making progress, but it was stilted, and perhaps not quick enough.

And when they reached the maze, they had that to contend with once more. There would be no markers left inside, and they would have to negotiate it with failing flashlights and tired reflexes. It was the worst obstacle they could face at this time.

At least, that was what Ryan assumed. Events were soon to prove him wrong.

Chapter Twenty-Three

'Oh, great, just when I thought things couldn't get worse.' Mildred sighed, unable to keep the sardonic weariness from her voice. 'At least we won't have to find our way through that bastard, I guess.'

They had reached edge of Atlantis and were confronted with a set of obstacles that they could never have imagined. For some reason, which had little to do with logical thought, they had assumed that the booby traps laid by Odyssey to undermine the ville would have ended at the point where the chem-damaged wasteland stretched out to the enclosed labyrinth.

The insane megalomaniac leader, however, had harbored different ideas. For him, the maze was the delineation of his territory, and he had extended his chain of explosives to run beneath the labyrinth. The signs hadn't been good for the companions as they reached the edge of the built-up area. They had been greeted by the sounds of crashing masonry, coming from in front of them. At this point, it would have been safe to assume that any such noises would be at their backs. Unless...

They came face-to-face with the ruins of the maze. Parts of it had already disappeared into the gaping holes that were opening up in the earth. Other sections remained, but were distorted and crushed out of shape by the damage and stress of moving ground.

Perhaps this could have been a good thing. With the maze now in pieces, the roof fallen in and many of the movable walls no longer in place, it was in theory easier for them to pick their way through. If that had been the only damage, then it would have been simple. But it wasn't.

The chem-damaged earth was brittle, the soil hard-packed but dry and prone to crumble to dust when disturbed or given space. The fissures that had been opened up by the collapsing sewers and tunnels beneath the ground had given the fragile earth plenty of space to move, and it had taken this option to an alarming degree. Large cracks split the ground in front of them, in places almost three feet in width, breaking up the remaining ground into tiny islands. The edges of these were visibly crumbling, and there was no way of knowing how fragile these islands may prove to be. To get across to the maze area, and a potentially safer ground, they would have to risk leaping from island to island, hoping that it wouldn't collapse beneath them.

They could tell some of the islands were obviously safe as they were already being traversed by wild beasts that had been freed from the maze by the collapse of the structure. Some they had chilled on their way in, others had perished beneath falling walls and sinking earth. But many still survived, and howled pitifully as they gingerly stepped from island to island. At first glance they seemed to be helpless, blinking in a light that was almost blinding to those who had spent so long in darkness, tentative in a world that was larger than that to which they had been so long accustomed.

Yet they were still savage beasts, for as soon as they caught wind and sight of the group of seven standing at the edge of the open ground, their snouts were raised, their cries became higher and more keening, and their determination to get across the islands became doubled.

Ryan swore to himself. They could stand here and pick off the creatures, but that would take time. If they waited too long, all the islands would collapse, and the ground rolling beneath their feet suggested that rest of the ville wouldn't be far behind. They had no choice but to try to move across the rapidly diminishing ground while avoiding or chilling the creatures.

'Ryan—we get past, then we take route,' Jak pointed out.

Ryan looked at him. Could the albino be memorizing each island that the creatures were using safely? Jak's eyes were fixed on the creatures, and Ryan had no doubt that this was the case.

'Okay, let's go,' he said decisively, making to take the first island. Jak held him back.

'No—let me. Fucker collapses, mebbe I'm quicker than dust.'

With a fleeting grin, Jak took the first step onto one of the islands, his blaster ready to take out any of the creatures that came near. They were spread out across the islands of dust, numbering twelve in total. Some were feral cats bred large, others looked as if they had once been dogs. They were keeping their distance from one another, wary of fighting when a food source was near. That might work in the companions' favor. If they were too nervous of nearing one another, then they were unlikely to attack as a pack. So it was probable that they would only have to pick off the beasts individually.

Jak landed on the first island, found it firm and

picked another, scanning those around to see which seemed the most secure. As he leaped for it, so Ryan began to follow, with Doc and Affinity following. Mildred stayed back to assist the still shaky Krysty, with J.B. bringing up the rear. As Jak found a new berth, so they moved slowly in file, until they were strung out in a line across the islands of dry earth.

It was an unpleasant feeling to be standing on dry earth that could give way beneath your feet at any moment, pitching you into the maw that gaped on all sides, dark beyond the point of showing true depth. Unlike the relatively solid ground they had just left, this new footing gave the impression of being about to dissolve at the slightest breath, making landings particularly nerve-racking. The previous incumbent might have survived, but would your footfall be the one to break the fragile island into a cloud of dust?

And all the time, the beasts closed. Ryan counseled his people that it would be best to leave them until they got with a couple of island lengths before firing. There was no telling what the recoil impact of a blaster would do to affect weight, balance and the fragile footing. Best to wait until the danger was imminent.

The ravenous creatures, overcoming their fear of the open and the light as the scent of the group became too tempting, weren't as cautious. One, the size of a wolverine and with jaws to match, although there was something about its snout that bespoke of a distant Alsatian heritage, found the prospect of fresh food too overwhelming. Throwing caution to the wind that had carried the scent, it charged for Jak, bounding across three islands with a sudden turn of speed. The second one began to collapse under impact, but the creature hardly touched the surface, such was the power of its initial leap.

It was in midair when Jak loosed a shot from the Colt Python. The silver Magnum revolver barked, its deadly load ripping into the throat and thorax of the creature as it flew. The trajectory of the heavy slug spun the beast in flight and it landed between islands, the bloodied head thudding on the edge of the dirt patch where Jak stood. The impact was enough to start a reaction in the earth, the dirt crumbling away beneath the albino's feet. He had to leap quickly, without being able to choose where he landed.

He was lucky. The island held up beneath him. Not so lucky for the others, who had a much wider gap to traverse now. Not so lucky for any of them as the first beast to break for the companions spurred the others to action.

From all sides the wild creatures began to spring from island to island, all caution lost to the bloodlust that inflamed their senses, the scent of the chilled wild dog mingling with the odors of the companions to drive them into a frenzy.

'Shit, just take the fuckers out,' Ryan yelled, bringing the SIG-Sauer into his hand and firing in one smooth motion. The others joined him as soon as they were able to free their blasters.

The shot charge from Doc's reloaded LeMat took out two of the creatures that were within an island of each other, their caution over the other's presence lost in the melee. Most of the shot was wasted in the gap between them, but enough on each edge of the metal cloud hit its respective target to chew lumps from their flesh and consign them to the darkness that split the islands, their howls lost in the encompassing depths and the explosive roar of blaster discharges around them.

J.B. ripped a feral cat into bloody chunks with a blast from the mini-Uzi and, changing his direction slightly, was able to stitch holes across a couple of dog-descended beasts that were within a few yards of each other.

Affinity, less sure of his marksmanship skills but keen to make every shot from his handblaster count, waited until his chosen target was within a few yards of him, then carefully placed a shot between the creature's eyes.

Mildred and Krysty weren't as lucky. They got a couple of the creatures, but the combined recoil from the ZKR and the Smith & Wesson was a little too much for the fragile ground beneath them to absorb through their body mass. They had to jump for the nearest islands, opting for one each, unwilling to risk their combined weight on untested ground.

Ryan and Jak were efficient, picking off their shots with care, trying to catch their targets before they came too close. Their ability to stay calm, and their good fortune in having sound footing—albeit second-time lucky for the albino—enabled them to take out more than their share of the creatures.

It was over in a matter of seconds, yet it had seemed like forever. And now they were strung out across the islands, with Jak, Millie and Krysty separated from the cluster of Ryan, Doc, J.B. and Affinity. The air was filled with the smell of blood and cordite, the islands scattered with the remains of what they hoped would be their last obstacle.

'You get here, then follow path taken by beasts,'

Jak yelled, gesturing to the trail left by the deceased
animals.

Moving as quickly as they dared, yet unwilling to
waste time and sometimes just hoping that the ground
would hold, the rest of the companions reached Jak's
island as the albino forged a trail across those secured
islands he had noted as being used by the wild animals.
With nothing now to stop them, except perhaps the final
dissolution of the ville, they made rapid progress.

It was as well. The earth beneath them belched with
disfavor at the amount of land it had been forced to
swallow, each deep roar presaging another tremor underfoot. They reached the maze, scrambling over the ex-
terior walls, which were now only a few blocks high.

'We follow the solid floors as much as possible,
going over the walls and keeping as straight as possible,' Ryan told them. 'Watch for the pit traps and any
bastard holes that have opened up. Guess the rest is shot
to shit.'

It was an arduous trek, but made easier by the way
in which the stone floors had managed to keep the surface together a little longer in this part of the ville.
There were moments when it felt as though the tension
between the floor slabs was all that was keeping them
upright, as they buckled alarmingly as the companions
crossed them, suggesting that underneath the slab was
empty air. It was a thought that each was keen to dismiss from his or her mind, preferring to concentrate on
keeping going.

They were soon through the maze and onto the
chem-damaged ground that lay between the labyrinth
and the forest that was their target. The earth was broken in places, with fissures that spread halfway across

the empty ground, but it was obvious that this was residual damage, and Odyssey's infernal self-destruction devices had halted at the maze.

They kept running and didn't look back. Behind them, there were more rumblings and crashes, and it was only when they were safely past the last fissures and on the edge of the woodland that they paused to look back.

Beyond the shattered labyrinth, it was now easy to see the remains of the ville. Little was left intact, and the combined weight of the vessel and Odyssey's temple in the center of the ville now forced their remains through the fragile shelf of topsoil, Atlantis falling finally into the ground, the destruction spreading until it reached the maze, the stone floors finally succumbing to gravity. As they watched, the last of Atlantis vanished into a pit in the ground. It was the second time within weeks that the companions had seen an entire ville wiped out. It had no less an impact when repeated.

'All those poor bastards chilled, just because of one mad bastard,' J.B. whispered.

'The madness of power has always the same result,' Doc said softly, with an edge to his voice that made Krysty turn and stare at him. Was this an admission of something? Not noticing her reaction, Doc continued. 'And now we can claim to have seen Atlantis fall, just as it must have the first time. At least there were witnesses to its demise this time around.'

THEY STOOD THERE until the sun fell and twilight began to gather. Only then did they turn to go, each wrapped in his or her own thoughts.

'What can I tell them in Memphis?' Affinity ques-

tioned. 'They will rejoice that Atlantis has fallen and
that we are now free to go about building our ville in
peace, although there will be many family left behind
to mourn. But then again, to many of us, they were
gone as soon as we escaped. But how do I explain that
Lemur was chilled by Cyran, and that she was princi-
ple of the spies among us? How—'

Ryan took the young man by the shoulder. 'A word
of advice, son. Sometimes—just sometimes—it might
be better not to tell the whole story. They bought the farm
during the chilling of Odyssey. Mebbe that's all the people need to know. It's still true. If the people think that
Lemur and Cyran died like martyrs, it'll give them a
symbol to rally behind. Any other way, and there'll be
doubts. And that's no way to keep a community together.'

Affinity considered this, then nodded. 'You are right.
Come back with me, help me to tell them. Help us to
build. We would welcome the experience and wisdom
you bring.'

Ryan smiled and shook his head. 'There's many
wouldn't agree with you on that. You don't need us.
You've got all the wisdom you need, and you've seen
enough to be able to handle anything that comes at you
now. You're all the leader you need to be... They'd be
stupe not to have after this. Hey, you're the man who
survived, right?'

'Perhaps,' Affinity mused. 'But what of you? Will
you not at least come back to Memphis to recover your
strength?'

Ryan considered his exhausted troops. He and Mildred were wounded; J.B. and Jak were shattered from
leading the line, as he was himself. Doc seemed to be

back to sanity, but was now harboring a darkness within himself. Krysty was regaining her mental strength, but was still shaky.

He shook his head, realizing that Affinity was regarding him with a bemused glance.

'Yeah, mebbe we will. I figure that we need some time to rest.'

Mebbe more than that.

Only time would tell.

Death is unleashed from above with no way to stop it...

SKY HAMMER

It is brilliant technology from the space-race days that was shelved long ago in favor of more sophisticated weaponry. No nukes, no warheads, just simple rods of stainless steel corralled in space and sent jetting into Earth's atmosphere at Mach 2 to hit select targets with white-hot balls of molten metal. Cheap to make, impossible to stop and easy to deploy, it has fallen into hostile hands. Across the globe, a demonstration of the accuracy of Sky Hammer leaves little doubt that this could be the endgame for Stony Man...and the world.

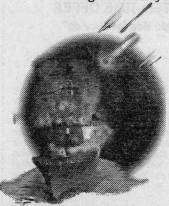

STONY MAN®

*Available
February 2006
at your favorite retailer.*

James Axler
Outlanders®

The war for control of Earth enters a new dimension...

REFUGE

UNANSWERABLE POWER

The war to free postapocalyptic Earth from the grasp of its oppressors slips into uncharted territory as the fully restored race of the former ruling barons are reborn to fearsome power. Facing a virulent phase of a dangerous conflict and galvanized by forces they have yet to fully understand, the Cerberus rebels prepare to battle an unfathomable enemy as the shifting sands of world domination continue to chart their uncertain destiny...

DEADLY SANCTUARY

As their stronghold becomes vulnerable to attack, an exploratory expedition to an alternate Earth puts Kane and his companions in a strange place of charming Victoriana and dark violence. Here the laws of physics have been transmuted and a global alliance against otherworldly invaders has collapsed. Kane, Brigid, Grant and Domi are separated and tossed into the alienated factions of a deceptively deadly world; one from which there may be no return.

Available at your favorite retailer.